THE SECRET ROMANTIC'S BOOK of MAGIC

Also available from Titan Books

FANTASY

Rogues

Wonderland: An Anthology

Hex Life: Wicked New Tales of Witchery

Cursed: An Anthology

Vampires Never Get Old: Tales With Fresh Bite

A Universe of Wishes: A We Need Diverse Books Anthology

At Midnight: 15 Beloved Fairy Tales Reimagined

Twice Cursed: An Anthology

The Other Side of Never: Dark Tales from the World of Peter & Wendy

Mermaids Never Drown: Tales to Dive For

CRIME

Dark Detectives: An Anthology of Supernatural Mysteries

Exit Wounds

Invisible Blood

Daggers Drawn

Black is the Night

Ink and Daggers

Death Comes at Christmas: Tales of Seasonal Malice

SCIENCE FICTION

Dead Man's Hand: An Anthology of the Weird West

Wastelands: Stories of the Apocalypse

Wastelands 2: More Stories of the Apocalypse

Infinite Stars

Infinite Stars: Dark Frontiers

Out of the Ruins

Multiverses: An Anthology of Alternate Realities

Reports from the Deep End: Stories Inspired by J. G. Ballard

HORROR

Dark Cities

New Fears: New Horror Stories by Masters of the Genre

New Fears 2: Brand New Horror Stories by Masters of the Macabre

Phantoms: Haunting Tales from the Masters of the Genre

When Things Get Dark

Dark Stars

Isolation: The Horror Anthology

Christmas and Other Horrors

Bound in Blood

THRILLER

In These Hallowed Halls: A Dark Academia Anthology

THE SECRET ROMANTIC'S BOOK of MAGIC

EDITED BY
MARIE O'REGAN & PAUL KANE

TITAN BOOKS

The Secret Romantic's Book of Magic
Hardback edition ISBN: 9781835410912
E-book edition ISBN: 9781835410929

Published by Titan Books
A division of Titan Publishing Group Ltd
144 Southwark Street, London SE1 0UP
www.titanbooks.com

First edition: June 2025
10 9 8 7 6 5 4 3 2 1

This is a work of fiction. All of the characters, organizations, and events portrayed in this novel are either products of the author's imagination or are used fictitiously. Any resemblance to actual persons, living or dead (except for satirical purposes), is entirely coincidental.

INTRODUCTION © Marie O'Regan & Paul Kane 2025
THE FALL GUY © Olivie Blake 2025
THE DUBIOUS LADIES OF MIRADOR © Melissa Marr 2025
UNTIL DECEMBER © Kelly Andrew 2025
THE KING'S WITCH © Tasha Suri 2025
DESIGNATED VIRGIN SACRIFICE © Kelley Armstrong 2025
SECOND CLASS MAGIC © Kamilah Cole 2025
BAMBOO, INK, PAPER, CLAY © Eliza Chan 2025
SLAY THE PRINCESS, SAVE THE DRAGON © A. C. Wise 2025
SAN'T MARTEN'S BOOK OF MILD MELANCHOLY © A. G. Slatter 2025
GOOD DEEDS AND THEIR MAGICAL PUNISHMENTS © Hannah Nicole Maehrer 2025
THE LARKSPUR © Megan Bannen 2025
ROSEBUD © Katherine Arden 2025

The authors assert the moral right to be identified as the author of this work.

No part of this publication may be reproduced, stored in a retrieval system, or transmitted, in any form or by any means without the prior written permission of the publisher, nor be otherwise circulated in any form of binding or cover other than that in which it is published and without a similar condition being imposed on the subsequent purchaser.

A CIP catalogue record for this title is available from the British Library.

EU RP (for authorities only)
eucomply OÜ, Pärnu mnt. 139b-14, 11317 Tallinn, Estonia
hello@eucompliancepartner.com, +3375690241

Typeset in Baskerville 12/18pt.

Printed and bound by CPI Group (UK) Ltd, Croydon, CR0 4YY.

TABLE OF CONTENTS

Introduction | By Marie O'Regan & Paul Kane — 1

The Fall Guy | Olivie Blake — 5

The Dubious Ladies of Mirador | Melissa Marr — 41

Until December | Kelly Andrew — 67

The King's Witch | Tasha Suri — 111

Designated Virgin Sacrifice | Kelley Armstrong — 135

Second Class Magic | Kamilah Cole — 165

Bamboo, Ink, Paper, Clay | Eliza Chan — 191

Slay the Princess, Save the Dragon | A. C. Wise — 221

San't Marten's Book of Mild Melancholy | A. G. Slatter — 247

Good Deeds and Their Magical Punishments | Hannah Nicole Maehrer — 273

The Larkspur | Megan Bannen — 309

Rosebud | Katherine Arden — 335

About the Authors — 363

About the Editors — 369

Acknowledgements — 373

INTRODUCTION

By

MARIE O'REGAN & PAUL KANE

It's no secret that, as far back as anyone knows, romance and fantasy have gone hand-in-hand.

You only have to think of the legendary Perseus' love for Andromeda. Or Arthur and Guinevere, not to mention her dalliance with Lancelot. Indeed, many medieval romances relate the adventures of a knight as he tries to win the hand of his beloved by going on a quest – often defeating monsters, like dragons or giants.

Most recently, the term 'romantasy' has been drawn on to describe fiction that combines the two. Used as early as 2008 on Urban Dictionary, nobody can deny the explosion of such work in 2023–24, with authors like Sarah J. Maas (*A Court of Thorns and Roses*) and Rebecca Yarros (*Fourth Wing*) leading the publishing charge.

So, after editing fantasy anthologies like *Cursed*, *Wonderland*, *Twice Cursed* and *The Other Side of Never* for Titan Books, it just seemed like a natural progression to delve into this particular realm.

To that effect, we've gathered together some of the best and brightest authors around today, with one remit: to deliver their own individual spin on Fantasy Romance. And boy, were we bowled over by the results!

In this book, you'll find a very different spin on the damsel in distress story, as Kelley Armstrong (A Rip Through Time novels) introduces us to the 'Designated Virgin Sacrifice'. While Melissa Marr (the Wicked Lovely books) touches on the gothic for her tale about a fantasy relationship that doesn't begin the way you'd expect.

A dragon does indeed crop up in *Wendy, Darling* author A. C. Wise's contribution, but again there's more to the proceedings than meets the eye, and Kelly Andrew (*I Am Made of Death*) makes time to show us special powers that might take you anywhere.

In 'The King's Witch' Tasha Suri (The Burning Kingdoms trilogy) explores the complexities of arranged marriages. Hannah Nicole Maehrer (*Apprentice to the Villain*) muses about just what it means to be a good person – in this world or a magical one – and Olivie Blake (*Januaries*) proves that trust can be a hard thing to come by in love, lust and fantasy societies.

The author *of The Undercutting of Rosie and Adam*, Megan Bannen, gives us a tale about luck – good and bad – will and predictions, where love is the key. Meanwhile, Eliza Chan (*Fathomfolk*) is inspired by a famous legend for her deeply moving piece, and A. G. Slatter (*The Crimson Road*) concerns herself with both the living and the dead.

Finally, Kamilah Cole (*This Ends in Embers*) tells us a tale of rivalry on a magical island that only appears every century… And Katherine Arden (*The Warm Hands of Ghosts*) warns us about searching for love in the echoes of the past.

We can honestly say we had a blast putting this one together and sincerely hope you, too, will fall in love with these adventures. Enjoy!

Marie O'Regan & Paul Kane

October 2024

THE FALL GUY

By

OLIVIE BLAKE

The truth of the matter lives somewhere between devotion and foolhardiness, right at the midpoint of yearning and valor. Although don't tell Mer that right now or he'll die.

Mer, an otherwise rational being, has apparently been so destabilized by the sudden reappearance of Lady Lilari Barzya, Countess of Setain, in his life that he's managed to achieve complete disregard for not only his vocation, but also the paltry matter of life and/or limb. Why, after all, risk everything Mer's worked so terribly hard for – indeed, the variety of indignities he's suffered by the profound personal compromise that is his loyal service to Moromaso, the Duke of Gonjain; to whom, by the way, *Lady Lilari Barzya* is now betrothed, rendering everything all the more upsetting – when he could have lived a long life unencumbered by disaster, disrepute, or distress? The only plausible conclusion one can draw from Mer's split-second decision to intervene in LADY

LILARI BARZYA(!)'s kidnapping is that he wants – he evidently *craves* – the opportunity to do something so hopeless and stupid it ruins him for life.

Is it clinical, perhaps? Madness, or the like? Is he just tired of catering to Moromaso's ill-begotten imperial wealth, his craven lifestyle, the never-ending cycle of indiscretions that invariably become Mer's job to dutifully sort? Is Mer *bored*, is that the problem? The nature of his work as an imperial scribe (soon to be ordained by the Aramisman Brotherhood, provided Moromaso keeps to his word) is highly methodical, mind-numbingly so. In order for Mer to perform his work, he must find a very quiet room – so quiet that nothing worth doing could possibly be happening within a radius of at least fifty feet – and he has to think about absolutely nothing except the task at hand. No wandering around in his memories of what LaDy LiLaRi bArZyA (he can't keep doing this; when he'd known her, prior to the magical epiphany that has been Imalian imperial governance, she was simply Lilari, not a lady, not a Barzya, barely even 'of Setain') had once been. The efficacy of scribal magic depends, necessarily, on clarity of purpose – that is, single-mindedness to the point of forgetting even to breathe. Survival is not always a given. It is barely, truth be told, a necessity. Scribes fall down dead all the time.

Not that he's going to say any of that to Lilari. Even after Mer, through a yawn, catches a hissing tone of danger from the drawing room when he arrives, concealed by the servants' entrance, to deliver the nightly spells; even after he clears his mind as best he can from the dankness of the hidden corridor and scribbles the Imalian word for 'explosion' onto a slip of parchment; even after he slides the spell into the room, resulting in a very loud bang, a great deal of property damage, a dead intruder, and a very stunned Lilari – who says only "Mer?" in a barely audible croak that spiritually resembles Mer's interior echoing of LLLLAAAADDDYYY LLLIIIILLLAAAARRRIIIII BBBBAAARRRRZZZYYAAA – even then, Mer still can't think of a better explanation for his actions than a lie. Which is somewhere between cowardice and coping mechanism.

"Hazards of the profession," he pants.

At the present point in time, Mer and Lilari have stolen a horse. One horse, singular, because Mer can't actually ride a horse, and the scribe thing has its limits. For example, Mer can't write down the word 'horse' in Imalian and expect to be capable of doing it (it would produce a horse). He could conceivably write the word 'learn,' but who knows how long that would take; too amorphous, not necessarily instantaneous. If he writes the word 'ride' there's no real guarantee he'll ever stop riding, and who knows how long his concentration would even hold before he simply dropped dead of exhaustion.

Really, this is the reason being a scribe is so stupid, and why Mer has continued working for Moromaso despite disliking nearly every bone in the man's body, because entrance to the Aramisman Brotherhood at least presents access to magic that's actually useful. Unfortunately, the Brotherhood is so exclusive it involves a rigid moral code that's characteristically Imalian. What a dreary hellhole the continent must be. The pseudo-religious orders and purity of thought and noble service are compulsory requirements for initiation. (How else, Mer supposes, could the worldly, scholarly elite be joined by a lowly scribe, particularly one who exists only by the grace of a wealthy, pious patron?)

The point is, post-rescue, Mer lies. He claims his leap to action in Lilari's defense is required by some imaginary scribal code of conduct. Heavily implying that he's undergone reputable combat training at some or any point in his life. Flagrantly suggesting he might make a worthy bodyguard as they ride away from his mess and toward her prospective safety, a journey that spans the remaining shrouded hours of the night.

⁓

So deep in his lies is Mer that he hasn't even considered whether Lilari might also be lying. Which she is. And this is the problem with imperial ethics, which Lilari would have gamely pointed out if Mer had asked. But instead, her mind was screeching MMMEEEEEERRRRR!! as if all the angels in which her dead husband so improbably believed had touched down from on high with a personal blessing. A chance to turn back time, to try to set things right.

But that's not what this is. It can't be, and it won't. Because for Lilari, the truth has no business in this equation. The only way out of this mess she's made is a man, one who could conceivably be Dometico, and Mer's the only one in line.

Ironically, Dometico wouldn't have happened at all if not for Mer — Mer the beacon, Mer the silver lining of Lilari's shadowed past. Isn't that hysterical?

Anyway, they digress. Right now, as they ride strenuously through the night, Mer pretends to be capable while Lilari pretends to be innocent, and they both pretend not to be aware of the proximity of their beating hearts, hers felt through his chest. His through her spine.

More sad, undignifying truths: Mer doesn't know how to use a sword or a knife or his fists. Theoretically, anyone with even a drop of proclivity for magic could do what Mer can, provided they were allowed – or so Mer would say, modesty being one of the core doctrines of the Aramisman Brotherhood. The Brotherhood puts a great deal of emphasis on service. The tenets of fraternity: loyalty (no empire could survive without it), service, and purity. In exchange for transcending to a higher plane of humanity, the Brotherhood are functionally sorcerers. Mer can write things down, sure, a glorified clerk. But the Aramisman Order is capable of real magic, the kind that doesn't require a quiet room and proper hydration, and anyway, he doesn't have anything worth staying for here.

Or at least he didn't, until now.

No, he still doesn't. Lilari is marrying his employer and Mer is still Mer, no matter what happens today.

Mer is thinking about all this (or rather, trying *not* to think about this) when he and Lilari finally stop in the crispness just before dawn. Presently, fog obscures the bustling port of Setain, as the Imalians call it. Eristoh is (was) a chain of islands whose ports make it so valuable – worth throwing money at or dying over, depending on who you ask.

When Mer wonders aloud why he and Lilari have returned to Setain for refuge, but not to Lilari's estate there, he suffers instant retribution. "My husband has a son from his first marriage," Lilari replies without feeling. She doesn't even look at him. Instead, she pets the horse as if he's the only male in the world with any compassion at all.

Ah. Of course, Lilari needs to marry Mer's revolting boss (gods save him etc. etc.). Her husband is dead and now she has nothing. She couldn't have inherited land or money, even if her husband had thought to set it aside. So, she needs one man to talk to another man and offer a substantial sum in transaction, or as substantial as can be expected when the person in question is a woman, a widow, and Eristo'ah, all of which count heavily against her price.

Which does beg a second question. Mer coughs, through which he manages vaguely to form the words: "Explain the... er... kidnapping?"

Lilari turns to Mer with a look of dark amusement. "You think I'm not worth kidnapping?"

"I didn't say that," offers Mer. Humbly, purely, idiotically. "I just meant—"

"No, put it in explicit terms, please," she says. Her beauty is a savage otherworldliness, a momentary collapse in what is, or can possibly be, real. Her eyes, dark as the night, flash incandescent with fearsome fury. "I'm not worth any money, so why would anyone go through the effort of kidnapping me? Is that it?"

Mer wants to curl up and die, this goes without saying. "I beg," he states, quite literally, "your pardon. I only meant—"

"I think we both know what you meant," Lilari snaps, and strides dismissively away.

꩜

More sad, petty truths: Lilari isn't insulted at all. It's a perfectly logical question. It's not a *flattering* question, but she can't blame the man she's leading to his death for questioning things when they don't make sense. None of this makes sense! She still doesn't understand why Mer even offered to protect her. Not that it matters what his reasons are, because at the heart of his unflattering assumption, he's correct: she needs him.

Even if she wasn't planning to set him up, the presence of a man, even if that man is Mer – which isn't to say Mer is in any way *unmanly* – he has one of those Imalian beards, like Moromaso's, only Mer's is thick and virile and unruly, and the long hair that's so fashionable on the continent is, on Mer, sleek midnight at the root and a careless, non-egotistical knot at the nape – which doesn't *sound* sexy necessarily, so you'll just have to trust her, that Lilari can see all kinds of carnalities in him – goodness, once you let them go these wretched truths simply overspill! – but Mer is also... visibly a scribe.

Which is to say, Mer thinks he's getting away with something that he absolutely isn't. But Lilari's got secrets of her own, so, you know. A little truth, a little lies.

For example, the kidnapping. It wasn't, per se, a kidnapping.

Well, listen. You know Adelion – the governor of what used to be Eristoh, which is now just more of Imalia. Everyone knows Governor Adelion is both zealously pious and corrupt as all hell, which is a common irony if not a pleasant one. Anyway, Adelion's in charge of tax collection and of course he skims a little off the top. He's a bully and he's violent (it's gotten incalculably worse since his wife was, ahem, murdered – the story is she fell victim to Dometico's pirates, the 'lawless scum' who line the new Imalian ports and tradeways) and he's got spies all over the thing that used to be a country that's now the savage landmass in his care.

Adelion has one particular spy, Kasalka, who happens to have discovered something damaging about Lilari, a secret he'd tried to use against her in what could fashionably be called a bribe for his silence, until Mer blew him up. Now the threat of Kasalka is gone, but that's arguably much worse. Because what comes after Kasalka is Adelion, and that is... very bad for Lilari.

What she needs now is Dometico, which Mer is not. But he's here, which is the next best thing.

"Mer. A warning." Lilari pauses abruptly. "This place... it's not too welcoming to strangers." Certainly not strangers who dress in Imalian fashions or wear their hair like Imalian aristocrats – she can't understand how or when that happened, especially as Mer was once so proud to be precisely what he was. Anyway. "I'm going to need you to play along, okay? Don't ask questions."

Mer gives her a look, like, okayyyyy.

"Everything will be fine as long as you follow my lead," Lilari says as they prepare to enter the grungy tavern with shuttered windows and clear evidence that all might not be well inside. So, another lie! But who's counting. At the very least, part of that lie is true – things will be fine for the time being. She trusts Nicano Asco, even if he does have his lackeys assign three blades to each of their throats the moment she and Mer walk through the door.

※

"Well, well, well," says a person Mer doesn't recognize until they step into the dim morning light, which sluices entropically through the tavern's shoddily-boarded windows. And then, gradually, awareness sinks in. Nicano Asco, wanted for trespass, felony robbery, felony burglary, assault on Imalian officers, and arson.

He's much handsomer than his wanted poster suggests, not that such things matter to Mer. Certainly they don't matter *more* than the reality that Mer could bleed out from an incautious swallow. "Lady Lilari Barzya."

(Mer marvels a little at how Nicano Asco seems to have no trouble saying her full name without wild interior strangulation.)

"Nicano," says Lilari. She seems unbothered by the knives presently threatening their necks, possibly because she's already survived one attempt on her life over the course of the previous twenty-four hours. Mer considers that, perhaps, he should do his best to become accustomed to danger, as it seems part and parcel with the consequences of his actions. "I need a favor."

She's doing a purring thing with her voice, something Mer recognizes as flirtation the way an astrologist might speculate about the stars. It seems strange now to think she was using the same tones with Moromaso hours earlier, on the other side of the study door from where Mer sat alone, trying not to feel things, attending to his pile of requested spells. (Most of Moromaso's household has been replaced with spells, which are single-use, which really means that Mer inherited that work. Granted, it's different work. He's never scrubbed an antique Imalian fireplace grate and will probably never have to, thanks to his benefactor. But he does have to write the Imalian word for 'clean' about a thousand times per night. Or he did, until he wound up here, with Lilari, at knifepoint.)

The notorious criminal Nicano Asco begins to circle them slowly, something Mer recognizes as a tedious game that Moromaso also plays. The issue with mortal peril is that eventually, you adjust to it, which leaves room for other things, like annoyance with the peacocking of a man who could just slit your throat and be done with it. Which would at least express adequate respect for everyone's time.

"So," Nicano murmurs to himself. "This is the great Teorestro Dometico, is it?"

"Ha," says Mer, because Teorestro Dometico is – much like Nicano Asco – a very famous criminal. A pirate of some sort, out for blood and bounty, though Mer's only interest in him is as a kind of bogeyman who haunts Moromaso's enterprises. It is Dometico who supplies Mer with his steadiest administrative tedium: the inscription of 'safety' for every trader Moromaso invites to the port of Gonjain.

Objectively speaking, there's almost no chance that Mer could be the sort of brawler known for brutality and senseless violence. But is it just him, or does Nicano Asco look… scared?

By the time Lilari purr-whispers, "Nicano, don't be jealous, it's incredibly unattractive," it occurs to Mer this might be exactly what she meant by following her lead.

⁓

Give or take some twenty knives later, after they're deemed acceptably unthreatening and the nest of Nicano's gang makes itself comfortable again, singing their bawdy tunes and getting characteristically drunk before mid-morning, Mer and Lilari are shown to their room above the tavern. Mer, not unpredictably, whirls on Lilari – who intends to say nothing, thank you very much.

"Why." It's the start of a sentence, but Mer's voice is so terse and clipped that Lilari can only hear it in tiny chopped up bits, like pickings for a stew. "Does. NicanoAsco." (This, meanwhile, is a single, ostentatious word.) "Think I'm. Some kind of. Master criminal?"

There's a note of absurdity in there, as if even by asking, Mer has defied the usual constraints on reality and must therefore take several steps backward. He sinks into the mattress behind him, a faint look of confusion crossing his enviable features. Not that Lilari is thinking about Mer's handsomeness at the moment, but truth be told, she loves a pretty thing, and Mer is very pretty. The way his lashes sweep across the high bones of his cheeks; the graceful look of his elegant fingers; the impeccable furrow of his scholarly brow. She enjoys this feeling, the one where she allows herself to admire a person, to wonder at the scent of salt and linen and the lovely ordinariness of a body, the way it can so easily be brought to pleasure. The way running a finger along the curve of one thigh can make anyone shiver, done patiently enough.

Lilari doesn't even mind the thought of sleeping with her new betrothed, Moromaso, who is an objectively terrible man. An attractive one, to be sure – thick and brawny, with ice-blue eyes and girthy thighs. Lilari likes to think she's capable of complex thought; for example, she can temporarily turn off the part of her brain that dislikes bullies in favor of the dumber, primal one that enjoys an expert cock. Yesterday, she was confident she could be perfectly satisfied with marriage to Moromaso, at least for the six or so weeks before things inevitably took a turn.

But then, today, Mer. Whose natural loveliness is undeniable, and lingers even when he scowls. It's really for the best that she turns traitor. How else would she otherwise go on?

"Look," Lilari begins, doing the thing where she says something with a lot of certainty so that nobody presses her or asks questions, a tactic that worked very well over the course of her marriage and on all the lovers she took during that time. "I think we can both agree that it's better if nobody tries to kill us. No offense, but they might very well succeed."

Mer mutters something like excuse me, I saved you earlier this evening in a display of impressive masculinity (Lilari doesn't actually hear him, but she assumes based on experience and context cues). "I'm just trying to make things easier for us," she lies before he can say anything else. "Nobody's going to come for you if they think you're Dometico."

"Oh, really?" says Mer, with a dull blow of a glance. "Interesting. So, not the Imalian police, or the Imperial Navy, or Adelion, or—?"

"The truth," Lilari cuts in, "is that Adelion thinks I have something that belongs to him." That actually *is* true, sort of. "And unless I can get it back, he's not going to leave me alone. Especially once he learns that Kasalka is dead." There! That's a cogent point. "Honestly, better for you to be Dometico than for you to be the man who killed the governor's favorite attack dog."

This is a very strong argument, such that even Mer seems to buy it.

Rather than imagining Mer's head being separated from his body, as will ultimately transpire, Lilari tries to guess what matters to Mer at this stage of his life. She's never known him this... obedient. Perhaps that's not a fair assessment, given that she's been away from him for half their lives, but she does feel as if she knows him, or that she used to know him, once.

Mer was an orphan (Lilari, by contrast, one of too many children) who seldom engaged with anyone, something Lilari observed whenever she came to the orphanage as part of her father's routine ministry. Mer's natural stoicism was why Lilari committed nearly everything he *did* say to memory, incidentally inscribing his every thought on the very meat and marrow of what she was. As a boy, Mer only ever spoke to come to the defense of others. He suffered no fools, and would say one word where other boys would use hundreds.

Mer, even at eleven or so, could be incisive to the point of humorlessness, as if in his estimation, nothing was ever funny. But Lilari always knew that wasn't true – that in quieter moments, Mer had an easy smile, and a full and throaty laugh.

But this is not the time for remembering. There will be plenty of that later, and for ample guilt as well. Lilari clears her throat at the sudden piercing jab in her chest, brought back to the present circumstances.

"There is one other thing," she says. "Dometico is… Well, he has a reputation."

"Yes," Mer agrees. "For carnage." Pointedly, he whistles a little shanty about Dometico the monster, who makes the seas run red with blood.

"Well—" Lilari swats this away for the nonsense it is, not that she's getting into it right now. The violence that colors the name Dometico is very necessary, even for someone who could conceivably understand the truth. "I mean more along the lines of Dometico's… *reputation*."

Mer looks blankly at her. "You just said that."

"Yes, but—" Lilari tosses herself beside him on the bed with a sigh. "I'll just say it. You're going to need to, you know. *Woo* me." Fuck me, she means.

It looks for a moment as if something inside Mer has briefly disconnected, like maybe his brain is no longer attached to his ears. "What?"

"Nicano and I were lovers for a time," Lilari says. She can't help a smile at the thought of it. Halcyon days, truly. How she longs for the inattentiveness of her dead husband, who didn't believe her capable of real – or any – harm (because she was a woman and therefore incapable of complex thought). Moromaso, by contrast, will keep her locked up tight; it's why Dometico is no longer an option.

A momentary sinkhole fills her chest. Then: "Nicano will only help us if he believes you're Dometico, plain and simple. And you're already testing the constraints of believability," she adds with a lying sweep over Mer's physique, as if his aesthetic is in any way disappointing aside from in this single, stupid regard.

Mer's face is blank.

Lilari feels an impatience that is actually, definitely, guilt. Mer deserves better treatment, and a far better fate, but at what cost? Her life? Even if that was a price she was willing to pay for anyone or anything, how could she explain her predicament to him? The loneliness, the desperation, the unavoidable fallout from years and years of self-imploding lies?

"You said you wanted to help me, didn't you?" she snaps. "I never forced you to come along."

"Do you *necessarily* require criminality from your lovers?" Mer poses archly. "Nicano Asco the thief, Teorestro Dometico the murderer—"

"He isn't—" Lilari grits her teeth, then gives up before she starts. "Fine, do as you like. I'm only asking for a bit of... *mmmmm*." She moans, taking several thunking strides around the room, choreographing a prelude to lovemaking of the most desperate, rutting kind.

"Oh, Dometico," she says, throwing her head back, "*yes*—"

"They can hear us," Mer mumbles, his eyes fixed with apparent mortification on his lap.

"Well, precisely," Lilari hisses at him. "Didn't you listen to a word I said? Oh, Dometico, yes, there!" She gives a shrill, almost yelping sound, which startles Mer into looking up at her. "Okay, now you'll want to—" She gestures for Mer to toss her gamely into the wall, but Mer seems to comprehend none of this. So Lilari does the work herself, yanking Mer up so that at least two sets of footsteps will be heard tripping over themselves. "Dometico, oh, *ohhhhh*—"

She feels her cheeks heat for real when Mer's eyes slip down to the top of her dressing gown, the one she's been wearing since Kasalka cornered her last night. It's designed for maximum enticement, so as to procure her betrothal to Moromaso, and it's very clear now that it works. Mer's hardly breathing, which amuses Lilari, but also excites her, a bit. She's spent so much time with shameless lotharios that she's forgotten just how lovely restraint can be.

"It would be just magnificent if you'd contribute to the performance," she says, managing to remember the context of their imaginary tryst.

Though the words come out… breathless, which she didn't plan. She didn't factor in the possibility that Mer might have an effect on her, not when she's been so unmoved by so many people over so many years. But she can't very well have Nicano overhearing, can she? So when she speaks, she murmurs in Mer's ear, her lips warm and soft and practical beside his bearded jaw.

In answer, he lets out a barely audible groan. Oh god, but what a groan it is, all manly and rough and intoxicating in its ambiguity — in the fact that Lilari can't tell if he's acting or if it actually escaped him, slipping through the clutches of even his extravagant restraints.

"Yes, good, like that—" Another hot breath in his ear, meant to be reassurance, though it comes off as sultry praise, almost as if she'd like him to keep going, *yes, yes, good, never stop.* "Perhaps another, if it wouldn't trouble you too much—"

She yanks him flush against her, and he trips. He falls, actually, into her, and they collapse together against the door with a satisfying thud. But because Mer is genuinely not expecting it, he fumbles for her waist to catch himself, to keep them both upright. The sound that leaves his mouth when he touches her is nearly feral, a strangled gasp that slips through his teeth.

"Yes, that's perfect, you're doing so well," Lilari whispers. Mer chokes on something, maybe a laugh, maybe something deeper, darker, more intimate. He has his eyes closed now, one hand balled in a fist, the other floating carefully over her bodice. Ready to catch them again if necessary, but offering nothing more.

There's a tenseness to his jaw and Lilari touches it softly, with a fingertip, before moaning again. "Oh, yes," she whines. A sensual whine, a heady panting. "Yes, YES, YES— Now you'll want to, you know," she whispers to Mer mid-performance, gesturing wordlessly to the fact that by now, they'd be rutting straight into the wood with every intention for property damage. Mer looks blankly at her and she throws her head back, miming the throes of pleasure. "You know? Like… YES, DOMETICO, HARDER—"

"You can't seriously think this is how I would do things." Mer's got a slightly hangdog look to him, a palpable disappointment. At first Lilari thinks it's directed at her, clocking that she's a shameless harlot after all, but then she realizes that isn't it.

"I would never—" His eyes rise painfully to hers. Beautiful, pleading, sad.

Then his gaze caresses her lips. "Lilari," he says, his voice brittle, as if he's managed to fit half a lifetime of craving between the cracks.

For a moment, Lilari falls silent. She forgets the theater of it all, though she knows Nicano is still listening. She tries to imagine what this moment would be if it were the continuation of their playacted sex, but now she can only think of it as it is, which is also, somehow, sex. She can already see the two of them coiled up in sun-soaked sheets, the sweat glistening on Mer's shoulders, the way he'd pull away just to stare at her, the kind of honesty that edges perilously close to fealty, or love. But that's not the kind of sex she unilaterally decided they were having, and now she understands Mer's disappointment, that she didn't properly understand the way he would have done this with her if it were real.

She surprises herself when she leans forward and catches his lips with hers. Another sound escapes him, something helpless, impossible to commit to memory or articulation. Like chasing after fate and finally catching up.

He breathes into her mouth. She sighs soundlessly into his.

"I'm not—" he begins. "I can't—"

Then there's a knock on the door behind them.

"Open up, my bloodthirsty lovebirds," says Nicano. "I've found that lost trinket of yours."

The unspoken is becoming more noticeable, weighing on Mer as he considers the events of the past twenty-four hours – the real things and the false ones, the abject lies and their incidental truths. As is his practice, he feels the presence of the uncomfortable and instead edges blindly around it, as if he doesn't see it and can't be made to look. He focuses his attention on the information Nicano Asco has given them, which is that the thing Adelion wants from Lilari – the thing that can potentially save her life, Mer's procurement of which would be heroically within the bounds of his forthcoming oaths to the Brotherhood, despite the impure thoughts he had while pressed against her – is located in the home of the Earl and Countess of Coricain, just north of the port of Setain.

"Your little problem was delivered to Lady Sabiyana Seraysra," Nicano says with a glimmer in his eye, his gaze repeatedly straying to Mer's. "And lucky for you, we happen to know she'll be with the Medericos this evening."

"How exactly is it that you know," Mer responds gruffly, not quite managing to summon the questioning tones necessary for the conversation. He's still struggling a bit through the physical effects of being so close to Lilari. Of toeing right up to his vows and lingering there, suspended on the tepid safety that is the distance between pretense and meaning. The difference between breaking and broken, at least by technical constraints.

"Between the two of us, Dometico, I think you understand the sorts of questions that should and shouldn't be asked," is Nicano's reply before he saunters out the door. He's put on ample bravado, probably for Lilari's benefit, which is banal enough to Mer's sensibilities to offer him space to focus.

Certainly more so than... other things, like the feel of a satin bodice, or being flush against that door.

"What are you writing?"

Lilari interrupts Mer's train of thought then, which is best, as the spell he's crafting might very well go awry if he thinks any harder about the thing he's trying to avoid thinking about.

"What?" he asks.

"What's the Imalian for?" she repeats, frowning down at what must be the sixteenth protective spell Mer's written out. He doesn't want to be caught at knifepoint a second time, so the words for 'explosion' and 'armor' seem equally relevant, under the circumstances. Lilari holds a blank slip of parchment in her hand, contemplating it.

"They're spells," Mer begins to explain, "you know, given all the mortal peril—"

"No, I mean – why Imalian?" she corrects him, and Mer looks blankly at her. "If you wrote them in Eristo'ah," she clarifies, "would it not work?"

It's been a long time since anyone around Mer has referred to his native language by its name. He has to fight the urge to look over his shoulder, however pointless that would be. "I was taught this way."

"Well, yes, understood," Lilari presses him, her presence a veritable chokehold on his ability to process thought. She has bathed, and smells of flowers and the sultry soddenness of freshly wet earth. "But haven't you ever—?"

"I can't write in Eristo'ah." Mer feels embarrassed about admitting this, even though it's not his doing. He was an orphan. And it's illegal.

Lilari laughs. "But surely—"

Then she sees his face and stops laughing.

"How did you...?" She seems unsure what question to ask, specifically.

"There's an exam for magical proficiency," is what Mer says, because he doesn't know how to answer the real question. "I wasn't supposed to sit for it, obviously, but I had a patron."

"Who?"

He winces. But what does he have to be ashamed of? It's not as if he had a choice about who'd noticed him rather than leaving him to starve. "Adelion."

He feels rather than hears Lilari suck in a sharp, critical breath. "Oh," she says, and thankfully this line of questioning is over.

They've both succeeded, in the absence of the other, to the extent of their respective limitations. Lilari married a rich Imalian noble, positioning her to marry another. And if that isn't power or freedom, it's at least luxury, which is better than many other fates.

Mer had the equivalent happen to him. As the new patron of the decaying orphanage in which Mer lived, Governor Adelion paid for Mer to sit the scribal exams, and then assigned him to Moromaso for the duration of his noble service. What did Adelion see in Mer that no one else would or could? In the end, it didn't matter. Mer spent a great deal of time around Adelion, which meant being grateful, despite never needing to ask Lilari why she'd run from him at the start.

But of course, Lilari heard the name Adelion as if Mer had spelled out *I'm a traitor* in calligraphic script, and why shouldn't she interpret him however she likes? It doesn't matter what she thinks. They'll hardly speak after tomorrow. He'll get back this stolen thing for her and then he'll write the spells to warm her bath until he's summoned to the Brotherhood, which had better be fucking soon.

The ride north from Setain is not very long, so Mer doesn't have to think too arduously about the shape of Lilari's waist below his fingers. He doesn't have to think about the way her breath changes when his chest meets the line of her spine. He doesn't have to think about the party they're about to attend, which Nicano Asco is none too sparing about.

"You know those rich bastards," he says in confidence to Mer just before they take their leave. "Everything is ever so cutesy and demure until they get behind closed doors."

"Meaning?" Mer hazards to ask. He's grumpy for unknown reasons, having seen Lilari and Nicano try to sneak a private moment, a heartfelt and/or lusty farewell.

But Nicano gives him a light smack on the arse, to which Mer barely withholds a disgruntled "oof."

"Enjoy the orgy," Nicano says, and kisses Mer full on the lips before winking at Lilari and sending them on their way.

It's not like Eristoh is, or was ever, perfect. A preternaturally warlike bunch of clans can't really be trusted with unified statecraft. But Imalians are just so *hypocritical*. There are so many rules, so many varying degrees to the hierarchy, who bows to whom, which titles are appropriate, which mistresses can be acknowledged and which ones nobody speaks of aloud.

They can be terrific fun, though, if you happen to be one of them. Which Lilari is with limitations, and which Mer thoroughly is not. Thank the gods he's so handsome they probably won't mind,

Lilari thinks, assuming they don't recognize him as Moromaso's servant. Which is unlikely. All the Imalians populating the fresh spoils of empire are new to their titles, and eager to prove they rank too high to concern themselves with other people's staff. Still, even the most horrid snobs can be occasionally astute.

"Stop fussing," Lilari says as she adjusts Mer's borrowed (stolen) clothing, grateful for the occasion of a masked ball and the fact that Nicano has an eye to current fashion. Imalians are incredibly fussy, especially the men. Layers and layers of brocade and velvets and silks, all of which are ill-suited for a life in Eristo'ah humidity.

Mer's underlayers are already saturated with sweat. He keeps pulling at the voluminous tie around his neck, an Imalian symbol of dignity, which is characteristically ostentatious.

"Am I really necessary for this?" Mer asks – tired, Lilari supposes, of the meager stakes of her life and/or death. "And surely there's no way I can just walk in and claim to be an enemy of empire—"

"They may eat with Adelion, but they fuck with Dometico. They're gluttons, Mer, and they're new to their money, and they're bored." Lilari is a little too rough as she secures Mer's vest, and he releases a withering sigh. "Relax – it's a *masked ball*, Mer. They won't even be paying attention to you. You just have to get Sabiyana alone." The final piece in her carefully laid trap.

"And then what?" prompts Mer, as Lilari snorts a laugh.

"I'm sure you can imagine what."

She turns away, irritable all over again, though whether with him or herself is unclear. After all, she's guilty of just as many betrayals as he is, if not more. She's the one who lays with the enemy as a matter of survival. She hates Adelion and she still sat with him at her late husband's table. Surely she will be on her best behavior when Adelion attends her wedding to Moromaso.

So why does she hate this thought so much – the one where Mer bends his studious neck obediently, performing the dutiful Imalian scribe beneath Adelion's approving gaze?

Because Mer's smart enough to know why she's angry, and possibly that's the worst of it. She's had so many handsome idiots and beautiful sycophants over the past decade of her life. She's forgotten, for the purposes of survival, that sometimes people who are good and clever and kind still bend the knee to monsters. It's unbearable, this awareness of the truth, and frankly, she's almost thrilled she's sending him to his death!

She moves with clipped, unsteady anger until Mer reaches out. Not touching her, but the motion pauses her just the same.

She thinks an apology is coming, or worse. She braces herself for whatever it will be. The thing that leads her to forgive him. The thing that means she can want him again, because her anger is already so flimsy as it is.

Instead he says: "I'm a candidate for the Aramisman brotherhood."

She scoffs: "What, you mean those hooded Imalian creeps?"

Mer mumbles something like assent and Lilari is relieved, overjoyed, to be able to hate him. Delighted to tell herself he has it coming, with the way the universe bends. "What absolute nonsense," she tells him. "Aren't those assholes completely celibate?"

Mer meets her eyes and she realizes he is angry. No, not angry. He's *hurt*. She's insulted him and it's annoying, the way she feels sorry. The way she feels anything at all. Doesn't he know the Aramisman Brotherhood is just another avaricious cult? Speaking of hypocrites! The Brotherhood claim to be sorcerers, but really, they're bankers. They charge for their services and collect interest on the debts. They're worse than Imalian nobles, which is saying something.

Ha, and Mer is angry with *her*? Lilari wants to scream. (She wants to ask forgiveness.) She wants to strangle him. (She wants him to lie with her in a world where survival doesn't mean compromise; where inevitably they starve to death for their high-minded ideals.)

"Well," she says, a spark of cruelty in her voice, "then I suppose you'll be useless, won't you."

She turns away and he takes a breath so sharp she feels it in her lungs, like the puncture of a rib. "Come here," he says. Softly commanding. Gently tempting.

As if in a trance, she pivots to face him. As if, in this moment or any other, he has only ever had to ask.

Mer scrubs one hand around his mouth, the thickness of his beard. The look he gives her is one of pure, slow delectation. His dark eyes follow the curves of her waist. Lilari feels a sudden, inescapable awareness of her nipples. His lips part and so do hers. He leans ever so slightly toward her and she doesn't move, doesn't breathe.

Then she takes a step to close the distance.

Then another, because the first didn't seem like enough.

"If what you want from me is the seduction of another woman," Mer says calmly, "then yes, you'll find me quite useless. I have only ever wanted one woman." He leans away, such that she can grieve the distance. So that she can watch his eyes linger with palpable curiosity on the motion of her throat.

Then he leans forward again, his nose ghosting along the edge of hers. His lips tracing the curve of her cheek.

He turns his head to speak in her ear, one hand rising to span the edge of her jaw, the line of her throat. "If anyone had offered me a choice, I would have chosen you," he says. "All of you."

His thumb brushes the edge of her lip and she is ravenous, delirious.

"Mer." It has a cooling sound, some semblance of refreshment. Like this moment, if she allows it to, can offer her some hard-fought peace.

So when he steps away, it's like dousing her with a bucket of ice. She realizes, belatedly, that the pain is still there, in his face. On his lips.

"I rather think I'll do fine in there," Mer says, adjusting his ludicrous tie. "Don't you?"

Right, she thinks, and catches her breath, recommitting to the fallout of her plan. After all, it's too late now to stop it.

Mer regrets his behavior. To a degree. Not the things he said (which were true) or the things he did (honest, if misleading and unchaste). What he regrets is not doing more. He regrets not taking Lilari by the shoulders and saying for heaven's sake, it's not as if he *wants this*. How can she possibly believe this is anything but the best he could scrape together of a life? One hardly dreams of these conditions as a boy. Certainly Mer hadn't, too haunted was he by dreams of a girl he hardly knew (you know which one).

Imagine if he said that. If he got down on his knees and said Lilari, fuck the empire and their promises of sorcery and power, I'll die with you in poverty and treason if that's what you ask. Can you imagine? If he said I'll die for you, how could she say anything short of okay cool, then die? He knows there is no future here, even if half an image blurs the edges of all his thoughts. The partially materialized fantasy where he loves and is loved by the woman who was a friend long before she was a daydream. Who is, perhaps, the only friend Mer's ever had.

But anyway, that isn't real, and worse it's painful, so now here he is in the Mederico family's private drawing room, sweating straight through all these fucking brocades, pretending to be the kind of man who can sweep a lady off her feet. Which, worst of all, is going well.

"God, but you can't even imagine how terrible it all is," sighs Lady Sabiyana, who wears a delicate birdcage mask. She's fingering the heavy jewel around her neck that Mer feels sure must be Adelion's stolen trinket. Now that he thinks of it, he actually recognizes the jewel – he's seen it before, in a portrait that hangs in Adelion's house, around the neck of his late wife.

Mer ponders how he's going to slip it from around the neck of this beautiful, horrible duchess and regrets not writing the word 'seduce' on a slip of parchment while his mind was more at ease.

"It's as if I don't matter at all, do you know what I mean? I'm just an object," complains the wealthiest woman in three counties, "and you wouldn't believe how disgusting it is here, the unrelenting heat. And the natives! And Vorcanto's so utterly draining, all his unavoidable wants and needs, his constant desperation for reassurance—"

"Indeed, has anyone considered how you must feel," Mer manages, adjusting the black silk mask tied over his face until it sops up some of the sweat beading at his forehead.

"Yes, but it's that precisely!" says Sabiyana, as Mer ponders whether he's capable of whatever Moromaso would do under these circumstances. Kiss her? Disrobe her? Colonize her homeland? He misses Lilari as he thinks this. He can almost hear her laugh.

Before he can say anything, though, someone enters the room behind them, and Sabiyana gives a horrified little gasp that Mer realizes is pure theater. But then she realizes it is her friend, the Lady Elemora Mederico, and becomes bored with it all yet again.

"We're busy," Sabiyana says, reclining into Mer to the point of altering his balance. He fumbles for the chair behind him as Sabiyana purrs, "Was there something you needed?"

Elemora, in sharp contrast to Sabiyana, is nearly panting with apprehension. "What are you doing in here? Never mind. Dometico's just arrived," she says, hurrying to stash what appears to be bottles of liquor in the nearby drawer of an antique Imalian cabinet.

"Dometico? The pirate?" Sabiyana straightens as if to augment her bosom, a look of delight on her features. "Where?"

Mer's chest tightens. His hand moves to the waistcoat where he's stashed the spells for escape, wondering whether he's light-fingered enough to grab the necklace at the same time. He'll have to find Lilari, too — why did they ever agree to separate?

He realizes abruptly they never even made contingency plans for if either of them got caught.

"Somewhere. Anywhere. How should I know?" Elemora's eyes slip to Mer before dismissing him in the same glance, and he's relieved about what that means for Lilari until it occurs to him that, actually, he's the only one who's taken on any kind of risk. It's not a crime for her to be here. There's the kidnapping danger, of course. But if she was worried about her safety, why leave Nicano Asco's at all?

Hmm.

"Fix your face," Elemora snaps at Sabiyana while Mer contemplates things very slowly in his head. "Adelion's just ridden up to the gates—"

"Adelion?" Sabiyana straightens with alarm, her first real sign of apprehension. She scrubs at her garish lipstick, shoving Mer aside to check her appearance in the glass. "What's Adelion doing here?" she shoots over her shoulder.

"How should I know?" Elemora is fretting, hiding things, pointlessly tidying the room. Sabiyana, meanwhile, is busy adjusting her bodice, pulling it up until it almost looks prim. "Someone must have tipped him off—"

A brief, unsolicited image: Mer finding himself one slip of parchment short as he was writing the spells for this endeavor. Another: whatever was slipped furtively from the folds of Lilari's gown into Nicano Asco's waiting hands.

"Who?" Sabiyana cries, then throws her hands up in an apparent wail of suffering. "Oh, those ignorant sluts! We're all going to be in for such a tiresome lecture, not to mention all the blasted fines—"

"Whoever it was had better hand over Dometico," Elemora agrees. "Otherwise who knows how much interest he'll shove onto the next tax—"

With that, Mer dismally concludes his math. Lilari was never being kidnapped. Of course no one here would summon Adelion, who'll employ all methods of pious usury now that he's caught them in the act. And Lilari never needed something so banal as a necklace. What she needed was to pin Dometico's crimes on Mer and then leave him behind for Dometico's fate. But why? To save her real lover, the murderous pirate?

It doesn't make sense, but at the same time, of course it does – the part where it isn't Mer. Mer, stupid Mer, who burns with something now, a confluence of shame and grief. All this time she was everything to him, and of course he was never anything to her.

Why had he ever possibly believed he might be? Just because for a single moment in a burning room, she'd almost looked at him like she could dream another future in his eyes?

The door suddenly slams shut, burying Mer in the consequences of his actions. So resigned is he to his doom that he scarcely notices the figure that materializes in the room, half-hidden in the shadows.

"Ladies," says a cool voice that, despite its unlikelihood, Mer recognizes instantly. "If you wanted Dometico, all you had to do was ask."

<hr />

Let it be known! Lilari did not intend to do this. Mislead Mer, firstly, but also, the bit where she spent years impersonating a pirate.

Or rather, *as* a pirate, impersonating a man.

The truth is, Adelion's butcher Kasalka came to the home of Lilari's new betrothed to deliver her a private warning, which was that he knew who she was and what she'd done, and that Adelion would soon find out unless she paid his ransom. The price: the jewel of Adelion's kingdom. But of course, Adelion didn't care about actual, literal jewels. Adelion cared about the trinket he'd kept behind bars, which Lilari had stolen a long time ago.

So, the big truth: Teorestro Dometico as a person isn't real.

Never was. But his influence is real enough, because Dometico has a specialty: he makes people disappear. Senseless tales of brutal murder are really the only way imperial police don't keep looking when a body fails to materialize in the sea. What matters is what people believe, which is that Dometico is a monster, a seducer, and a heartless nightmare of a man, which is all very critical and convenient.

If Kasalka were to reveal to Adelion that Dometico was actually a disinherited former noblewoman named Lilari, well, suddenly everyone who's 'lost' gets found. And it's a hard life for an Eristo'ah woman under Imalian rule. Which is to say, Adelion's murdered wife is Eristo'ah, and the truth is she's alive somewhere, hopefully at peace.

"Dometico." Lady Elemora Mederico's eyes narrow. She's not a bad person. Not nearly as annoying as Sabiyana, who's vain and flighty and dull. But Elemora would happily sacrifice Mer if she thought he was Dometico, which was Lilari's plan until… well? Now.

Lilari, prepared to flee the moment she saw Mer and Sabiyana slip away, had been besieged by thoughts of the way Mer looked at her. How he touched her, like she was treasured. Like, if it were possible to make themselves another future, he could already see it taking shape. And then Lilari had thought: *What life am I saving here, exactly?* She imagined herself a week from now. Moromaso's wife, bowing left and right, kissing rings, without even the promise of Dometico for distraction. *What will be left of me when the beacon of Mer goes away?*

"What are you doing?"

It's Mer, unhelpfully, as he was meant to take this opportunity to escape. Lilari wants to scold him, and meets his eye to signal something, possibly *run, you idiot, run!* But then she finds she can't look away.

There is something so knowing in his gaze – a quirk of amusement, not mocking but sweet, as if he's pleased and suitably chastened to learn she was never really in need of his help. In truth, it rearranges things for him, the realization that she resents his hypocrisy because she isn't a hypocrite, just duplicitous! She's a liar but not a traitor. In the look that passes between them, the one where they wordlessly exchange their respective tales of survival, they understand that the story which defines them is not one of cowardice. Because yes, survival, that's all this is! And look how beautifully they've been doing it.

Without each other. For all these long, long years.

It was Mer who'd put this fire in Lilari's heart, this desire for something close to rightness. This longing for the kind of purpose that is inextricable from sacrifice.

Where is Adelion's wife now? Who knows. Nobody, and that's the point. It's her secret and Lilari plans to keep it that way, even if her own contrivances now demand that she do so with her life.

∼

The march of imperial footsteps approaches – the sound of a dozen guards. Adelion. The doors burst open and Sabiyana screams, one hand flying to her necklace. Mer fingers the spells inside his vest, the swamp of it almost curdled by now. He faces his patron, who looks only at Lilari, piecing it together the way only a brilliant, cruel person can. Seeing the truth in what was once a clever but not quite convincing mask.

"Where is she?" he says in a voice loaded with the danger that sadism can pose. He won't kill Lilari, not yet, not while he can still enjoy her suffering, and who could say when that kind of appetite will ever be sated?

Horrifically, Mer understands. He wants something from Lilari too, and how can that end? Thus far it is terrible, and consuming, and lifelong.

Admittedly, the end result is quite different. Mer loosens a piece of parchment from the fabric of his vest, holding delicately at the front of his mind to the promise of a different outcome. The welcome embrace of a very different life.

"She's dead," says Lilari. "And I'm afraid the dead are out of even your exhaustive reach, Governor."

"Is she?" Adelion looks amused before letting his gaze travel to Sabiyana. "Where did the Duchess Seraysra get that, then?" Adelion steps forward, fingering the jewel around Sabiyana's neck before he lets her go, turning to Lilari. "Sold, I imagine, to buy safe passage? With the right motivation, such transactions are easy enough to trace."

Mer reads on Lilari's face that this is, unfortunately, true, and an unforeseen consequence. The plan was different when Mer would be the one caught with the necklace, because then it was meant as a device to frame him. Mer doesn't actually know the answers to any questions Adelion might ask – but Lilari does, and the word 'confess' on a slip of parchment can make a terrible difference when it counts.

So shortsighted, Mer thinks, shaking his head at Lilari, at her foolish, wonderful bravery. Changing the plan on a whim to save Mer's life was a dangerous move, hardly masterly. A grave and disastrous error.

Which Mer understands, because he's willing to risk the same.

When Adelion takes a step toward Lilari, Mer leaps boldly between them, the parchment now clutched tight in his hand. "Lilari, run!" he shouts, and resigning himself to the end, he throws the spell at Adelion's feet – close enough that Mer, too, will be met with the blast.

Adelion's face goes white. His hands rise helplessly to shield his face. The paper kisses the ground, and then…

Nothing.

Moments pass, and…

Nothing.

The spell is too sodden with sweat, Mer realizes. The painstaking handwriting has all but washed away, smeared by the disgusting eccentricity of Imalian tradition, and by fabrics that don't fucking breathe.

"Well." Adelion turns to Mer with mirth in his eyes. "I'd intended to deal with you later. You're still very useful to me, you know. More so now that I have compelling reason not to share you with that idiot Moromaso, or to pass you along to the Brotherhood. And as for you," he says, with a menacing step toward Lilari, "you will tell me where she is, or you will die begging me for mercy—"

"Like hell I will, Imperial scum," spits Lilari, and Mer, unthinkingly, lunges forward to take her hand. It's another moment of disaster, one in which he blurts aloud the one thing that comes to his mind. A thing he almost never allows himself to think, because it has so long been gone from him, from even the outer edges of his reach.

Safety, he thinks in Eristo'ah. He clutches Lilari's hand and whispers devoutly, in the language they spoke as children, "Home."

It's as if he called down a wildfire. As if all the gods of his birthright have finally answered.

As if they've only been waiting to be given this one chance to let these false idols burn.

<hr />

The truth is, it was probably a long shot anyway, the idea that Mer could have joined the Brotherhood, what with all that magic for others to exploit. And as for Lilari, well, there are a lot of deaths, and marriage can sometimes be one of them. So really, it was all for the best.

After the mysterious fire that night, Moromaso is the new governor, which complicates things, given his familiarity with both Mer and Lilari, but conditions could certainly be worse for two wanted murderers. After all, Moromaso's spent so many years reliant on his loyal scribe – how can he possibly summon the effort to hunt down criminals now, in addition to the tedium of statecraft?

And crime is really out of hand these days in all the port cities. The coasts are positively festering with pirates. The looting's gotten so bad that many Imalian nobles have gone back to their imperial court, seeking refuge in their country of manners. These new lands, they're just so savage and unruly. You can never really be sure whether one Dometico or another will choose today to scour the seas.

"So, who gets to be fearsome today?" Mer calls across the room, which Nicano Asco has so generously provided in exchange for permission every now and then to watch. Mer's beard is trimmed now, though his hair is still tied in a scholarly knot at the nape of his neck.

Lilari turns to look at him. Not a lady, not anymore. Wedded and bedded, though. Mer happens to like keeping to the solemnity of vows.

(That other future they both foolishly saw: it's honest and simple. Precious and shared.)

"Don't be stupid, Mer," she chastises him fondly, reaching out to cup his cheek. "I'm always the fearsome one. You're just wonderfully combustible."

The truth of the matter lives somewhere between devotion and foolhardiness, right at the midpoint of yearning and valor. Although don't tell Mer that right now. He's going to bed.

THE DUBIOUS LADIES OF MIRADOR

By

MELISSA MARR

～ ALWEN ～

The cloisters were dim this time of day, lit by flickering oil lamps, and Alwen was hurrying toward the gardens. The new sprouts from the root vegetables were already an inch tall, but Alwen was still worrying over them. One frost or surge of beetles or too much water… there were a dozen ways to lose her new crop.

And Alwen was *terrible* at failing. She abhorred it. Mother Superior thought it was a kind of pride, a sin that she'd rather not see in any of her charges, but it wasn't that. Alwen simply didn't like to let anyone down. She'd been tasked with gardening, so she would excel at it. If she were tasked with maintaining the linens, she'd be just as thorough. However, the sisters had summarily removed

Alwen from cleaning, from cooking, from laundering. Her desire to be… *thorough* made most of the sisters dislike sharing tasks with her. So, Alwen tended to the plants outside, away from the others.

She had dreams of doing something more exciting. Every sister at the convent trained in combat and seduction, make-up and manners. In the years since she had come of age, though, Alwen had not been sent on a single mission – even reconnaissance. Hers was a quiet life, but she had accepted it. Some days, she even liked it. So what if her temper wasn't well suited for subterfuge? She was where she was, and it would be foolish to wish for a different life.

Alwen thought about the small measures of her past that she recalled. A mother who was afraid of sunlight; a home in a cave where Alwen felt cold and damp every day. Her memories were scant. Since she'd been a child, she'd lived here.

Vows will come, and this will be my future. My past. My present. My future.

Occasionally, the thought bothered her, but what other life was there?

Today, turnips. Tomorrow, checking the chicken wire.

"Alwen."

Her name echoed in the silence of the cloisters. To speak *here* was verboten, but there was one woman who could change the convent rules at will. Alwen pivoted. Mother Superior headed toward her. She had the shape of an old oak, wide and tall and square. No one could pass her in a hallway, and she had the sort of glower that meant no one attempted it, either.

Alwen dipped in a curtsey of sorts, bit her lip to try and stay silent. That was one of the many rules she struggled to follow.

Too loud. Too thorough. Too inquisitive. Too hungry. Too much. I am always too much of everything.

After a long, still moment, Mother Superior said, "You will go to Helgren."

"*Me?*" Alwen stared at the head of the order, hoping that her question wasn't terribly impudent. "On a mission? Alone? Outside the convent?"

Mother Superior gave a solitary nod. "I prayed on it. We all did. You are the right choice."

"Yes, but—"

"Do you doubt me?" Mother Superior's glower grew deeper and her voice louder.

"Of course not!"

For a moment they were at a standstill, before Mother Superior said, "Mirador is swayed by a pretty face. I was certain the time would come, Alwen. Your path simply took longer to become clear. Your beauty will lull Mirador to peace. You are the weapon we need to contain her."

Alwen swallowed against the praise. She'd seen her reflection a few times, and although no one had commented on the matter, she'd seen the looks from delivery folk. They were interested, hungry, curious. That mattered little, though. Alwen had never been assigned any duties that required disrobing. Some novitiates had, of course. The convent served the greater good, and many of the novitiates had seduced enemies of the crown or enchanted a wayward noble to attain compliance.

Alwen, however, had never left the convent grounds. In the two decades she'd lived with the sisterhood, she'd stayed within the walls. Anxious now, she asked, "Are there rules?"

"The more experienced sisters will dress and instruct you." Mother Superior caught her gaze and held Alwen fast. "You will contain Mirador however you must, Alwen. She's become a menace, and the crown would rather word of her *kind* not reach alarming levels."

"I vow to serve the good of the kingdom and the peace the Divine has decreed," Alwen said clearly. She'd made the promise often in the two decades since she'd been gifted to the convent, but not for *this* sort of mission. To take a life, even one such as this, was a heavy burden.

Perhaps there is a non-fatal answer…

"I've sheltered you as long as I could, Alwen, longer than perhaps I ought to have, but…" Mother Superior sighed. "Can you do whatever it takes to contain her?"

"I will. My vow." Alwen bowed her head briefly, but her temper flickered. She looked up and caught Mother Superior's gaze. "I am thorough in every task I am assigned."

"That you are." Mother Superior chuckled. "Too much so at times. Sister Bernadette still mentions the reorganization of the larder."

Alwen flushed. "It was haphazard."

"True." Mother Superior patted Alwen's cheek fondly. "You are the right choice for this mission. I trust you."

A trickle of some unfamiliar feeling came over Alwen. "Will I be welcome here after?"

"If you choose to return, yes. If you can, yes." Mother Superior pulled Alwen into an uncharacteristic embrace. "Your service to the kingdom and the Divine do not make this easier to accept. I feel honored to have guided you." Mother Superior sniffled suddenly. "Be careful. See yourself to the armory and then to the wardrobe."

"I was planning to weed the west garden and—"

"Another sister will mind the turnips. Go." Mother Superior turned in a half-circle as they embraced, so that when she withdrew her hold, Alwen was facing the depths of the convent instead of the door. Then she gently pushed her forward.

And Alwen went to prepare for a battle with a creature that was no longer human, no longer able to accept the Divine's grace.

What sort of depraved wretch will Mirador be? Will that make it easier to kill her?

～ MIRADOR ～

I woke to find an eagle perched on the dresser. The creature had shredded the fine wooden top with its great talons, carving patterns as it studied me. The bird and I had an uneasy truce so far. Admittedly, I was unsure whether the animal was aware of the truce. Being cursed as I am does not grant me the gift of conversing with creatures, or much of any true benefit. I do not die. I do not stay injured. Those are certainly assets – heightened senses and strength – but my familial longevity comes with neither magic nor money.

Nonetheless, I like to feel the fresh air when I wake, and the eagle liked to rest indoors. We had an accord of sorts. The beast had fashioned an eyrie atop my wardrobe, a tangle of woven twigs creating a frame lined with the stuffing from a settee I used to like.

"A bit late today, aren't you?" I could see the last swaths of red and purple in the sky. The sun was set, and I was awake. My feathered guest had returned to the room she thought of as her own. All was as right as possible in my routine.

And yet I am overcome with sorrow…

The bird made a harsh, guttural noise, then sharp and high. For all I knew, she was answering me – or mocking my maudlin mood. The creature stalked toward her nest and settled in; her gaze was fixed on the cliffside view from my window.

Eagles could rip flesh from bone with their knife-edged beaks and talons. I'd watched this one shred a few fish and a small rodent-like carcass efficiently. Still, when she hopped closer to the edge and tilted her head toward me, I dutifully stroked the ridge between her eyes. There were few things that could kill me, and unless the eagle severed my head from my body, anything else was an injury that would heal.

The bird made a low noise that was not a purr, but surely seemed like one.

"I need to go to Helgren, eat, talk to humans." I stared into the distance, where the lights were tiny beacons. "Soon. Not tonight, but soon."

The anticipation of talking to someone human was almost as keen as the desire to have a companion for the night. No one had warned me that loneliness and longevity were hand-in-hand companions, but I could see no other option.

What depraved soul would want to hide away in seclusion with a creature like me?

I considered my features. I was under no illusion that I was hideous to behold. I was not ghastly, nor was I beautiful. An average woman, slightly too tall and muscular to be found ladylike. Far too adept with swords and fists to be mistaken for a damsel.

Inside, however, I am something Other. Not merely mortal. Who could love me with my madness and peculiar diet?

Somehow, my parents and the rest of my family had found

love, but I was seemingly unlovable. Decades had passed with nothing more than fleeting touches – or purchased ones. I learned languages, dances, painting, writing, and still I was unlovable. The women who sought my embrace were often doing so as a last adventure before marrying. I was their proverbial summit to scale, their sea to tame, before they settled into mundane lives.

Where is the one who will want me to be their companion in a mundane life?

"She's out there somewhere," my mother had assured me time and again.

"Waiting to torment you for eternity," my father often added when they were at odds. "Why rush? Go to the pub, Chrissy. Enjoy your freedom while you have it."

Despite their quarrels, my parents were often blissfully happy. I wanted that. In fairness, I also wanted my one true love to be a fair maiden with coffers that overflowed. My mother had found that when she married my father. *That* money lasted for almost two centuries.

"Stop shredding the furniture," I grumbled at the eagle. "I have no money for a new settee."

The eagle did not so much as glance at me. I was no threat to her. I was a madwoman in a mountaintop eyrie, not so different from her.

Castle Mirador perched atop a mid-height peak, the summit of which had been sliced away by glaciers cutting through this valley long before the records of my besmirched family began. A magician who spoke to the land had come out, drawn his runes and whatnot, and declared the ground stable.

He'd not declared my ancestors stable, mind you, just the ground.

My sense of what was madness and what was bravado was tainted by a lifetime of secrets. My mother had walled my father into the west tower some years ago. He'd betrayed her – and had done so clumsily at that. Mother had no patience for that sort of thing. She still visited the tower, castigating him from outside the barrier. I suspected her of the explosion a decade later that sent her and my father – and a section of the tower – plummeting into the ravine. Mother had been maudlin without him, so I suspect it was no accident that she and the tower went over the ledge one afternoon.

They'd heal. Father had the same longevity and health as Mother after their bond. Such was the way of our family: mad and eternal.

My extended family was no saner than my parents. My cousin, who had lived here along with a half-dozen assorted relations, married a pair of sisters. They were happy enough for almost two decades, until the first sister grew ill. Now, they three had left for a mission to find a forest witch. Last I'd heard, they were seeking a particular root that had to be found under a new moon in the Salt Cedar Grove far west of Helgren. Cousin Colin swore that he'd cure his wife, or they'd all crawl into a grave together.

I miss them, but I cannot blame their choices. My family loves with a sort of folly, a lack of self-preservation, and there's little I can do to escape such a fate. My solution, such as it was, hinged mostly on spending any naked time with women of ill repute and spending any remaining hours trying to rebuild the family's fortune by my sword. Unfortunately, sword-for-hire had the awkward difficulty of rarely getting paid all that had been promised – especially if one were on the losing side or had seduced the general's daughter... or wife... or mother.

I waved in the loose direction of the tower's remains, where it was jumbled in a ravine. "Good evening, Mother. Father."

They were not yet healed enough to answer – or perhaps they had healed and were on another honeymoon. One never knew when it came to a Mirador.

Perhaps fate has decided She's had enough of my family. Perhaps I'll never find love...

Somewhere out there, Fate laughed at my hubris. I'm now sure of that because two nights later, I was forced into an unexpected reckoning, the woman of my dreams standing in the alcove near the door of the pub like a trembling rabbit who had wandered into a den of wolves and vipers. If not for the daggers I could smell hidden somewhere on her, I might have been as deceived as the humans all were. The daggers, however, made her interesting. Beautiful *and* deadly? She was *exactly* my type.

Typically, this was my cue to introduce myself and separate her before this lowly pack of swindlers and reprobates could swarm, but I swayed on my barstool. In the moment, I could only marvel at the wide-eyed innocence. Fine, I also marveled at the fact that her breasts were seemingly intent on escaping her low-cut blouse and her hips had a curve that was just right for grasping – but I was *first* struck by the wide-open eyes and parted lips. Her throat was bare, pulse visibly thrumming like an invitation. Everything about my future wife was custom made to draw my eyes. She had berry-stained lips, charcoal-lined eyes, and hair lightened by some mix of sun and citrus.

Honey trap, my mind filled in. Other less logical parts of my body could only think, *so what?* Helgren was low on women I hadn't already *known* by this point in my too-long life. I drank of so many throats in the area that I could identify most of the women by their scent alone.

"Another," I grumbled at the barkeep.

Cyrus was a surly old man with a chest as thick as the barrels he tapped and served. When I'd started drinking here, he was a babe in his mother's arms – or maybe that was his father. Mortals died so often that I couldn't keep track of all of them.

"Bad as your grandmother," Cyrus said as he slid the rot-wood rye my way. The tankard was chipped. My memory summoned up various barfights over the years, but at this point, they rolled together in a long image of skirmishes.

The grandmother, of course, was *also* me. The stories of my long line of ancestors? Still all about me. Longevity requires a bit of subterfuge.

The last time I'd brought true wealth to my estate was when I married an ailing old man. He thought I was the granddaughter of a soldier he'd fought with, until I slipped up and he caught me out. We'd wed, consummated the deal even, and I had hope of friendship at the very least, but age makes some soldiers bitter.

Two months later he'd died of blood loss. I was alone again. That was eighty years ago, and my only companion since was an eagle.

I stared at the young woman at the door again. I lectured myself against it. I reminded myself of the dangers. She stood there as if she was unsure of her next move.

Such perfect prey – or my inevitable demise.

Then she lifted her head and caught my gaze. When she smiled at me, I swear I felt the good sense leave my body in that moment. Self-preservation died. She was the One. I felt it as the surety of madness that washed over me.

"Mine," I said clearly as I stood and bowed to her from across the room. I might be a debauched liar, but I was still chivalrous when circumstances demanded.

"Friend of yours, Mirador?" Cyrus asked.

"My future wife." I couldn't look away from her. I needed to know her name, her interests, her enemies, everything about her.

She stared at me as she slid forward into the sea of men struggling to find the words to approach her. The man at her side, who had been attempting conversation, stood there with his mouth gaping open like a suffocating fish, and I could do nothing but smile back at the young woman I would marry. She veered around his now-outstretched hand, dodged another man's doffed hat, and stepped delicately over the extended foot of a third would-be suitor.

I hastily uncorked a vial of mint extract and brought the miniature glass bottle to my lips. When your diet is mostly blood and booze, you learn to carry a few less noxious things to assist the lingering scents.

"Hello." She stood at my side now. Radiant. Tempting. Her pulse beat faster, and I couldn't look away from the thin skin covering that thrumming blood. "I'm Alwen. You are?"

"Brash," I observed softly.

She smiled in a way that danced toward laughter. "Curious name."

"I am Christabel, Lady of Mirador." Again, I bowed, bending slightly. She was so close, however, that the movement meant my face was hovering above her nearly bared bosom. I smiled despite my best intentions. "Hello."

Alwen laughed as my word ghosted over her bared cleavage. "Cheeky."

I glanced at her face again. While I had no skills that would bring me the fortune I needed, I *did* have a few that kept me warm at night, talents that were appreciated by more women than dared to admit their proclivities in public.

So instead of doing anything remotely logical, I dropped to my knees and said, "Marry me, Alwen. Come live with me and be my love."

~ ALWEN ~

"Are you prone to madness?" Alwen asked, staring down at the woman currently asking for her hand in matrimony. Mirador was striking. Cheeks drawn with a knife's edge, eyes that glittered in a way no human's did, and a mouth that... did not make Alwen think of assassination.

Mirador was a monster. Alwen knew that. She'd spent her entire life learning about the terrors that faced the world. Mother Superior and her convent of holy soldiers protected the kingdom, spying and seducing as needed. The Sisters of Peace answered only to Her Majesty, the queen herself.

And so Alwen knew when she'd been given the mission to neutralize Mirador that taking a life was the likely next step. She had even suspected that a bit of seduction would be necessary to get Mirador alone. This, however, was not the expected plan.

"Marry me, Alwen of... Do you have a surname or family name?" Mirador knelt on the tavern floor. No ring or gift offered.

"You are not amusing," Alwen muttered, looking around at the crowd now watching them intently.

Several people called out.

"Stop carrying off women, Mirador."

"Mirador, you wretch."

"Greedy bastard. Leave a few for the rest of us!"

In a level, uncompromising-sort-of-voice, Alwen asked, "Do you carry off many women?"

"I had done in the past, but now that I've found you, I swear to devote myself to your pleasure and happiness." Mirador's gaze slithered over Alwen in a way that ought to have greatly offended her, but instead was making her feel joyous.

Is that a magic the monster has? Disarming me with a look...

"You know nothing of me," Alwen protested. She did not lie and say she knew nothing of Mirador. She had, of course, read the entire file on Mirador. The Sisters of Peace were a thorough order, and research materials were always plentiful. Instead, she asked, "Do you assume I'll fall prey to your wiles?"

"You're a hunter, not a lamb." Mirador took her hand, seemingly not noticing the thunder of Alwen's pulse. "I was rather hoping we could both fall."

Her skin is so soft...

Because she is a monster. That was the detail Alwen must repeat in her mind when she felt weak. *She is built to lure unsuspecting victims to her lair.*

Mirador reached out with both hands, capturing Alwen's face in the cup of her palms. She stood there, holding Alwen gently. "I want to drown in you."

A thought flickered in Alwen's mind that she ought to draw her dagger and end this now. There were too many witnesses for the convent's preference, but the alternative was drawing Mirador away from here. Somewhere private so Alwen could behead her.

I cannot say that's wise... or safe... or anything other than tempting.

"I'll learn everything, so I know you as no woman ever has," Mirador murmured, her lips a breath away from Alwen's mouth. "I'll make you happy, my love. I will spend all my hours adoring you until you can no longer remember a life without me. I'll bathe you in—"

"Enough!" Alwen's face burned in embarrassment. A life in the company of the Sisters had provided sufficient evidence that some women were meant for other women's love or, at the least, their affection. She'd known that she was just such a woman, and felt no shame in that. Desiring a blood-drinking monster, however, was an entirely different matter.

She took a steadying step away from Mirador's plump lips.

One ought not bite the target...

Alwen's eyes were cast low, gaze firmly on Mirador's lips.

"Shall I prove my intentions toward you?" Mirador tempted, but Alwen could not glean how exactly one proved the intent to marry a complete stranger. "Say the word."

"Fine, but—"

Mirador stood, took Alwen's hand, and led her to the bartender. "Cyrus, be a love and mind my future bride." Then the monster leaned close and brushed a soft kiss over Alwen's too-fast pulse. "I will overcome every soul in here to prove that I can protect you!"

Alwen's entire body leaned toward the stranger she'd been dispatched to kill. She wasn't a wilting flower in need of protection, but it was still charming. Alwen's gaze danced over Mirador's taut arms, her legs where the trousers strained against them, and she bit back a sound of appreciation.

Then Mirador was gone, hopping onto the pitted bar top and

yelling, "Behold, I present my intended, Alwen, future lady of Mirador! If you can pass me, I will not besmirch this fair damsel. If you cannot, she will be mine..."

Besmirch? A shiver of anticipation followed the thought.

Mirador leaped at a man, landing so she was on his shoulders, high above the crowd. Using her feet against his midsection, she threw him off-balance and dismounted with the grace of an equine soldier.

Alwen gasped, but a laugh rang out as Mirador ducked and dodged fists and flagons.

I ought to study her fighting style, since I probably will need to kill her.

But there was no style other than improvisation and daring. Mirador moved in ways that were obviously not human, and the crowd just went with it. The melee was absurd. Bottles flew through the air, and tables were upturned.

At her side, Alwen heard Cyrus say, "Are you sure about this, girl? You could slip away if you need."

"Does Mirador hurt people? Kill them?"

"Nah. Maybe hurt 'em in a brawl or kill 'em for a job, but she's well-liked by everyone 'cept the man whose wife or intended she's luring to her bed at that moment. Never met anyone – man or woman – who can tempt the ladies into their arms so often." Cyrus gave Mirador an admiring glance. "The rest of us only wish we had her charm. It's definitely not her money. That one doesn't have a pot to piss in or a working door to toss it out of."

Cyrus chuckled, his attention as riveted as Alwen's. Absently, he added, "Haven't seen her as cheerful as this before, though. I'm impressed she kept you a secret. Maybe she was worried you wouldn't show. Did you have a tiff?"

Alwen shook her head, but she wondered at what Cyrus had inadvertently revealed. Curious now, she prompted, "Why do you ask?"

"Mirador's been——" He glanced at Alwen and rubbed the back of his head. "—*active* more the past few months. Woman after woman, most of them ones she ought not tangle with, and in between she's like a hurt fox retreating to her den. She's been… sad and drunk or naked, not much else." He stared back at the fight as Mirador crowed in joy. "She's not a bad fellow. Glad you showed up."

Alwen didn't know how to ask if Cyrus realized that Mirador lived on blood, or that she likely wasn't *seducing* women but drinking their very life essence. Alwen shot a look at the way the woman fought, arms bared now as her sleeves hung in tatters, and thought perhaps there was some seduction going on, too. The definition in those arms brought a gasp to Alwen's lips.

Monster though she might be, Mirador was undeniably beautiful, and her joy in the fight was intoxicating.

"You're as bad as the rest, aren't you?" Cyrus muttered.

Alwen couldn't argue. Her attention was locked onto Mirador in a way that might make this mission more complicated than she had expected. How was she to snuff out a light as vibrant as Mirador's?

"Are you ordained still?" Mirador called over the ruckus. "Cy!"

"I am," Cyrus bellowed, batting a log out of the air. He glared at the young man who'd hurled it. "Watch yourself."

"Marry me, Alwen," Mirador half-asked, half-demanded.

"You are absurd," Alwen shouted across the room.

"Yes." Mirador leaped onto a table. Her cheeks were flushed, and her lips were red. And Alwen couldn't remember having ever seen anything quite as alluring.

What harm was there in a wee wedding? If she had to kill Mirador, she'd be a widow – one with a castle. *I don't want to kill her*, Alwen admitted to herself. *The mission is to* contain her. *So if we are married…*

～ MIRADOR ～

I knew she was mine before she did. I hadn't understood it until today, though my parents and cousins had spoken of it. My heart felt as if a shaft of light had pierced it, cut clear through me, when she smiled at me that first time.

Of course, I also knew what she was: a hunter. She had all the markings of one of the holy sisters that the queen commanded. I could smell the metal weapons on her, and my nose tingled at the garlic, salt, and seeds sewn into her skirt hem.

Fate has a perverse sense of humor.

"Behold my oath that I will take no one as my wife except you," I intoned as I stepped over several bodies where they were nursing bruises and egos. "I take you, Alwen, as my faithfully conjoined wife to have and to hold until the end of my life, and I give you my word of this, if you should accept me and my vow."

"You don't know me," Alwen said, even as she stepped around the bar and came to my side.

When she said nothing more, I added, "Ubi tu gaius, ego gaia. Where you are, there am I. If you have me, I will take only you."

In a shaking voice, Alwen answered, "I take you, Christabel of Mirador, as my faithfully conjoined wife to have and to hold until the end of my life, and I give you my word and vow of this, if you should accept me and my vow. No other vow before yours."

"I pronounce you wives, by the powers and all the rest," Cyrus bellowed. "Let no person put them asunder."

I met Alwen's gaze, knowing what other vow she must mean. My fated bride was here to destroy me. I couldn't mention it in the company of so many who had no idea what I was. So I took Alwen's hands in mine and vowed, "I will give you no cause to heed other vows that came before this day."

I felt the tremble in her as she asked, "Why?"

"You were destined to be mine, and I will dedicate myself to proving that I can be worthy of that fate." I pulled her closer to kiss her, but a boot hit my temple.

I pivoted. "Truly? A muddy *boot*, Emil?"

"Not throwing my mead." Emil scowled from where he sat against the wall.

"A round to celebrate my nuptials!" I grinned at Cy. "Put it on my tab!"

"Mirador!" Cyrus glared at me, but before he could come around the bar, he was swarmed by drunks in search of a free pint.

I lifted my wife into my arms and ran from the tavern. Alwen wrapped her arms around my neck, laughing and chastising me at the same time.

"To our castle, my love!" I found a strong pair of horses, boosted Alwen into the saddle of one, and discovered both a bottle of some vintage and a bit of coin in the saddlebag of my own chosen steed.

"Do you always bring a second horse?" Alwen asked.

"Never." I wasn't lying, and I rather liked that. I lied so often to convince unsuspecting maidens and matrons to slip into the shadows with me. There were no restaurants that served what I ate, so what was a woman to do? And I often left them smiling for other reasons as a gratitude for their kindness. I suspect more than one of them had whispered enough that my appetite drew the Crown's attention.

My bride and I rode out of Helgren and into the dark.

"Keep a dagger at hand, my love. There are dangers aplenty in the shadows."

"A dagger?"

I opted not to answer. We both knew she was armed, and now *she* knew that I was aware of her weapons.

As the moon rose higher and we grew closer to home, the castle showed her best face, and I heard the whispered, "It's gorgeous," from my left side. My bride stared up at the behemoth, and I paused to let her awe wash over me.

I could already feel my body reacting to her. We were wed. That started the bond. And as long as she drank no blood, she'd remain more or less human. The choice to change would be hers alone.

"Mirador?"

"The view *is* spectacular," I offered.

My skill at flattery was far less impressive than my adroitness with weapons and naked intimacy – but I couldn't say that to the bride staring up at my ancestral home so cheerily. She was a strange one, not complaining, not objecting. A wiser woman would flee, if not from the foreboding castle, at least from the scarred wife she'd landed.

Instead of leaving me like a sensible woman would, however, Alwen was staring at the structure as if it were grand. Maybe to her it seemed thus. I tended to see the ancient edifice as a crumbling pile of debt and decay, dressed in curses and ornamented by bad decisions. Yet my smiling bride was gazing at it with the sort of wonder she seemed to reserve for heinous things.

Luckily for me.

"I can't believe I'm going to be lady of the manor," Alwen said, awe bleeding toward a sort of joy that I found rather disarming.

"Castle Mirador is not perfect," I started to explain. "Neither is her master, as a matter of record."

Alwen laughed. "You speak as if I'm unaware of the whispers, Christabel of Mirador."

I flinched at hearing my full name spoken by my sweet bride with her hidden daggers. I was helpless before her at that moment, filled with respect for her machinations and audacity. One second of mad love, and here we were. Married. Bound together. I could no more will my heart to stop than rout her out of it.

"We must release the horses," I told her, gesturing at the path. "If we try to ride at this hour, we might as well step off the edge."

She laughed again, a musical note that I was coming to value in a way I knew was a deepening of the bond. "I'll follow you, Mirador."

We stepped onto the path. It was longer than it appeared. The switchbacks were blade-sharp, and the ground littered with what I hoped were sticks illuminated in the moonlight. The occasional bone of my parents' meals – rodents and serpents mostly – had been washed out of the rubble of the tower that functioned as their cairn.

The walk was as quiet as things ever were here at Mirador Castle. Coyotes yipped and sang in the nearby canyon, and strange bird cries cut through the night. Something wailed. I thought it was a creature, not a relative come home, but one never knew here. Only one thing in the night was likely to be murderous, and I'd already tithed this season.

My wife's breathing was not heavy. Nothing we'd done had

taxed her. Not when I had hastily married her, not our abrupt departure from Helgren, and not the steep walk to the castle.

"You have a soldier's stamina," I remarked.

"And aim," Alwen added.

"Ah, are we confessing now?"

"I know what you are," Alwen allowed.

"Sister of Peace," I rebutted.

"And yet you married me…" She continued at my side, calmer than most women when they learn of my predilections.

"I drink blood," I blurted out, darting a glance at her.

"So I was warned." She smiled. "Do you always marry your victims?"

"No. Never."

We fell quiet as we continued the walk.

Ambiance matters. If one were to find her way up the winding road at the front of a cliff, following switchbacks that were designed to invite gasps, and focused attention lest one plummet to certain doom, the castle would be revealed slowly – as if a maiden were oh-so-casually lifting her skirt higher and higher. At first the heart speeds slightly, but as more is exposed, gasping truly is the only option when the viewer glimpses an ankle, shapely calf, or a bared knee, if one were risqué.

Or in this case, the viewer would see a solid foundation topped by dark stones and eventually, at the summit, the ramparts. Castle Mirador looked elegant when strategically revealed under the right lighting. Like bruises on our fictional courtesan's leg, Mirador's evidence of a rougher past aren't apparent in low light. I knew the crumbling turrets and parapet walks with their missing stone and gaping roofs were hidden by shadows at this hour.

My home, such as it was, had seen better days. Then again, so had I. My armor hid more scars than anyone elegant was meant to see.

Alwen interrupted my gloomy thoughts. "Do you suppose we should've brought food?"

She pressed close to my side, but I didn't answer at first.

"All I need is you," I swore. That, like everything I said, was only half of a lie. Her blood would sustain me in a way food could not. Oddly, though, what I wanted was her kiss.

I had the bottle of wine and a few sundries from the saddlebags in hand. I hadn't stolen the bags, and I'd released the horses. The money and provisions I'd kept. I gestured to the makeshift sack over my shoulder. "But I can provide for you, Alwen."

She stared at me, shoved her hair back so her throat was bared. "In exchange for this?"

"If you are willing, but... what I most want, what I would give anything in my power to have, is a taste of your lips." I stepped in front of her and waited.

~ ALWEN ~

Alwen ought to say no. She ought to focus on the mission. Those details were the reality she should be embracing, but Mirador was staring at her with hungry eyes. Her lips parted, a glimmer of white teeth.

"Is this about bedding me or my blood?" Alwen blurted out.

"My kind has a destined partner in the world, and mine – *you* – were hidden away from me. I knew on some level that you were out there, but I despaired." She stood in front of Alwen, sharp-edged teeth plainly visible now, hiding nothing. Her fangs glimmered in the light of the full moon.

"I've been in the convent."

Mirador nodded. "They undoubtedly knew you were meant for me."

Alwen thought back to Mother Superior's odd words. "Perhaps."

"I am yours, Alwen of Mirador." She stepped even closer. "Let me show you how happy we can be."

"I don't love you."

"Yet."

"I was sent to kill you," Alwen pointed out.

"I will give you a little death as often as you want. Will that satisfy this obsession with killing?" Mirador's eyes glittered at this short distance.

"Maybe." Alwen let out her breath in a sigh. "Show me, and I'll allow a kiss."

And Mirador dropped to her knees in the dirt, gazing up at Alwen in adoration. "Perfection."

She lifted Alwen's skirt, pressed a kiss to the vein that pulsed under the sword strapped there, and guided Alwen's leg over her shoulder. It was scandalous to be doing such a thing out in the open along a path under such a bright moon, but Alwen reminded herself that the path led only to the castle.

Then Mirador pressed a kiss to the juncture of Alwen's thighs, a lick, a small bite, and in a matter of seconds, Alwen thought of nothing at all.

"Christabel…"

~ MIRADOR ~

"Mirador. Christabel." Alwen shook me roughly. "Wake up."

I grabbed a sword from the hold above our heads. In a blink I was armed and upright. All traces of sleep were gone.

My bride was as naked as I was, but she was staring at the eagle currently perched on the windowsill.

"We're going to have to talk about where you nap," I muttered to the bird.

"You have a pet eagle?"

The beastly thing let out a loud noise, seemingly in objection. Increasingly, I thought the feathered pest might understand our language. It mattered little, though.

"She's mine. She lives here now," I told the bird.

I felt cheerier than I ever had in my lifetime, the bond fully and surely upon me. Her blood was still a sweet memory that brought a smile to my lips. I glanced at the tiny red marks on her inner thighs.

"How often do you need to eat?" she whispered.

"Monthly."

"Oh." Her cheeks pinked. "So I suppose you don't want to—"

Her words got lost when I bent to cover her lips with mine, slanting gently over her still kiss-swollen mouth. Alwen melted at my touch, and the longevity of my curse suddenly seemed like a gift. We'd have centuries together, which I ought to tell her, but if I spent all of them adoring her, I would still want more. She was my world now, my sun and moon, my pulse and breath.

When I pulled away from kissing her, I asked, "I must know everything, Alwen. Everything. What pleases you? Do you read? Sew? Sing? Garden? Do sums for pleasure? Dance?"

She laughed. "Most people start there."

I shrugged. "I am not most people. You came to kill me, my love. I was entranced."

"Madwoman," she breathed.

"Sometimes." I gazed in wonder at her, naked and in my sheets. "Tell me."

"I love gardening, reading, and I enjoy a swordfight or fisticuffs. I cannot cook well. That was usually done by..." Her voice trailed off. "I loved the convent. The community."

I paused. My home was vast and empty. I had enjoyed the years when my family was near, so I understood. "Would the sisters want the East Wing of the castle? There's a turret, a hall, bedrooms and—"

"Truly?"

"Will they try to kill me?"

"No." Alwen smiled. "That was to be my mission." She suddenly gave a scowl. "Will you drink of them?"

"No."

"Anyone in Helgren or elsewhere?" she pressed.

"Only you," I swore, adding part of my vow aloud again. "If you have me, I will take only you."

Alwen's glower vanished. "My mission was to 'contain' you. Have I done that without your death, Mirador?"

"I am yours," I swore again.

She gave me another kiss, this one at no prompting by my touch or word, and I thanked the Divine for sending her my way. Fate. The Divine. The Crown. The deadly Sisters of Mercy. I would be faithful to all and each because they had brought this wonder to my side.

"I will rebuild the library," I offered.

Alwen beamed. "The convent will pay rent, of course. What you choose to do with it is up to you."

"The decision is up to *us*," I corrected. "We can ride to them or send a messenger."

The Sisters of Peace already knew where Castle Mirador dwelt. Our castle home was far from spectacular right now, but with work and grace, it would be repaired.

The eagle made a low noise and looked away. The bird settled on her nest, and I wondered if we could restore another room so she could have this one for herself. My castle would be filled with family, but that was no reason to ignore the one creature who had shared my home of late.

But then my wife pulled me close and whispered wicked requests of me, and I thought no more of anyone or anything else. She might not know me fully, nor I her, but she already had my heart, my body, and my castle at her command. In merely a day, Alwen had eradicated my loneliness and claimed my heart.

"Mirador?"

I paused in my kisses.

"Love me," she ordered.

And that was the order I had waited to hear all my life. The destined keeper of my heart had demanded that I love her, and so I did, I would, and until our deaths, I would continue to do so.

UNTIL DECEMBER

By

KELLY ANDREW

December

It's 8 a.m. and Orson Auclair is staring. This is nothing new. He usually does. He's made the act of leering into a veritable art form. He glowers with the best of them, scowls with the greats. It's studious, the way he's applied himself over the years, like a war general assessing the foundation of a castle for cracks.

Looking for ways to bring Georgina Wells crumbling down.

It's been like this for six long years — since their disastrous first meeting in junior year of high school. She'd been new in town — a former military brat, nomadic and friendless, fresh from several years of homeschooling. She'd gone to school determined to make a good first impression. To put her best foot forward. Instead, she upstaged the school's resident genius in a quiz on which Latin conjunctions were best to use when drifting.

She hadn't meant to do it. One minute, she was rattling off conjunctions – *et, que, sed, neque, aut* – and the next she was pinned by that colorless stare. Striking. Cold. Like the first breath of a winter's day. She'd felt an immediate shiver run down her spine.

After that, she'd done her level best to avoid eye contact altogether. Head bowed. Eyes on her paper. The room around her crackling with frost. For the most part, her plan had worked – until just after class, when she found herself cornered by the lockers, those quicksilver eyes inches from her face. *"Next time Professor Archambault calls on you, play dumb."*

It hadn't taken her long to figure out who he was. Tempus Academy's golden boy. Before Georgina, Orson Auclair had been staunchly unopposed. Brightest in his year. Valedictorian hopeful. Class president. A nepo baby, whose father had an entire wing dedicated to the Auclair family name.

Georgina hadn't been born into it. Not like him. She'd discovered the art of drifting quite by accident – one day she'd been thinking of her mother, floating on a navy vessel somewhere in the Baltic Sea, and the next she'd been there, listening to the slap of waves against the hull, her mother's startled gasp as she launched from her bunk.

The sight of her standing there, tangible and close, had startled Georgina right back into her own body. She'd snapped into her bones like a rubber band, and that had been that. Her father, a professor of philosophy at a nearby university, had declared she'd moved well beyond his ability to teach, and promptly enrolled her in Tempus Academy's School for Gifted Children.

Orson Auclair's ivy-clad kingdom.

Unlike Georgina, he'd been born into a *family* of drifters. His father had been a spy during the Third World War, before drifting became as commonplace as any other career. He'd slide out of himself and into enemy territory, pinning his coordinates just by looking at a photograph. Auclair's mother had the ability, too, though she'd preferred to use it for more personal tasks. She'd drift to Aspen in the winters, Martha's Vineyard in the summers — spend her days among the bright blue hydrangea blossoms and the clapboard cottages, watching the tide rush in.

As a result, Orson Auclair knew how to drift well before he could walk. She'd heard a rumor that he used to slip right out of his bassinet and into the playpen, wake the entire household with his vast arsenal of toys.

Georgina couldn't imagine him as a little boy. In her head, he'd always been this: cruel, cold, and clever. His arm at her windpipe, his head bent in close. *"If you know what's good for you, you'll stay out of my way."*

She used to tell herself that once high school was over, she'd be free of him. Instead, and by some unfortunate turn of events, they'd landed at the same university. In the same field. Matter transmogrification. Energy sciences. Ways to unlock the brain, to widen the drift field. To perfect the art of stepping outside oneself, and into the vast ether of the electromagnetic current connecting all humanity.

Today's class is centered around the mantis shrimp; an ugly, iridescent creature that processes the world through twelve channels of color. Twelve, where the human limit is three. Professor Elrod has thrown up several slides that look, to the untrained eye, gray. The day's instructions are simple. Clear your mind. Think of the proper conjunction. The most accurate verb. *Vide.* See. There's a color here beyond human perception. Perceive it.

She isn't sure how she's meant to unlock anything with Auclair staring so intently.

There's something markedly different about the way he's watching her this time. He isn't leering. Not today. Today, he looks wary. Nervous, even. He keeps trying to catch her eye. She stares dead ahead at the slide of gray. She doesn't see a single color.

Here is the worst part about having a nemesis like Orson Auclair: he's a natural. His talent is hereditary. Innate. He makes it look easy.

And Georgina? She's well-read. She's intelligent. She's very, very good at studying. But she's never been able to drift. Not on purpose. Not when it counts. Not when it matters. For her, drifting is as accidental as a sneeze, a totally involuntary occurrence. Three years into university, and she still hasn't managed to recreate what she did the first time she transported herself to her mother.

By the time class ends, she's in a horrible mood. She didn't see a single shred of color. She packs up her things in a huff, shooting a sorry half-smile at Professor Elrod. Georgina can already predict the consolatory email she'll receive later this afternoon. *Your electromagnetic field is powerful. You are brimming with raw energy; you just need to learn to tap into it. We'll get there. Keep trying.*

Her one solace is that Auclair didn't see anything on the slide, either. He couldn't have. He was too busy watching her flounder.

As if she'd summoned him, he appears. He's sloppy today – dressed in gray sweats and a t-shirt – like he rolled out of bed late and raced all the way here. It's not at all in line with the Orson Auclair she knows – fastidious to a fault. She's fairly certain he's been seeing someone. Several days in a row, he's been late to class. Sometimes, he doesn't show up at all. Once or twice, he even arrived with love bites on his throat, which is the most undignified thing she can possibly think of. Georgina expected better from him. A shred of self-respect, at minimum.

Now, his lanky frame swallows up her path. He looks as though he's been waiting for her. She tries to skirt around him, but he doesn't let her through.

"Can we talk?"

She draws up short, forced to look up at him.

The worst part about Orson Auclair is how beautiful he is. Long, full lips and dark lashes, with cheekbones that could rival the work of Michelangelo. Back in high school, there'd been a rumor that his mother delivered him alone in a freak November blizzard. Mid-drift. In the middle of a snowy Manhattan side street. She'd gone into labor in the back of a taxi cab and tried her best to transport herself to the nearest hospital. The result was a baby born in snow.

Wind-whipped. Cold. Brutal.

Glowering up at him, it's difficult not to believe the stories, ridiculous as they are. He looks as if he's been whittled by a biting wind. His features are pale and sharp beneath a close crop of dark hair. Usually, he wears it in a severe part. Today, it's a mess, the ends peeking forward over his ears. Like he rolled out of bed and came straight to campus. She hopes whoever it is he's been seeing comes to her senses soon.

She hopes this mystery girl takes his heart out and stomps on it.

"I can't imagine what you could possibly have to say to me," she tells him.

Shouldering her bag, she shoves past him, determined to escape into the December cold of the quad. From there, it's a short jaunt to her car, then a five-minute drive to the tiny attic apartment she shares with her geriatric cat and her turtle, Hank. Georgina visualizes the coziness of her apartment — the teakettle on the stove, the knitted quilt from her grandmother, and the gentle slope of the ceiling — and wishes, for the umpteenth time, that she could drift as easily as her classmates.

It would be so nice, to blink herself away where Orson Auclair cannot follow.

As it is, he's following her now, tailing her down the stairwell and out into the lobby. He cuts her off at the pass, skidding just slightly in his sneakers. Sneakers. Another thing she's never seen him wear. It's always dress shoes. Glossy and expensive.

"Georgina, wait."

This makes her stop. Georgina. *Georgina?* In the six terrible years she has known Orson Auclair, he has only ever called her Wells. He seems to notice his slip-up at the same time. His cheeks color — something she didn't know they could do; she'd always thought him bloodless, like a vampire — and he clears his throat. He doesn't take it back.

"I'd like to walk you to your car," he says, instead.

She stares up at him, stunned. "Excuse me?"

His throat clicks as he swallows. He seems impatient. "Let me walk you to your car, Georgina."

Georgina, again. "Have you suffered a blow to the head?"

"What? No." He searches her face in that same, unsettling way. "Can't I be nice?"

"I wish you wouldn't. It's like seeing a fish walk on land."

"Be serious."

"Do I look like I'm kidding? By the way, no, I do not want you to walk me to my car. I'm being so sincere when I say I'd rather eat lead."

But he's already tugging on his coat. As he slips his arm into his sleeve, she catches sight of what's scribbled along the inside of his forearm.

Her name.

Georgina.

She blinks. Blinks again. It's impossible. *Impossible.* Not just because it's her name, cramped and intimate, but because of who wrote it. His arm disappears into the sleeve, but there's no denying what she's seen.

Her handwriting, on the inside of Orson Auclair's arm.

His eyes lift to hers. He knows she's spotted it. He seems on the verge of saying something. Something ruinous. Something horrible.

She doesn't let him.

She flees.

As it turns out, Orson Auclair is a tough person to shake. He's waiting outside her apartment when she arrives home. Worst of all, he looks infuriatingly casual about it, slouched against the old brick tenant house with his hands stuffed in the pockets of his coat. It's snowing heavily this morning, and somehow – irritatingly – it suits him. He looks made for this weather, like some sort of wicked Jack Frost. Like he stepped out of a cold front and onto her stoop.

Angry, Georgina tugs her collar up around her throat and forces herself to approach. It rankles that she drove all the way here, skirting traffic, slipping on ice, and all he had to do was picture her building, and there he was. Effortless. Innate.

It begs the question: how *did* he know what her apartment looked like? She didn't even think he knew where she lived.

"I'm going to call the police," she states, as she lets herself in.

"Go ahead." He slips in after her, just before the door can shut. The sight of him standing in the narrow foyer, dusting snow from his shoulders, turns her stomach. Or maybe flips it.

"I mean it, Auclair."

"So do I. Call them, I don't care. It won't make a difference."

There's something ominous in the way he says it. Something inevitable. She doesn't trust it. She darts toward the stairs in a desperate but futile bid to lose him. He falls into easy steps alongside her, taking one long stride for every two of hers. Tailing her to the converted attic she calls home. Light pours in through the windows at each landing, snow gathering in fluffy drifts against the glass. Beneath her chest, her heart beats at a clip. Orson Auclair is in her complex. Orson Auclair has followed her home.

It feels like a fever dream.

He doesn't even live anywhere near here. Last she heard, he'd moved out of his parents' chalet in Courchevel and into Boston's glittering Seaport, into a studio he bought – bought, not rented – with his mother's money and his father's influence. If the roles were reversed – if *she'd* followed *him* home – she would have been denied entry by a doorman.

At least her cat is waiting for her upstairs in her apartment. Morgana hates everyone, even Georgina. She wouldn't put it past the vicious old alley cat to chase him out.

When she steps into her kitchen, so does Orson. He slides through the narrowing gap, entering the space – her space – as if he owns it. She's never been more conscious of her things. How small they are. How secondhand. Her tiny vintage fridge, the dated green backsplash, and the slim black cat with murder-yellow eyes perched atop the tile. She braces herself for criticism – for him to sneer and mock and deride.

He doesn't. To her great and unimaginable horror, he squats down and scratches Morgana between the ears. Morgana, who detests being touched. Morgana, who only lives here because she followed Georgina home one day – fat with kittens and days away from giving birth – and then never left, even after the rest of her litter had been rehomed. Morgana, who won't even let Georgina pet her without drawing blood.

"Did I hit my head?" she demands, dropping her bag onto the counter. "What is happening here?"

Sensing tension, Morgana slinks into the bedroom. Slowly, Auclair rises to his feet.

"You don't remember," he says. "I'm too early."

Unease bleeds through her. "Is this a riddle?"

"What? No."

"A game? Have you developed a new and inspired way of screwing with me?"

Annoyance flickers across his features. "No."

"Okay." She pulls the apartment door wide. "Then get out."

He hesitates, his focus drifting to the window. To the snow, gathered thickly on the sill. It's begun to slow. The first needles of sunlight poke through the glass.

"It's all the same," he whispers, and for an instant, he looks as afraid as she's ever seen him. As helpless. "We never had any control at all."

Her unease deepens. "What are you talking about?"

"Do you think it hurts?" His cold eyes flick to hers. "Dying?"

"Okay, seriously, Auclair. You've always freaked me out, but you're taking this to a whole new level."

His head cants to the side. He looks tired in this light. Tired, and forbearing. "Be gentle," he says. "Okay?"

Before she can ask him what the hell he means, he's gone. Not through the door, the asshole, but in a blink. A shifting of the ether. An effortless drift.

"Showoff," she snaps, and shuts the door with a slam.

That night she dreams of snow.

*

It blizzards in the night. The following morning, the world is crisp and white and glittering. It takes Georgina an hour to dig out her car. By the time she makes it to campus, she is soaked through and shivering, her mood sour.

Her first class of the day is Transference, which is by far her weakest subject. It isn't the testing portion that eludes her – it's the practical application. Drifting physically is one thing – conceptually simple, even if she's only ever managed to do it once. Drifting mentally is another thing entirely. Six years of study, and she's never mastered the art of slipping behind someone else's eyes.

Orson Auclair, of course, is exceptional at it.

He picked up on transference from his father, who utilized the talent often behind enemy lines, hopping in and out of the heads of soldiers and politicians alike. She doesn't know if he inherited his natural aptitude, or if his prowess comes from a lifetime of practice.

Either way, it's yet another skill he possesses and she doesn't. The total disparity of it rankles her beyond measure.

Auclair is already in class when Georgina arrives. It took her so long to dig herself out, there's only one open seat remaining. And just her luck, it's next to him.

He sighs when she sinks into the chair beside him. "The one day you're late, Wells, and it's the only time I'd prefer to sit with anyone but you."

Her eyes jolt to his. "What?"

"Nothing," he says, and kicks his feet up onto the table. "Never mind."

Professor Souza arrives a few short minutes later, muttering about the weather and shedding her outer layers. She breaks the students off into pairs, setting a hunk of blue chalcedony onto each table. A conduit of communication. An organic amplifier.

To Georgina, it might as well be a piece of coal.

"Start small," says Professor Souza. "Open yourselves up to one another. Think of a shape. Something simple. Visualize it. Its edges. Its corners. Its color."

Auclair settles deeper into his chair, hands laced behind his head. Deceptively casual. He's dressed to the nines again this morning, not a hair out of place, as if yesterday was just a momentary lapse. He looks unfairly handsome in a pair of pressed slacks and tooled brogues, his cable-knit vest the exact shade of blue she'd imagine him wearing... if she thought of him at all.

Next to her, he smirks. It's halfhearted, lacking its usual cruelty. "You think about me all the time," he says. "Don't lie."

Her heart plummets into her stomach. "That's not fair."

"It's quite literally the assignment."

"We're supposed to be thinking of shapes."

"Think of a shape, then, and stop fantasizing about me in blue."

Anger builds inside of Georgina like a blister. She wants to pop it – to let her temper ooze out – but instead it feels like a modicum of normalcy. A return to their usual rapport. This version of Auclair – persistent as a pest – is far more 'palatable' than the Auclair she'd encountered in her kitchen, blinking over at her like a man coming out of a trance. Petting her cat like he knew her. Speaking in riddles.

"Why was my name on your forearm?" she asks, before she can stop herself.

His smile flickers. He takes far too long to answer. "Wouldn't you like to know?"

"Are you obsessed with me or something?"

"Come on, Wells," he says. "You don't need to be a mind-reader to know that."

His answer sinks into her. She doesn't need a mirror to know her cheeks have gone pink. Just as she doesn't need to meet Auclair's eyes to know he's watching her squirm. She thinks she'd rather be bleeding internally than sitting here beside him, weathering his scrutiny.

The sound of his feet dropping from the table in twin plunks draws her eyes to his. He leans in conspiratorially, fingers closing over the chalcedony. This close, Georgina can smell the toothpaste on his breath. Can hear the scrape of stone over laminate as he pushes the rock toward her.

"Why don't I think of the shape, and you try to work it out? You clearly need the practice."

She wants to argue, but he's right. "Fine."

"Fine." He sits back, kicking out his feet. "Go ahead."

She meets his gaze and holds it, wishing she'd arrived early enough to work with her usual partner, Constance Abernathy. As it is, Constance is engaged in a fruitful session with Eustace Papadopoulos just two tables away, and she's stuck here. Staring down a viper.

"A viper," says Auclair dryly. "Really?"

"Stop that."

"Stop shouting all your thoughts at me, and I will."

"It's not me, it's the chalcedony."

"Of course it is. God forbid you ever take responsibility for something, Wells."

"Just shut up and think of the shape."

His brows lift. "I've been thinking of nothing else."

Georgina bites back a retort and squares her shoulders. Stares deep into his eyes. The minutes bleed away from them, charted by the loudly ticking clock at the back of the room. And then, like the feel of sinking into soft sand, there's a shift. A giving way. Her focus snags on the outer edge of something – a circle. Not flat, like a drawing, but soft and pink. There's movement, too. The heave of a breath. The arch of a spine. Not a shape at all, but a girl. A girl with a fine curtain of hair, strawberry blonde. A pert, freckled nose and heavy-lidded eyes. Hazel eyes. *Her* eyes.

She topples back into herself as though shoved. In the opposite chair, Auclair is tight-lipped.

"Here we go," he says ruefully.

"That's all you have to say for yourself? *Here we go?* What sort of sick fantasy was that?"

But even as she says it, she knows it's not true. That wasn't a fantasy.

It was a memory. An impossible, implausible memory.

Across from her, Orson Auclair looks as stoic as she's ever seen him. There's something fatalistic in his eyes. His face is stone, his jaw is set.

"Georgina," he says, and nothing more.

She reaches for the chalcedony and grips it hard, the jagged edges biting into her palm. She casts out of herself, searching for the riptide pull. That esoteric shift. This time, there's no uncertainty. This time, she dives. Distantly, she hears Auclair curse. Something heavy topples to the ground. Professor Souza shouts her name.

Georgina doesn't heed it. She is looking down at herself – at her arms pinned above her head, her wrists shackled in a long-fingered grasp. The same grasp that once held her notebook aloft over the cobbled well in the Tempus courtyard. *"Trust me, I'm doing you a favor."* The same hand that once cut off her escape the night after the solstice gala. *"You're an explosion waiting to happen, and no one sees it but me. If you had any brains at all, you'd drop out before you kill someone."*

In the memory, his hands slip down to cup her face. There's a glimmer of bronze. A fall of books. The clatter of wood against a hard floor. She is flush with color, a name breaking at her lips. *"Orson, quick. We have to be quick."*

She plunges deeper. Knifing into his head. Chasing after his most private thoughts.

Another memory. A window, ferned in frost. Her, seated on a leather couch, a blanket around her shoulders. Her voice, curling through the ether like smoke. *"What if I'm just going to keep killing you? What if this is all there is?"*

A hand at Georgina's wrist wrenches her back to herself. She is on her feet, blood trickling freely from her nose. She swipes at it with her own free hand, knuckles coming away bloody. Professor Souza's grip is ironclad, her face white. All around them, the rest of the class has gone silent. Only Auclair makes a sound.

A horrible, gasping noise.

He's on the floor, his head tipped back, foam gathering at his lips.

Professor Souza's voice comes out tight. "Someone, call an ambulance."

There's the sound of running footsteps. It's followed by a great and terrible quiet as, on the floor, Orson Auclair — the object of Georgina's rage, her ire, her most deeply buried affections — goes still. His spine, previously arched, falls flat against the floor. After that, everything happens in staccato. Professor Souza kneels at his side. Checks his pulse. Shakes her head. *No*, Georgina thinks. *No. No. No.*

"She killed him," someone says. Constance, maybe. The words echo horribly.

Souza reaches down and shuts Orson's eyes. He looks like he's sleeping this way, the tension gone out of his face. For a single, manic moment, she thinks maybe he is. Maybe this is some elaborate, awful prank. It wouldn't be the first one he's played. It wouldn't even be the cruelest.

But that was when they were children.

They're adults now, and his chest is still.

His skin has gone the color of stone.

"Everyone out," orders Souza.

No one argues. They leave their things, making their way toward the door in a desolate single file. She is left alone in the room with Professor Souza and the body.

His body.

Panic creeps in, cold and absolute.

"Ms Wells," says Souza. She's directly in front of her. Blocking her view. All Georgina can see is the limp curl of Auclair's fingers. *"Ms Wells!"*

She staggers backward, her thoughts wobbling, as if she's only managed to partially reattach her consciousness. Another step, and she collides into a chair so hard she sends it clattering to the floor. The room is tight. Airless. Her mouth is ash. Her chest is a gulf.

Georgina flees, shoving out into the hall. Breaking into a run.

There's no escaping the thoughts she ripped clear out of him. No outrunning that cold, careening feeling of being stuck inside Orson Auclair's head – as if he'd died within her, still entombed inside her mind. She sees flashes of moments that aren't hers. A long, dark hall, a man at one end. A voice, sharp and bitter. *"Your footwork is abominable. Get up. Do it again. You have the Auclair legacy to uphold."*

A woman with hair gone silver and a sharp, displeased face. The lights of a Christmas tree glittering behind her as she pores over the honor roll, parchment stamped in Tempus Academy's familiar seal. *"Outranked by that charity case of a girl again? Orson, sweetheart, really – it's as if you enjoy the humiliation."*

She sees herself, seventeen years old and standing outside a makeshift door. A lesson. High school. Senior year. Her brows are furrowed, her nose crinkled. Nothing happens. Nothing at all. She hears the woman's voice again, disembodied this time, memories colliding one into the other like thunderheads. *"I've heard a rumor that she can't even control her abilities. A girl like that ought to be locked up in a cell before she kills someone. Keep away from her, Orson. I mean it."*

Georgina sees it all in ribbons. In tatters. In broken skeins of memory, pooling at her feet.

She trips down a set of steps, clinging to the railing, unsure where she is, where she's going. Blinded by memory: a bed, early morning, snow piled high against the window and her hair spread out like a halo beneath the glow of a sunrise. The voice of Orson Auclair twining around her spine. *"This moment, this moment."*

Up ahead, she spots a door. In memory, perhaps, or out of it. She trips through it, toppling out into the sunlight. Into wind. Into a quad of dull green grass and a sky that is bleak and white and vast. The snow is gone. A last gasp of leaves still clings to the trees in brittle cups of brown.

And in front of her—

In front of her—

"Don't tell me you finally managed to drift, just to get in my way," says Orson Auclair. His jacket is expensive. Suede. His hair is windblown. A stray lock hangs down into his eyes. Georgina knows, immediately, that something is terribly wrong.

"You're alive."

It's not what she means to say. It comes out anyway, surprising both of them.

"Should I be otherwise?" He peers down at the cardboard cup in his hand. "Did you slip poison into your latte when I wasn't looking? Very good sleight of hand, Wells. I'm impressed."

Slowly – too slowly, perhaps – she pieces it together. Because the coffee he's clutching is her coffee – with her name scribbled onto the side. She can recall, with perfect clarity, how he'd plucked it right out of her hand on the way to class that morning. *"Is this for me? Wells, you shouldn't have."*

Today is Wednesday, November nineteenth. Wind-whipped. Cold.

One week, three days, and two hours before Orson Auclair dies. Before she kills him.

"It's your birthday," she ekes out.

He looks at her strangely. "It is."

"But that's impossible."

"That's the thing about time, Wells. It marches ever on."

Her mind is a sieve. Her grip on reality runs away and away. "We argued in the student center," she says, remembering. "You and I. Just a few minutes ago."

"You are a paragon of equivoques today," he notes, around a sip of coffee. "Not to change the subject, but weren't you just wearing a skirt?"

In all her studies, she's never come across anything like this — drifting against the current. She's always been taught that time is a river, flowing fast. Everyone is carried along in its torrent. Some people — people like Orson Auclair and, theoretically, Georgina — can cross the stream. She knows the process cold, even if she can't make herself do it. A capable drifter knows how to find the shallow places. The muddy banks. The fords. An experienced drifter can find a way across.

But there is no swimming *against* the current.

That's time travel, and it's impossible.

"You were definitely wearing a skirt," confirms Auclair, who has been having a silent epiphany of his own. "It was far too short for a puritan like you. One sharp wind, Wells, and anyone could see up your—"

She stops listening. Across the quad, she sees the door to the student center open. Out comes a rush of familiar faces. And with them, red-faced and coffee-less and looking for a fight, is a girl with a strawberry-blonde ponytail and a pleated gingham skirt. And she's headed straight this way.

"Shit."

Auclair raises a 'brow. "Pardon?"

"Hide."

When he doesn't spring immediately into action, she grabs a fistful of his jacket and tugs him after her into the gap between buildings. They're wedged unceremoniously between the metaphysics building and the freshman dormitories, the narrow space dotted with shrubs.

"You know, Wells," says Auclair, "if this is your way of finally making a move, it's not your best."

"Quiet," she snaps. Then, too late: "Wait, *finally*?"

But Auclair doesn't answer. He's spotted what they're hiding from. She watches, horrified, as his eyes bounce between Georginas. If he has any sort of reaction, he doesn't show it. He is as calculating as ever, his mouth thinning into a tight line. He doesn't say a word to her at all until the other *her* has disappeared into the building. A cold feeling overtakes Georgina as she realizes the earlier version of her is heading into Professor Elrod's morning seminar. Auclair hadn't attended that day. She remembers spending the entire class watching his empty chair, gripped by suspicion, her throat pinched tight.

Across the alley, he's studying her closely. Too closely.

"Georgina Wells," he says, and suddenly — horrifically — he's smiling. A wide, beatific grin that sets her blood racing. "You've done something bad."

It's late afternoon by the time he finally stops making Georgina repeat herself. She sits perched on the edge of a leather couch – the same leather couch she'd glimpsed in his memories – too afraid to move even a muscle. She's imagined Orson Auclair's apartment before. Mostly, she's imagined it burning down. Bulldozed. A wrecking ball flying straight through his window just as he's finishing his breakfast.

She never, ever imagined this.

The sun through the window is pale and feeble. A late November's glow, casting the shelves upon shelves of books in a wan, buttery light. It feels entirely too personal – being here, seeing his things – but there'd been no getting around it. He'd practically wrestled her into his car back on campus: *"Use your brain, Wells, where's the one place you* won't *be?"*

His apartment smells like leather. Leather and old books, the slight smack of coffee grounds. She wished she didn't like it so much. She wished it didn't make her miss him. Horribly, awfully, humiliatingly, even though he's standing right in front of her.

Twenty-four hours ago, the sheer luxury of his accommodations – a penthouse studio overlooking the harbor – would have made her loathe him even more. She would have thought of a thousand cruel things to say about privilege and nepotism. She would have rented a crane herself.

Today, Georgina can't stop picturing his face as he collapsed. She can't stop thinking about her name, written along his forearm. She wonders if the future is inevitable, or if the sheer cataclysm of what she's done has eroded the banks of time enough to form little tributaries of possibility. She wonders if she'll ever find her way back to December.

"Tell me again," he says, bracing his hands against the back of the adjacent loveseat.

"Which part do you want to hear?"

"All of it."

"I've gone through it twice. What else could there possibly be?"

His eyes flick to hers. "You're leaving something out."

"I'm not."

"You are." He studies her closely. Too closely. "I've known you a long time, Wells. You don't think I recognize when you're hiding something?"

Georgina debates her options for a fraction of a second. She could lie. She could evade. She could open the window and fling herself out of it. In the end, she settles for the truth. "The transference of your memories was... personal."

"Personal," echoes Auclair.

"Private."

"*Private?*"

"Would you stop repeating everything I say?"

"Would it kill you to be a little more forthcoming?"

"They were intimate memories, Auclair. Of an... of an intimate nature."

Auclair blinks. "Sex."

"God." Her cheeks flame. "Yes."

"You and I, having sex."

She doesn't know which is worse – that he says it so easily, or that there's no question at all as to whether the second participant was her. He is as sure of it as anything. *You and I.* Even the way he says it is awful. Flat. Blunt. Apparent. As if he's saying, *who else would it be but you?*

"Do you have to be so forward? This is hard enough."

The chilly look he slants in her direction borders on incredulity. "Let me get something straight. You murdered me—"

"Not *yet*."

"—and you want me to censor myself? So that you can be more comfortable?"

"None of this is comfortable."

"You're telling me." He regards her coldly, and she sees the exact moment a new idea occurs to him. A new and terrible idea. "I could kill you."

"Are you insane?" She lurches to her feet. "Out of the question."

"Not *you* you, of course," he muses, and falls to pacing. "The *you* on campus. You're not very strong. Your abilities are unpredictable. It'd be easy."

"Easy?"

"Practical, even."

"*Practical?*"

"Now who's repeating who?" He rounds on her in a flash. His eyes are brighter than she's ever seen them. Wilder. "Think about it. If I take you out of the picture today, in November, you won't be around in December to shred my brain to ribbons."

"Except you'd be killing the me that's here in front of you, as well."

His smile flickers. "That's not really my problem, is it, Wells?"

"You're seriously considering it. I can't believe you."

"You killed me first."

"What I did was an *accident*. This would be premeditated."

"Trivialities." He yields several steps in her direction. "You, Georgina Wells, are a living, breathing fucking accident. It's you or me, and I choose me."

He's too close, crowding her against the glass. Against the wide, mirrored window she'd just moments ago considered flinging herself out of. She can hear the click of his swallow. Can see the hammer of his pulse in the hollow of his throat. The setting sun leeches the colors out of the apartment, until everything goes gray and formless.

Everything but Auclair, set ablaze by the dying light.

"You won't do it," she finally says.

He's watching her too intently. "Won't I?"

"No."

"You seem very sure of yourself."

"I am." There is nothing left between them but a sliver of rapidly fading sunlight. "For one, we have no idea if anything we do will have an impact on the future. You could kill me now, and something else might kill you that day in December. You'll slip on ice. You'll choke on your supper."

His mouth quirks. "Can you give me a dignified hypothetical death, at least?"

"For another," she adds, ignoring him, "I saw your memories."

She's close enough to see his pupils dilate. "They were that incriminating, were they?"

"You seemed to be having a good time," she says and immediately regrets it. The words hang between them, incendiary and irretractable. She blinks and sees her legs, hitched around his middle.

"Tell me," he demands.

"What purpose would that serve?"

"It would satisfy my curiosity."

He's too close. Too close, and there's nowhere to run.

"Nothing good will come of it," she whispers.

"They're *my* memories, Wells."

"Not yet, they're not."

His smirk screws into a grimace. She's known him long enough to recognize it for what it is – sheer determination. Her fight-or-flight kicks in and she tries to snake out from beneath him, but he's too quick. He snatches her forearm, folding it into the small of her back. She's spun out, her chest cracking against glass. The glittering palindrome of Boston Harbor falls away from her in a dizzying scope.

This time, there's no shifting of sand, no soft, subdural landing. He knifes clean into her head. She's back in Souza's Transference seminar, pondering the resignation on Auclair's face. He'd known what was coming. He'd known, and he'd let it happen.

She can feel everything – the hunk of blue chalcedony in her fist. The clumsy toppling of transference. And then they're in his memory. A matryoshka nightmare. She sees herself in that dark room, bronze glimmering over her head. The fall of books. The clatter of wood. Her back pressed against a shelf, her eyes glazed gold.

She's buffeted from all sides, caught in a frantic shutter-reel. Her bloody nose. His body on the floor. His father. His mother. Her own face, four years younger and screwed up in frustration. Faster. Faster. Faster. And then, all at once, slow. Everything careens to a stop in a mess of white, tangled sheets. And there, before her, is her golden coronet of hair. Her sun-glazed skin. His mouth at her throat.

"This moment. This."

Another drop follows. A physical one this time. She slams to her knees in the chilly penthouse. A thin shard of chalcedony clatters to the floor. Outside, the sky is full-dark. Her reflection in the glass is tear-streaked and trembling. Georgina doesn't need to look over her shoulder to know that Auclair has recoiled from her. She can feel the loss of him, like a limb. Can hear his voice, tight, empty, cold.

"Get out."

She sleeps in the campus gym, huddled on a bench in the locker room. She showers there, too, dressing in a hurry. She sticks to the outskirts of campus, avoiding crowds, her stomach rumbling. She left her bag behind the day she fled Souza's classroom, which means she transferred with nothing but the clothes on her back. There's a strange sort of dissonance, having no form of identification. No wallet. No keys. No meal card. She feels unsettlingly adrift, nameless and out of place. A lost, hungry ghost.

Pilfering snacks from the canteen is out of the question. For one, getting caught will attract unwanted attention. For another, there's a chance she might run into November Georgina, sleepy and unsuspecting, and there's no telling what sort of damage that will do.

Auclair finds her just past lunch, hungry and irritable and holed up on the third floor of the campus library. He doesn't greet her when he arrives. He only drops a stack of books atop the table and sinks into a vacant seat. He looks as terrible as she feels.

She flips through a dated textbook on theoretical physics, striving for nonchalance. "How'd you know where to find me?"

"I know all your hiding places, Wells." He tugs a book toward him and flips it open. She catches a glimpse of the spine: *The Problem with Causality*, by M.K. Alastair. "Not very clever of you to hang around your usual haunts, given the circumstances."

"I have a lecture with Donovan," she assures him. "I won't come this way for hours."

"Let's hope you're right." He thumbs to the back of the book and falls to reading. Georgina watches him scan the index out of the corner of her eye. He is alien to her like this. Quiet. Courteous. *Cooperative.*

"Are you *helping* me?"

"I'm helping me," he corrects, without looking up. "I'd prefer not to die."

"You should be more careful. To your point, I might have been November Georgina."

His mouth twitches in a near smile. "Is that what you're calling yourself?" He lets the book fall shut. "I saw November Georgina rushing off to class on the way in. You're wearing a ridiculous parka today, by the way."

"You told me I looked like a picnic blanket," she says, remembering the encounter. "You said if I sat too still, I might attract ants."

"That was mean," he admits, grinning. "The truth is, I think you look pretty in everything. Even a picnic blanket."

All the air gutters out of her. "Why would you say that?"

"Here's a thought," he continues, as though he hasn't heard her. "What *would* happen if you ran into yourself?"

"I don't really know." She shuffles through her assortment of books, desperate for something to do with her hands. "I've been researching all morning, but I can't find anything on time travel."

"I'm not so sure it is time travel," Auclair contests.

"What? What do you mean? I started in December, and now I'm in November. I went backward. That's the literal definition."

"It's the definition of drifting," corrects Auclair. "Only, you swam downriver. Not across." He punctuates this with a stare that feels like a kick in the gut. She wonders if he's thinking of the peculiar carousel of memories between them. Of the seamless way they'd fit together.

It's all she's been able to think about.

"Tell me about the first time you drifted," he says, as though he doesn't already know. As though it wasn't all anyone could talk about, when she first transferred to Tempus. Georgina Wells, freak of nature.

"My mom was deployed," she says. "I'm sure you've heard. She'd been stationed in the Baltic Sea during the sanctions immediately following World War Three. We had minimal contact. We exchanged letters whenever we could, but hers usually came back with entire sentences blacked out. It used to really upset me – more than it should have. It just felt like they were keeping her from me. I'd cried myself to sleep the night it happened. I remember wanting her so badly. I needed my mom, and then there she was."

She lifts her eyes from where she's fallen to fiddling with her sleeve. Across the table, Auclair is giving her his undivided attention. Elbows braced on his knees, fingers steepled, a stray lock of hair falling into his eyes. Georgina wishes he would look anywhere else.

"Do you know how hard it is," he finally says, "to drift overseas?"

"I'm aware, yes."

"I mean it, Wells. They talked our ears off about it back in high school, but in practice it's an entirely different beast. My dad used to be flown as close as possible to his drift location. He'd spend days beforehand studying photos of the location. Blueprints. Maps. Satellite images. All of it. He'd memorize every angle, and even then, he sometimes ended up in the wrong place."

"I know," says Georgina, growing impatient. She doesn't need him to explain. She'd taken all the same classes. Read all the same books. She knew how it worked. She knew, too, that what she'd done — exploding out of her cluttered little bedroom in Rhode Island and reappearing below decks on an aircraft carrier four thousand miles away — was an anomaly.

A hiccup.

It was an uncontrolled spasm of power, and it couldn't be replicated on command. She'd learned that lesson the hard way. Over and over again.

"Your trigger is emotional," says Auclair. "It makes perfect sense. There are few bonds stronger than that of a mother and daughter. You were upset that day. You wanted your mom, so you went to where she was. When I died—"

"Don't say it, Auclair."

"Why not? We've both seen it. What's the point in pretending otherwise?"

"It's a false memory. A–A distortion. We saw something that never actually happened."

"Yet," says Auclair.

She launches to her feet. He trails her.

"You followed a bond," he presses on, undeterred. "*Our* bond. Like it or not, Wells, that's the reality. There was no bank to cross to reach me. You can't follow the dead. So, for the second time in your life, you did what no drifter has done before—"

"Shut up."

"Get over your pious fucking hang-ups, Georgina, this is important. It's—"

"I'm serious," she snaps. "Someone's coming."

He falls silent, listening. The sound of laughter trickles in from the hall. Her laughter. November Georgina. His eyes jolt to hers.

"You need better hiding places."

"Shoot. I forgot Donovan finished early today." She's gathering up her things. Shoving books into her bag. "Move. Quickly."

To her immense relief, he follows her lead. They clear out just in time, sliding through the nearest door and pulling it closed just as she catches sight of her parka, oversized and flannel, and very much like a picnic blanket, rounding the corner. The door snicks shut. They're left shrouded in the dark, hemmed in by industrial shelves piled high with toilet paper and cleaning products.

"A closet," intones Auclair. "Nicely done, Wells. You really thought this through."

"I panicked," she snaps, wary of his elbow poking into her stomach. Able to think of almost nothing else. "What if I see myself and my brain breaks?"

"Like you broke mine?"

"Not on purpose."

"Nothing you do is ever on purpose." There's a grunt, and she feels him turn, fitting himself into the narrow space as best he can. "Maybe that's your problem. You need to start assuming some responsibility."

"I'm not going to fight with you inside a broom closet."

"Why not?" His breath gusts across her face. He is dangerously close. "It seems as good a place as any. Out of curiosity, how long do you think you'll stay out there?"

"Until Theosophy, at least."

"Ah, so we're trapped. Excellent. Fucking Wells and her books."

"I can hear you."

"You were meant to." The industrial shelf rattles beneath his lean. She can picture his slouch. The seamless slide of his hands into his pockets. After a brief but loaded silence, he falls to humming. It's a dangerous sound. A provocative sound. He knows she hates it when he hums.

"Do you think," he finally says, "the first time I kiss you, it'll be because I saw it in a memory or because I want to do it?"

Georgina's pulse skips several beats. "What?"

"It really brings all thoughts of predetermination screaming to the forefront, doesn't it?"

But she's still stuck on what he said. "Who says you're the one who kisses me?"

His surprise is palpable. Or maybe it's only that she's so attuned to him, after so many years of furious scrutiny, that she knows him blind.

"Well, it certainly wouldn't be you," he says, after a moment's consideration. "Everything you do, it's because you stumble into it. When I kiss you, it'll be on purpose."

Heat gathers in her cheeks. Simmers just beneath her skin.

"Come to think of it," he muses, before she can chastise him, "if everything is predetermined, one could argue that we don't possess free will at all."

"Auclair."

"Yes?"

"Can you stop waxing philosophical for a second and—"

"Kiss you?"

The world, and everything in it, comes screeching to a halt.

"That's not what I was going to say."

"Wasn't it?" He's moved without her noticing. The thin strip of light from the door illuminates the bridge of his nose, the devastating curve of his mouth. And then, suddenly, he's touching her. Barely. Just. His hand skims the curve of her hip.

"Look around, Wells," he murmurs. "Look at where we are."

His directive brings the shadowed opacity of the closet careening into focus. Bronze winks down at her from a box of brass fixtures on a topmost shelf. Directly over her head sits a series of dated encyclopedias, haphazardly stacked. And beside her is a broom, its wooden handle splintered. She is, all at once, both within a memory and outside it, Orson Auclair's touch skating up, up, up – over her ribs, along her clavicle, up the soft underside of her throat – until finally, finally, he reaches her mouth. His thumb presses a shallow indentation into her lower lip. A single, cut breath escapes her.

"It's fascinating, isn't it," he notes. "What came first, do you think? Our awareness of this moment, or the moment itself? Here's a thought experiment: if I lean in and kiss you now, is it because I've been led to do it, or because I want it all on my own?"

Sense eludes her. Her entire world has winnowed down to this: the pad of his thumb scraping along the edge of her teeth. She tilts back. Just a little. Just enough to get her bearings.

Her voice comes out tattered. "*Do* you want it?"

"Hell yes," he breathes, and kisses her.

It's different than it was in recall. That was all impressions, gently faded. Mental indentations, twice removed. This – this perfect, treacherous pocket of stolen time – is as raw and as immediate as anything. As insistent. She charts it all in hazy awareness. His knee pressed between her thighs. His mouth trailing along her throat. His hands in her hair.

"Touch me back, Wells," he orders between kisses.

And she does. Her hands skate over his chest – over the hard hammer of his heart, the cords of his neck. Georgina meets him in a kiss that obliterates what shreds of self-preservation remain, leaving them both fumbling with the buttons of his shirt, grasping at the hem of her sweater. Shedding outerwear and undergarments with an urgency that borders on panic. The books go toppling to the ground as his hands slide along her thighs. As her legs hitch around his waist. As memory collides with experience.

"I'm sorry," she gasps, as they move together. "I'm so sorry."

She hadn't realized how truly sorry she was until this moment. Until they're notched together in the airless dark, his arm belted around her back, both of them splitting and fracturing in a thousand different directions. A slight shift, an explosion of starlight, and everything, everything, everything clicks at last into alignment.

"Georgina," he says, "look at me."

She obeys. He's watching her the way he always does. Like he can't quite make sense of her. He's watching her that way, still, as she tips over the edge. As he follows, taut and trembling.

When it's done, they dress in silence, then sink side by side onto the floor. They wait, his fingertips tracing the lines in her palm.

"I always knew you'd kill me one day," he says. "It was inevitable."

There is no word in the English language for this feeling in her chest.

"I'm going to fix it," she promises.

He threads his fingers through hers. Brings the back of her hand to his mouth. She can feel him smiling, and she doesn't deserve it.

"I know," is all he says.

⁜

They're a week into researching when they finally find it: the first glimmer of hope.

She's curled on the couch in his apartment, hemmed in by a growing fortress of books. A useless, dusty hoard. She's gone through everything. Annals. Records. Periodicals. Anything they can get their hands on. Anything at all. Every last resource has turned out to be a dead end.

In three days and two hours, Orson Auclair will die at her hand.

"We've been going about this all wrong," declares Orson, bursting through the front door. He unravels his scarf and drops onto the couch, tugging her into his lap in the same fluid movement. He smells like the first snow, crisp and cold. His hair is still damp with it when he leans in to nuzzle her neck. "Hello."

She lifts her chin to grant him access, shivering as he peppers her throat with kisses. Caught between this slow, intoxicating bliss and a sense of stifling urgency.

"Orson, we should focus."

"I am intensely focused," he murmurs into her sternum.

She presses him back into the couch, shifting until she's

straddling him, her knees notched on either side of his thighs. "You've learned something new."

"Maybe." His touch scores Georgina's hips. His eyes are bright, his mouth bruised with kisses. "I've been thinking about Parmenides."

It takes her a moment to understand what he means. "The Greek philosopher?"

"Yes, and how he believed reality is intemporal."

This again. "Orson—"

"Just wait. Hear me out. He thought the universe was the same, all throughout, yes? If true, that would mean time is static. Everything is happening all at once."

She thinks about what he's saying. "Except that line of thinking has been disproven."

"No, there's *a lack* of proof. That's different. Think about it, Georgina. We've been taught to envision time as a river, ever-flowing. But what if what we've been taught is wrong? What if it's a pool?"

"I'm not sure how this gets me home," she says, driven to distraction by his touch. "A pool, a river, a puddle. The analogy doesn't matter. I'm still stuck here. And even if I manage to go back to the moment I left, you'd still be dead."

"But what if you haven't left at all?" asks Orson, his fingers tiptoeing along her spine now. "If all time is static, then right at this moment there is a very distraught version of you sobbing over my corpse."

"I didn't *sob*."

"No, you're right. You'd be far too traumatized. It's a common symptom of shock."

"That's not funny."

He grins and tips back against the cushions, his hands bracketing her hips. Peering up at her in that studious way of his. With a steadfastness strong enough to snap her in two. They spend some time sizing one another up, basking in the glow of a feeble November sun. Lost in thought. Steeped in dread. Comfortable in the feel of one another, in spite of everything that has happened. Everything that will.

"I saw you today," he finally says.

"Were you horrible to me?"

"I tried not to be, but I think you're suspicious."

She blinks down at him, another piece clicking into place. Another epiphany, popping into sparks.

"I wasn't suspicious," she admits. "I was jealous."

"Jealous?" He looks unreasonably delighted for a man approaching death.

"I thought you were seeing someone."

"Ah."

"Don't gloat."

His eyes glitter. "I didn't say a word."

"You don't have to. It's all over your face."

He reaches up and presses Georgina's hair behind her ears. "You can read me that easily?"

"Like a book, Auclair."

"Give me an example."

She considers him, shivering as his thumb traces shapes along the underside of her jaw. "The day I killed you, you knew what was coming. I've never seen you look so resigned."

His touch stills. "I'll know this time, too."

The way he says it – as if it's an inevitability – puts an awful pit in her stomach. "So, is this it? We're trapped in this loop forever?"

"I don't think so," he says, after a moment's consideration. "You didn't know what was coming, which means you must have drifted *somewhere*."

"But where?"

"That's the mystery. If we're operating under the assumption that we exist at all times, in all places, then theoretically you would have had to slip back into some version of yourself, at some moment in time. The fact that there's two of you existing simultaneously in the same moment is a glitch."

"A hiccup," says Georgina.

"A hiccup," he agrees.

She thinks of all she's seen, the flickers, the variances, the memories. The answer feels like it's right there, on the tip of her tongue. At the edge of her consciousness. She reaches for it. "You came to my apartment the day before you died. You seemed distressed."

"Distressed?" echoes Orson, frowning. "That doesn't sound like me."

"You were wearing *sweatpants*," adds Georgina, as though this is further proof of how calamitous the entire situation had been. "It seemed like you'd been there before."

Solemnly, he says, "I have never been fortunate enough to receive an invite to the great Georgina Wells' apartment."

"Don't joke. This is serious."

"Well, yes, if I was wearing sweatpants, then it must have been extremely serious."

"Orson, stop it. This is important – you were in my kitchen, and you said something strange. You said a lot of strange things, actually, but there was one in particular – oh!" She snaps her fingers. "'I'm too early.' That's what it was."

He gives a short bark of laughter. "Wells, you genius. This is how we do it."

"It is?"

"Yes. Don't you see it? We follow the memories. We use them as a roadmap. Think about it – when you shifted back home, that first time in Rhode Island, what did it feel like?"

"It hurt," admits Georgina. "It felt like I was slamming into myself."

"What if you were?" asks Orson. "When I drift, I take all of me. What if when you drift—"

"It's just a portion," finishes Georgina, considering.

"If you've rattled a piece of yourself loose, you'll need to put it back."

"You make it sound like my soul was searching for yours," she says. "That's not science, Orson. That's poetry."

His throat clicks in a swallow. He searches her face. Finally, he says, "'The steeds that bear me carried me as far as ever my heart desired'."

She falters. "What is that?"

"It's poetry." His smile is crooked. "Parmenides, to be exact."

When all she can summon in response is a scowl, flat and dark, he leans in to kiss it away. "We must have found proof of it the last time. Georgina," he speaks into her mouth. *Think*. Why else would I have been expecting you on that day of all days?"

"Desperation?"

"Have a little more faith." He pulls back to look at her. "Out of curiosity, what color are your sheets?"

"White." She cuts him a sideways glance. "Why does that matter?"

"During our last transference, I saw us. Together. In a bed with white sheets. I said—"

"'This moment'," she finishes.

"'This moment'." Their eyes clash. The anticipation is a held breath. "Let's recreate it."

※

They go to her apartment in the late morning, once she's certain November Georgina is safely on campus. Without her key, she's forced to ask the super for help. Giulia Marino is a stout, Catholic woman. She scowls up at Orson as she lets Georgina in.

"I will pray the Rosary," she says. "And bring you a lasagna. You are too thin."

"She didn't like me," notes Orson, once they're alone in her kitchen.

"Don't take it personally," says Georgina, setting down her things and gesturing for him to follow. "She gets jumpy if I have any male guests over. I think she missed her calling as an abbess."

Orson tails after her, ducking to avoid hitting his head on the dramatic slope of the ceilings. "And does that happen often? You having male guests, I mean."

"I'm sure you'd love to know."

Her bedroom is small and somewhat unimpressive, like everything else she owns. There's just enough room for her half-poster bed and a singular dresser, atop which sits a burbling tank. Inside, Hank the turtle suns himself on a rock. Morgana lies curled on the bed in a patch of sunlight, looking furious to find Georgina back home again so soon.

For the next several minutes, they stand side by side at the foot of her neatly made bed. Contemplative. Uneasy. In the quiet, everything veers into too-sharp focus. The creak of the floorboards. The clatter of her downstairs neighbor. The distant scream of a kettle.

Orson Auclair, delineated in the midday light. Marked for death.

"What else does Parmenides say?" she asks, because she feels the need to say *something*.

She expects him to crack a joke. To make light of it. Instead, he thinks for a minute. When he speaks, he's uncharacteristically quiet. "'And there is not, and never shall be, any time other than that which is present, since fate has chained it so'."

The verse ebbs between them. It doesn't make her feel any better.

"This feels wrong," she says. "Something's off."

"You're just nervous," he offers, but he feels it, too. His voice comes out tight.

"That's not it." Worry worms into her, cold and wriggling. "There's not enough snow."

"What do you mean?"

"Look at the window. In the memory, there was snow piled on the sill."

A yellow goldfinch chooses that precise moment to alight on the sash. It lingers there for an instant, bright and ephemeral beneath the dripping spikes of ice. It feels like a sign, though Georgina has never believed in signs.

"We don't need to recreate that moment," says Orson suddenly. "You need to drift to it."

Fear clots in her veins. "I can't."

"You can." His confidence is catching. The air crackles with it. "Georgina, you *can*."

"Not on command."

"Not on command," he agrees, turning to face her. "To me."

He looks so despairingly confident. So infinitely trusting. So utterly doomed.

"And what if I fail?"

His smile is thin. "Then I die."

"Not funny."

"I agree. I don't want to die, Georgina. I want to live. I want you. That moment — you and me and the snow covering the window — that's where you need to be."

She can't do this. Can't stand here in the glow of his unearned confidence. She paces away from him. Paces back. Her stomach is sick. Her words come out bitten. "The fact that I have a very concrete memory of watching you die suggests that I missed that moment. Maybe more than once. Maybe an infinite number of times."

"So, don't miss it this time." Like it's as simple as getting off a train at the right stop. Smiling faintly, Orson leans in and kisses her right on the mouth. It's slow and sweet and fleeting. When it's done, he tips his brow to hers. No singular moment has ever felt more colossal. More catastrophic. In a whisper, he says, "My life is in your hands, Georgina Wells."

He steps back. Her heart feels like it's collapsing in on her.

"Wait." She lunges for her dresser, scrabbling for a pen in the messy top drawer. Reaching for his arm, she presses up his sleeve. He looks on as she scribbles her name along his forearm. *Georgina.* Another roadmap for them to follow.

"What's this?"

"In case I miss again. Show me your arm. Tell me what happened."

A muscle works in his jaw. "You'll never believe me."

"Try. Promise me."

"I promise." His eyes travel over her. Cataloging her. Sizing her up. Like always. "Well," he says, with a lift of his shoulder, "I'll see you when I see you."

And then he's gone. Out the door, down the stairs, leaving her alone. She wants to race after him. To tell him to stay.

But that way ends in death.

Gripped by a cold intensity, she shoos Morgana off the bed and lays down on top of it. Flat on her back, arms cast to the side. Afloat. She thinks of everything she's been taught. *Summa.* Drift. Everything she's read. *Fluito.* Float. Only this time, instead of envisioning a river, she envisions a pool. Flat and blue and still. Sky mirrored in its depths. On the other side stands Orson Auclair. Object of her ire. Her affection.

Singultus. Hiccup.

She thinks of its other meaning. Death-rattle.

She sinks. Into cool waters. Into fathomless depths. Into endless, winking starlight, reflected both above and below, like the night sky refracted off a flat, clear pool. She shuts her eyes and imagines the feel of fitting back into herself. What it might be like, to pour out of a pool and into a body. This fractured soul-piece into flesh and blood. This hungry, spectral girl into skin and bone. And there it is — a surge, a plummet, a strange, subdural *click*. The rush of awareness, of sheets against skin. The kiss of cold air on her chest. The frost against the window. Her breath, harsh against the quiet. And then, quite impossibly, a breath, breaking over her throat.

"Please," whispers Orson Auclair. "Please, let this be it."

And then he's there, her wrists shackled in his grasp, sheets damp and legs tangled. She opens her eyes and finds him peering down at her, his own dark eyes searching. At the look on her face, his mouth turns up in a smile.

"Like a fucking book, Wells," he whispers.

Later, wide awake, she traces circles into his back and watches Morgana bat her paw at Hank's water. In the window, the sun turns the snow to diamonds.

"I know how *I* got here," she says, "but how did you?"

Sprawled flat on his stomach, Orson doesn't open his eyes. "I'm very charming."

"You've never charmed me."

"Evidence suggests otherwise." He flops onto his back and peers over at her. "You told me you were jealous. I used it to my advantage."

"You seduced me?"

"More like, I talked you into a one-night stand."

"I can't *imagine* how you decided to broach that topic."

"I find it's best to be direct," he says, and his grin is sharp enough to cut into her. "I suggested we fuck each other out of our systems."

"Ew." She plucks a pillow off the bed and lobs it at him. "I can't believe I fell for that."

"Oh, please. You were looking for a reason."

Georgina pulls her knees to her chest, contemplating him sidelong. "Did you?"

"Did I what?"

"Get me out of your system?"

The look in his eyes is solemn. "Never."

They lapse back into silence, each of them ruminating over their victory, however uncertain. It's Orson who speaks first, rolling onto his side to face her. "I've been thinking about the theory of predetermination."

"What, right now?"

He ignores her. "It's a load of crap. All of it. We're proof of that – you and me. We did it. We changed something."

"We don't know that for sure."

"We do. Today is Tuesday. Tomorrow is the day you kill me."

"I won't," she swears. "I'd never."

He rolls over her until she's pinned beneath him, leaning in to press a kiss to her brow. Everything, everything, everything sits in perfect alignment. The beat of their hearts. The flow of time between them. Their breath in tandem. Their fate, chained.

"I know," he says, and smiles. "That was just a hiccup."

THE KING'S WITCH

By
TASHA SURI

The soldiers come for me as I am scribing *Histories of the Peninsula* by lamplight. The mouser cat, Numen, is snoring on my feet. She spent an edifying hour chasing fireflies before succumbing to sleep, but hours have passed since then, and the night's insects are now a rich froth on the lamp, unhindered by her curious paws.

The light is so dimmed by gossamer wings that I ruin my copy of *Chapter Three, The Rise of Kings* long before the soldiers thunder up the stone steps, rattle my door, throw it open and fling themselves to their knees around my desk. Still, I blame them for the damage, my voice trembling, as Numen launches herself across the room and claws her way into her preferred hiding spot on top of my wardrobe.

"This is a hermitage," I say shakily. "How dare you disturb this sanctum – my manuscript is *ruined* – I – I cannot fix it – the azure ink alone cost me five gold talons—"

"Mistress Silver," the first soldier says, as I flounder for words. "A thousand apologies. But it is your time, ma'am. The old king has been dead six moons, and the wars of succession are done. You've been chosen."

I push my spectacles up my nose, and inhale deeply. My lungs, and my head, are suddenly quite empty.

"There's been some mistake," I reply, when I find my voice again. "There are twelve other potential brides." And any new king, approaching their coronation, would pick from those twelve before choosing me. I do not claim this out of any desire to denigrate myself. I simply know my worth. I have carefully cultivated my value, after all.

"The new king chose you, Mistress Silver," the soldier says. "The ceremony of faces was held – your portrait was presented – and when I bowed before the king, I was given your image and tasked to seek you out."

The first soldier – the commander of this group, I realise now – removes a miniature from his stiff jacket to confirm his claim.

In the hazy light I peer at a palm-sized copy of an oil painting of myself. I remember sitting for the original; it was painted eleven years ago when I was still only a girl of eighteen, and the artist did me the great disservice of rendering my likeness with painstaking accuracy. There on the miniature before me is my own face, pinched and thin, my black hair scraped severely back, my Tyrene-marked orange eyes narrowed behind gold-wired frames. There is my unsmiling mouth, my stiff shoulders, my grey gown embellished with crescents of green thread. I embroidered the gown myself – even in miniature, my lack of skill with a needle is glaring.

I take the painting from him, and it is a miracle I do not drop it. My hands are quite numb with shock. I cannot imagine any new king, still steaming with blood from the battlefield, looking at my sallow and unlovely face and thinking, *Ah yes, this is the bride for me.*

The soldier has been speaking, but I have not been listening. I force myself to pay attention.

"...proxy marriage will be carried out here before dawn, and then we will accompany you back to Anamora."

"A proxy marriage," I repeat.

"Contractual and symbolic," the soldier says, voice placating. "A priest has come from Anamora to stand in the king's stead. You must understand, the king cannot risk travelling with the throne so freshly blooded."

The sting of being lectured about kingly marriage practices – me! Lectured! On topics I am clearly, necessarily expert in! – returns my good sense.

"I understand," I say. "Take me to the priest."

※

How is a crown born? How does a nation decide upon its rulers?

I have lived and studied long enough in the hermitage in Braithen to know that every land has its tales of how it came to be, and its reason for crowning and worshipping the mortals they raise above the rest. But in all the fourteen entwined regions of the Helvell Peninsula, they say a ruler is made first by their well-blooded sword, and second by their marriage to one of magic's heirs.

This is how to gain a throne: when the previous king dies, an ambitious warrior must slay all other would-be kings, those likely lords who think a crown would suit them well. But then a king must lay down their sword, and take a spouse from Tyrene's bloodline to bed.

Magic's wiliness. Might's steel. These are the words engraved into the king's crown, and into the spouse's wedding torc. No king can rule without their witch.

And I, it seems, am to be the witch of our new Anamoren ruler.

There are many *descendants* of Tyrene – she was a lusty thing, and fecund with it – but precious few of us are born with both her mark and her magic. Thousands of years have thinned the blood to the faintest spark of holiness, rarely ignited. I showed my blood, as we all do, in my eyes first: rust-coloured, lambent as a cat's. The magic came later, when I reached adulthood, long after I joined Anamora's grand monastery at age five.

The blood shows young in us all, but not every heir of the First Witch is discovered in a timely manner.

I was there when the last heir joined us. I was seventeen years old, and nigh on nocturnal. It was past midnight when the gates of the grand monastery where I was raised clanged open, and a monk strode in with a girl wrapped in her arms. The girl was bleeding. There was a tumult of noise in the courtyard. I, seated on a window ledge with a book in my lap and a candle at my hip, hurriedly snuffed out the flame and watched the monks converge on her, lanterns in hand.

When the lanterns were dimmed once more, and the courtyard was empty, I crept down to the sickroom. I could hear the monks singing. Prayers would keep them busy.

The girl was lying alone on a pallet. She was bone-thin, with collarbones like knives, and hollows for cheeks. Her hair was ragged, a short auburn, her skin brown, and her eyes very much like mine – a flame-bright umber, blazing in her gaunt face. Someone had bandaged her arms and left a tonic by her bed. She was entirely alone. The monks were at pre-dawn prayers, and they would not return until sunrise began.

"My name is Lark," she said, and grinned. Her teeth were limned in blood. She wanted to scare me, I think; her grin certainly faltered when I simply poured her a glass of thinned ale, and placed it neatly on her bedside.

"Drink," I said. "You'll feel better. The blood must taste vile."

"It isn't my blood," she said. "I bit off some bastard's ear."

"Then you'll feel much better when you can't taste any more ear blood, won't you?"

She gave me a long look, and then she drank, deeply and violently, liquid pouring down her throat and her tunic. She placed the empty cup on her bedside with a clang.

"It's polite to tell me your name, when I tell you mine," she said. There was something dangerous in her voice and the curl of her mouth. "Do you think I'm not deserving of politeness, little monk?"

"My name is Silver," I said. "I am not a monk. Like you, I'm a child of Tyrene."

"Is that what I am?" When I nodded, she gave an ugly laugh. "All these years, I've been clawing to survive, and all I had to do was come here and tell these sheep I have witch blood?"

"They should have brought you here when you were small," I replied. "It's their fault you suffered. I'd be angry with them, too."

Lark's eyes narrowed. She gave me a considering, piercing look.

"Do you want to know how I got hurt?" Lark asked.

"No."

"Oh, you're a terrible liar." Lark sounded delighted. "You'd be eaten alive in the city. There'd be babies gnawing on your bones."

"I don't care for hyperbole," I said stiffly – I was then, as I have always been – and did not know what to do when Lark laughed.

"How's this then? The city's a hole," said Lark. "Ugly, full of shit and people who'll slit a throat for no more than a copper talon. I tried to steal a talon or three, and the bloke who I stole from wasn't well pleased with me. He tried to throw me into the Gel, but I stabbed him in the throat and ran to the monastery gates hoping someone would save me." I shuddered. The Gel was the river that ran by our monastery, and it was a beast of rocks and churning waters. "He's dead now. What do you think of that? Do you think I'm brave?" she asked. "Or do you think I'm a monster?"

"Monsters aren't real," I said to her. "There are just people who choose chaos or order, compassion or destruction, for their own ends."

"How wise you are!" Lark exclaimed. I was not sure if she was mocking me, and that made me bristle.

"I am not wise," I said. I could not stand incorrectness. "I'm quoting *Serene's Ethics*."

"Ooh, you *read*." She sounded delighted. She reached forward, adder-swift, and grasped me. "We are either going to be friends or great enemies, Silver," she said solemnly, her hand over my own. I looked down at our clasped hands – her bruised knuckles, my ink-blemished skin.

I did not know what to do with such a dramatic pronouncement. "We may be neither," I said.

"We may," said Lark. "But I'm rarely wrong. You'll see."

In the end, she was right, but so was I. At first, Lark was my dearest friend. And then she became something else entirely. I am not a poetic woman, but she was like a bard's song to me. I believed we would live and die together.

But she has been gone for ten years now. And I have been in Braithen ever since.

There are fourteen regions of the Helvell Peninsula. Braithen is the thirteenth, and an unforgiving land. Its proximity to the sea should make it a wealthy trade port, and the mountains that rise sharply from the salt-green shore should be rich in seams of ore. Instead, the mountains are cold, impassable and worthless, and the sea is known for nothing more than flinging ships against deep rocks, costing many a trader their crew and their livelihood.

The hermitage lies between the tooth-sharp spires of two mountains. The priest who will serve as my proxy spouse and king stands in the shadow between them both, before a stone altar, at a holy space where sky and land meet.

The monks wanted to attend the ceremony – there's precious little to do in the hermitage, and this is the most excitement anyone is likely to see in decades – but the soldiers insisted that the priest requires privacy. So I walk now to my wedding – my *proxy* wedding – alone.

The darkness is lit by golden torches, flickering wildly in the fluting wind. Against the backdrop of the sky, with the contract unfurled upon the altar, stands the priest.

Priests are different from monks. Monks serve knowledge. Priests serve power. Knowledge and power are often the same god, but sometimes – often – they are not.

The Anamoren priest wears a gilded mask of the First King,

priceless rubies embedded in a flourish like blood at the brow. I do not know their gender, or if they have one at all. They have not tied their gown in a typically feminine manner, or a masculine one, or marked themself with the braided belt or epaulettes typically used by Anamoren folk of other genders. Instead, their gown is a sweep of black, without belt or drapery – a great spill of night.

I walk to them, and bow. "Welcome, priest," I say. They reach for me and urge me to stand, their hands on my arms at first – and then around my own, clasping them tight.

"You are not Braithenese," states the priest. In their grasp, my hands look small. Their fingers are callused, flecked with scars, and sun-darkened; my own are pale, with a single callus at my writing finger, a blush of ink stains beneath my nails.

How do they know? I suppose my accent revealed me.

"I was born in Anamora," I reply. They have not released me. "I came to this hermitage in my nineteenth year."

"A decade in this place is a fate I would not wish on anyone," the priest murmurs. Only their eyes are visible through the mask, and they are dark brown, penetrating.

Of course the priest knows my age. Likely every official in Anamora knows everything about me. I am chosen, after all. But a disquieting feeling slithers through me. Those eyes look at me as if they know me.

"Why did you come here, Mistress Silver?" The priest's voice, turned hollow by the mask, is prying. "Were you exiled to Braithen as punishment?"

"I chose to come here."

"A strange choice for an heir of Tyrene," says the priest.

"Not so strange," I reply. "In this place, I may copy manuscripts and study magic without interference. I have a quiet life, with food and shelter and a very fine cat. Many would envy such a life."

"As you say," the priest offers eventually.

They turn from me abruptly, toward the marital contract, pinned to the stone altar with four palm-sized stones.

"Does anything stand in the way of your marriage to our king?" the priest asks. The words are brusque and formal. Their quill is ready, beaded with golden ink.

I almost say, *Yes. I love someone else, steadfastly. I always shall. I would rather die than marry another.* But love and marriage rarely co-exist when crowns are involved, and I am not actually interested in my own death, so I simply shake my head.

"Nothing," I say. "Give me the quill."

The priest signs the contract, then places the quill in my hand. I sign too, the words blurred in front of me.

The priest exhales. The mask lifts.

I see, in the torchlight, the shape of a strong jaw and a full, lush mouth. No more. The priest presses their lips to my knuckles. Their mouth is soft, skin hot. No part of me has been kissed in a decade, and the touch is a shock, a revelation. I hadn't realised how much I missed tenderness.

I should be affronted. But I do not pull away as the priest's mouth lingers, then leaves my skin.

"You do not have the right to kiss me," I say.

"You should read contracts before signing them," the priest replies. Their mask is back in place, their voice unreadable. They've released me. My hand is tingling. "Follow me," they order.

How did I come to love her, Lark of the city, Lark the talonless, Lark with russet hair and blood on her teeth? Well, I ask you – how could I *not* love her? I had lived a regimented and sheltered life, safe in the gold-limned walls of the monastery. Lark was like a creature from another world entirely. I was fascinated by her. She was the rarest manuscript ever placed tantalisingly before me. I wanted nothing more than to take her in my hands and read every part of her.

Yes, even when I was seventeen. Luckily I was too shy and awkward to act upon my desires, at first.

Our love story began with lessons. I was the only one she allowed to teach her to read. She could not perform magic without her letters; magic, after all, begins in writing and ink. But she taunted the monks, and was indifferent to our fellow heirs of Tyrene. It was only my guidance she wanted, and I was glad to give it.

Soon enough, we truly were friends. When I entered our dormitory or the prayer hall, she would turn to me first, a smile on her mouth. For a girl like me, of little charm or beauty, her attention was a heady thing.

It took me a long time to realise my gaze followed her too. I watched as she grew stronger, her gauntness giving way to muscle. I watched her train with swords in the courtyard, skin gleaming with licks of sweat, and she watched me scribe letters for her in the cool quiet of the library, her gaze attentive, her shoulder pressed against mine.

We watched one another, orbiting each other as celestial bodies do. It should have been a cataclysm when we finally collided. But oh, it was sweet instead. Sweet and welcome.

It was my eighteenth, my natal day, and the monks had arranged for an artist to paint my portrait. Accordingly, Lark and

I had run from the monks and escaped to the roof. We sat together and watched the clouds stretch their pale bodies across the city below – all its smog, and squat houses, its churning river. Lark pointed from here to there, describing places she had lived as a child, the place she had broken a bottle over someone's head, and the shingled rooftop where she'd slept under the stars. There, she pointed, was the tavern where a true lord of the underworld had offered her a place in his gang, when she was only twelve. "But I said no. I knew better than to get tangled up in that shit."

"Of course you did," I said fondly. "You're too brave to put yourself under anyone's power."

Her gaze was fixed on the distance. Her smile was thin, almost a flinch.

I watched her – her wild hair, curling at the nape of her neck. Her glowing eyes. The movement of her mouth, and her hands.

I realised she had fallen quiet.

"You're not looking at the city," Lark said, voice tentative. She turned her whole body to face me, hesitated, then leaned incrementally forward, not quite touching me. Not yet.

I was used to Lark's confidence. I was not used to her vulnerability. She looked at me nervously, hopefully. Her fingertips touched my cheek.

I lurched forward and kissed her.

Our kiss should have been awkward, but it was not. We melted into each other like two halves, softness and fire. Lark's hesitation was gone. She tangled her hands in my hair. She dragged me close, using her fresh strength to haul me into her lap. I gave a squeak, and she laughed fondly, her nails pressing sparks of fire into my scalp.

"My Silver," she murmured, her breath a caress against my lips. Then she kissed me once more.

Later, I was painted. I sat stiff in my chair while my portrait was sketched. The artist was not interested in me, and I was not interested in him. Melise, another heir, had spent days braiding their hair and applying blush to their cheeks before their portrait. But they wanted to draw a king's notice, and win a king's torc. I wanted no such thing. I was headily in love. In my heart, I was sure that Lark and I would stay with each other forever – wreaking chaos in the monastery, kissing in the shadows, loving one another all our days.

We had six months of happiness.

※

I follow the priest.

They do not guide me back to the hermitage. There is a makeshift camp at the entrance of the monastery, with horses tied to stakes, and soldiers milling by campfires. Of course. The hermitage is not large enough to host them all, so they must make their own shelter. They nod their heads as the priest passes.

There is a large tent. The priest enters. I know I must follow.

I think of the priest's mouth against my fingers. I think of Lark on the rooftop. Lark of the kisses, Lark of my heart. I cannot imagine the king I am married to. I can only think of Lark. Lark of my grief.

I stand frozen before the entrance of the tent. I cannot enter.

※

Six months passed.

Lark woke me in the night. She hushed me with a fingertip to my lips, then released me and lit the stub of the candle by my bedside. I rose onto my elbows and looked at her. She was fully dressed, a coat over her gown.

"What's wrong?" I whispered.

"Nothing's wrong." She reached for me. "I stayed for you, Silver," she said, holding my face tenderly between her hands. Her eyes were strangely dark in the candlelight – more black than orange, like ashes after a great fire had burnt out its rage. "When you know all of it – just remember, I stayed for you. If they hadn't found him – I would have stayed forever."

"What do you mean?"

She leaned down and kissed me; the lightest, sweetest brush of her mouth against mine.

"I'll tell you everything," she said. "But not now. We don't have time. When I'm gone, wait until the candle burns low then come to the courtyard. I'll meet you there. We'll leave together."

"Leave?"

"Yes, Silver. Leave." Her gaze was imploring. "We can't be happy here. There's no future for us in the monastery. We have to go. I just... need to clear the way."

I swallowed. I had many questions, but none of them compared to my trust in her. "I'll come when the candle burns," I promised.

Lark kissed me once more, and then she was gone.

I waited for the candle to burn low. Quietly, I dressed, and packed everything I had of value. A few pieces of jewellery. Some vials of ink. A small pouch of bronze talons. I'd never had much need for talons in the monastery. I regretted that now.

I crept out into the courtyard, and was met by blazing lights. All the monks and a dozen guards were there, yelling at one another. My stomach dropped. I feared Lark was in some terrible danger. Behind me, the other heirs emerged, drawn by the sound.

One of the monks was waving a vial around. It was full of a strange liquid – virulently orange, the colour of my eyes.

"She was a fraud," the monk was yelling. "Bloodflower ichor, applied to the eyes with a dropper. That's how she took on the look of Tyrene's bloodline. No wonder she avoided her magic lessons." The monk's face was a rictus of disgust, her lip curled. "She belonged to an underworld lord who sought to steal the riches of our monastery. Our talons or jewels – our children. She was a cuckoo planted in the nest." She pointed in my direction, and suddenly all eyes were on me. "She would have taken Silver. We all know it."

The other twelve heirs muttered fearfully; some, like wise Elara, said nothing at all. Rion, not as wise but far braver, frowned.

"She was here for years," said Rion. "If she wanted to kidnap any of us, she could have done it long ago."

"You're a sheltered boy," the monk answered. "You know nothing."

There was more talk. Some of the monks questioned, like Rion, why Lark had remained here so long, feigning the First Witch's gifts. I remembered Lark's voice.

If they hadn't found him—

Lark had come here to steal from us. But she had not. She'd stayed. She'd stayed for me, clumsily avoiding magic, playing with her swords. Loving me.

And then her master – the man who'd sent her here – had been captured and revealed the truth of her.

Rion looked at me, seeking my eyes. But I could not look at him.

"Where is she?" I asked. "Where is Lark?"

The gates shuddered open. A guard walked in, soaked through.

"I chased her," he said, panting. "I caught her. She fought. She had two knives — aimed one right at my gut."

"Where is the girl?" the monk asked, echoing my words. "Bring her in."

"I cut her throat and threw her into the Gel," the guard said grimly. My knees buckled. Elara caught me by the arm and held me upright. "Don't look at me like that — she'd have died one way or another, by the king's justice or ours. Everyone knows the price of trying to steal an heir of the First Witch. At least she won't harm any of you now."

I did not weep. That frightened my fellow heirs. They sat at my bedside and held my hand. Once, Rion climbed into bed and held me. I came close to weeping then, from his kindness.

The minute they left me alone, I forced myself to stand. I shoved my feet into my boots, and walked out of the dormitory toward the monastery's gates.

I don't know how I escaped unnoticed. I just know that I walked and walked, my body aching with grief and exhaustion. The Gel lay before me

She's there, I thought. *I'll find her. I'll bring her home.*

I dove into the water.

The Gel tried to swallow me. I was not a strong swimmer. It was only luck that brought me back to the shore, coughing water and shivering.

I threw myself back in.

The guards found and saved me. They brought me back to the

monastery, trembling and heart-sick. Two days later, I fled again. This time, I searched the city – ramshackle, narrow buildings, full of strange faces. I saw no sign of her. I paid a child with hair as russet as Lark's two talons to look for her. They stole my money and never returned.

I ran away so many times over the months that followed. On my final escape, when a furious guard dragged me back home, the monks gathered around me, their faces tired and solemn.

"What must we do to protect you?" they asked.

"I won't stay here," I said. I didn't recognise my own voice, it was so cold. "Send me to a quiet hermitage. Send me far, far away. I will not remain where she was murdered. When a new king is crowned, they can come and collect me if they want me." But I knew no king would seek me out. If I were lucky, the current king would live a long, long life and I would remain undisturbed, hidden away where I could grieve in peace.

Braithen became my home. I stayed in my room. I did not scribe. I barely ate. I felt paper-thin.

Then one of the cats in the hermitage had a litter of kittens. The runt of the litter, black as soot with eyes as orange as my own, barely grew. I fed it milk with a dropper, but it would not drink. The poor thing, I was sure it would perish. I felt the warm weight of its body, and could not bear it.

That was when I finally opened my books once more, took up my quill, and turned to the art of magic: runes and letters, limned in good ink, blessed by the magic of my hands. I wrote my magic, urging the kitten to flourish and live. The next day, the kitten recovered her strength, the film fading from her eyes, and began finally to eat. I rejoiced, and named her Numen.

That was when I decided how I would pass the many long years to come.

˜

Hands on my own urge me back into my skin; into the present of the cold night, and the tent before me.

"Follow me, Silver," the priest urges. "The tent is warm."

There is kindness in their hollow voice. Perhaps that is why I step forward into their arms. Their breath hitches, and they hold me, guiding me into the warmth of the tent. They release me as I enter, and I step forward as they draw the curtain entrance of the tent shut behind us. I can still feel the echo of their heat, and the soft velvet of their dark robes.

The tent is lushly appointed, with a large bed and a vast rug unfurled on the floor.

"You deserve a fine room on your wedding night," the priest says from behind me. They're so close. I could step back into their embrace again.

"This is not a wedding night," I reply. "Merely the night of my proxy marriage."

"You're married to the king," the priest says.

"I am."

A faint laugh.

"I told you. You should have read the contract," they say. Then they're behind me, their fingertips on my shoulders. An ache like relief fills me at being held, even by this stranger.

"You have no right to me." I say it like a question.

"I thought you would know me anywhere," they murmur, voice

low against my ear. "I thought you would recognise me the very second you saw me. But here we are, on our wedding night, and you do not see me. This was no proxy marriage, Silver. This marriage is real, and it's ours."

I turn to face them, horrible hope ringing in my skull, as they step back and reach for their robe. That night-dark robe unravels, undone by a hidden knot. The cloth spills to the floor, and I see beneath the ruse of priesthood. The figure before me is broad-shouldered and narrow-hipped, garbed in black armour over a gown cut to severe feminine angles. I see bare arms, scarred and sun-darkened.

The priest – who is not a priest – removes her mask.

I should have known her. But how could I? Ten years has whittled me down to the smallest version of myself, far too small for vain hopes or wild daydreams. I could not tell myself she was here. I thought it impossible.

But time has honed her into the sharpest version of herself, brilliant where I am dull. There is her face, no longer gaunt but striking – strong jaw and hollowed cheekbones, elegant sweep of brows.

There is a mark on her throat. The scar is a rope as silver as my name, deep and livid. But she speaks, and she *lives*.

"Lark," I say. Or try to say it; the name is more a sob. I struggle for breath, seeking to find my strength, my voice.

"If you are stealing me from the king," I begin. But then I realise – of course the king does not want me, cannot want me. This must be some trickery – a heist to pry me from the hermitage. So I say, "If you're tricking the hermitage, they'll see through your ruse. They'll accuse you of kidnapping me, and you know the price is your life. And I–I can't allow you to be hurt again." My voice shakes. "You must go."

Lark stares at me, her brown eyes blazing, her lush mouth a thin line.

"I dragged myself from the Gel. Threatened an old friend from my time before the monastery until they helped me heal up. I stole some talons, and left Anamora behind. For five years, I served a warlord in Bersalt," she says, naming the eighth region of the peninsula, where disorder runs rampant. "I rose in their ranks until I was their most trusted advisor. Then I killed them and took their place. I destroyed everyone who stood against me. I amassed power and wealth. When the king died, I was ready. I raised an army. I bathed in blood, and won a crown. And I won you. This is no ruse, Silver. I am king, and you are my bride."

I do not know how this wolf of a woman can look at me with such hunger, such avarice, as if I am as silver as my name.

"Perhaps you no longer love me, Silver," says Lark. "Perhaps you never did. But here I am. I am yours, and you are mine."

She moves closer to me. Her hand on my jaw, her other on the small of my back. She holds me like I am fragile glass, her touch light but firm. I think I could break her hold in an instant, but I cannot move. Every fingertip against my skin marks me as indelibly as ink on vellum.

I touch her in return. I trace the contours of her face. Her youthful softness is all gone. She is as unforgiving as Braithen's rocks, eyes as stormy as the Gel. She is so dear to me still.

"Why ten years?" I ask, shakily. "I did not know you lived, but if you knew…"

"I wanted to be sure that no one would have the power to

separate us again," says Lark. "And I admit it, Silver – I wanted revenge against fucking Anamora, against every person who wronged me. Now I'm king, I can have it."

"Am I a person who wronged you?"

"Did you look for me?" Lark asks. And finally, I see something of the old Lark beneath the scars, the muscle and knife-sharp self-assurance. She is accusing me, yes – but she is also *asking*. "Or did you simply forget me?"

That time is an old wound. I fear to open it. So instead I ask her a question in return. "Why wed me?"

"You know very well the price for attempting to kidnap an heir of the First Witch is death," says Lark. Her scar is a stark reminder of how close she came to paying that price. "But I have not kidnapped you. I am king, and you are my bride, and no one can take you from me."

Her voice is fierce.

"You cannot have become king for me alone," I whisper.

"When I was young, I was a thief, and proud of it," Lark replies. "Then I met you, and I changed all that I was. I became the kind of girl who would have said no to a crime lord." A wry twist to her mouth. "And then I became this – for you. You're the moon that pulls the tides of my nature, Silver. That's the truth of it." She draws closer to me, no distance between our bodies. "What did you become for my sake?" Lark asks. "Perhaps my loss did not change you at all."

When I do not answer her grip tightens, her voice darkness. But I hear the tremble in that voice – the fragility.

"We will never be apart again. Even if you reject me, I will protect you. Even if you hate me, I will love you. You may have all the manuscripts you like – all the solace you desire. But I won't let you go, Silver. You need to understand that. No matter how little you think of me."

I have always been a good student. And Lark was always my favourite subject. I look at her now, and I know her – all her fractures, her darkness, her wounds.

Ten years, she avoided me from fear. Fear that I had never loved her, or stopped when I learned the truth of her. Fear that I would turn her away. Only now that she is the most powerful person in the peninsula, only now that her armour is thicker and stronger than a mountain's heart, can she bring herself to stand before me once more and ask if I looked for her, *grieved* her, when a guard callously cut her throat and left her for dead.

I know my words could break her like the great prow of a ship against Braithen's rocky coast. But I have never wanted to hurt Lark. My heart breaks for her instead, and for me.

"What nonsense," I say, finding my voice through the pain. "If I am the moon, then you're beholden to me. You'll let me go if I desire it. But I don't. I never shall."

Lark stares at me, dark eyes fixed upon me.

"I looked for you," I say. "I ran away a dozen times, and a dozen times I was dragged back to the monastery in Anamora. I vowed to them I wouldn't stay. I vowed to them I would find you. But in the end, I told them I accepted you were dead and gone. At last, they allowed me the seclusion of Braithen. I decided it was enough. But I never forgot you, Lark. And I have proof. Send one of your soldiers to collect my manuscripts," I tell her. "Or take me there. But you must see them. Please."

Lark gives me an assessing look, then walks away from me to

the entrance. She barks out an order, and there is a flurry of activity beyond the tent.

My manuscripts are brought to me, carefully piled, swaddled in silks. They're placed in the tent. Lark watches the soldier, face forbidding. They bow and leave.

I pick up the first that comes to hand. *Serene's Ethics*. "Open it," I urge. "Look."

She turns the pages. I know what she sees. They all follow the same pattern. Ten pages, exquisitely rendered, all looping Braithenese-style script and luminous art of all manner of fine creatures. The hart, the hare, the russet fox. Then two pages of errors: just enough to ensure no monk would seek to add my copies to any hermitage or monasterial library. Many monks have sighed and shaken their heads over my work, but they accepted my failures. I am not valuable because of my penmanship, after all.

Then, finally, the pages no one thinks to look upon. Page upon page of tight scrawl, humming with power. Every page is a spill of ink and magic. Magic for seeking out ghosts. Magic for protection. Magic for luck, and safety, and shelter. All of it threaded through with Lark's name.

"What you felt, I felt," I tell her. "I have dreamt of you every day since we were parted. I spent my magic secretly seeking to protect you." I swallow. "I didn't know if you lived or not. In truth, I thought you were dead. But I never stopped trying to keep you safe."

As she reads, I see the understanding blaze across her face.

"You blessed me," says Lark, voice awed. "Every time an arrow narrowly missed my throat – when a blade went through my chest and missed my heart – all of it was your will and your magic."

"I hid here because I grieved for you," I say to her, never looking away from her face. "I missed you. I loved you. I *still* love you, Lark. That will never change."

We stare at one another over the books. And then suddenly Lark shoves the manuscripts aside. They fall to the floor with a flurry of pages, the thud of heavy spines. She grasps me and I grasp her, as she nearly lifts me off my feet and presses her mouth hungrily to my own.

She has fought wars for me, and killed for me. I do not know how to be worthy of that devotion. But I do not think worth has very much to do with what she feels for me, and I feel for her.

Magic's wiliness. Might's steel. When we return to Anamora, we will have a wedding before the city, and she'll place a golden torc marked with those words around my throat. I have never thought of myself as wily, but I will be whatever I need to be to keep Lark safe.

"My king," I whisper, when our mouths part.

"My wife," Lark says in return, voice hungry. And then she kisses me once more. In her kiss, I feel a portent of what may come: a world blood-red with Lark's vengeance, led by a woman with cold iron in her bones and a sword in her hand. But there is another future, folded into her kiss, where the world is made anew. A kinder world, where those with magic in their blood are not bound to monasteries and service to the crown. A world where girls like Lark need not choose crime or falsehoods or a sharp knife.

The choice lies in my hands. And I know what I will do. But our future will wait until morning.

"It's our wedding night," I say. "Will you celebrate it with me, Lark dearest?"

She removes my spectacles, carefully folding the fragile arms at their hinges, then places them aside. It's a miracle we haven't broken them yet, in truth.

Without them, her face is blurred and soft, her smile radiant.

As I told Lark long ago, there are no monsters. There are only people who choose chaos or order, compassion or destruction, for their own ends. But Lark could never be anything but goodness, to me.

I will give you the world, I think, already scrawling spells in my head. *A world of love, my darling. And all the vengeance you desire.*

She draws me close, into the strength of her arms, and I think no more.

DESIGNATED VIRGIN SACRIFICE

By

KELLEY ARMSTRONG

My mother taught me how to see monsters. Not everyone could spot them, she said, but with the proper training, it could be done. When I was a child, her lessons were far too advanced for me, and so I immersed myself in monster stories instead. Every time a bard came to our village, I'd pester them for new stories to add to my collection, and then I'd secrete each away like a precious jewel, to be pulled out and studied and pondered from every angle.

What I noticed was how often girls were the victims. Occasionally, I would find one where she was the hero, and those were my favorites, but I was astonished by how many young women ended up sacrificed – or wedded – to beasts, always to benefit someone else. They gave their lives to save their village, their parents, the prince, the kingdom, and they accepted this as their fate. Their purpose in life was to die, and that never seemed very satisfying, especially when the beast only returned for more girls.

All this studying primed me for my mother's teachings. When I finally understood her lessons, I began to see the monsters, and I decided this would be *my* purpose in life. I would kill monsters.

At sixteen, I went into the world and discovered that monster stories are everywhere. Every fiefdom and kingdom has their tales of the beasts who will only be sated by the sacrifice of a young woman. She has to be young so you can be sure she's a virgin, but really, this only proves that it is men making these decisions, men who have conveniently forgotten they deflowered their first virgin at thirteen.

Oftentimes, the monsters exist only in lore. They are nothing but bedtime stories to keep girls from dreaming too big. Be careful, be small, be invisible, or the king/knight/bishop will select you to feed/wed/pleasure the dragon/werewolf/hydra in our mountain/forest/sea. In those versions, there were no actual monsters, which is a relief, because if all those stories were true, there wouldn't be a virgin – or presumed virgin – in the world.

But sometimes, the stories *are* true. Other times, they become true, the beast waking from sleep and demanding its due from an overly fat kingdom. That appears to be what has happened here, in this tiny realm whose name I have never encountered before, so tiny it's barely more than a city. That city is surrounded by mountains, which is where the beast – a gryphon – lives.

After the last sacrifice, the gryphon slumbered for generations, awaking only now, when the rulers had discovered precious metals in its mountains. Some say it woke greedy for its share of the spoils; others say the mining disturbed its slumber. Either way, mining has ceased until the sacrifice is made.

This may explain why I have barely entered the city gates before I am pounced upon by locals.

"You're new," an old man says as he falls in beside me, his worn sandals clacking on the cobblestones. "From one of the villages?"

I lower my gaze and speak shyly. "I lived with my mother in the woods, but now she is gone and..." I blink, as if holding back tears.

"You are alone," an old woman says, falling in on my other side, enveloping me in the acrid odor of laundry soap.

"How tragic," the man says, in a voice that suggests the word he wants is not *tragic* but *fortunate*. Fortunate for them.

We continue along the main road, the castle shining ahead, the hovels on either side shining... a little less. The smell of baking bread mingles with the stench of slaughter, and I step gingerly over a rivulet of blood that I hope comes from a pig.

"How old are you, dear?" the woman asks.

"Fifteen, I think. At least, that's what my mother said." I actually passed my nineteenth birthday last month, but no one looks a gift sacrifice in the mouth to check the wear on her teeth.

Another woman, this one with a baby on her hip, appears from a doorway, as if she overheard us. "Fifteen," she says. "What a lovely age! I suppose you're looking for a husband."

I duck her gaze and whisper, "I can only hope to someday catch the eye of a kind man."

Another woman hurries out with a basket of apples and offers me one, which I take with whispered thanks.

"I hope your journey was easy," the young mother says. "You did not... encounter any difficulties, did you? Perhaps near the mountain?"

"Oh, no. I stayed away from the mountain. My mother always said a gryphon lives there."

The locals exchange a look.

"Did she?" the old man says, his voice neutral. "And what did she say about it?"

"That it has been sleeping for over a hundred years, but you never know with monsters. They can wake at any time."

"True, true," the old woman says, nodding. "You were wise to avoid the mountain, dear. It seems the gryphon is stirring."

I shiver. "Oh!"

"Do you… know how the gryphon is returned to its slumber?" the woman with the apples asks.

"It can be returned to slumber? Oh, that is excellent news. I had not heard such a thing could be done."

"It can," the old woman says. "We know why it has woken. Because the prince has not yet taken a wife."

"The prince? Oh! I have heard he is very handsome."

"Very handsome and very rich."

"And kind," the young mother interjects. "Very kind."

"So he needs to find a wife?" I sigh. "Imagine what a lucky girl that will be." I perk up. "Do you think there might be a royal wedding soon? I should dearly love to see it."

The old woman smiles. "Oh, I am certain it will be very soon. Now, come, child, there's someone you need to meet."

⁂

The problem with local legends is that all the locals know them. If a gryphon lives in the mountains and requires a virgin from that particular royal family, you are not going to trick any city girl into marrying the prince and being sacrificed before her wedding night. You could reach farther afield and find a foreign princess, but diplomatic relations tend to suffer when your daughter is eaten alive hours after her wedding.

The solution is to find an outsider with no knowledge of the legend and convince her that what the gryphon really wants is for a commoner to marry the young prince. Because the world is full of stories where *that's* what the monster wants – one ordinary girl to be elevated to royalty. If only monsters were so thoughtful.

The procedure rarely changes. I find a place in need of a naive sacrifice, and then I show up, as innocent as a newborn lamb. Next, I will be introduced to some palace official, who ensures I fit the criteria for a prince's bride. Of course, I am perfect. What luck! Then I am taken to meet one of the royal couple – in this case, the queen – who questions me further. When she declares me perfect – what luck! – she takes me to meet the prince. That is where we are heading now, and I know exactly what I will find: some slouching and bored young man who can barely look at me without the urge to scrub his eyeballs clean.

The queen finds the prince in the gardens. However, he is not sitting – or slouching – by the pond. He is off to one side, kneeling and planting shoots for an elderly gardener. He has a pleasant face, with a shock of bright-yellow hair, and long, nimble fingers that expertly work the earth.

"Eraric!" the queen calls.

The prince jumps up. Then he sees me, and something almost like guilt flashes across his face. He hurries over and holds out his hand.

"Eraric!" The queen passes her son a handkerchief before I can shake his dirt-streaked hand. With a deep sigh, she waits for him to clean it and then says, "This is Marielle. Your future bride."

"Ah." That look again, furtive, his gaze sliding away.

His mother clears her throat meaningfully.

Eraric gives me a slight bow. "So pleased to make your acquaintance. Thank you for your, uh, assistance in this matter."

"Yes!" the queen says. "We are delighted that you have agreed to marry our son and settle the gryphon. Eraric really should have been married last year. He *is* nearly twenty! But you know how boys are – so particular."

As she prattles, Eraric shifts from one foot to the other, looking discomfited.

"Eraric, do you have something to say to Marielle?"

"Uh, yes. Would you like to go for a walk? Perhaps to the stables? One of the hounds has new pups and—"

His mother cuts in. "That is not what I meant."

"Er, yes." He turns to me with a slight bow. "Thank you, again, Marielle, for your generosity. May I bestow upon you this token of my esteem?"

He reaches into a pocket, pats it with a frown and then tries two more as his mother sighs again. Finally, he withdraws a pendant – a brilliant ruby in an ancient filigree setting, on a chain that shines like newly-forged gold.

"Oh!" I clap my hands to my mouth. "Oh! That is beautiful."

"The pendant belonged to my grandmother," Eraric explains. "We have fitted it on a new chain, with gold from our mines."

"An apt symbol of past and future," the queen says. "The prince's past and your shared future."

"So lovely," I coo.

Eraric lifts the necklace. "Please, let me put it on you. And then we can go for a walk—"

"You will have plenty of time for walks after you are married, Eraric. For now, we have a wedding to plan. Come along, Marielle."

She taps my back, guiding me like an errant lamb. I glance over my shoulder to see Eraric watching us go, his face wreathed in dismay. He catches my gaze, and then quickly looks away, but not before I swear I see him mouth, "I'm sorry."

***

I do not get a chance to speak to my bridegroom before the wedding. Oh, he tries – with at least a dozen excuses for why he must talk to me alone – but his mother thwarts him at every turn. I could try harder to meet with him, but I don't understand the point. Does he wish to apologize for the fate I am about to face? If so, that's hardly helpful.

Oh, I fear we are about to sacrifice you to a gryphon. Terribly sorry about that.

No, if he feels some guilty compulsion to warn me of a fate I cannot escape, then that will only annoy me. It certainly won't fix his kingdom's monster problem, and I am determined to fix it.

The harder Eraric tries to speak to me, the more I need to fight against something I hate feeling. Hope. Hope that he is a decent person who would not sacrifice a stranger to keep his family's hold on their throne. But I cannot help it. I always hope.

Two days later, I am in front of the bishop, pledging myself to Eraric. I'm impressed by how quickly this has happened. Normally, they take a few days to prepare the gown while I bask in the luxury owed to a future sacrifice. But no, I have one day to be pampered and spoiled, and then it's off to the altar.

I have collected a few jewels along the way. That is always useful. Eliminating monsters is a thankless — and profitless — occupation, and I take every bauble I can get my hands on. In this case, I have the necklace, the wedding ring, a set of earrings, two bracelets and a handful of jewels that I liberated from the queen's quarters while she was having me primped and primed in her boudoir.

After the wedding, I expect a meal. Truly, it is the least I deserve, and shouldn't the royals and the nobility celebrate my sacrifice in grand fashion? There is usually a feast, sometimes even dancing, but I get none of that. Either they're in a very big hurry to sate the gryphon, or they're too miserly to waste a party on a fake wedding. I have barely said "I do" before the queen is at my side, herding me away.

"Your honeymoon awaits," she says.

"Already?"

"No time to waste, my dear. We have such a voyage planned for you. A grand ship awaits beyond the mountains."

"The mountains?" I say uncertainly. "With the gryphon?"

"Yes, the gryphon who has been waiting for Eraric to wed. We must show you to it, so it knows we have upheld our end of the bargain."

"Oh, all right, then."

The king pats my back. "Such a good girl. Now, let us get you into your riding clothes."

We are on the road by dinner hour. That means not only do I miss my wedding feast, but they do not even feed me before plunking me into a carriage, where I am seated with Prince Eraric and his parents.

"How far is it to the coast?" I ask.

"You will be there by noon tomorrow," the queen answers.

I frown. "Forgive me, Your Majesty, but if the ride takes a half-day, why not depart in the morning?"

"Because we choose to depart now."

She turns to look out through the window, waving to her people. I notice they do not wave back. They do not even line the street to watch us depart. They go about their lives, as if the royal family is not passing in a grand coach.

"The gryphon ceremony must take place at dusk," Eraric murmurs. "We will stop at the place, complete the ceremony, and then sleep the night."

"And eat?" I ask.

The queen turns to glower at me for my impertinence, but Eraric smiles.

"And eat," he says. "The meal is packed on top of our coach. A wedding feast." His eyes sparkle. "Would you like me to tell you what there is?"

"Eraric, please," his mother says. "You are a prince, not a steward."

"We start with the soup," Eraric says. "Turtle soup made from the rare bellini turtle. It is quite good... though I do worry about the turtles. Their populations are in decline."

His father huffs. "Which is why only kings and queens eat them." He smiles indulgently at me. "And princes and princesses."

"Yes, well, it is very good soup," Eraric says. "Next we have a salad made from the most delicate shoots…"

⁂

Soon after, we pass the deserted mine. I stare past the massive guard station, into the darkness beyond.

I frown. "It is a very well-guarded mine."

"Because it is a very valuable one," the queen says, with exaggerated patience, as if speaking to a very dense child.

"But there are no guards here now. Anyone could slip in and steal from you."

The king smiles. "It is not as if the earth's wealth lies scattered on the ground, child. Obtaining it is very difficult and requires specialized equipment and specially trained men."

I do not ask more. I am only needling them, and I really should not indulge the urge. I know why it is only guarded when the miners are present. But when I go silent, Eraric frowns.

"Why *is* it so well guarded?" he asks. "It seems excessive."

His father clears his throat. "Might we discuss this later? It is your wedding day. A time for joyous conversation, not dull matters of business."

Eraric nods, with obvious reluctance, and we fall back into silence.

⁂

"What the devil is that?" the king says, when the pounding of hooves has us all sitting up.

He's putting his head out the window when the coach comes to a stop so suddenly the queen shrieks and pulls him inside.

Eraric throws open the door. His mother reaches for him, whispering, "Bandits!" but he only dodges her hand and clambers out.

"Sergeant Hauge?" Eraric says. "What is the meaning of this? Where is the rest of your troop?"

I hike my riding skirt and exit the coach to see a young man scrambling off his horse. About Eraric's age, he has tan skin, dark hair, and a scar running from his temple. He's dressed in military attire, with a sword at his side. His uniform is torn and filthy, and a bloody slice on his cheek promises him a second scar.

"Oh!" I say. "Are you all right, sir?"

"Not *sir*," Eraric murmurs gently. "Remember you are a princess."

"Oh, yes. Of course."

"I second my bride's question, Hauge. What the devil has happened?"

The young sergeant struggles for breath. "Gryphon. It was – it was the gryphon, sir. It attacked. They—" He swallows. "They are all gone, Your Highness. Dead."

Eraric blinks. "Dead?"

"I— I think so. The beast took Captain Basara, after slaying my other two comrades. I tried to chase after it, to free the captain, but I could not keep up."

Eraric takes a moment to compose himself. "I am sorry to hear about your comrades, and I hope Captain Basara survives. This is my fault for not taking a bride sooner. But I have done it now, and the beast will be satisfied. No one else will die. You have my word."

His mother makes a small noise, as if to remind him that

someone else will indeed die. His new bride. Best not to tempt fate with broken promises.

"Are you well enough to join us, Sergeant?" Eraric says.

"He must be," the queen says. "He needs to accompany you and Marielle."

"Accompany us where?" I ask.

Eraric doesn't look my way, only murmurs, "The last part of the journey is along a road too difficult for the coach. We shall be leaving my parents behind. Captain Basara and his men were to accompany us the rest of the way. Now it seems it will only be Sergeant Hauge. Unless you are not up to it, Sergeant? I am certain I could protect the princess myself—"

"Absolutely not," his mother says. "Hauge will go with you."

Is it my imagination, or does Eraric sag at that?

"Fine," he says. "He will have the night to recover and then—"

"No," the queen says sharply. "Two of our men are dead. Probably three. We cannot delay any longer. You will leave right after the ceremony."

My brow creases. "But the ceremony will stop the gryphon, will it not?"

Silence, as the queen works on an excuse. Surprisingly, it's the king who comes to her rescue.

"It should," he says, "but the gryphon is obviously enraged, and we cannot take the chance it will attack our son." He clears his throat. "Or his new bride, of course. We must get you both out of the kingdom as soon as possible. Now, everyone back in the coach. Dusk will fall soon, and we must hold the ceremony at sundown."

We've travelled partway up the mountain, where the road ended at a small plateau. I'm standing on the edge, looking out.

"Careful, my lady," a voice says, and I turn to see Sergeant Hauge. His lips twitch in a tiny smile. "It is a beautiful view, but take care you do not stand too close to the precipice. It is dangerous."

I inch toward the edge. "Perhaps I like danger."

"Perhaps you ought to like it a little less." He catches my elbow and tugs me back, whispering, "Take care," as his dark eyes meet mine.

"Please remove your hand from my bride."

We both jump as Eraric strides over.

"I moved too close to the edge," I say. "Sergeant Hauge was concerned."

Eraric's nod is curt. "Thank you, Sergeant. I will tend to my wife's safety now."

The young sergeant nods and steps back, then turns to head for the coaches, and I need to drag my gaze away from him.

"It is a beautiful view," I repeat, looking out over the bluff. "You can see the city from here."

Eraric moves up beside me. "You can, and it will be even more gorgeous at night when the city is lit. We hold all our important ceremonies here, where we can look down at our kingdom and be reminded of our duty to its people."

It is a pretty sentiment, but from up here, you cannot see people. Only land and distant buildings. The kingdom as a concept, a thing to be owned and ruled, the people inside it lost, as the individual trees are lost in the blanket of green below.

"Eraric?" the queen calls. "Marielle? We are ready for you."

We head over to what looks like a giant stone table. That gives me pause. I have seen such things, where the monster apparently requires humans to conduct the actual sacrifice. When I slow my steps, Eraric takes my hand and squeezes.

"That is where we will have our wedding feast," he says.

"Except there will be no feast," his mother cuts in. "We will pack you a basket."

Eraric's shoulders slump. "I think we could spare an hour to—"

"We cannot."

The queen leads us past the empty stone table to a narrow path. The king and queen go first. Eraric follows... until he sees Sergeant Hauge slipping in behind me. At that, Eraric moves me in front of him, murmuring an apology for momentarily forgetting his manners.

We proceed through a rocky passage and come out beside a beautiful waterfall.

"Oh!" I say, hurrying forward.

Again, it is Sergeant Hauge who stops me, this time only stepping into my path. "Take care, my lady," he says as he motions to the sheer drop a few feet away, the waterfall rushing down into a distant pit.

My heart stutters. I thought I understood how this would go. I know the local legend, at least, and it does not involve the new bride being slaughtered on a stone table or pushed into a waterfall. Still, the legend and the reality often bear only a passing resemblance to one another, the story third cousin to the truth.

"It is fine to stand where you are," Sergeant Hauge says, his voice low. "I will stay where I am. You are safe."

"Of course she is safe," Eraric snaps. "She is with me."

Hauge only nods and stays between me and that precipice. The king and queen walk farther, onto a jutting rock, and I hold my breath, ready for them to call me out there. I did not expect this, and I'm not ready. If they—

"Oh, great gryphon," the queen intones, lifting her hands. "Bear witness to my son's new bride, a common girl, as you demand."

I brace, and Hauge does, too, but Eraric stays relaxed, and the queen makes no move to summon me over. She keeps babbling nonsense, and I soon realize it is for my benefit. After all, they have said the gryphon only wants Eraric to marry – so thoughtful! – and therefore they have invented this little ceremony to tell the beast that the deed is done, and they hope it is now satisfied with our nuptial bliss… as it munches on the corpse of poor Captain Basara.

"Please accept the gift of this ring," the queen says.

When she reaches for me, Hauge sidesteps, just a little, as if ready to stop her from pulling me into the pit. She gestures with impatience.

"Your ring, girl. The beast must have your wedding ring."

"What does it want with that?"

"How should I know?" she snaps.

I lift my hand and frown at the very fine ring with its very fine stones. "But this is the symbol of my marriage. If I take it off, I am no longer married, and the beast will be angered."

"Just give me—"

"No, Mother," Eraric says. "She is correct. We cannot take the chance of the gryphon thinking Marielle has thrown away her vow with her ring. Use one of yours."

The queen sputters. Oh, I understand why she wanted my ring. It is obviously a valuable heirloom. Either she would pretend to toss it in and palm it like a sideshow magician, or she would toss it onto a ledge, where she could retrieve it later.

"I will buy you a new piece of jewelry, my dear," the king says to his wife. "Let us be done with this."

She takes forever to choose a ring and then pitches it into the pit. "There. The ceremony is complete. Now off with you."

"Our dinner basket?" I say.

The queen growls and starts to stomp toward the coach, which only has a single bundle atop it, leading me to suspect I was never getting a fancy dinner.

"Allow me to help you, Your Majesty," Hauge says, striding after her, and I hold back a smile. At least someone is making sure we get a proper dinner tonight.

The king wishes us well on our 'honeymoon,' and then Hauge returns with an overstuffed basket. He bows to us.

"Shall we be off, Your Highnesses?" he says.

Eraric nods curtly and leads me to the single horse tied behind the coach.

"Where is yours?" I ask, looking around.

"You will ride with me," Eraric says.

The better to ensure I do not flee. I only smile and say that sounds lovely, and then I let him help me up onto the steed.

※

Eraric is troubled. Yes, perhaps one should be troubled by the fact they are about to sacrifice their new bride, but in my experience, princes just want to get this part over with so they can get back to their normal princely lives. The fake wedding and real sacrifice are terrible inconveniences, and even more inconvenient if they begin to suffer pangs of guilt.

I had one – a young king, actually – who became so incensed by his own emotional reaction to committing murder that he decided to blame me for the whole thing. Worked himself into a foaming frenzy insisting it was my fault for being a young virgin, upon which I told him that I absolutely was not a virgin and it was his fault for making such a ridiculous presumption based on my age and gender. That one did not go well.

"I need to confess something to you," Eraric leans forward and whispers in my ear.

I sigh. Part of me does not wish to hear this confession. It is easier if I can simply continue playing the role of the dewy-eyed virgin sacrifice until the last moment. However, there is always the risk of the prince being caught in the crossfire, and I would hate to do that if he did not deserve it.

"Yes, my lord?" I say as I shift, trying to get more comfortable. I am seated in front of him, which is damnably *un*comfortable. But if I were riding behind him, I could slip off and flee, so I am here, ostensibly safe in his arms.

"Hauge!" Eraric calls, the sudden shout making me jump.

The sergeant looks back.

"Ride on ahead," Eraric says. "I wish to speak to my bride in private."

Hauge's gaze meets mine, and Eraric's arms tighten, but Hauge only nods and spurs his horse ahead.

"I fear you are in danger," Eraric whispers. "There is..." He sucks in breath. "My mother did not reveal the whole of the legend."

"Whatever do you mean?"

"It is... possible the gryphon may still come for you. That it may demand, well, you."

I twist to look at him, all innocence and fluttering lashes. "What would the beast want with me?"

"Er..." He tugs at his collar. "I... do not know exactly, but I fear... I fear it would harm you."

"Oh dear."

"Yes. That is why my parents wanted us to ride this way at night. It is also why we were supposed to have a full quartet of guards, to ensure I did not try to save you if the gryphon comes."

"Oh my."

"But I will," he says hurriedly. "Fate has intervened, leaving us with only one guard. Hauge is not the commanding officer, so it is unlikely he knows the exact instructions. We are supposed to ride through a certain mountain pass, in case the gryphon wishes to take you. I am going to suggest another route."

"But won't the sergeant tell your parents the truth?"

"I have jewels. I intended to try and bribe the captain, but instead, I will pay Hauge. He will need to flee the country, of course, but he will have the wherewithal to do so."

"And then?"

"Well, then we shall tell my parents that the gryphon took him but left you alive, which must mean that it wishes for you to live."

And then? I want to ask. Pure curiosity, of course. Eraric seems like a lovely young man, but I very much doubt he would ask me to stay, and even if he did, I have a fate to chase, monsters to slay.

Perhaps he does not specify our future plans because he does not wish to address them. What would he say? That he has fallen madly in love with me on the barest acquaintance? That is not how things work, but I am a young woman, naive and hopeful, and I might be crushed if he did *not* say that.

I am secretly pleased by his plan, though. It is terribly sweet. I will still need to slay the beast, for his kingdom's sake, but I am unreasonably delighted to find a young nobleman who does not wish to sacrifice me to a monster. They are so very rare. It gives me hope that Eraric will be a good ruler, one who will break from his family's traditions. I would dearly love to see that.

"Your Highness?" Hauge calls from ahead. "I should not be so far in advance for too long. May I return?"

Eraric sighs. "Yes, yes. Come back."

When Hauge approaches, he is studiously looking away from me, but I can see the worry in his eyes.

"All is well, Sergeant," I say. "We have seen no sign of the beast, but my husband has a question for you. Did Captain Basara tell you which route we are to take?"

Eraric gives a soft chuckle, and he squeezes my arm, obviously pleased at my show of intelligence.

"Yes," the prince says. "I was debating the routes, and I was not certain what the captain's plan was."

"He did not say."

"Good. Then—"

"However," Hauge cuts in, "the queen was clear that we are to take the main mountain pass. I am" – Hauge clears his throat – "not certain I agree. I hate to question Her Majesty's order, but that pass is where the beast flew. I tried to say so, but she was adamant."

"You are right to question, my good man. My mother knows many things, but she does not know these mountains. I explored them for years before the gryphon woke. I have another idea of a passage we might take, though it is steep."

"My horse is surefooted," Hauge says. "Elevation will allow us to see the creature, if it comes. Please, Your Highness, if you would guide us, I would appreciate that."

※

We dine before we ascend the mountain path. Earlier, I could sense Eraric was troubled. Now it is Sergeant Hauge giving off the same sharp aura of distress. That concerns me. He'd seemed happy with the change of plans, but now he clearly struggles not to keep looking back at us. When he does — and I see his expression — I send a warning look of my own. If this goes awry, I cannot afford to make Eraric suspicious.

I hope it will not go awry. I hope I am spotting a glitter in the dirt, the rare jewel of a good ruler. Yes, despite everything I have seen, I remain an optimist. It's the only way to survive, really, or disillusionment drags you into darkness.

The horses climb the steep ascent, and Eraric scans the sky for the gryphon. The moon is full, the way bright, with no need of torches, and yet Hauge carries one aloft, a beacon in the shadows.

The higher we climb, the uglier the view grows, the trees gnarled and stunted, sharp rocks lining the trail like teeth waiting to snap. I twist, hoping to see a magnificent vista behind us, but all is darkness. I shiver, and Eraric wraps his arms around me.

"All is well," he says. "You have my word on that. No harm shall come to you."

I nod and blow hot air into my hands as a bitter wind whips over the mountaintop.

"Soon," Eraric whispers. "Once we are down the other side, I will have Sergeant Hauge build a fire." His lips go to my ear. "I saved you another glass of port, as well."

I smile. "Thank you, my lord."

"Eraric. Please." He takes my hands in one of his, warming them. "Whatever you choose after this, Marielle, know that I will see you are cared for."

"Whatever I choose?"

I feel him shrug against my back. "We will discuss that later. I wish you to have choices. This all happened so quickly."

"I am not the only one who did not have a choice."

He gives a soft laugh. "But I am accustomed to that. Choices are not for princes. We have our duty, and that comes first."

He moves closer, his body warm against my back. Then, as we reach the peak, he calls, "Take care, Sergeant. There is a chasm to the left."

"I see that. It is dangerously close to the path."

"I was going to suggest we walk our horses for this part."

Hauge grunts. "Agreed."

The sergeant swings off his steed. Eraric reins his to a halt and then helps me down. We tread carefully along the chasm edge. When I move closer for a look, Hauge seems ready to leap over his horse to stop me. I step away, and he shakes his head, but he keeps checking on me, to Eraric's obvious irritation.

"Stop up here," Eraric says. "There is a cloak in my saddlebags. My bride is chilled."

Another worried look from Hauge, but he moves to the right once there is space. When Eraric takes my elbow, Hauge tenses, but Eraric only leads me farther from the edge and points to a rock.

"Sit there, Marielle," he says. "Where it is safe."

Eraric pulls a cloak from his saddlebags, and I relax at that. As he's handing it to me, he goes still and turns, slowly, toward the chasm.

"Did you hear that?" he whispers.

"What?" Hauge whispers back.

"The beat of wings." Eraric looks my way. "Stay there, Marielle. Please."

Eraric carefully edges toward the precipice. Then he peers down. When he turns, his gaze goes to Hauge. "There is something down there. Large and dark, with a white head. Is that what you saw?"

Hauge nods grimly. "The body of a lion with the wings – and white head – of an eagle. We must take cover." When Eraric leans out farther, Hauge rocks on his toes. "Your Highness."

"I am not certain what I see is truly the gryphon."

Hauge strides over. "Whatever it is, sire, we should take cover. If it has come for the princess—"

Eraric grabs the sergeant's arm. I leap to my feet, but Hauge is already hurtling forward with a cry of surprise as Eraric whips him over the edge.

I scramble toward them, screaming, as the sergeant disappears, his cries quickly dwindling to silence. I race for the precipice, but the prince puts up a hand to stop me.

"You— You—" I say. "You threw—"

"I did what needed to be done, Marielle. His sacrifice will distract the gryphon while we get you to safety. And now there will be no witnesses to your flight." He marches back to me. "I can tell my parents that he died trying to save you."

"But— But you already planned to do that. You said you would bribe the sergeant—"

"I did what I needed to do." Eraric straightens. "I protected you."

My mouth opens and shuts as I stare at that chasm.

"He is gone, Marielle."

I still walk toward the edge. Eraric grabs my arm and yanks me back. When I try to push him off, he grips me tighter.

"Come," he says. "Let me get that port from my saddlebags."

"I do not want port. You just killed—"

He yanks me to him. "I insist," he says through his teeth. "You are cold. You should drink more port."

"Because the sedative did not work the first time?"

He stares at me, and my heart drops. Hope, it's such a fragile thing, so easily and so often shattered. I can see now that his earlier kindness was designed to win my trust and make this easier on him. If I trusted him, I would drink the port and fall into a gentle sleep, perhaps not even waking when the gryphon tore me apart. That would be so much easier for him – no traumatic memories of me wailing and begging for mercy.

I free myself from Eraric's grip and step back. "The sedative did not work because I tipped out the port. I noticed you were not partaking, and I wanted to believe you when you said you needed to be clear-headed, but I was still careful."

"Sedative? What childish nonsense—"

I snort. "It's a bit late for that, my lord. I saw your reaction when I said it. The port contains a sedative. You murdered Sergeant Hauge because you suspected he would interfere with the sacrifice."

"Sacrifice?" Eraric tries for a laugh. "What foolishness has someone put in your head, child?"

"I'm not a child. I am, however, an expert when it comes to local monsters. Your legend says that when the gryphon rises, it requires a virgin princess. The convenient way to do that is to make a princess — some commoner no one will miss. I have done this before, my lord."

"Done what before?"

"Played the designated virgin sacrifice." I purse my lips. "Well, I'm not actually a virgin, but that part never seems to matter. The point is that this is my job. I get rid of the monsters."

Eraric stares. Then he goes very still as a distant sound fills the air. The beat of massive wings.

He reaches for his sword, but I get to it first, yanking the blade free and dancing backward as I wield it.

"Let me do my job," I say.

His mouth opens. Nothing comes out but a squeak, nearly drowned beneath the thunder of those wings.

"The gryphon comes for you," he says. "You must accept your fate. For the country."

"You can accept your fate. I create mine. And mine is not to be killed by monsters." I scramble onto a rock and face the chasm. "Run, little prince. Before the beast comes."

Eraric gapes at me. Then he turns and starts to flee. I hold his sword aloft and watch as the gryphon rises from the chasm. First comes white-tipped wings. Then the top of a white head, with blood-red eyes. A yellow beak follows — a beak bigger than my arm. And last comes the body, with its four legs, the hind ones furred and clawed, the front with wicked talons. A lion's tail whips behind the creature.

"Wretched beast!" I shout at it. "Take me if you can."

The gryphon's mouth opens, and what emerges sounds suspiciously like a low chuckle.

"The people will suffer no more!" I shout. "The monsters must be purged from this land, their evil and their greed extinguished forever." I lower my voice and point the sword. "He went that way."

The gryphon dips its head, lets out a terrible shriek, and wings off after Prince Eraric.

I wait until the screaming has stopped. Then I walk to where Eraric lies bloody and dead, and the gryphon… Well, there is no gryphon. Just a young man, wiping blood from fingers that had, moments ago, been giant talons. He looks at me, his eyes shifting color in the moonlight, first gold, and then blue and then black as night. His skin shifts too, from pale to dark and every shade in between, as if unable to settle on one.

I walk over and touch his bare arm. Fur springs up, and when I rub it, the texture changes from fur to scale and then back to skin again.

"That was messy," Volkir says, his lips curling in distaste.

I lean in to kiss his cheek. "It was also much too close. You should not have let him lead you to the precipice."

Volkir shrugs. "I knew I could transform in time."

"What if you struck your head? Hit the cliffside? You take too many risks."

His brows arch. "*I* take too many risks? You're the one who kept getting near the edge."

"I was testing the prince. Hoping…" I make a face and look at Eraric's bloodied corpse. "Always hoping."

Volkir pulls me into a hug. Beneath my fingers, his skin changes, to fur, to scale, forever shifting. The curse of a doppelgänger. They have no true form and can only take on that of others. A gryphon. A young sergeant. Whatever they wish.

People call them monsters. Unnatural and inhuman. But my mother taught me how to look for true monsters, how to see the evil shimmering behind jewels and crowns and even kindness. I saw that monster shadowed in Eraric, and yet I still hoped I was wrong.

There are beasts in this world – gryphons, dragons, doppelgängers and the like. But they do not go around demanding virgin sacrifices. Like all of us, they just want to exist in peace. It is the humans who won't allow that. Two years ago, I had found Volkir sentenced to die in an arena for the entertainment of nobles. After I helped him escape, I discovered the most precious jewel of all – someone to love and trust, someone who loved and trusted me back.

There was never a gryphon in these mountains. Only gold and jewels and greed. When the enslaved miners revolted, the king and queen resurrected the old legend to frighten the miners into obedience and then planned to find a virgin sacrifice among the miners' daughters. So Volkir and I gave them a real gryphon, swooping overhead and insisting – through messages from a hermit druid (also Volkir) – that the proper sacrifice would be an ordinary girl who wandered in from the forest.

"Now, I believe you issued a challenge earlier, Mari," Volkir says. "Take you if I can?" His brows waggle.

I rap his arm. "Later. First we need to divest the prince of his jewels. Then we must finish eliminating the monsters."

Volkir bows. "As you wish, my lady." He transforms into Sergeant Hauge. "Or would you prefer me like this?" Another suggestive brow waggle.

"I prefer you as yourself, at least until we reunite with the king and queen. Now, could you please check the saddlebags? I will see what I can find on our prince."

The king and queen are still where we left them, awaiting the return of their son. Volkir had changed into a raven to confirm they were there. Now I run up the mountain, gasping, my dress torn and speckled with blood.

"My king!" I pant. "My queen!"

They've been lounging in their coach, and now the king flies out, sword in hand. Seeing me, he blinks.

"My king!" I stumble toward them. "Tragedy! Horrible tragedy! The prince is dead. The gryphon— The gryphon has murdered him."

The queen clambers out. "What nonsense is this?"

"The prince!" I wail. "The prince is dead! Killed by the terrible beast!" I turn and raise my hand. "There! It comes! The gryphon comes! Save yourselves!"

As I run, the queen hikes her skirts and races toward me. "Get back here! The beast has come for you, girl."

I spin. "No, Your Majesty. But fear not. All shall be well. Your sacrifice will not be in vain."

"What— What sacrifice?"

"I will see that your legacy is honored. I will free the slaves you took to work the mine, and the riches from those mines will go to improving the lives of your people."

She sputters. "What nonsense—"

"All will be well, and they will remember you." I meet her eyes. "They will remember you and ensure they never see your like again."

"What—"

The gryphon grabs her then, whisking her into the air.

"Oh!" I shout after her. "Captain Basara and his men are fine! Let that be a comfort to you!"

Her screams say it is not a comfort, but still, I can always hope.

༄

Killing the monsters is only the first step. Then comes days of work to ensure our efforts weren't for naught. While Volkir and I have never actually met a real hydra, tyrants come close – lop off one head, and another appears to take its place. We need to be sure that does not happen.

The king, queen and prince are recovered and laid to rest – so sad! The gryphon appears to have left the mountain – so happy! The enslaved miners are freed, and the kingdom tears down the guard towers and restarts the mines for the people, just as their rulers wanted, according to what they told the hermit druid before sacrificing themselves to the beast – so… unexpected!

This is where poor Volkir is run ragged, playing endless roles to ensure success, as much as such a thing can ever be assured. Once we have done our part, we retreat to a sumptuous inn, where I thank Volkir in the way he likes best. With hot baths and rich food and fine wines. No, that is not the way he likes best, and this is why I am happily very much *not* a virgin. But he still gets the hot baths and rich foods and fine wines, because he deserves them.

"We both deserve them," he says, when I tell him this, and he pulls me to him in bed, legs entwined with mine, whispering words of sweetness and love.

This is what it means to hunt monsters. Sacrifice, in its own way, and certainly danger, but reward, too. Fate has rewarded me with the satisfaction of knowing I help others, but it also gave me this for myself. A partner who happily joins my quest and believes in it as much as I do.

I kiss him, smiling at the soft changes of his lips beneath mine. Then I nudge him back on the bed and straddle him.

"I have an idea," I say.

He grins. "Please share."

"For something new."

Volkir's brows waggle. "Most excellent."

"A mission where I am *not* the designated virgin sacrifice."

His brows arch. Then his grin grows. "Ah. We do this, then?"

He shifts forms into a sweet maiden, with tan skin and long copper hair.

I laugh. "No, sorry. You still need to play the monster. I cannot do that. But I have heard there is a wyvern terrorizing a realm, and the bishop is holding a contest for the prettiest virgin."

Volkir rolls his eyes, having shifted back to his quicksilver shape. "Of course he is. Winner is sacrificed to the wyvern. Runner-up gets to warm the bishop's bed."

"Likely. Now, I cannot win a beauty contest, so I propose we rescue the winner and slay the monster. Then we can send the winner off with money from the bishop's coffers." I consider. "Perhaps set all the girls up on their own. All the contestants."

He rises to press his lips to mine. "An excellent plan."

"Good."

"But are you sure you don't want…" He shifts back to the comely maiden, copper brows dancing.

I laugh and lean down to kiss him. "Why not?"

SECOND CLASS MAGIC

By

KAMILAH COLE

Margot Stern didn't know what to pack for a trip to an island that hadn't existed for a century, so she brought a little bit of everything.

At thirty years old, Margot was what her parents bleakly called a 'professional assistant.' After graduating with honors from Hexenhall, one of the best magical universities in St Izabeta, she'd found her calling in field research. Bouncing from one expedition to another, mooching off of grants for other people's work, she supplemented her magical education during long nights in exotic locales, despite the efforts of her field leaders to exhaust her on their experiments during the day.

Margot was born sixth of an impressive twelve children, and so she was well-accustomed to living her life in the margins of someone else's. Her mind was both ravenous and fastidious, content to wait for a magical mystery worth sinking its intellectual teeth into.

Harlan Langford and Elixane Isle were that mystery.

Langford had been the Archmage of St Izabeta – a title basically equivalent to a court magician, and thus the second most powerful man in the kingdom after the king himself – for a memorable week over six centuries ago. He had resigned from his post by creating an island off the coast of the country which existed in its own magical subdimension, after which he and the island disappeared. One hundred years later, when almost everyone he knew was dead, Elixane Isle had reemerged, and Langford had made his first of six open calls for assistants – to be returned, of course, intact and to the time of their choosing – to help with his private research.

None of those chosen had breathed a word of what they'd done or how long they'd been gone. The last had died decades ago without giving a single interview.

Margot intended to be the next to go.

Her suitcase contained outfits for each of the four seasons, six books (three textbooks and three romance novels), a reasonable collection of shoes, toiletries, an umbrella, a wrapped bundle of letters, her second-best teddy bear, her third-best winter coat, a notebook and pen, and her resumé. She'd also managed to wedge her tea box inside with a bit of creative spell-work. By the time she'd said goodbye to her plants and left her seaside cottage, Margot was thoroughly prepared for anything.

Anything except Jesy Bellchant.

༄

Seeing Jesy on the docks was something akin to finding dog shit on the bottom of her shoe after she'd already tracked it through the house.

Jesy was surrounded by a small crowd, which made Margot scowl. There had once been a time when she would have stood there, too. She and Jesy had graduated from Hexenhall together and gone on to become assistants on many varied expeditions, but Jesy was always doing better than Margot. She would only rank first if Jesy wasn't in the running. She got her pick of the research trips that Jesy hadn't already selected. There were even rumors that Jesy had secured her first credit on a paper, due to be published in the fall.

They were from the same town, a decimal point in the valley of two mountain ranges in north St Izabeta, and that had seemed, to Margot, more than enough reason to send that first letter.

> *To Miss Bellchant,*
> *As a fellow Sunderlandian, I attended your recent panel on the restrictive elitism of hermetic magic, and I found your points on literacy and library access to be particularly sound...*

Her first message had been four pages long. Jesy's had been five, beginning with 'Have you been home recently? They've got a petting zoo!' and ending with 'Call me Jesy.' Sixty-three letters exchanged over five years, interrupted by deadlines, expeditions, study and – in one memorable case – a wayward spell that had disintegrated all paper within a four-mile radius of the encampment.

They'd traded hopes and goals. They had dissected each other's research and proposed new inquiries to explore. They'd confessed their insecurities and dark histories: Jesy orphaned and Margot overlooked. She'd sent Jesy pictures of her siblings, and Jesy had mailed her the homemade granola clusters she feasted on during late-night casting sessions.

And then they'd actually met, and it had been disastrous.

Now Margot inched around Jesy's admirers, her gaze on the weather-beaten wooden planks of the dock. Elixane was due to appear within sailing distance at some point today, and Jesy Bellchant and her cult were far from the only ones who had come to see it. Tripods were mounted with accordion-like cameras, flanked by reporters who were smoking while their unattended pens scribbled across the pages of their notepads. Merchants wove through children and families packed on the beach, offering ice-cream cones, soft pretzels, or fruit-infused water. The sapphire sky was blocked by airships, eager to catch the first glimpse of the island.

It was so chaotic that it was embarrassing Margot could tell a Jesy Bellchant crowd from a regular one. But as Margot passed, the throng parted and there she was, wrapped in a fitted black suit with a shimmering silver waistcoat. Her voluminous curls had been artfully pinned to cascade down the right side of her head and kiss her collarbone, and her large brown eyes were alight with mischief when they locked on Margot. Her amber skin was clear and dewy. Her smile could have lit the sun. Before Margot could hide, perhaps in the water, Jesy was right there, towering over her by four inches, smelling of mint and fresh parchment paper.

If Jesy Bellchant was a tornado, then Margot was a wooden shack on the plains. There was no escaping the devastating force of her.

"Stern," said Jesy. "Are you going to Elixane, too?"

Margot's panicked thoughts screeched to a halt. "'Too'?"

"It's a once-in-a-lifetime opportunity, so I knew you'd come along."

Margot blinked owlishly. If Jesy wasn't just here to watch

Elixane appear, if she was actually eager to become an assistant, then what chance did Margot have of impressing the Archmage? No one living in St Izabeta would hire Margot Stern when they could have Jesy Bellchant. Why would Harlan Langford be different just because he'd turned his back on the country to live in magical solitude? Jesy would charm him easily. Margot would fade into the background, a misspelled name on a half-hearted letter of recommendation.

Her hands tightened around the strap of her bag. She felt like a little kid who had woken up on Yuletide to an empty stocking. Her eyes burned with the need to cry.

Jesy's smile widened obliviously. "I'm sure we'll work well together, at least. We were always best at that part."

Margot should have said something cutting, maybe something about how Jesy had been the one to ruin the other parts, how small and stupid Jesy had made her feel the last time they'd seen each other, but she never got the chance. Mist gathered on the horizon, blurring the blue of the ocean with what looked like moving clouds. A hush fell over the crowd as the fog crept closer and closer, swallowing the rippling ocean waves. Camera flashes erupted in the corner of her eye. Tomorrow, the newspapers she hopefully wouldn't be around to read would be covering nothing but this: the moment Elixane emerged from the haze, all emerald foliage and golden sand, slate-gray mountains and rich brown soil.

And standing on the shoreline in a navy-blue overcoat was Harlan Langford.

Margot had read as much literature as she could about Archmage Langford. He'd been born in Cardinal, the capital city, to two professors who had fostered his love of learning and magic. He'd had a falling out with his older brother which resulted in Langford becoming Archmage just to spite him, a falling out from which they never reconciled. He had a fondness for dark chocolate and black teas, which he'd claimed in a rare interview helped him to think.

Since the last photo of him was a century old, she cast a quick magnification spell and cataloged the differences between then and now. His salt-and-pepper beard had turned fully silver. There were crow's feet by his hazel eyes and frown lines by his full lips. He was an inch shorter than Jesy, from what Margot could tell, and he was solidly built, his overcoat fluttering open to reveal a simple white t-shirt and black stretch pants.

One of the greatest magicians in history stared out at the onlookers and scowled like he'd just found a bunch of children on his lawn.

"Which one of you is my apprentice?" he said, his voice carrying across the water as easily as if he were standing right in front of them.

Margot dropped the spell and hurried forward. "Right here, Archmage."

"And here," said Jesy, stepping up beside her with more grace than Margot had ever known how to emulate.

Langford sighed. "I only need one of you this time."

Margot looked at Jesy. Jesy looked at Margot. Panic sliced through her — only one? — but neither of them withdrew their bid.

"Come," Langford said, turning his back and disappearing up the beach.

Two boats shimmered into existence at the end of the dock. Margot ignored Jesy to claim the first one, gasping in fascination when it began to race toward Elixane the moment she sat down. She could hear Jesy's boat sloshing along behind her, but she forced herself to ignore it. She'd shown initiative, which was sure to have made a good first impression. If she could keep it up, maybe the Archmage wouldn't send her back in the same ship before the day was over.

Margot had expected setting foot on the island to feel more momentous. It had been created by magic and the will of a man who was over six hundred years old by St Izabetan standards. She'd read of it and dreamed of it and wanted it so badly, it had become a thing of legend to her — and shouldn't that make her legendary, too, being here right now? But when she stepped from the boat, her boots sinking into the wet sand, she felt no different than she had when Elixane was just a smear of colors emerging from the mist. It was solid in a way it hadn't been in her daydreams. The scent of brine and vetiver filled her nose, and the same breeze that pulled the waves up and down the beach tangled in her braids. Nothing about the island screamed magical, unless you counted a complete absence of birdsong.

"Creepy, isn't it?" said Jesy, disembarking beside her. "I think his house is this way. Come on."

Margot smoothed down the folds of her skirt and followed, still waiting in vain for that spark of rightness to light up her soul.

Harlan Langford lived in a townhouse on a cliff overlooking the rest of Elixane. It was impossible to sneak up on him without being seen from a mile off, and even still the house was surrounded by a massive hedge with no visible gate. An arched doorway appeared when they arrived, closing behind them in a crinkle of foliage.

The yard was decorated with rows of flowers, paved paths, hanging cypress trees, and reflecting pools. The birdsong that had been missing from the rest of the island chorused in this haven; wrens and thrushes, sparrows and robins all hopped from branch to branch, calling to one another or watching Margot and Jesy pass with their unnervingly steady gazes.

The Archmage waited for them on the wraparound porch, his scowl firmly in place. "As I said, I'll only be needing one assistant. If neither of you want to cede the position to the other" – he glanced at them hopefully and, when silence followed, deepened his scowl – "then I suppose we should have some sort of exam."

Margot's spine stiffened. "Would it really be inconvenient to take us both?"

"I hate people," said Langford, as though it should have been obvious. Margot was glad her dark skin hid her resulting blush. "What were your university marks?"

Jesy had beaten her by half a point, but Margot had been valedictorian because Jesy "didn't have time for any kind of speech". She left that out when she added the accolade, and, thankfully, Jesy didn't correct her.

"What have you been doing since you left school?"

Jesy's expeditions were with some of the most respected names in the magical field, but Langford clearly didn't recognize any of them. Margot listed the results of her expeditions rather than the personnel, detailing the experimental magic she'd been lucky enough to work with. It was only impressive until Jesy followed up with a similar answer – and the magic she'd researched made Langford's thick eyebrows climb his forehead.

He stroked his beard. "Which one of you talks more?"

"I do," Jesy easily admitted. "But not when I'm working." She paused, and added, "Stern talks to herself as she works."

"I—" Margot's face burned. "I don't *have* to do that. I can keep my thoughts in order in all kinds of ways."

For a long time, he simply studied them as though there were a particularly complicated summoning circle. The panic returned with a vengeance as Margot overthought all of her answers, unsure if she had given the Archmage anything close to what he was looking for. Would it help to express how much she wanted this apprenticeship? How much she *needed* it? Or would that only make her sound desperate?

Margot had never understood how the very act of wanting had become so vilified. It seemed like the height of privilege, to look down on someone for wanting anything desperately. Sometimes, she felt like she was nothing *but* want, wrapped in the skin of a woman who worked herself to the bone for scraps.

There were many theories about the origin of magic. Some scholars thought it was the earth's gift to humanity, the stewards of the world given the power to shape it. Some reasoned that magic was an excess of soul inherent to everyone, their own lifeforce to manipulate without extinguishing. Less secular theories involved spirits that had created the planet and everything on it, spirits who rewarded their most devout followers with power beyond compare.

Margot had always cared less about the origin of magic than she did about her origin as a magician. The first time she had successfully performed a spell – a simple charm to float a cookie jar from the top of the fridge to her outstretched hands – it had felt like everything was awash in new possibilities. With nothing but her word and will, she had left an indelible mark on her world.

That was what magic meant to Margot: a legacy.

And as one of twelve children, those weren't easy to carve out.

Would it help her case for Archmage Langford to know that? She couldn't tell, and so she said nothing.

Finally, he said, "We'll do this another way, then. Two months. You'll stay in Elixane and we'll work together for two months. At the end of that trial period, I'll pick my permanent assistant. Does that sound fair?"

Margot couldn't say yes fast enough. She could feel Jesy's eyes on her, but she didn't dare look at the other woman. Starting now, every word she said and every move she made mattered too much to be wasted on their petty rivalry. She would kiss Jesy Bellchant on the mouth right here if it got her access to ancient magical knowledge and a letter of recommendation.

"You'll both stay in the cottage," said Langford. "It's around back. Now, I don't want to see you again until dawn."

───※───

The cottage was smaller than the townhouse, yet no less luxurious. It had enough bedrooms for six apprentices, as well as three bathrooms, a fireplace and stone chimney, and a thatched roof. Ivy curled around the curtained windows. Cobblestones lined the path that wound from the main house to the front door. A vegetable garden hid in the shadows of the cottage, bearing several plants that were out of season yet ripe and plump and ready to eat.

"So," Jesy said as soon as they were inside, toeing off her shoes by the door. "Truce?"

Margot watched her balefully from the fireplace. "We're not at war. Just because we don't like one another doesn't mean—"

"Who says I don't like you?" Jesy quirked an eyebrow. "I highly respect you, as a matter of fact."

"Now it sounds like you're trying to start one."

"One what?"

"A war."

Jesy's teeth flashed as she smiled. "I wouldn't dare, Stern. Not while you have access to me as I sleep."

Margot rolled her eyes. Any magician worth their salt would ward their door to protect their possessions – and, especially, their research – from enemy hands. If Jesy was arrogant enough not to, she deserved to live with the paranoia of thinking she might wake up with Margot's hands around her throat.

She hadn't lied, she thought, as Jesy carried her bags down the hall to claim a bedroom. She *wasn't* at war with Jesy Bellchant. There was no point in fighting a losing battle. But the first time they'd met, Margot had swiftly realized that there was a world of difference between letters – which could be written and rewritten, every word chosen with care – and being in front of a fellow intellectual, whose body language and patronizing tone could cut sharper than any sword. After suffering two hours of Jesy's condescension, Margot had excused herself to the bathroom only to return and find her pen pal talking about her to the other scholars at the benefit.

"She's boring," Jesy had said with a little sigh. "Her mind is sharp, but she has no charisma at all. She won't get very far in any field that requires connections."

"How disappointing," her companion, a man with a small brown mustache wearing a bowler hat, had said. "We need a professor at Hexenhall, but I'd prefer someone with leadership qualities."

"Margot Stern has no leadership qualities whatsoever. She'll only ever be a follower."

Margot had chosen then to clear her throat, taking a sick sort of satisfaction in the way Jesy and the man had paled. The small throng of scholars had fallen silent, their eyes darting between her and Jesy. It was one of those moments that Margot wished could be like a scene from her romance novels, where she would have flung the perfect caustic response at Jesy's feet and walked away triumphant. Instead, her eyes had filled with tears, and she'd made some sort of odd choking sob that she could still recall with enough clarity to hate herself for. Jesy had said her name, and the pity wrapped around the syllables had sent Margot running to catch the first coach back to her hotel.

The next time Jesy had written to her, Margot responded:

To Miss Bellchant,
Do not contact me again.

She'd burned Jesy's letter without reading it.

Now, standing in front of a different fireplace in a different cottage, Margot wanted to be as insouciant as Jesy was. She wanted to smile and laugh and act like those words — *Margot Stern has no leadership qualities whatsoever* — didn't live in her head, waiting for any chance to hurt her again. But Jesy was the one with the charisma, the one who could strut into a room and have everyone in it fall for her elegance and wit.

Margot, one of twelve, from a decimal point of a town in the valley, was lucky to be in the room at all.

"Not this time," she murmured to herself, grabbing her bag.

This time, she would not accept scraps. This time, she would *win*. This time, it would be Jesy Bellchant leaving in disgrace.

She would make sure of it.

                                                                                ∽

At dawn, they arrived on the wraparound porch to find two lists of chores with their names neatly printed at the top. This sight would dictate the first few weeks of their stay on Elixane. The chores ranged from mopping the porch and mucking out the rafters to gathering herbs for the Archmage's potions and making chalk for his summoning circles. All the while, Langford was like a wraith, appearing in the distance to watch Margot in silence before shaking his head as he disappeared, as if she was already disappointing him.

She gritted her teeth and walked even further into the forest, not returning until her basket was brimming with leafy greens.

She rarely saw Jesy during the day. She often returned to the cottage much later than Margot, filthy from whatever sludge Langford had made her crawl through for his materials, and she fell asleep shortly after taking a long bath.

Two weeks in, Margot gathered some extra items and, when Jesy stumbled through the door, she had a cauldron full of stew simmering in the fireplace. The cottage smelled of potatoes and homemade sausages, parsnips and mushrooms, carrots and a pinch of red wine. Margot brought a spoonful of the brown liquid to her lips, wrinkled her nose, and added more salt.

When she looked up, it was to find Jesy staring at her. "What's this?" she asked, eyes round as dinner plates.

"We made it through the first fourteen days," said Margot, setting the spoon atop the mantel. "I thought we should celebrate."

Jesy took a step forward then seemed to think better of it, hesitating in a way Margot could only describe as awkward. "I didn't know you could cook."

"I live alone, so it was cook or die."

Firelight danced across Jesy's face, bronzing her high cheekbones. Her hair was pulled up into a bun today, a mane of curls sitting like a cloud over her head. She wore a pale-blue button-down smeared with mud, black trousers that were smeared with mud, and black boots that trailed mud across the wooden floor. Leaves were caught in her hair – yet the most arresting thing about her was her gaze and the way it rested, unblinking, on Margot.

She understood even more why Jesy was always surrounded by admirers. Her focus was a heady, intoxicating thing. Margot was drunk on her attention.

"I can't cook," said Jesy, scratching at a dry patch of mud on her pointed chin. "But I can wash dishes."

"Wash yourself first. You smell."

She didn't, not really, but Margot could no longer stand the feeling of those long-lashed eyes so fixated on her. She wandered into the kitchen to get away from them, hating the way the lingering awe on Jesy's face made her chest warm. As if, even now, she still longed for Jesy Bellchant's approval.

Once she heard the water running, she went to her room. Everything in her bag had been transferred into the trunk at the foot of her bed. It took her no time at all to find her bundle of letters. Sixty-three letters that she could recite from memory, and Jesy had dismissed everything that they had been to each other to talk a Hexenhall professor out of offering Margot a job.

Her fingers traced the letters, the careful way Jesy had written her name and addresses on the envelopes, and anger flared to life in her chest. She stoked it into something constructive, building a wall between herself and the way her heart wanted to soften at the sight of Jesy Bellchant and her impossibly beautiful face.

༺༻

Two weeks of chores turned into a month of them, as if Archmage Langford had realized that two hands were better for getting to the end of his bottomless to-do list. It wasn't until the last day that Margot and Jesy were assigned to the same item, and, of course, Langford had picked the worst day for it. His library took up an entire floor of the townhouse, his enchanted books giggling as they purposefully left their own shelves to visit friends. They had until the end of the day to sort them alphabetically ahead of their lesson the next morning. Rain splattered the island, making the trees bend and the paths flood. The library had three balconies, and the wind slammed each of their doors open, letting water pool across the carpet toward the texts.

Margot and Jesy barely arrived in time to save some of the rarer parchments, which had moved from their displays in order to get some summer sun.

"You catch them, and I'll sort them," Margot said, her eyes narrow as a dictionary skirted around a shelf to place itself between an almanac and a grimoire. "You're fitter than me."

She had meant to say *faster*. Her mistake echoed through the room.

"Thank you," Jesy said without meeting her eyes. She went to lock the balcony doors, leaving Margot to consider banging her head against the shelves until a blissful darkness claimed her.

The sun had gone to sleep before they met in the center of the library, both of them breathing hard from exertion. Jesy had dutifully chased the books and parchments around the room, strapping them down when necessary, and Margot had found an arrangement for the shelves that allowed them to be alphabetical and near to their friends. Even the displays were facing the doors, safe from the elements while still able to see a gorgeous view of the dark island. Rain continued to pelt the windows, but it felt cozy rather than threatening. The clouds were dark purple, but no lightning cracked through them. The wind had calmed from a howl to a whimper.

Jesy dragged her arm across her forehead, wiping sweat on the sleeve of her button-down. "We start lessons tomorrow. *Finally.* What do you think he'll teach us?"

"I can't even begin to guess," answered Margot, eyeing a nearby armchair and wondering if it would be rude to sit while Jesy was standing. "But it will be the start of our final month here, so it better not be a spell to get bats out of the attic."

Jesy laughed, a bell-like sound that Margot immediately wanted to hear again. She sat in the armchair, folding her hands in her lap. She could feel Jesy watching her, but didn't want to look up to see how much more the woman could tower over her. Margot was exhausted, both from the physical labor and from the abrupt realization that she was no closer to being chosen as Langford's assistant than when she arrived.

"What if he doesn't plan to choose either of us?" Margot whispered. "What if this is all he intends to use us for before he sends us back with nothing?" Her nails dug into her palms. "I can't leave here with nothing. I just *can't*."

She felt Jesy settle onto the arm of the chair. She could feel the heat wafting from Jesy's body, smell her mint shampoo. Her throat was dry, and she wasn't sure it was just from the desire to cry.

"You don't have nothing, Stern," Jesy whispered back. "I've followed your career over the years. You've made incredible advancements in the use of magic in the field. You invented a spell to multiply food without the need for a word anchor. You've never left an expedition that didn't speak highly of your contributions. Archmage Langford needs you far more than you need him."

"Too bad I lack leadership qualities."

"I—" When Margot looked at her, Jesy's face was grim. "Am I finally allowed to explain myself?"

"No." Margot stood, but she didn't get more than a step before Jesy's hand caught her wrist. Lightning of a different sort zinged up her arm, but she kept her face blank. "Let me go."

"You were wasted on Hexenhall," said Jesy fiercely. "They would have kept you there, kept you small. You had the world waiting on you to do great things, and the school knew that. They didn't want to give you a job. They wanted to clip your wings before you could fly too far from their influence."

"You don't know that."

"Of course I do! So many of the greatest minds of our age are on the staff there, confining themselves to classrooms and tenure, instead of going out and innovating. Somewhere along the line, they chose safety over creation, and I couldn't let that happen to you. Not you."

"Dedicating oneself to academia is a *noble* pursuit. Sharing knowledge instead of hoarding it, inspiring the next generation of magicians, that's every bit as important as innovation in the field." Margot tugged at her hand, but Jesy held tight. "And you don't know me, so what I do or don't do is none of your business."

"I know everything about you." Jesy caught her other wrist, gently pulling until there was only a couple of inches between them. She was still sitting on the arm of the chair, allowing her to gaze upward at Margot with an intensity in her dark eyes. "I know the names of all your siblings, and I know how you like your tea. I know your soul is as restless as mine, and I know that you could have never stayed in Sunderland when you could learn so much more beyond the borders of our small town. I know that you contain yourself because you're used to not standing out, but I know that when you're in a room, you're the only thing worth looking at."

Margot tried to swallow, but couldn't around the sudden lump in her throat. "Even if you were right about Hexenhall, you – you were cruel. I bared my soul to you in every letter, and you humiliated me in front of our peers."

Jesy released her, and Margot was almost disappointed. She put enough space between them for her to breathe, watching warily as Jesy combed her hands through her hair until her wayward curls began to curve toward the ceiling.

"I know," Jesy finally said. She was standing now, her hands in her pockets. "I wasn't expecting— I wasn't my best that day, and I took it out on you. I've wanted to apologize, but I also wanted to respect your boundaries."

"Until now."

At this, Jesy's lips ticked into a smile. "I'm not here because of you. I just didn't avoid it knowing you'd likely be here."

"Why do you want to be the Archmage's assistant? You have everything in the world! Why do you have to have this, too?"

"Everything in the world?" Jesy scoffed. "You say that I don't know you, but it's you who doesn't seem to know me."

I don't remember my parents, Jesy had written her once. *But I know they were magicians. When I left the group home to go to university, I read as much as I could about them. I want to follow in their footsteps, to become the best magician in all the world. Maybe then I'll feel close to them. Maybe then I'll remember that they loved me. Or at least what it's like to be loved.*

Jesy Bellchant was always surrounded by admirers, but they had bonded over that once, how easy it was to feel alone in a crowd. Margot's loving parents and supportive siblings had always been underfoot, but there had been so many of them that her family had once forgotten her birthday. Meanwhile, Jesy had shuffled from home to home, surrounded by children who came in and out and guardians that never quite felt like parents. Both of them had felt reduced to their accomplishments, defined by them, chained to them.

It wasn't that Margot had forgotten. It was just that she hadn't wanted to care anymore.

Guilt churned in her stomach. "I didn't mean it like that. I know – I know, all right? But I need this."

"So do I," said Jesy, and now her tone was cold. "I'm not leaving, Stern. Get used to it."

And then she was gone, leaving a ringing silence in her wake.

※

If he noticed the glacial tension between them at the start of their final month, Archmage Langford elected to ignore it.

"Magic on this scale," he said, gesturing at the island behind him, "requires more than words and will. It requires delusion."

They were on the beach, a cheerful sun bearing down on a miserable Margot. She hadn't slept, so she knew that Jesy hadn't returned to the cottage the night before. She also knew she had no right to ask where she'd been instead, especially not when Jesy hadn't even looked at her since they'd gotten there. Water licked at the sand, leaving behind colorful shells and strings of algae every time it retreated, but there was no sign of St Izabeta in the distance. Just the endless horizon, wreathed by clouds.

"You must reject reality as you know it so you can build your own," Langford continued. One foot tapped against the sand. "In the right mindset, this can all become glass with only a thought. Bellchant, you can go first."

Jesy stepped forward. She was in another one of her suits today, this one rose pink with a beige collared shirt beneath. The jacket tapered at her narrow waist, emphasizing her curves in a way that Margot hated to notice. Jesy's eyes fluttered shut, her chin tipped toward the sand. It remained a glittering gold, indifferent to her efforts.

"Stern," Langford said after five painful minutes of silence.

Margot didn't step forward and didn't close her eyes. She had never needed to block out the world to reject her reality. She lived in a one-room cottage with nothing but plants for company, had more siblings than she could count and exhausted if well-meaning parents who frequently forgot to visit. She got one of every twenty field research trips she applied for, and she'd failed to land a grant on her own every day since graduating Hexenhall. It was only by rejecting reality that Margot had gotten this far, so if she wanted the sand to be glass, then she would damn well *force* it to be glass.

At first, nothing happened, other than sweat beading across her forehead, as though the sun were laughing at her efforts. Then, a spiral of crystal-clear glass swirled out from under her foot, stopping a meter away from Langford.

He made an approving sound. "Very good." And then: "Bellchant, try again."

Jesy tried and tried until the sun began to set. She had no effect on the sand at all. At one point, she begged to use words — a word anchor to direct magic was the most common form of spell-work — but Langford refused. "Magic can't be limited to the words of any language. You contain your power and, in so doing, you weaken it."

"Yes, Archmage," was all Jesy said, but Margot could read her frustration in the lines of her body.

When the sun began to dip below the horizon, painting the ocean gold, Langford dismissed them for the day. His townhouse, and the dinner he'd been looking forward to cooking, were waiting, and spells cast by the light of the moon were an entirely different lesson. He wound his way up the path without waiting for them, and Jesy began to follow.

This time, Margot caught *her* hand. "Let's work on it together."

"What's the point?" Jesy scoffed.

"A wise magician once said that we've always worked well together. And I know you can do this." She paused, allowing Jesy to see her earnestness, her contrition. "I know *you*."

Jesy studied her for a long moment before nodding minutely. Margot nudged her toward the high tide, kicking off her shoes so she could sit in the sand with the water streaming over her bare feet. Jesy followed at a more measured pace, shedding her suit jacket and rolling up the sleeves of her shirt. Margot's gaze bounced off her bared skin, focusing intently on the rippling black sheen of the ocean.

"I think Langford was right about rejecting reality, but it's not just for magic of his scale. All of magic is a rejection of the world as it is, a creation of the world as we want it to be." Margot drew her knees up to her chest, resting her chin atop them. "Think of what you want most and what you would do to get it. Somewhere between desire and desperation is the ember of power you need for this."

"What I want most," Jesy repeated slowly. Margot glanced at her to find that Jesy was already looking at her, eyes half-lidded and mouth quirked into a small smile. "I've never heard magic put like that before."

Margot's cheeks reddened. "Archmage Langford said it first."

"No, he didn't. Not like that. Why do you always diminish yourself like that, Stern?"

You know why, Margot wanted to say. Instead, she licked her lips. "Are you going to try the spell or not?"

Jesy was still looking at her, but that intensity was back, the focus that pinned Margot in place until Jesy decided to let her go. She saw movement from the corner of her eye and realized a second too late that it was Jesy's hand, rising to cup her hot cheek. She watched Jesy's throat bob as she swallowed. When she leaned into the touch, Jesy's lips parted in wonder.

"What I want most," she breathed. "Why would anyone want anything other than you?"

Margot had no response, because that smiling mouth was pressed against hers in a kiss both sudden and inevitable. Jesy tasted like bergamot. She kissed like this was a debate and she was responding well to Margot's arguments. Her other hand grabbed a fistful of Margot's braids and tilted her head so that Jesy could slide her tongue into Margot's mouth, claiming her beneath the watchful moon. Heat flared in Margot's chest, that sense of rightness settling into her bones. Every success and every failure had led her to the golden beach of Elixane Isle, to be kissed by Jesy Bellchant, and in that moment every painful experience was worth it. She groaned as Jesy pressed her back against the beach, her brief flash of annoyance over the sand she would get in her braids immediately overwritten by the feel of Jesy's hand on her breast.

"Don't think this means I'm going home," Jesy murmured against her neck, followed by a hint of teeth that made Margot whimper. "If anything, I'll be more determined to beat you."

"I expected nothing less," Margot breathed, dragging her nails down Jesy's back. "I can't work if you're here, putting your hands all over me."

Jesy's thigh slid between her legs, pushing up her skirts to press right against where Margot needed her most. "We won't need to work for a few more hours yet. And my hands aren't the only things I want to put all over you."

Margot ground against her thigh, sparks of pleasure lighting up every nerve ending. "Do it, then." She yanked at Jesy's collar, and three buttons popped free. "We have a lot to make up to each other, don't we?"

Jesy laughed into the next kiss. Then Margot's hand found its way inside her trousers, and there was no more laughter at all.

If he noticed the searing tension between them the next morning, Archmage Langford had elected to ignore it. He walked the length of the beach, making thoughtful sounds at the way the sun reflected off the ridge of glass that now marked the line of high tide. As it turned out, Jesy's desire to master the spell was equal to her desperation to get Margot fully undressed. With that motivation, Jesy had turned her stretch of sand to glass with hours left to go until sunrise – hours she subsequently spent making Margot cry out with pleasure until her voice had gone hoarse.

Now Margot's spiral of glass and Jesy's ridge cut through the grains that Langford studied, crystal proof of exactly how well they worked when they did it together.

"Very good, Bellchant," Langford finally said, stroking his beard again. "Next, I'll have you both change it back. Who wants to go first?"

This was only their second real lesson, and already Margot could see the future that raced toward her. The rest of the month would bring more lessons rooted in monotony, enough to learn from but not enough to engage them for longer than a few weeks. Langford would continue to avoid the pair outside of his daily magic practices, as if he were allergic to the company of other people, leaving them to their own devices. She would still be forced to spend her nights and mornings in Jesy Bellchant's company, perhaps teaching her how to cook, perhaps turning to her for magical help, perhaps performing a different kind of magic all together.

But for the first time since she had arrived, Margot didn't look ahead and feel anxious about what was next. The prospect of the competition didn't seem daunting. She still planned to win, but the desperate edge to her want had eased. She didn't need Archmage

Langford to make her feel important, not when Jesy Bellchant gazed up at her from between her spread legs as though she were worshipping her own personal god. She didn't need to prove that she had leadership qualities when she knew now that she had only ever cared to be a support system, a part of something greater than herself. She didn't need to return to St Izabeta a hero, because she had already seen things that no magician in her lifetime had seen just by being here, right now.

The sun emerged from behind a thin cover of clouds, making the glass too bright to look at. Margot turned away from her spiral to catch Jesy looking at her with mischief in her eyes. She remembered the first time she had seen her again, a month ago, and how she'd taken that look as a challenge. Now, she saw the warmth that softened Jesy's expression, the way that gleam in her gaze said *play with me, play with me.*

Margot smirked, gesturing imperiously toward the glass. "You go ahead, Bellchant. I need to know what not to do."

Jesy laughed, that twinkling, addictive noise which had quickly become Margot's favorite sound.

"All right," said Archmage Langford, and for a moment Margot could have sworn that he was smiling, too, "begin."

BAMBOO, INK, PAPER, CLAY

By

ELIZA CHAN

~ WILL ~

"Look," the performer says, sensing someone who would linger. From the lacquer chest he lays out a wraparound top, a long outer skirt embroidered with peonies, a gossamer overrobe with flowing water sleeves and scarf in blush pink. All in miniature. A tiny outfit that would fit only a child's doll. Beside the garments, he neatly places a pair of silk slippers and an ornate headdress. Then he pulls clay from his hands.

He pinches the wet slurry from his forearms, scoops it from his cheeks, moulds it with deft movements into a noblewoman with a round face and upturned eye. A puppet to inhabit the clothes he has left her. In an instant, the clay dries, porcelain white as fresh snow.

A glaze shines upon her features. He makes her swoop and wave, holding tiny hands demurely to her mouth. And then a second puppet: a young man with thick caterpillar eyebrows and an earnest expression. His immovable gaze happens upon the noblewoman. Everything changes. With only a few strokes on their painted faces, the moment is still palpable. The instant they fall in love.

The performer slowly retracts his hands, like spinning a plate upon a stick. The puppets remain, animated by the magic in his clay. The life it gives them. They move towards each other, admiring the willow branch that drips above them. Tilting their heads, gesturing with flat hands that will not bend nor point. They do not speak and yet their story is clear.

A mother and daughter, striding purposefully towards the vegetable stall, stop to gawk at the show. A couple of children sit cross-legged on the dirt before the makeshift stage.

"A story of forbidden love. A beautiful merchant's daughter fell in love with her father's clerk. But she was betrothed to another!" The back of his hand arches melodramatically to his forehead. The two women giggle but wait, reeled in. Others wander closer, their feet magnetised by the sight. A magical puppet theatre is rare in a town as small as this. Most of the magic users gravitate towards the capital, to its highborn households and businesses, if not the emperor's court. The two puppets fold into each other's arms, the noblewoman's head on the man's shoulder. The performer strikes a gong. It trembles through the mesmerised crowd, up and across the whole marketplace. The puppets are yanked apart, as if an invisible barrier has come between them.

The performer leans in, voice quietening conspiratorially. "Betrothed to a leather-faced Mandarin, twice her age! Her father locked her away, building a fence around her pagoda. The girl cried day and night until her maid relented. On the night before she was due to be married, the couple ran away together."

He winks at me from across the market square. I scowl, annoyed he has caught me looking at all. My own stall is bereft of customers, unless I count the lonesome cockroach which skitters from my broom.

"They lived contentedly, for a time. She kept the house; he wrote poems to her beauty." I roll my eyes, resisting the urge to stick two fingers down my throat. The performer's mouth wrinkles upwards at my response. Behind him, the puppets dance as he speaks. "Alas his skill with words was simply too great! His fame gave away their hiding place. The merchant and his men arrived with torches and blades, ready to destroy the couple."

Vermillion-red and burnish-orange silk scarves flutter behind the puppet couple. The puppeteer cuts slivers of clay from his thumb, a faceless mob chasing after the pair. "As flames licked the walls of their humble home, the lovers looked into each other's eyes and took their own lives."

Even the children and street dogs are silent, sensing the sombre atmosphere. Knowing they are all riveted, the man clasps his hands together, letting a single tear roll down his cheek. "The gods looked down from Mount Kunlun. In their mercy, they transformed the couple's souls into birds." He flings his hands open and porcelain birds fly out. Their bodies are pure white with powder-blue wings. The mesmerised crowd clap and cheer, filling his bowl with the clink of coins.

Before the sun is at its zenith, he has made more than I have in a week in this town. He whistles as he packs up the puppets with care, smoothing down their robes before putting them to sleep in a box. My temper flares, and despite myself, I stamp across the courtyard. The porcelain birds flap their wings in a panic and flutter onto his shoulder as I approach.

"How dare you?" I hiss.

Weifeng's hair falls across his eyes as he beams up at me. Three years have passed since I last saw him. He has not changed. The same lopsided grin that made me like him in the first place. The nick on the shell of his ear that was entirely my fault. Goddess of Mercy help me, I was an idiot then and it appears I have not shed the habit.

"I dare. You would not have approached me otherwise. I will take your anger over your indifference." His cheeks are hollow where he gouged from his own body. The toll of his tale is apparent.

"You would spout this nonsense, to make money?"

Weifeng shrugs indifferently. "Better to confront the story than to hide from it."

~ LOW ~

The girl was not very young nor very foolish... but she was *just* young enough to still be giddy. Balancing on the toes of her silk slippers as she walked on the low pavilion wall, she peeled layers from herself with the recklessness of youth. Folded the paper into boats to spin on the lily pond. Stretching up to place paper cranes on the branches of the plum tree, whilst the gardener shook his head but pretended not to notice. Chattering away like one of her birds as she left mud-stained scraps of paper and scrolls scattered around like moulting feathers. Everything was simple. Mistakes scrunched up into balls and quickly forgotten, torn paper easy to replace. On the cusp of adulthood, everyone indulged her. She would have time enough to grow up later.

Her mother had passed away not long after she was born, but her father had the gift of bamboo. Wooed by every business from construction to fabric, each winter he would cut the fingers from one hand to give her the finest things. His delicate paper flower, the most exquisite in the garden. She had tutors in calligraphy and poetry; could embroider a perfect chrysanthemum and perform the peacock dance; handle a sword, a bow and a flute. Her days were filled, but although she did not want for anything, there was a want all the same.

He arrived with the end of the rainy season, like summer had been tucked under his collar. An apprentice clerk to help her father with his books. His skin was inkstone. Words and pictures flowed from his touch. She brought him lychees damp with morning dew; freshly steeped tea; she danced and sang until all the household staff whispered, but she paid them no mind. She peeled scrolls from her legs, wide as the drapes on a canopy bed, folding her desire into paper lotus blossoms.

Paper and ink. They were fated to be. The destiny and purpose Meiyu had dreamed of. She had read all the great romance poems but had yet to experience it herself. To live one. Write one. The anticipation so sweet that she could subsist on it: the desire to fall in love.

～ WILL ～

"Did you follow me?" I ask sharply.

Weifeng strokes one of the porcelain doves on his shoulder. His creations do not have a voice, but the bird shakes its wings as if to puff out against my wrath. Even though I know it is clay, the fine feathers look soft and real. Its head is tucked behind his earlobe. I resist the urge to pick it up and dash its fragile body against the ground. The willow story has pursued me in the months and years since we last crossed paths. No matter where I go, they are retelling it: in poems and song, sighing over the doomed lovers as they plant out the rice, as they mend fishing nets and shore up broken walls.

"Would you believe me if I said this was a chance encounter?" The dove hops onto Weifeng's cupped hand and he gingerly places it into the low branches of a nearby tree. "But since I am here, have dinner with me."

My traitorous heart skips a beat even as I frown. There is no escaping him in this small place. I fold my arms. "You are paying."

He drags a stool over to my stall, mending the frayed hems of the puppets' garments as I shuffle my wares in the hope of enticing new customers. Weifeng looks intently at his work, words as if not for me. "I always thought it would be papercutting."

"I have not since…" My voice falters but he does not push me. We both know how far we've evolved from the tale his puppets tell.

"Lovers transformed into birds, butterflies," Weifeng says, amusement tingeing his voice. He cleans the face of the noblewoman puppet, dabbing at the unseen tears upon her cheeks. "We are obsessed with flying."

"Maybe we just want to be free."

"And you, Meiyu? I kept away as you asked. How does it feel to be free?" I look at him finally, really look at him. The dark circles under his eyes, the marks on his arm where he pulled the clay from his own body. My hand aches to slip against his, to peel a layer from myself to bandage his wound. The memory of his skin's warmth is suddenly as tangible as the bamboo fibres I am holding.

"Difficult," I answer honestly before I can stop myself. A laugh escapes my throat. I gesture at the misshapen paper on my stall. "The world may be mine to explore, but I know not what to do. Nor when to quit."

Weifeng picks up a damp piece of paper. The sheets are warped, undulating where they should lie flat and straight. It feels like he is weighing my soul. I clamp down on any excuses for the clumsy handiwork.

"You are better once you get started. The deckled edges are more even on the later sheets."

His compliment undoes me entirely. I tell myself I do not need it, and yet I fold it into my chest like a precious gift, only to be unwrapped under the cover of darkness. I let my imagination soar. What could have been. I nod, hoping my voice will not give me away. "It always comes out this shade of grey. I was thinking of using flowers or leaves to dye it."

"Willow leaves," Weifeng says. I recognise the twinkle in his eye. He is trying me. Mocking us.

"Willow trees and pavilions." The teasing brings me back to earth, solid and gritty underneath my nails. It reminds me that I do not need him. I do not need anyone.

~ LOW ~

Meiyu was in love. The birds knew it, singing her lover's name from the branches of the willow tree. The koi fish knew it, coming to the surface of the pond to kiss her as he had kissed down her neck. Only her father did not know it. He took her hand and talked of ambitious men and naïve young women. The fragility of paper, so light it could be swept away by a breeze. Of freedom and boundaries and finally, when she still refused to pay him any heed, of sending her lover away in disgrace.

Meiyu did what all the great love stories had taught her. She shouted and wailed, locked herself in her room and refused to eat, apart from the three sweet buns that her maid smuggled into her room, vowing it would be the last morsel to pass her lips this month. And the congee in the morning, but that was mostly water. Also the nashi pears she pilfered from the garden, but they hadn't come via the kitchen so hardly counted at all.

She wrote letters to her lover, peeling sheet after sheet from her chest until she was raw. About the quality of his lips and his skin and his brow and being upstanding as a tree, or was it a mountain peak? In any case she wrote across the pages, the ink hardly having time to dry. Her maid returned with the smuggled responses. Declarations of love and devotion in bold sword strokes. She read them in bed, embracing them like her lover, but in the morning the ink had stained her skin and clothes, clinging to her.

After a few weeks, she had run out of things to say. When all was said and done, they had hardly exchanged more than three awkward conversations. For all she had imagined him saying to her, and all she had imagined responding, there were gaping holes in her knowledge. He was a porcelain figure that she had placed upon the shelf. The folded paper flowers she had made for him tore between her finger and thumb, yielding under the slightest pressure. Perhaps, she thought, her father might have a point. Her lover's letters still came. *Ours* and *mine* almost unreadable in chaotic characters that filled an entire sheet. Demanding more paper than she could make, than she wanted to give.

After a month, she gathered up the letters she had stopped sending back, holding the fragile paper in her hands. A part of her she had been willing to give away. She enjoyed the notion of being in love, the new taste upon her palate, more than the meal itself. She tore the letters into shreds, the pieces like blossom petals around her. A moment of infatuation to be savoured like all the other moments unfolding in her life. One by one, she placed them on her tongue, absorbing them back into her body. Then she peeled another sheet of paper from her skin. A strip all the way down her arm. Blank as yet.

A new interest filled her days. She honed her paper cutting, delighting her maid with flapping butterflies and cranes; bringing back her father's laughter with papercut dragon and tiger. In winter she filled the garden with paper peonies and in summer, frogs to jump across the pond, never minding that her paper could not survive the wet and cold. Her bond with her father grew stronger, and everything was as it should be.

"I fear there will be no one to look after you once I am gone," her father said, holding up the papercut tiger. Once sharp and precise, a tiny spill of tea and it was ruined, paws soggy and beyond repair.

"I will manage on my own," she protested. "Look how badly love turned out for me!"

Her father shook his head, the silver in his whiskers more prominent now. "Paper is too delicate. Let me introduce you to someone. There are more people in this world than one young clerk."

"What if he is cruel and warty and old?"

Her father tucked a strand of hair behind her ear. He was indulgent. "Then you may turn him away. Cast him away with a hundred paper cuts. Make him wait under the willow tree for the rest of his days."

Then one morning the double doors opened and he was not cruel nor warty nor old. Weifeng was the other half of her heart, although neither of them yet knew it.

~ WILL ~

At dinner, I have a second bowl of rice. I eat the ribs with my hands, licking the juices that run down my fingers. I have no qualms in helping myself, scraping the bottom of the dish clean with my spoon. The warmth of the food is a novelty in my belly. Hunger was something I had only learnt about of late. I had thought myself acquainted with the notion, but in hindsight it was nothing but boredom. True hunger, the type that gnawed on my insides, that distracted so I can barely put one foot in front of another, is an experience I only learnt after leaving my father's home.

When I finally come up for air, Weifeng is watching. He has ordered all my favourites, the ones he recalled from the old days. It is like he has found a version of me, dusty and forgotten, wedged down the back of the cabinet. The girl who likes sweet more than salty, who has not yet experienced bitter and sour.

His long, black hair lies loose around his shoulders, no longer pulled back into a tight bun now we have both fallen from grace. It suits him. Once I mocked him for being so upright, as if he was a guardian lion at one of the temples. It was only later I realised the stiffness was because of me. The off-hand comments and requests that scattered from my mouth like wild seeds grew under his care, fragile roots becoming tougher than the hardiest weeds.

"Stop looking at me like that."

"Like what?" Weifeng says. He does not stop. Does not blink.

"Like I am the sun in the sky."

He quirks an eyebrow at the notion. "More the lonely moon."

"Weifeng," I say, and his name on my lips sends an unexpected shiver through me. I try and fail to blank out the memory of when I last said it. Aloud at least. I do not want to admit how many times I've said it in my dreams. Wondering if I regretted the decision I made. The anguish it caused us both.

"Why do you keep torturing yourself with that story. Surely there are others?" I ask, honestly wanting to know.

His answer is a long time in coming.

"I had this notion, that if I kept telling it, it would no longer hurt. I could purge it. Mock it. Confront it."

"There will be none of you left at this rate." I bite my bottom lip.

"Only the centre that is yours." His eyes crease with his smile, making me blink. Paper walls are flimsy at the best of times.

"You are an arse," I snap back, another paper cut upon his cheek.

"And a fool," he agrees without missing a beat.

~ LOW ~

"Paper is delicate. More fragile than butterfly wings. A single mistake and it is ruined. I long for something more robust, that can be handled without fear of breakage," Meiyu declared. She had almost forgotten Weifeng walked at her side, until he mumbled, so softly that she had to lean in to hear him.

"You are too strong to break." He did not look, eyes trained into the distance. Meiyu wondered if she had imagined it entirely. Only the flushed spot upon his cheeks told her otherwise. They kept walking in amicable silence, their long shadows touching on the ground before them. It made her smile, to imagine how he would jump for them to be so close. The smells of the market filled her senses and for a moment they both took it all in. A stallholder ran across the way, chasing after a couple of chickens. Meiyu leapt back, Weifeng steadying her with hands upon her arms. Steam from the huge bamboo steamers glistened on his cheek. Close enough to press her lips against his skin, the notion dizzyingly tempting. They sprang apart.

"What about you?" she asked in the awkwardness that followed.

"My family business is in pottery. Earthenware and porcelain." His response was exact and rehearsed like a wind-up music box.

"But what do you dream of?" she persisted. His eyes widened, and Meiyu realised perhaps her question was too personal. His pale face softened like wet clay. A dimple appeared on his left cheek as he smiled.

"When I was a boy, I wanted to be an opera singer. An actor upon the stage with a pair of pheasant feathers in my hat. An orator of great renown. A puppeteer, even. I wanted to make my mark on the world, and not just pass through it."

"But you are so quiet!" Meiyu blurted before she could prevent herself.

"Only around you," Weifeng confessed. It was only then that she realised jade warms slowly against the skin, the veins of colour more apparent when held to the light. His stiffness not a formality after all, but nerves.

"I would come to all your shows."

He found courage in her response. Looking around, he beckoned her over to a stall selling various ornamental trinkets: household deities and porcelain statues. He pointed at a striped tiger on the table and then uncurled his hand. With a pinch and a pull, he made its sibling. The tiger's rear paws still fused into his skin as its tail swished from side to side. It pounced, clumsily separating its feet as it tumbled from his grasp. Somehow Meiyu reached out in time, catching it before it broke upon the ground. The tiger prowled, pawing at the branching lines written upon her palm.

As she looked up at him, a new feeling blossomed within her ribcage. One she did not dare define for fear of getting it wrong once more. A new story. One that might not sell poems or inspire operas, but was honest and true.

And then she saw him, her first lover. Watching her from a distance behind rickshaws and ox-drawn carts. The scowl contorting his features like a blot of ink.

"What's wrong?" Weifeng asked.

"It's... nothing. Someone I once knew. From another lifetime." Her maid had kept bringing her letters months after Meiyu stopped. Long, flowing letters with perfect calligraphy that filled page after page. She sent a polite but curt response back, not wanting to hurt the heart that she would once have done anything for. It did not end. The ink bled across the sheets of paper until it was unreadable. One unending mistake.

~ WILL ~

"This is what you see yourself doing? Now and into the future?" Weifeng asks after the meal. Between us, we carry the chest filled with handmade paper up the narrow stairs to my rented room. The question was asked without inflection, and yet I hear the scorn all the same. How I have fallen from my place as the daughter of a noble household. My father's legacy died with him. They would not trade with a woman, and certainly not one without bamboo in her veins. I had tried my hand at many things. Cobbled shoes, made candles. Trundling my cart into the next town where they would crowd my stall at first, always looking for magic and instead seeing only the clumsy missteps along the way. The paper I make is grey and uneven. Nothing like the smooth sheets I pull from my skin. It will never be enough.

"It's just a way to pass the time…" My response is reluctant. Sullen. Weifeng places the chest down at the foot of my bed. His eyes take in the chaos of the room, stooping to pick up strewn clothing and folding it neatly in a pile. I realise where we are, the expanse of the unmade bed between us, the door narrowly ajar. I turn to light the lamp, hiding my fluster with busywork. The warm glow simply brings out the contours of his robes. How they fall against his lean frame. The hint of stubble upon his chin and upper lip. He catches my eyes upon his mouth, gaping like a koi fish in a pond.

I could take a couple of steps forward, put my knee upon the corner of the bed, press his head against my chest so he can hear how quickly my heart is beating. I could pull him up next to me and take off his layers, his air-dried exterior crumbling in my hands. Kiss him, let desire and need write us a new chapter. Let the years and distance slip away. The hunger in his expression tells me he will not say no.

I move forward. One step, then another. Then my eyes snag, not on his face, but the hanging scroll upon the wall. A battered, yellowing thing with the image of two birds upon a tree branch.

A musing on love written in vertical columns. I have seen many hanging in a tavern room on my travels. Each time I cannot help but shudder. Weifeng's hand is halfway to my face when something tells him to stop. He follows my eyeline and his shoulders droop. Unhooking it from the nail, he rolls the offending scroll up. Tightly. Pulls clay from the V where his tunic folds between his collarbones, moulding a cylinder to hide the scroll in.

I sit on the edge of the bed, no longer thinking about the warmth of his skin. Only of the paper and the ink, of the story that had been written a hundred times. Weifeng says something before he leaves but I do not hear his words. His scent lingers, the heady amber of sandalwood. We barely touched and yet the air between us is infused with the memory of him.

～ LOW ～

Weifeng toured her around the pottery studio, to the family warehouses. They walked up and down between the shelves of drying pots, where porcelain was packed up to be sent across the seas. The earthy smell reminded her of a garden after the rain.

Shyly, he showed her the secret models he had made. A mythical qilin that galloped around the table on lopsided legs; a huli jing whose nine tails were too heavy for it. He was not the most skilled of potters, but everything was done in earnest. Each piece a glimpse into his vulnerable interior.

"I made you something," Weifeng said, nerves causing him to blink. They had taken to a riverside walk each morning, before the town stirred. The rose of dawn still in the sky and the long curtains of willow branches shading them from view. Inside the neatly wrapped cloth parcel were a few sheets of handmade paper decorated with rose petals. "I thought, with your paper cutting…"

"But I can—" Meiyu started, peeling paper from the back of her hand. Confusion furrowing her brow. Weifeng's hand rested atop her own, stopping her, his skin cool clay.

"You *can*, but you do not have to. You do not have to offer all of yourself, all of the time."

His words were a revelation. Too many times had her father cut off a part of himself, his body used to make houses and boats, instruments and weapons. His health had started to falter of late, spread too thin, always worrying if his daughter would be provided for. It had never occurred to her that he could say no.

Meiyu imagined the effort Weifeng had gone to. Pressing the petals into the pulp before it dried, each placement precise. The paper was uneven, the surface curling at the edges. Imperfect and personal. A gift that offered her a different point of view.

She had made him something in return. It unfurled in the palm of his hand, like a flower blooming only one night a year. The paper cutting stretched out, all the folds and cuts springing apart like clockwork pieces, the gaps empty cups waiting to be filled. A miniature willow tree grew before their eyes, long branches sweeping down to Weifeng's fingers. And there, underneath the umbrella of its canopy, a couple, snipped not simply with the sharp blades of her scissors, but with the longing of her heart. Foreheads touching. Hands holding. The magic stirred within her, ached from the narrow strips she had taken from across her chest where her heart thrummed loudest. She had not given him all of her, but enough that he would know, now and always, what he meant to her. The paper figures leaned in closer.

"Meiyu," Weifeng said, his voice thick as he reached for her. His hand shook in hers. Slipped like he could not quite hold himself together. Laughingly he wove his fingers between hers, steadying them both. It was so different from her first lover. It did not explode and end like fleeting fireworks in the sky. It grew, slow and steady when she had least expected it. Everything in her body responded to that touch. A ripple in a pool. Everything in her mind responded, also. An endless scroll of their lives together. She leaned forward to press her lips against his, knowing that she would never regret the decision; not seeing the other branching paths their lives would take.

The house was a bustle of activity to prepare for the wedding. Her father coughed into his sleeve but vowed to be a part of the celebration, cutting bamboo limb after bamboo limb to pay for it all. Inviting the finest cooks, tailors and entertainers so he could give them the best wedding the province had ever seen. Each day passed in a glowing haze, Meiyu's smile aching her cheeks and yet she could not stop beaming if she'd wanted to. The stream of well-wishers and tradespeople made it easy for someone to gain entry to the house. For her ex-lover to gain entry to her bedchambers, even. It was, after all, the true love story. The one that was written.

The only one that mattered.

~ WILL ~

I cannot sleep, my back and shoulder aching upon the hard mattress. I snap at the tavern owner, even though I have had no issues all the nights previous. The empty space upon the wall where Weifeng removed the hanging scroll mocks me.

The chest thuds heavily down the stairs, the steps protesting at their mistreatment. It was easier with another pair of hands to help. The treacherous thought floats on the surface of my mind, but I ignore it, setting up my stall. Each day the chest only gets heavier as I make more paper I cannot sell. Not when my handiwork is amateur at best, thick and thin in places. The couple of sheets I have sold are to those who take pity on me, who hope a few coins might broker a friendship, or at least a story from my past. They are always curious. My clothes are finer than the average stallholder, even if they are now threadbare and out of fashion.

Today Weifeng does not have his puppet show. Instead, his stall has rows of ceramic ornaments on display: dragon and phoenix, qilin and tiger. He watches me struggle from across the way but does not approach. I am glad of that mercy.

Everyone expected him to take over the family business, to make porcelain plates and vases to sell across the seas. Once, I worried he would be like my father, stripping himself to the bone to provide for others, but Weifeng has not made that mistake. He has taken his clay and made something new.

I ignore the rest of the market, spreading out the damp paper from the day before to dry on rods. The grey tinge could be forgiven, but the uneven patches have dried into pockmarks. I could be good at this, if only my fingers didn't keep getting caught. Snagging against the deckle as I lower the frame into the pulp slurry. Paper pieces flake from me onto the wet sheets despite my best efforts, impossible to pick out. My cheek flaps open like the pages of a book, even as I press it back in. When I scratch the itch on the nape of my neck, squares of paper flutter from my back. The townsfolk are staring now, pointing at the magic that I refuse to use. What is wrong with her? Why would she waste such a gift?

The wind blows mockingly, scattering stray seeds and curled leaves into the wet paper. I throw another ruined sheet to the ground in frustration, kicking it away from me.

At midday, I finally give up, my fingers raw with all the paper that has come loose. No matter how I try, parts of me stick to the mould, messing everything up. I pour the remaining pulp water into the ditch. When I turn back, I see something small moving out of the corner of my eye, and smack at it instinctively with a stick. The porcelain rooster squawks wordlessly at me as it hops out of reach. Its ornate tail has been sweeping paper into a pile. A clay rabbit and rat gather the fragments of paper in their jaws. A pig rolls a crumpled ball with its snout.

Weifeng is busy with customers, as he has been all morning. I gather my paper-making frame to hide the tears that threaten my eyes.

~ LOW ~

It took Meiyu a moment to place him. It had been years since she'd set eyes on her father's clerk. Since she had sent him extravagant love declarations about running away together. She had all but forgotten the features of his face, blurring into a watercolour stroke on the paper. A story from a lifetime ago. She had forgotten there was a time before Weifeng took up all the space in her heart. But perhaps, Meiyu thought as her ex-lover slid the bolt shut on her bedroom door, as he smothered her in an embrace, time passed differently for them both.

"How long they kept us apart." His words are discordant against her ears.

"Wh-what are you doing here?" Ink was blotched on her ex-lover's sleeves. Words ran up his robes, vertical and horizontal lines that crossed and clashed against each other, as if he could not wait to find the paper to write upon. The ink in his body burning to be released.

"Your father said I wasn't good enough for you. I kept writing to you, every day, every week, even though he prevented us from communicating. I knew you felt the same way. I knew you would wait for me, even if he forced you to write those false missives rejecting me. We are meant to be together. To write the story of our love." He had built himself around an empty husk.

"I stopped responding. My feelings changed."

"Of course, that is the version you tell, to retain your virtue and standing in this community. I understand, Meiyu. But you are meant to be mine. Paper and ink."

"I am not," she said defiantly. "We build these images of love in our minds. Of what great poets and songs tells us it should be. Paper and ink sounded so sweet together, so right. But we never knew each other, not really."

"You are my true love. My first love."

Meiyu pitied her ex-lover and the story he now clung to. Voice soft as she cut through his delusions. "You were my first love, but not my last."

His eyes turned to flint, his grip on her tightening. The ink on his fingers stained her paper skin, binding her wrists in thick cuffs. She tried to explain, digging trenches with her words. "Leave it as a sweet memory. Let us part as friends."

"There is no more parting in this tale." His words may have meant to bring her comfort, but it did not.

"I am betrothed to be married in two days," Meiyu said, trying to keep the fear from her voice. Perhaps in her taciturn tone he heard something else. Perhaps he would only ever hear something else.

"They will not force you into it. I have arranged for us to leave, tonight. We will be free." His eyes, which once she would have called deep pools of affection, were unfathomably dark.

~ WILL ~

I sleep through the afternoon, my body moulting layers of thin paper like a silkworm cocoon. I curl up, trying to ignore the growl in my stomach. Things will be better at the next town. I might as well dump the poorly made paper and start again. It is too fragile to carry around. It is, after all, what I have done for years; never quite finding a purpose the way Weifeng has. Instead, I sell off pieces of jewellery to eke out my money. But I have left it too late to depart now. One more night, and I will pack up in the morning. That is the promise I make myself, pretending it is practicality and not the hope of seeing him once more.

Downstairs, the dining room is empty. All the shutters are thrown open, letting the wan light into every corner. Round stools are pushed under round tables. He is not here. Has probably made the more sensible decision to leave whilst the sun was high. I think of asking the server which way he has gone, but am I not the one who pushed him away in the first place?

I pick at my meal. The mustard greens too salty, the steamed egg not silken smooth. The rice is overcooked, mushy when it had been fluffy the night before. I tell the server as much, but he looks incredulously at me. At the same table, on the same stool as my meal with Weifeng. Hoping to reenact our dinner together even though I am alone. It is preposterous how easily my papercut heart tears.

~ LOW ~

Her ex-lover held a blade to her neck, marching her through the hallways towards the end of the pier. They passed rooms filled with wedding decorations and gifts, strings of red lanterns swaying in the breeze. Meiyu kept her mouth shut, knowing that any explanation would not be believed. Instead, she peeled paper from her fingers, all she could reach with her bound hands, scattering them behind her in a breadcrumb trail. The scraps of paper danced and swirled like cherry blossom petals, all the way to her father's room.

The first calls of alarm were sounded as her ex-lover pushed her into the boat. Gongs rang and voices yelled. Her father stumbled from his quarters. His legs were stiff, bamboo not yet regrown from where he'd lopped it off. His voice wavered querulously into the night. It was hard enough for him to know they would be parted after the wedding. The grief was too great. The heavy thud of his body audible even above the shouts and running feet.

Weifeng's family had boats and resources to spare. They chased into the night, but the channels were narrow, and their vessels designed for the open seas. They could not navigate around the mangrove trees and marshy inlets. And even when they could, they did not. The union between the two families had not been completed. There was no profit in carrying on the pursuit, the embarrassment of an absconding bride better to be buried and forgotten.

"They are comparing us to the Butterfly Lovers. The Cowherd and the Weaving Maid. The great love stories," her ex-lover said. He did not stop writing, for sleep or food or anything so mundane. It was his duty to transcribe their story. Their great love. He came back from the market with tales as if they were gold coins, evidence that he was correct, despite Meiyu reiterating that she no longer loved him. He was inspired by it: writing couplets in vertical columns, pacing the room as he searched for the right word. It mattered not that his inspiration spat at him each time he approached, that he tore strips of paper from her tongue each time she spoke against him.

Weeks passed, and Meiyu realised there was only one way out. She scattered the idea like seeds upon the fertile earth. A great romance does not end with a happily ever after. It should end in tragedy. He swallowed the narrative like an ornamental carp, not seeing how small the pond of his imagination truly was.

~ WILL ~

It is late. Even the patrons who ordered jars of baijiu stumble off to their beds. The locals mutter at the sudden downpour of rain, straw hats and tattered paper umbrellas shielding them. The server blows out every candle except the one on my table, retiring to bed. I was the first to arrive and will be the last to retire. Moving the congealed food around my bowl. Stubbornly hoping he will come for me, even though I know he is long gone.

The door sweeps open, rain and wind blustering in through the gap. Shapes like thick snowflakes swirl towards me in a blustery stream, reaching out to hold me in an embrace. I grasp at one, holding it between finger and thumb. Paper. Squares of paper in every shade. Big enough to make kites, small enough to fold offerings. The paper comes to me from Weifeng's arms, leaping across the distance. I do not understand. I do not need any more paper. I am saturated in it. And yet the paper finds me. It sticks to my cheeks and forehead, circles my chest and legs. Cool from the rain, like a balm.

Weifeng dumps out heavy bundles of paper from the woven basket upon his back. Wrapped up in waxy banana leaves and tied in string like steamed parcels, keeping them mostly dry from the rain. Pile after pile, he stacks up before me, not saying a word. I am swaddled in a cocoon of scattered sheets, only my face free of the patchwork pieces.

"Why?" I ask finally.

"Because once it made you happy. I believe it can make you happy again. You do not have to bleed with every cut. You do not have to do everything yourself, the hard way." Weifeng's clothes are wet and stained. His face is lined with exhaustion, clay rolling off him in fat drips to puddle on the ground. Nevertheless, his face shines with triumph. He has been to the next town and back to buy me this gift.

I untie the bundle on the table, touching the topmost square of cream paper. I imagine what I could make with it. Folding and cutting fine floral details on the back of a dragon or circular motifs as round as mooncakes. Without taking a piece of myself with every cut. Without worrying that everything has to be perfect. I can simply enjoy it.

My hands shake as I lift the sheet of paper. Trembling like a fledgling with wet wings. My eyes blur so that I cannot see what is before me, tightening my grip in fear. The paper crumbles in my fist. I cannot.

I tear the damp paper from my body, tossing each sheet to the ground. They adhere to my damp palms, to each other, desperate to cling on. I know not if I am tearing his paper or my own anymore. I mulch the clumps in closed fists, pulping it with my anger. Ruined. Everything I have ever wanted has only ruined me and those I love.

Paper is too fragile for anything else.

∽ LOW ∽

When Weifeng arrived, Meiyu's ex-lover had been dead for days. She vowed a suicide pact with him, convincing him the gods would transform them into doves. Stared at his body for hours as she used her teeth to tear her bindings loose. She had no desire to join him. The only birds she would choose were the ones she'd peeled from her skin over the preceding days. Cutting the shape of their paper bodies with fingers and teeth. A flock of them, benign to his eyes, until she had taken her magic and pushed them down his throat. Stuffed his mouth and nose with them until his bloodshot eyes finally saw that she was not the weak maiden he thought to rescue. Not his one true love. Just a trapped woman making him suffocate on his own lies.

Weifeng took it all in, saying nothing at the macabre scene. He dropped to his knees, arms already around her. Despite herself, Meiyu stiffened, pushing him away with a snarl. The paper flaked from where he touched it, thick manuscripts cleaving from her. Sharp-toothed scrolls battered about his head with all of her frustrations, all of her rage. Cutting him. She did not realise what she had done until he held his hand against one ear, blood trickling between his fingers. He came for her, despite his family's objections and her father's death. There was nothing here for him apart from her love. And she could not even give him that.

"He isn't me," Weifeng said finally. Logic told her his words were true. He had done nothing to deserve this suspicion. Yet, everything inside her that was lightness and joy had turned to amber resin. A well poisoned far beneath its surface.

"I won't be a puppet in someone else's story," Meiyu said. Vehemence made her brittle, paper cracking in her hands.

"You wouldn't be."

"You do not know that for certain!" She was tired of being told what her future looked like. By the father who did not want her to want, and yet laid the burden of his sacrifice upon her back. By the ex-lover who sought to mould her in an image not of her own choosing. And even now, by the man she loved, who wanted to make promises for a future that was not certain. "You cannot promise me that tomorrow will be the same as yesterday. That we will never make each other unhappy. That we will live together until we are old and grey. My mother made that promise to my father. A lie."

"It is true, I do not know how our story ends." Weifeng took his hand from his ear. The blood trickled still, a slow drip like a tear running down his face. "I do not want to leave you, but I will… if that is what you need."

Meiyu wished he was the tyrant the stories portrayed him as. The jealous suitor. It would make her decision easier. "I need time. Space to learn what it is to be myself."

"Take it. A week? A month?"

"A year," she said, turning her eyes away so she would not see the expression on his face. "A year to go through all the seasons, to find out what I want to write upon these pages. A year to prove I can be myself, and not simply fall into someone else's narrative."

Weifeng said nothing, so still that his features seemed but painted on. His throat bobbed finally as he wet his lips. "A year. I will become the person I wanted to be also. Let us meet, you and I, under the willow tree in your father's pavilion. A year today to see how we have grown, separately if not together."

⌒ WILLOW ⌒

The paper pulp falls in a ring around my feet. A gift he offered me, destroyed in the only way I know how. He wants me to be courageous, to jump back into the fray and follow those dreams as I once said I would. But paper is too delicate. Despite the lofty ambitions I once had, I do not know what to do. I am afraid.

"You did not come," he says finally. I expected it on the first day, when he saw me across the market square. When he cut me with the puppet theatre as I had once cut him with my paper. The accusation I deserved. I had promised to meet him, a year after we separated. "I waited. A whole week, just in case. Even when it rained, on a night not dissimilar to tonight, I waited. And then the next year. And the next."

"I could not find the person I wanted to become. All this time, I thought I was someone else's story, but the truth is, I am nothing. A blank page." I cannot look at him as I admit my shame. And then I lie, to push him further away. "I assumed you had moved on."

"A blank page. How wonderful," Weifeng says.

I stare at him. "No, it is a terrible thing. To lack the skill to write a real story."

"The Willow Story – the ill-fated lovers. Is that a real story?"

"For some."

"But not for you." Weifeng stoops to pick a handful of the pulped paper from around my feet. "Not for us."

He makes a space for himself, toe to my toe. Uses his fingertips to roll clay from his forearm, kneading it together with the ruined paper. Pinching and pulling out the resultant mix, until he makes a simple model. An arch.

"What purpose does it have?" I cannot help but ask.

"Does it matter?"

I have been so consumed with finding my purpose that I have forgotten to enjoy the journey. One that does not always have to be walked alone. He has always supported me. Listening and challenging me to be more ambitious, to create for no reason other than my own joy. Just as I never belittled his dreams. In all the narratives, I lost that thread.

His wet hair clings to his face, and clay drips from his chin, but he is everything I have ever needed. I ignore the bridge in his hand, but make a new one with my arms around his neck. Paper and clay are not the most obvious fit, but together, we are stronger than anything either of us could be alone.

"This," I say with certainty, "is where our story begins."

Weifeng smiles tenderly, clay tears glistening in his eyes. Beneath our feet, the paper and clay mix together to form something new. It stretches up with our magic, a willow tree. I am certain of many things: that the hand now clasped in mine will support, love and respond to everything I need; that we will grow together, branches intertwined until there is no way to separate the two.

It delights me.

It terrifies me.

He strokes my cheek, holding me until the trembling eases. Gently pushing the pages back into my jaw. He tilts my head up. "Look."

Above us, the paper-clay tree forms a shelter. A thick canopy of stretching branches and rustling paper leaves, like an umbrella overhead. Father, ex-lover, Weifeng – they all wanted to protect me. The feeling of being trapped tightens my throat. Restricted. Then I see why he made me look. The gaps. Papercut holes between leaves and branches. Triangles that let in the sunlight. Space to grow. Being together does not mean losing all of myself.

I understand now, what Weifeng was always trying to tell me. We do not have to follow the template of those that came before. Bamboo, ink, paper, clay. It is always a choice.

Our lips and hands touch. Clay and paper making something new. Not for the first time, and certainly not for the last.

Together, we will start a new story.

SLAY THE PRINCESS, SAVE THE DRAGON

✦ By ✦

A. C. WISE

The curtains were drawn, aluminum foil backing them, but the sunlight still found a way to slosh into the room, determined to do violence. Ev crawled out from under the covers. Her shitty bedroom, in her mom's shitty trailer, hadn't transformed overnight. She hadn't gone to bed a frog and woken a princess. Which meant that behind the balled-up mass of t-shirts, socks, and underwear in her top drawer, the dresser remained papered with letters informing her that the Royal Academy didn't have a spot for her, nor did Tower, and that even her back-up schools could offer little to no financial aid.

Even if she wanted to settle, she couldn't afford it.

Ev's mom worked her ass off at the plant, and had in fact just switched to night shifts for the pay raise. Ev herself worked at the local Gas Stop, and it still wasn't enough. It would never be enough.

Unlike the light battering her windows, her future wasn't particularly bright. In short, she was fucked.

It felt pointless, but Ev prised herself up, showered, dressed, and got on the bus regardless. Last semester, senior year. She'd come this far; even though there wasn't anything waiting for her on the other side, she might as well stick it out.

The hallways buzzed as Ev stood at her locker. The loudest, brightest cluster surrounded Carissa Hotthorpe – aka Princess Carissa – heir to the Hotthorpe Pharmaceutical fortune. Not an actual princess, but as good as. And – if Ev understood the rules correctly – if about twenty-some-odd people happened to meet unfortunate ends, Carissa could in theory inherit the throne.

Ev's shoulders rose, but voices from the knot surrounding Carissa found her regardless – cooing over her latest socials. Carissa dutifully tilted her phone, as though her coterie hadn't already seen and liked every single post. Now, though, they had the opportunity to shower their praise in person – Carissa's hair, her clothes, the light, her angles, all of it too perfectly perfect. And of course the gem in her social media crown, her ever-present, best accessory of all time, in the background of each picture – her dragon.

Ev hate-followed, since the algorithm seemed determined to shove Carissa's posts in her face regardless. It was barbaric, keeping a dragon as a pet. Worse still, Carissa's father likely harvested its scales, teeth, and claws on the regular, grinding them into potions and powders and tinctures, selling them to a diet-pill-popping, skin-tightening, glow-up-hungry public. Then again, Princess Carissa would probably never allow anything that might damage the aesthetic of her oh-so-perfect photos.

Ev kicked her locker shut. The bottom was dented inward where she'd once done so with enough force to jam it shut. The custodian had to pry it loose with an extra-long screwdriver, giving her the stink-eye the entire time. Princess Carissa's locker was probably perfectly smooth; she probably didn't own boots stompy enough to kick it inward, and if she did, she probably had magic flowing from her fingertips that would unstick it without any outside intervention needed.

Ev slouched down the hall, exclamations and cooing following her and tempting her to look back. She kept her eyes firmly forward, and her phone firmly in her pocket. Carissa Hotthorpe was too beautiful, too perfect. People like that shouldn't be allowed.

Normally she had a free period after her first two classes, but today the time was reserved for a session with the guidance counsellor. Ev scowled her way through those classes, dreading the thought, wondering if it was too late to cancel. But her bad mood wasn't enough to overcome the guilt that would inevitably follow if she failed to show.

She went, book bag heavy, dropping into the chair across from Ms Averill's desk, already glancing at the clock behind it. Just because she'd turned up, didn't mean she had to listen. Ev let Ms Averill's words wash in and out.

"...financial aid and scholarship opportunities from outside sources." Ms Averill's voice remained bright; Ev sank lower in her chair, arms crossed.

"What's the point?" The words slipped out; she'd meant that to be an inside thought.

"Okay." Ms Averill didn't miss a beat and Ev looked up. She'd expected an argument. "How about this, then? Rather than thinking about next year, let's think about the rest of this semester.

Your marks in chemistry are incredibly strong – how do you feel about tutoring?"

"I already have a job." Ev didn't mention that her hours had been drastically cut.

"It's one hour right after school, twice a week. If you can fit it into your schedule, it's a little extra cash in your pocket. That's not a bad thing, right?"

Ms Averill turned her screen to let Ev see the details. The contact information should have been temporarily hidden, but it glared out at Ev from the screen.

"Carissa Hotthorpe? Are you fu— I mean, are you serious?"

"Sorry." Ms Averill turned her screen back, flustered. "Pretend you didn't see that."

"It doesn't matter. I don't want the job."

She could think of no torture greater than spending her remaining after-school hours locked up in the castle with Carissa Hotthorpe. Besides, the princess couldn't possibly need a tutor. She was a legacy kid, her admission to the Royal Academy guaranteed; even if she decided to skip college, as her father's sole heir she could probably slide right into the fucking CEO position at Hotthorpe Pharmaceutical when he retired.

Unless it was a weird pride thing? Like it would reflect badly on the family name if she got anything less than A+ across the board, especially in chemistry? The only classes Ev shared with Carissa were drama and PE, not enough to determine whether she was a good student. But even if she was a genius, what incentive did she have to care or try, with her future all laid out for her? She could float through life, posting selfies and reels and collecting likes without a care in the world.

"Just think about it?" Ms Averill said.

"I need to get to my next class." Ev stood, shouldering her bag and heading for the door before Ms Averill found a way to wear her down.

Ev cut through the scrappy strip of trees dividing the cul-de-sac, where the bus let off from the trailer park. Once upon a very long time ago, the trees had been part of King's Wood, home to a whole host of magical creatures. Then the Royal Alchemical College, and its direct offspring, Hotthorpe Pharmaceutical, had discovered how much more useful magical creatures could be if they were cut up, skinned, and ground. The woods had been emptied, then razed. Shitty sub-developments had grown up in their place, and instead of being home to magic, they were home to potholes that never got filled and storm drains that backed up every time it rained.

Since her mom was on nights, she'd probably be sleeping. The trailer wasn't big enough to keep Ev from feeling that every creak and rustle of motion she made would steal her mother's rest. She swung to the right, stomping on in her stompy boots toward the train tracks at the edge of town. A straight line out to a glittering future, but only for other people, it seemed. On the far side of the tracks, the plant loomed — blocky buildings and tanks, pipes and catwalks, all glittering with lights like a miniature city unto itself. It used to belong to the Hotthorpes too, until they spun off the household division of cleaning products — everything from bleach to floor wax — and sold it in a multi-billion-dollar deal to Wodehouse & Farmer, so they could continue focusing on cosmetics, and what Ev thought of as vanity drugs. Hotthorpe no longer made things that were lifesaving or necessary, but things that people wanted desperately all the same.

The air here smelled like asphalt and identical houses, strip malls and parking lots and, of course, the plant itself – the stink of disappointment and failure. The plant where Ev's mother had spent her days, and now spent her nights. The plant where Ev's future lay, too, the only possible one she could see.

A beer bottle sat propped upright on the platform. After checking to make sure it was indeed empty and someone hadn't pissed in it and left it as a trap, Ev hurled it as far as she could. Of course it would never reach the plant, but it was the 'fuck you' gesture that counted. It arced short, struck the rails with a soft pop, and sent satisfying shards of glass spattering outward.

Maybe tomorrow would be the day that she didn't bother to go to school at all. Maybe tomorrow would be the day that she would blow it all right the fuck up. Maybe tomorrow would be the day to...

Slay the princess, save the dragon.

The idea rose up, terminally stupid and oh-so appealing.

Not literal murder, of course, but how glorious would it be if Ev could somehow free Princess Carissa's dragon and annihilate, or at least mortally wound, her online presence? If she got caught, then it would be a wondrous blaze of glory to go out on. And being dragged off by the Royal Guard was a better excuse for failure than a bevy of schools not wanting her. If she did, by some wild chance, succeed, then the dragon would be back in the skies where it belonged. Win-win for everyone.

Ev turned away from the train tracks to look back toward the town. The sky should be filled with dragons. Instead, the only thing visible was the glow of the castle. The sprawling glass monstrosity at the highest point of town was the most visible thing around, lit up with spell-light at all hours. Because when you were as rich as the Hotthorpes, why have electricity if you could have something twice as costly and half as practical?

Fuck it. She was going to steal a dragon.

‎ ‎

No wall surrounded the castle, not even a gate across the drive. The fireflies blinking lazily above the grass before twilight had even fallen were probably security drones, and the massive glass atrium – the source of the spell-light visible from the train tracks – was undoubtedly etched with protective runes. Stepping even one foot onto the property was beyond stupid. But if she could stay just outside the property line…

She'd come this far; she couldn't turn back now.

Even from the bottom of the drive, Ev felt the dragon, like someone singing at a frequency just on the edge of hearing. The sound lit up her spine, turning every vertebra into glass, her belly into a struck gong. She'd never had occasion before to experience the way dragons picked up and amplified human emotion. She felt it now. Like a cell signal plucked out of the air, the Hotthorpes' dragon sharpened and bolstered everything inside her and cranked it up to eleven. Reckless, unstoppable, ambitious, stupid.

"Kill the princess, save the dragon," Ev murmured.

She swung wide, keeping low in case any of the Hotthorpes happened to glance out the window. She wasn't sure where the property line lay, but no alarms sounded, no heavily armored hands dropped onto her shoulder to haul her away.

The dragon's song changed in pitch — a higher, more anxious register. Behind the castle, multiple levels of terraces stepped down the hillside. Ev picked her way carefully down the slope to the lowest level, and still no alarms shrilled. Maybe the Hotthorpes didn't even bother with security, knowing no one would ever dare. One foot on the smooth flagstones, and then before she lost her nerve, Ev crossed the terrace in one go and peered over the rail into the massive pit below it, also dug into the hillside.

Too perfect, too beautiful.

Spell-light gleamed off scales that were blue-purple-black-green-maybe-pink-sometimes. Princess Carissa's dragon was massive, even curled in on itself, snout tucked into its flank, sleeping. Ev ached to touch it; an overwhelming sensation of want, bordering on hunger. She needed to run her hands over those scales, needed to put one in her mouth. Warm, shiny, and smooth. Could something taste shiny? Yes. But just to be sure, she would launch herself over the railing and find out.

No.

Ev dug her nails into her forearms, letting the pinch against her skin bring her back. Unlike a dragon, she couldn't fly. Stupidly, she hadn't even brought the most rudimentary tools, and even if she had bolt cutters, they would be inadequate against the massive chains keeping the dragon in place. She was the worst thief ever, or certainly the least prepared. But the pull of the dragon remained, a need like air. What had been a passing whim now became a full-blown obsession with the dragon's influence feeding her. She would free the creature, but not tonight.

New plan. Fuck it. She was going to become a tutor.

Befriend the princess, save the dragon. How hard could it be?

Ev stared down the length of Castle Hotthorpe's drive. Somehow, it was even more intimidating in daylight. The band around her wrist marked her as belonging, no one would arrest her, but she was having second thoughts. And below those thoughts, the insistent burr of the dragon remained, like an earworm of a song, never entirely leaving her consciousness. Doubts or not, she had to suck it up. It was her best chance at getting to the dragon.

The door chimed and a screen lit up with the simulated face of a bored-looking security program.

"I'm the tutor?" Ev hated how uncertain her voice sounded.

"Scan your wrist." Contempt colored the electronic voice, even though Ev knew that was impossible.

"Oh. Right." Ev lifted her wristband and the door clicked open.

"Miss Carissa is in the atrium. To your right." The voice, and its condescension, followed Ev across the hushed marble entry hall.

Despite the weather outside, inside the atrium it was full-blown summer. Plants grew riot, dripping fragrant blossoms, all surrounding a pool lined in turquoise and emerald tile. Carissa lounged in a bikini at the far end of the room, legs long and tanned, toes and fingers glinting with matching mani- and pedicures. She didn't look up from her tablet, which was just as well, because Ev couldn't help staring.

Butterflies – Ev couldn't tell if they were drones like the fireflies or actual butterflies doped with chemicals or dosed with magic.

Either way, they hovered around Carissa's hair, lifting strands and looping them over each other in complicated patterns to weave together the most delicate of fishtail braids. It was ridiculous, impossible, showing off the Hotthorpes' wealth — magic taken so deeply for granted that Carissa seemed to barely notice the butterflies at their work.

Carissa spoke without looking up. "Are you planning on spending our whole hour just standing there?"

Ev tried to remember if Princess Carissa had ever addressed her directly before. Maybe she'd asked Ev to pass her a script in drama class, or to borrow a pen. The musical voice that lilted through the halls, answering the *oh my gods* and *so cutes* had been replaced by a cool indifference that felt almost studied. Voice as armor, a shield in stark contrast to her barely clad form. Carissa's legs were longer, sleeker, than Ev had ever realized, her stomach flatter. Her bellybutton was pierced, because of course it was — sparkly and drawing Ev's eye.

She hadn't spoken yet and Carissa finally looked up, impatiently waving the butterflies away.

"You can put your stuff down and sit there." Carissa used her tablet to indicate the chaise next to hers.

Ev briefly caught sight of a diagram on the screen, a complex-looking chemical formula she was certain they hadn't covered in class. Carissa needed tutoring, but she read chemistry books for fun? Seeing where Ev's gaze was directed, Carissa turned the tablet and held it against her chest, frowning.

"Now, what was it you wanted to study?" Carissa asked, as if she was the one doing Ev the favor.

Ev had the brief, absurd thought that they were back in drama class, and Carissa was play-acting as the very epitome of a spoiled upper-class brat. Because no one could be this, could they? But then her social feed indicated that yes, maybe she was, unless it was masks all the way down.

Annoyance – hers, Carissa's, the dragon's, all three pinging in a feedback loop. Ev couldn't tell the source, but it made her snap her next words. "I don't need this job." It came out pouty, defensive.

"Don't you?" Carissa swept her gaze over Ev, her smirk self-satisfied.

Outside, the dragon hummed, reminding Ev why she was here. She rearranged her face into something like contrition.

"Sorry. I mean, it's just, I don't understand why you need me, given..." She gestured to the tablet.

Carissa tried to glare, but a hint of blush crept through, caught out. She tilted her head so that her hair swung forward to hide her face, seemingly more comfortable that way.

"It was my dad's idea, not mine."

"So," Ev said after a moment when Carissa didn't offer anything further. "Do you always do your studying in here?"

"It's as good a place as any." Carissa's tone was guarded.

"It's just, all the pictures you post with your dragon, I figured—" The words felt clumsy, an obvious ploy.

Carissa scented it, her head snapping up, her glare real and unadulterated this time. "You don't need the job. So you're here for the dragon, then?" The frost in Carissa's voice lay atop bitterness, taking Ev by surprise.

She'd thought flattering, cooing like the coterie surrounding Carissa at school would open the floodgates of enthusiasm. Then she would let slip some key that Ev could use to set the dragon free.

Except clearly Ev had done it wrong. "No, I…" she fumbled.

Was there a chance Carissa had seen her skulking around the property? Or was it that she was used to people using her to get to her dragon?

"It was just a question."

How had she managed to fuck things up so thoroughly already?

It was going to be a long afternoon, a long semester.

When Ev arrived for their second tutoring session, she found Carissa in the atrium again, but at least this time she was fully clothed – jeans softened by multiple washings and a plain white t-shirt. A spike of annoyance went through her. The jeans were probably designer, distressed to look like an old, favorite pair. The t-shirt, too. How much money did it cost to look like you hadn't put a moment of thought into your wardrobe, that you didn't care?

Carissa's back was turned, butterflies once more surrounding her. Her hair was loosely braided, three strands thick enough that the butterflies couldn't possibly have lifted them unless she'd trained them somehow to work in concert. Carissa bent to set something down; when she stepped back, Ev saw it was a shallow dish of what was presumably nectar. So they weren't drones, then.

Rather than descending on the food, the butterflies continued to hover around Carissa. One settled on her braid and the others followed suit, arranging themselves so the subtle color gradation of their wings made them into a living hair accessory.

"Not me, the nectar." Carissa lifted her braid, shaking the butterflies free. "You need to eat."

Her shoulders tightened, matching the distress in her voice. Ev felt an answering echo from outside, a mourning note in the dragon's song. Carissa stepped away, waving the butterflies toward the nectar.

"Go on."

The butterflies circled, confused, as if something drew them to Carissa. She took another step, half-turning and noticing Ev. She started, but quickly smoothed it over with annoyance.

"You're sneaking up on me now?"

"I thought you heard me come in." Ev found her tone mirroring Carissa's again.

Carissa's cheeks flushed, defensiveness replacing the contouring and highlighting normally there in all her photos. Bare skin, like Ev had stumbled behind the scenes of her feed while she was still getting dressed. Too perfect, too beautiful – but not right now.

"What are you even doing?" It sounded slightly accusatory, not what Ev meant, but she couldn't seem to stop herself.

The butterflies flittered close again. Carissa swatted at the air around them, then immediately looked horrified at herself, scanning quickly to make sure she hadn't hurt them.

"I can't be in here right now." Carissa brushed past her.

She didn't invite Ev to follow, but she didn't tell her to stay put, either. She pushed through a glass door tucked within the greenery, leading out onto the terrace. Ev found her standing at the railing, arms crossed, body held rigid, conveying a mixture of fury and misery.

"My father switched my shampoo and didn't tell me," Carissa said. A frown pulled at the corners of her mouth, her head canted downward. Two more terraces sprawled below them, the lowest where Ev had stood overlooking the dragon's pit. Carissa's gaze was directed that way, but she didn't seem to be looking at anything at all.

Ev couldn't see the dragon from here. It must have an interior space it could retreat to, holding its body in the same knot of upset as Carissa. At least, that's what Ev guessed, based on the resonating song shivering through her bones.

"You're mad about shampoo?" She couldn't keep the scorn from her voice.

Just when Carissa had almost started to appear human, she'd revealed a new level of shallowness.

Carissa wheeled around, her mouth slightly open, anger flashing up into her cheeks again.

"He's product testing on me, and he didn't even have the decency to ask."

"What?" Ev floundered, lost.

"It attracts the butterflies, and now they're not interested in eating; they're only interested in my hair. They're going to starve to death so my dad can sell them as stupid fashion accessories. I even offered to look at the formula myself, but all he wants is for me to keep being an influencer, selling products."

Carissa's eyes shone, matched to the hectic flush in her cheeks. No longer too perfect or beautiful, but human in a way Ev had never seen from her before. "Wait." Her words finally registered fully. "You offered to look at the formulas? Doesn't the company have a whole lab full of people for that?"

"I like chemistry." Carissa's tone shifted to defensive, as if she expected Ev to make fun of her.

Ev was utterly lost. "Then why do you need a tutor?"

"Because I don't want it, *any* of it — the Royal Academy, the family business. It's all bullshit. Hotthorpe could and should be helping people, but they aren't, so I'm trying to blow it all up by failing my classes on purpose."

Carissa's anger, her despair, clattered hooked and spiky against Ev's skin. The terrace shuddered, the rumble preceding the audible sound as the dragon bellowed its response. Not a song this time, but a single, discordant note, setting Ev's teeth on edge. The letters papering the back of her drawer, a lifetime stretched before her of trudging out from the trailer park before dawn even pinked the sky, across the tracks to the plant, dark already gathering by the time she dragged her weary bones home to collapse into bed and do it all over again the next day. That was the future waiting for Ev.

"Are you fucking serious?" Her voice rose to match Carissa's. "You have everything and you're just going to throw it away like some spoiled—"

"What?" Carissa stepped closer, squaring up to Ev. "Bitch? Princess?"

Somehow, she made the second word sound worse than the first, imbuing it with all the snide dismissiveness with which Ev had always framed it in her mind.

Ev refused to feel guilty or sorry because fuck it, she had every right to be pissed. She opened her mouth to snap a retort. The terrace shuddered again, cutting her off, the faintest of cracks spidering across one of the flagstones. Ev stumbled, catching herself against Carissa, hand on her arm. The warmth of her skin was what Ev imagined she would feel if she could lay her hand against the dragon's scales — a furnace for a heart, constantly burning, so hot that it threatened to turn the body holding it to ash.

Ev realized she hadn't moved away, the closeness between them terrible. Carissa's eyes were a muddy hazel-green. She'd always thought they were a bright, almost turquoise blue. In all her posts, they must have been filtered.

"You—" Ev started without a clear idea of what she meant to say, but Carissa pushed her away. Ev felt suddenly cold.

"I'll make sure you still get paid," Carissa said, "but don't bother coming back."

A thrum from the dragon, not a roar this time. It spoke a counterpoint to the frost Carissa put in her voice, the hardness she tried to hold in her eyes and the line of her jaw. The guilt Ev had managed to dodge before slammed into her with full force. An apology stuck in her throat, and it was all her, not the dragon forcing emotions on her. They didn't do that.

Carissa held her glare, but Ev could see how dangerously close she was to cracking, like the flagstone, letting the tremor underneath show through.

"I—"

"Just go," Carissa said. Her smile turned sharp-edged. "And you can tell everyone at school what a disaster Princess Carissa is in real life. In fact, you'd be doing me a favor."

Slay the princess, save the dragon. It was what she'd wanted when she first took the job, but Ev had no idea what she wanted anymore.

Shit.

She couldn't see a way past Carissa's armor, cracked or not. Couldn't see a way to apologize, especially not when part of her was still angry, when the larger part of her was confused. Should she resent Carissa or pity her? The dragon wasn't helping either, swirling everything inside of her into a mass of anxiety, guilt, irritation. She turned, her bag cutting into her shoulder, a tuck-tailed dog slinking away.

⁂

Ev lay on her side, the only light the glow of her phone. She couldn't help it. Despite telling herself not to – she checked Carissa's feed. She hadn't posted anything all day, utterly unlike her. She scrolled through older posts, camera angled just so, everything cropped and filtered and carefully framed. None of it was her; Ev could see that now, and she couldn't help overlaying every image in the feed with the Carissa she'd seen this afternoon. She hadn't applied the filter to her eyes out of vanity, but to hide how much it hurt to post the pictures, to pretend to be somebody else.

A mask Ev had chosen to believe, because it made her feel justified in her jealousy that she'd let border on hate.

Shit.

She scrolled farther. Always in the background, Carissa's dragon. Both of them trapped and chained.

Perfect. Beautiful.

And when exactly had she dropped the *too* in her mind?

A laugh broke from her, a sound on the verge of becoming a hiccup or a sob, because it was all so ridiculous. Even if there was a chance that Carissa—

No. Ev cut off the branch of thought. No point hoping or wondering along those lines. But she could at least apologize. It wouldn't gain her anything, but it was the right thing to do.

Ev peeled back her covers, pulled on jeans and an old sweatshirt, her stompy boots, and slipped her phone into her pocket. Time to trespass on the Hotthorpe property again.

She followed the light, the atrium burning as bright as ever, night and day, guiding her through the streets as the houses got bigger, nicer, then fell away altogether until it was just the land surrounding the castle. The walk wasn't even all that far — so little space, and such an arbitrary line dividing Carissa's life from hers, yet they inhabited different worlds.

As she had the first time she came here, Ev circled around the edge of the property, but instead of descending the terraces, she approached the atrium from the side and peered in. She started at the figure seated on the ground. She hadn't really expected to find anyone. It took her a moment to recognize Carissa. Her head was completely shorn.

Her legs were folded to the side beneath her, feet bare under the hem of a floral slip dress. The thin straps showed off the slant of her shoulders. Her head was bowed, revealing a tattoo where her neck met the knobs of her spine, an intricate and lovely design formerly hidden by her hair.

Ev tapped the thick glass before she could think better of it. Carissa's head snapped up in a full-body flinch.

Carissa unfolded herself and came to the door. She opened it, but slouched in the frame, blocking the way. The spell-light of the atrium showed her skin was blotchy, as if she'd been crying before Ev arrived.

"What do you want?"

"I... to apologize," Ev said.

She looked down, because it was easier than meeting Carissa's eyes, but she could feel the princess weighing her sincerity.

"Fine." Carissa stepped back, leaving the door open.

"I won't bother you after this, I promise," Ev said, following her inside. "I just needed to—"

She stopped. The shimmer of stilled wings lay arranged in a mournful circle where Carissa had been sitting. Her butterflies.

"I was too late," Carissa said, running a hand across the stubbled remains of her hair. "I don't know if it was something in the shampoo itself, or if it was hunger, but I found them all over the garden and…"

She gestured, helpless, and the motion made her shoulder blades stand out beneath the straps of her dress.

"I really am sorry," Ev said. "For this. For everything."

If Carissa had wanted to make a statement or anger her father, if she'd wanted the attention, she could have posted a dramatic video of her shaving her head and crying, but she hadn't. She'd just wanted to save the butterflies.

Ev pictured her in a too-large bathroom as bright as the atrium, all marble tile and a double sink, even though Carissa was only one person. The thrum of the razor against her skull and the thrum of the dragon outside as a wall-length mirror shone Carissa back at herself and locks of her hair fell to the floor.

"I'm sorry, too," Carissa said. She looked over her shoulder at Ev, her voice defeated and tired. "It was shitty flaunting what I was throwing away. I know you won't believe me, but I understand what it's like to want something and feel like you'll never have it."

"Tower turned me down. The Academy as well," Ev said.

Carissa was the first person she'd admitted it to out loud. She hadn't even told her mom or Ms Averill, saying she hadn't heard back yet. It was both liberating and solidified the course laid out for her.

"It's a good thing your family sold the manufacturing plant. Otherwise, I'd end up working for you even though you fired me today." Ev tried to make it a joke, but she wasn't sure it landed given the expression on Carissa's face as she turned to her fully.

"You're going to work at the plant?"

"I guess." Ev looked away. "I don't have much choice. At least I like chemistry."

"You could leave," Carissa said. Ev looked up, surprised. "I mean, you could go somewhere else, right? You don't have to stay here your whole life."

"I... don't know." It had honestly never occurred to her before.

Her mother, her aunt, her uncle all worked at the plant. Even the father she'd never known had met her mother there before they'd decided it wasn't going to work and he'd moved on to another job, another town. Her mother had his contact information. They'd decided it would be Ev's choice if she ever wanted to reach out. Maybe she could look him up after she graduated, maybe they could even meet. She'd never been anywhere but here, but that could be a start. The possibility was both thrilling and terrifying.

"Anyway, I guess we both made some assumptions," Carissa said, unhappiness creeping back into her voice as she turned to survey the butterflies. "But if you want to keep pretending to tutor me for the cash to fund whatever you do next, that's fine by me."

"I wouldn't want to be in your way." Ev felt herself blushing, and was glad Carissa wasn't looking at her. "I mean, you've got your friends and..."

Ev trailed off, unsure where to go from there and even less sure as Carissa's shoulders stiffened.

"Not really," Carissa said, standing still. "I'm not sure any of them really know me, or even want to. They like my online cred and that I pay for shit when we go out together. They like that I have a dragon."

"Shit." Ev didn't know what to say, cheeks warming further, but with embarrassment this time when Carissa looked at her over her shoulder again.

Then the corner of her mouth lifted, a half-smile. "Yeah, that about sums it up."

Perfect. Beautiful.

Ev wanted to keep her talking and found her mouth running away with her, too conscious of the words, wishing she could stop even as they kept pouring. "I always figured because you were surrounded by people at school that you were happy and had everything. I figured the dragon was like an accessory and—"

Carissa snorted, cutting Ev off. "You thought I was a monster like my father, using _____ for personal gain." Carissa said a word in the middle of the sentence that Ev didn't understand. It blurred and shivered and sang in her mind. "_____," Carissa repeated, brushing her fingers over the tattoo at the back of her neck. "It's their name, my dragon. They should be free, but I begged my father to let me keep them as a pet. It's the only way I could think to stop him from experimenting on them or using them in his products. It's not enough, but I thought if I could save even one…"

Carissa let her hand fall to her side. Ev took a step closer, but stopped, feeling like she was intruding. Her hand tingled, the memory of resting against Carissa's forearm and feeling the heat of her skin.

"I'm sorry," Ev said again. "I wish I'd known all that. I mean, I wish I'd known… you."

She hoped Carissa heard the distinction in the last word, cheeks flaming now, hotter than the remembered furnace of Carissa's skin. The tilt to Carissa's smile grew, and she turned to fully face Ev, a glint in her eye.

"You could have talked to me, you know. If you'd wanted to get to know me."

Ev's mouth opened, shut; a landed fish. Was Princess Carissa teasing her?

"You didn't even know I existed until I showed up at your door to tutor you," Ev protested. "You would have laughed in my face, someone like me trying to talk to someone like you."

"You don't know that," Carissa said, the shine still in her eyes. "You could have tried."

She'd moved slightly closer now, close enough that Ev could have reached out to touch her arm again. The pitch of the dragon's song sat in her belly, like one of those bowls full of water that chimed when you dragged a special stick around the edges. Ev felt it all the way through her, like nerves, like falling, like want. Almost like what she'd felt when she first saw the dragon. How was it that the space between them could be so little and so vast, so impossible, all at once?

"You could have talked to me," Ev countered.

"*You* didn't know *I* existed," Carissa said. "The me you knew was the one you hated."

Her voice had grown softer, her look considering, or regretful maybe. Melancholy. Ev felt the urge to hold her breath. She wondered what the dragon's song felt like in Carissa right now, how she experienced the notes and what emotions it turned up. Hope bloomed between her ribs, but Ev scarcely dared to believe it.

"I didn't, I don't, hate you," she said. "I was jealous."

Carissa huffed a laugh. She tilted her head back, lengthening the line of her throat, a column Ev wanted to kiss. The architecture of her collarbones sang as loud as the dragon; it took all the will Ev had not to track her fingers along them. Carissa closed her eyes, giving Ev time to study the shadow of the stubble across her scalp.

"Okay," Carissa said. "I'm going to tell you something really embarrassing."

Ev waited. Carissa cracked one eye open, peeked at her to see if she was listening, then closed her eye again, letting the words out in a rush. "I had a crush on you back in freshman year." Pink crept up the bared expanse of Carissa's throat.

"Why?" Ev blurted the word before she could stop herself, and Carissa opened her eyes, smiling with a hint of self-deprecation.

"Because I had a thing for hot, quiet girls who are furious at the world, apparently."

"Oh." Ev wasn't sure where to look, what to do with her hands. Her breath snagged in her throat, fighting her as she rushed the next words out. "So had, like fully past tense and you're over it now?"

"Well," Carissa drew the word out, smile returning, but shy now. "We've already established we don't really know each other."

But.

Ev heard the word, hanging hope onto it, even though it was probably foolish. "We could *get* to know each other," she said.

"Sure," Carissa said. Her smile wasn't a promise, but it was a start, and the blooms behind Ev's ribs were now in full riot, a garden that threatened to stop her breath.

"Would it be okay if I took your hand?" Carissa asked.

"Yes."

Warm fingers against hers. Carissa's smile deepened. Ev's whole body was a sounding bowl now, shivering resonance from tip to toes. It was an effort not to shake physically.

"Would you like to meet my dragon?" Carissa asked.

"Yes." The thud of Ev's pulse nearly drowned the word out.

Carissa led her outside and down to the lowest terrace, fingers entwined with Ev's, palm against palm. At the railing, Carissa spoke the word that Ev now knew for the dragon's name.

A trilling chirp answered her, a sound she'd never known dragons could make. Their length unfolded from the shadows where they'd been curled, a sinuous motion like water flowing upward and upward, pouring themself along the stone until their head was level with the railing.

"Oh." Ev breathed the word.

Carissa laid her free hand against the dragon's snout. How it didn't sear the skin from her bones, Ev didn't know. She could feel the heat from here.

"They're beautiful," Ev said.

The dragon's scales sheened in the spell-light. Their eyes were everything – stars and the night sky overhead, every color Ev could name, and several she couldn't. Curiosity radiating from them, peeling back the layers of her flesh and bone, all the way to her heart.

"You can hold out your hand and let them get your scent, if you want, but I wouldn't recommend touching them just yet."

Ev held out her other hand under Carissa's approving gaze and the dragon breathed her in, pulling her out of herself.

"I'm going to tell you something, too," she said. "I'm not sure if it's embarrassing, or just horrible, or both." She took a breath. She felt Carissa's expression turn questioning, but she couldn't look away from the dragon, and she couldn't bear to look at Carissa as she felt the truth drawn to the surface of her skin.

"When I first took this job," Ev said, "I did it because I had this really stupid idea that I was going to steal your dragon and set them free."

She kept looking at the dragon, Carissa's gaze a physical presence leaning up against her.

"Do you still want to steal them?" Carissa asked.

Ev couldn't quite read her tone. She turned to look, and for a moment, Carissa's muddy-green eyes were the same as the dragon's, all stars and impossible colors, and Ev felt a truth she hadn't been sure of until this moment on her tongue.

"Yeah, I kinda do."

She expected Carissa to let go of her hand, maybe shove her away again, but she didn't. She went on studying Ev like a thing she couldn't quite puzzle out. Ev very much wanted to run her hands over the stubble shadowing Carissa's scalp; she wanted to kiss her, trace a hand over her shoulder and run it down her side to settle on her hip, not holding her, but asking her to stay close.

"I kind of want to steal my dragon, too," Carissa said.

"Oh." It was the only thing Ev could think to say, because the words sounded to her like something else — again, not a promise, but maybe an invitation, a door opened to *let's see where this goes.*

It would be a lot easier to steal a dragon with their princess on her side.

Ev let the silly thought flash across her mind, unable to stop the goofy grin that followed, because she also couldn't help picturing riding the dragon — was that even a thing one could do? — behind Carissa, arms wrapped around her, breathing her in the way the dragon had breathed in Ev. They wouldn't need the rails that led out of town for other people who were never her – they could go anywhere.

"Would it be okay if I kissed you?" Ev asked before she lost her nerve.

Carissa leaned in when she answered. "Very okay."

As their lips met, the dragon's song shivered and thrilled and rolled across all three of them, like they'd already taken to the sky.

SAN'T MARTEN'S BOOK OF MILD MELANCHOLY

By

A. G. SLATTER

The city, ancient and shining, runs on magic and paperwork, serviced by an army of mages and clerks.

Built high against and into the cliff side, the upper cantons of San't Marten live in the sun, constantly warm in the summer months and also the winter. The lower parts of the city (a series of tenements, really, short and tall) are not so fortunate, breathing mostly in shadow and chill, with even the harbour bathed in deepest shade. Sailors on a ship leaving the docks hold their breath until they reach the breach between the stone pillars that lead to the open sea; those on ships coming in do the very same thing until they are moored. The black is so profound that anything might rise from the depths with no light to bother it.

The current (most recent) king and his family concern themselves only with the bright places.

Those who inhabit the space below the sunline are left very much to their own devices – as long as they do not interfere with the upper echelons. Which is not to say the umbral city is unpoliced – quite the contrary – but the guardsmen who work this part of San't Marten know their assignment for what it is: a punishment for wrongs, real or perceived. They do their duty but are careful to look the other way when it seems safer. Their presence is less about preventing crime than corralling it; less about stamping it out than keeping it from surging upward into something that might become a revolution. Conditions are kept not bad enough, or sufficiently not awful, to avert such a thing from occurring.

Mindful of this, Millicent Broad, entrepreneur, tries to keep to herself. She runs a small business of an honest if rather (according to some) deplorable nature. Hers isn't the only one of its kind, but it is one of the most reliable. In fact, probably *the* most reliable and, if anyone were to be honest, similar services running in the sunshine levels cost more and deliver considerably less. No. No one has ever accused Millie B of being a fraud. Many other things, yes; a fraud, no. Had she been born under very different circumstances (well, she *was*, but circumstances are notoriously shifty) the young woman might have had a very different life. But the things that happened, happened. Anyways, Millie keeps her head down in the interests of keeping it attached to her shoulders.

The Bureau takes up the top floor but one of a smallish building down in Tate's Hollow – not the worst place, but certainly not the best; halfway up, halfway down in the dark places. Robberies tend to be less violent, committed more by those who'll make jests at one's expense while stealing purses and jewellery, yet leaving coin enough for a commiseratory drink. It's been a while since Millie's had to worry about such things — she's lived here long enough to not work with cash nor wear any jewellery, and the knives at her belt aren't for show (it only took two stabbings for word of that to go around). No money's kept on the premises (except a small purse hidden under her mattress, just in case). Anyone who wishes to use The Bureau must appear with a note from Billings Bank, stating that a particular sum has been deposited into Millie Broad's account there (the bulk of it thereafter disbursed to its branches in three different cities, just in case she's ever required to quit San't Marten in haste) before she'll allow them access to the services. No fool, Millie B.

But the building: the first floor houses a workshop for six seamstresses, sisters and aunts of varied connection; the second, a small distillery of potent spirits, supplied to local inns at a fair price, and to those above sunline for an exorbitant one; the third is The Bureau, divided into four small rooms (two on the left, two on the right), one large locked one at the back (the necro-room, but no one's allowed to call it that outside these walls, or at least not loudly), and a tiny reception area at the front. The top floor is Millie's home, comfortable and colourful, filled with books (those left behind by the Witches and those she's gathered on her own). It's shared with no one now, not even the occasional lover, because that's what joy-houses are for.

The reception area is where Millie sits during business hours behind an enormous wooden desk, balancing the accounts, darning socks, and occasionally reading truly terrible romances by Pirraleigh Portnoy (whose actual identity has remained a secret for twenty years); looking generally harmless in her full skirts and velvet corset tops and glossy brown curls.

The little space is painted a lurid purple, hung with lanterns and incense burners, the ceiling covered in a network of fairy-lights that come alive with a spell each morning. There are bookshelves here, too, containing only the harmless tomes. In each of the four small rooms used by the mediums (decorated identically, more purple with notes of scarlet – the rooms, not the mediums), the business of The Bureau is done and done well enough that those from above the sunline often risk the trip down through the winding streets to visit. The city is large, someone always wants something, wants to talk to someone, specifically someone who's no longer alive. Loved ones, lost ones, rivals, those who died with their secrets intact, those whose knowledge is worth its weight in gold if only there's a way to pry it from their cold, dead mouths and minds and hands. The lonely and the loveless, rich and poor, come to The Bureau in the hope that their departed will speak with them one last time.

One time only. Millie Broad is insistent, because the dead deserve to rest, and the living should simply get on with things. She's got no interest in syphoning away fortunes from those with broken hearts, welcoming them back and back again until both client and ghost are thin and worn. Others are not so scrupulous, but they never last as long as The Bureau has – too many summonings and a spirit might turn mean. A careless ritual might let something *nasty* through. Sometimes, the dead don't want to leave and that can lead to all manner of problems. Gods know, Millie B and her mediums have been brought in to fix the mistakes of others (at great cost), and lay such wicked and weary phantoms to rest. The Witches began the business, passed it on to Millie when they decided they had somewhere else to be. Custom did not suffer for the departure: Millie had been around since she was a child, she's known and trusted.

And that large, locked room at the back? Seldom used, only at great cost, only for a very small clientele sworn to secrecy, and only by Millie Broad. She herself isn't a medium. Millie is something else.

It's late in the day when the unexpected client arrives.

The other mediums have already left – Ana, Harriet and Louisa, who've been with Millie for three years now, very reliable and swear they'll never leave. All have been offered more money by rival operations, but working here is the best job they've ever had so it's not all about coin. Millie looks out for them, pays well, never argues about time away for illness or caring for children or elders. And Millie knows that finding true and skilled and wise mediums is a rare and wonderful thing – why wouldn't she keep them happy?

The fourth and newest? Pandora? She may or may not be a problem; Millie hasn't quite decided yet. The young woman is sensitive in her task, correct in setting up and aligning her table, careful with ritual, makes connections quickly and effectively. Tends to run over time, but Millie's not so worried about that – it never hurts to let clients have a little generosity. She has hopes for the girl, which lend themselves to fondness.

Pandora's instinct for other people, however, isn't so well-developed. Millie can spot a bad 'un a mile off; Pandora will welcome one and all without thinking twice. Doesn't tend to interrogate their requests, doesn't ask the whys and wherefores. On two occasions when Millie's been running errands, Pandora's taken in clients who've not presented their proof of payment, one of whom had given a name for summoning which Millie very well knew to be that of a demon. If the girl had done her study, she'd know the forbidden names, too. It was pure luck that Harriet and Ana had overheard and sent the supplicant away with a flea in her ear. Yet another had asked for a service only Millie could provide; when she'd refused, the girl had offered to do it, openly, right in front of her employer. Both of them were fully aware that Pandora was not then and is not now qualified for necromancy. She might be ambitious, but that doesn't equate to ability or safety. Millie senses the girl wants to impress her, so she's given warnings instead of dismissal, but the rule is three strikes and Pandora's only got one left.

This evening, she's running over yet again. Millie's about to call a gentle reprimand when the door of The Bureau opens and a shadow, broad and tall, darkens the doorstep.

"We're closed, I'm afraid," Millie says mildly. "Return tomorrow at half-ten."

Nevertheless, the figure crosses the threshold. The lights show a man, perhaps Millie's age or not far off, with a peerlessly handsome face, black hair, strange eyes, pale skin and a five o'clock shadow that's almost blue. And Millie can't do anything about the physical reaction that rolls through her at the sight of him, the heat that starts at her curling toes and washes up, spends a little extra time at the apex of her thighs, then continues its journey until her face blushes the pinkest of pinks. Oh! Familiarity.

"But I'm here now." The voice is deep, commanding, *different*, and immediately switches off any ardent desire that Millie might have had to see him naked and sprawled in her bed. He's looking through her with those eyes – black? With a flaring hint of something else, here, then gone? Surely that's not right? – and she realises the familiarity seems entirely one-sided.

"An unhappy circumstance," she says, standing, keeping the desk between them. She's not as tall as he is, but she's not some tiny thing to be intimidated, either. And he can also see the knives at her belt, the muscles in her bare arms that say she won't quit without a fight. "Pandora? Time to go."

Almost immediately there's a rustling in the furthest room on her left, and the door opens. A short, bearded man shuffles out, tears on his cheeks, but a smile making his features glow. He repeats *thank you, thank you, thank you* to the thin, red-headed medium who follows, and to Millie as he exits The Bureau without a glance at the newcomer. Pandora, running her hands down her dress front as if to ensure its neatness, gives the stranger a doubletake and says, "I don't mind one more client."

Millie gives the girl a look that says it's not up for negotiation. The girl reddens and her freckles briefly disappear, then she nods, and passes close by the tall man. The door closes behind her with a small slam that might be carelessness, might be a sulk. Millie doesn't take her eyes off the client.

"As I said, *sir*, we're done for the day. All my staff are gone."

"You're here. You're Millicent Broad." He's speaking as if the act is a recently learned skill. There's something wooden in his use of her name, as if he's dragged it up from somewhere, all unwilling. "You bring them back."

Millie's suddenly very cold; her talents are not spoken of so freely, not in the light. "Do you have your proof of payment?" she asks steadily, fingers itching to creep towards at least one of her knives.

Instead of a reply, he tosses a leather pouch onto the desktop; the noise it makes upon landing is almost a gasp, almost a protest. Millie can see the thing's weight has scuffed the polished wood; his expression says all's settled. That it's only a matter of money, as if she's a joy-house girl. "There's more than enough in there."

"Nevertheless, *sir*, that's not how it works. I don't take cash here. If you've heard of my business, you're aware that a proof of deposit at Billings Bank is required. Their tellers know my account, how much to transfer, they will give you the correct proof to show me. I make no exceptions."

"But I wish to engage you *now*. This very moment." His eyes darken even more and his forehead creases into a frown. The marks around his mouth grow deeper, like furrows of rage. "*You bring them back.*"

"You appear to be under a misapprehension. If I do not wish to take on a client, you don't get a choice. And therefore there's no point in you returning on the morrow."

"But I'm the—"

"—Crown Prince Augustus. I know who you are." Mind you, she didn't know it three weeks ago when they were entangled and the name he'd offered was 'Gus'; or at least, not at the start, although in hindsight perhaps she should have. Nor when they locked eyes in the anteroom of a joy-house close enough to the sunline that she'd be less likely to encounter anyone she knew, and apparently far enough from it that he'd been similarly convenienced. It was only after, when they'd begun to speak, that she noticed the tattoo behind his right ear, in the spot where princes and princesses are marked. That was when she made her excuses and ran. Despite knowing her name, however, he doesn't seem to recall *her*. "Your position entitles you to nothing here."

"I will—"

"You will not. You're alone, none of your guardsmen here to fight your battles, and I have no compunction about slitting your throat, *sir*, and stuffing you into the incinerator in the basement. By the time you're missed, your ashes will have drifted across the bay."

There's a spark in the prince's eyes. Millie realises it's a red tint that's been flaring in his gaze, and she remembers those eyes were blue three weeks ago. His hand goes to the hilt of the sword at his side, and she points at the polished floor with both index fingers, drawing a circle around herself that appears as a line of salt, fine but definite. Distinct. The crown prince – or the thing wearing him – recoils, then halts, steels himself, tries to pretend no fear. Millie makes no other move; no matter what she's said, murdering a prince isn't easy, and she'd have to lug his enormous corpse down a lot of stairs, not to mention clean up in here. All of which feels like too much trouble.

Crown Prince Augustus steps away, reefs open the door. He points a gloved finger at Millie and growls, "This isn't over."

Then he's gone and Millie's around the desk, slamming the door shut, and throwing the lock, breathing hard and wondering what she's done to deserve such a visitation. It hits her that she's not sure whether she's more annoyed about that or irked that the hours they spent, in and on each other, had not clung to his memory. Insult to injury, no matter that something was clearly using him as a skin-suit. Yet he came *here*; she'd not told him what she did, offered no more than her first name, never mentioned The Bureau, and certainly had not uttered a word about bringing back the dead.

Millie waits nearly an hour, and when she does finally leave, it's not the easy way.

A rope ladder she keeps for emergencies is rolled out the back window of the necro-room (which overlooks a tent-covered roof where rugs and carpets are stored for the shop in its lower levels), down to the street below. It's definitely not her favourite way to exit – rope ladders are snaky and wilful, and skirts aren't the most compatible with such activities – but it means she's unobserved, or most likely so. Once Millie untangles herself, she's able to slip along the cobbles in the darkness, towards the Inn of the Painted Face where she hopes there'll be some answers.

It's early in the evening, or late in the afternoon, and the tavern is already rather full. That, of course, assumes there was a time during the day – or the week or the month or the year – when it was ever sparsely populated, and that is a very big assumption. Millie drifts in behind a group of adventurers – all women, well-armed, dressed like pirates and smelling like a perfume shop – and uses them as camouflage until they're well into the large front room filled with tables and benches and folk rapidly sinking into their cups. Then she sidles to the left and into a narrow passage, following it along to a door banded with copper shaped like ivy. The passageway is long enough to discourage most people, to give them second thoughts about their direction when seeking a bathroom or bedroom or cloakroom or the kitchen to check where their meal is.

Millie Broad knocks three times (not being given a key still irks, after all these years). It takes an inordinate amount of time for the door to be hauled open, its inhabitant looming out. Faustus Belisarius, pallid and bald and skeleton-thin, squints blearily; either he started drinking early or simply didn't stop from last night, or the night before that. When he realises it's her, he looks surprised, then vexed, and tries to shut the door again.

"Oh, no *no!*" Millie wedges her boot into the gap, thankful for the steel-capped footwear because it's the sole thing stopping him from crushing her foot, the mood he's in. She quickly says the only words she knows will distract him. "The royal family." He grunts, lets her pass. She can smell the potent brandy he's been imbibing. The room looks small, overcrowded with books and all the tools of a bookbinder, but she knows that behind the shelving at the far end there are more shelves, more books, quite far back. Its tenancy was creatively acquired just after what's called in some quarters 'The Fall of the Last Great House' (the previous royal family), in others 'Marquette's Just Rebellion'. Millie takes the stool furthest from the fireplace where Faustus has a cauldron of something unidentifiable bubbling. In the event of an explosion, she doesn't want to be too close. The heat, however, is inescapable. Sweat breaks out on her skin quickly, soaks through her bodice, beads her brow and dribbles down her face through her makeup – she'll look like a clown by the time she's done – and bubbles on her spine, her thighs, calves. Ugh.

"Well? What?"

"The crown prince."

"Yes?"

"What's happened to him?"

"How should I know?"

"Because you keep an eye on them: King Marquette, his wife-of-the-moment, his nephew and heir. You know their every move. You did it with the last lot, you've been doing it with this one."

"They're less interesting than your family, that's for sure," he mutters as he stamps over to the other stool and drops heavily onto it. There's a book open on the table beside him, not yet assembled.

"You're in no state for fine work," Millie says gently. "You won't get paid if you ruin that." She knows he can't help himself – any money he'd had before the Just Rebellion has been spent on books and booze. He'll jeopardise his last means of support if he becomes unreliable. She also knows that he sold her to the Witches, and that money's gone too; that he makes deals with the innkeeper on his worst weeks. Millie doesn't like him enough to help out.

"Don't you think I don't know that?" he snarls, then calms. "What *about* the crown prince?"

She doesn't mention the joy-house or the things they did, how when they talked afterwards, she realised who *Gus* was and how her blood ran cold to have slept with the nephew of her family's usurper. Instead, she just says, "C'mon, Faustus. You must know something. Or suspect. He came to The Bureau. I didn't like him."

"In all fairness, you don't like many people."

"True but unhelpful. He wanted me to raise someone. He said 'them'. 'You bring them back.' And he wasn't right." She raises a finger. "And before you say anything stupid or dismissive, it was the red flashing eyes."

His expression becomes thoughtful.

"Well?" Millie prods. "Well, ex-Chief High Librarian of San't Marten?"

"There are days," he drawls, "when I very much regret smuggling you out of the palace before the coup."

"So you've said time and again. But you did it and here we are. The crown prince?"

He shrugs. "Lad's a reader, so I hear. There are dangerous volumes on those shelves," – the Great Royal Library of San't Marten – "and my sense is they're not too careful what they give him."

"Unlike you, who kept such things safely under lock and key."

She can't keep the tone from her voice, but he seems not to notice. Millie thinks, watching him stare into the flames, that he's remembering the sight of her wandering through the palace corridors, while behind her a ruckus erupted, the beginning – and frankly end – of the Just Rebellion. Faustus knew that he'd never survive the change of power – too closely aligned as he was with the old king – so he grabbed up the princess and fled through the hidden tunnels of the library, down into the dark part of the city. They got lost among the denizens and the lowlifes, hiding until the guardsmen from above the sunline stopped looking.

Within six months, he'd offered her to the Witches after hearing they were looking to buy a child. It could have gone horribly for Millie, but the Witches were kind, though very old, and taught her everything they could, nurturing the strange talent they detected beneath her skin, embedded in her bones. They'd taught her the ways of raising the dead, of reassembling blood and bone, of making the inanimate dance like life, and the even rarer skill of *remaking* them when all you had was the memory of them; no corpse needed. And, when she turned seventeen, they'd told her it was their time to go; that there were other places they needed to be. So they departed, leaving her The Bureau and their home, money in the bank and warnings she'd never forgotten ringing in her ears.

"Focus, Faustus. The crown prince, in the dark part of the city, wanders into *my* business by pure chance. The crown prince about whom there is the whiff of sulphur."

Faustus shakes his head. "I'll ask around, but it might take some time to… If he returns—"

"Don't answer the door. I know."

"Well, no. Try to trap him."

"Whatever's sent the heir into the dark? It's not going to be a good thing."

※

When Millie returns to The Bureau – clambering up the rope ladder and cursing all the way – she's surprised to hear voices, then a loud gasp. Two. She's careful to be quiet, making her way to the mediums' rooms. Pandora's door is open. Millie peeks around the frame to see her erstwhile employee seated at the little round table with its lace cloth, lit candles and focus crystal. Across from her is Crown Prince Augustus, surrounded by a blood-red aura that leaps like flames and flows between medium and prince. Neither look happy about it. Pandora's mouth is open in a scream and the prince's eyes are wide with fear.

Before Millie can cry out there's an ear-splitting *crack*. The air smells like petrichor, and Augustus is thrown away from the table, so far that he lands at Millie's feet. Freed of the crimson hold, he looks different, smells different, and the eyes that stare up at Millie are the pale blue she remembers. Millie reaches for him as she takes a last glance at Pandora – there's nothing left of the girl but bones held together with red lightning. An energy that pulses and pulses, pressing the air in the room outwards. Fingers hooked in his royal collar, Millie drags the young man into the short corridor between the mediums' rooms, her strength unreasonable, powered by fear. She gets him into the necro-room, swings them both through the window and onto the still-dangling ladder just as an explosion rips through The Bureau. The ladder is torn from her hand, but she doesn't let go of the prince even as they fly, even as they land somewhere softer than they should, and even as the impact closes her eyes.

⁓

When she wakes, it's to the press of a warm weight beside her, a sulphur-free scent (although there's a whiff of garlic and red wine) and a low rumbling snore. Every sensation casts her back to the joy-house, the room drenched in blues and greens like a deep-sea grotto, silks and velvets, cushions as far as the eye can see. Millie B moans, keeps her eyes closed, seeks the mouth that's oh-so-close to her ear, blowing hot air and a vague hint of stale breath. Not romantic, but that's not what she's seeking, nothing so ephemeral. No. She wants something solid though temporary, nothing as binding as commitment, nothing as clingy as romance.

And her companion responds with enthusiasm, which is when Millie realises she's in neither a joy-house nor her own bed, and her bottom lip is stinging like a bastard. She pushes away the body, its cunning tongue, hard muscles and all the other hard bits. Eyes flying open, she stares into a blue gaze set in a bruised and bloodied face. She won't be looking any better, she realises; touches a hand to her mouth that comes away wet and red. "Shit."

"You!" Even his voice is different – sounding less like he did a few hours ago, and more like he did a few weeks back.

"Oh, recognise me now, do you?" Millie can't avoid the snarky tone – then realises something's not quite right. They've landed by some miracle on the roof covered in rugs and carpets, on top of the tent (which they've managed to collapse), and she can see him very clearly. But it's night, and night down below the sunline is black as a goat's guts, and there are no torches on this roof because fabrics and flames don't mix. Millie sits up, feeling the ache in her muscles, her bones, but nothing seems broken. She turns toward the source of the light. "Oh, no."

The Bureau is ablaze, the top floor mostly gone, which means all of Millie's possessions – her livelihood – has gone with it. She thinks about all the books burned, all their spells released into the air, perhaps some fuelling the conflagration along with the contents of the distillery below... Millie hopes the rest of the building was empty, that no one was working late. No one except Pandora. Oh, Pandora. Millie imagines the girl, ambitious and defiant, waiting around on the street to see if the client might have an interesting request, sneaking in when all seemed quiet and paying the price for it. Millie rolls back towards the crown prince (who's reclining annoyingly casually, hands clasped behind his head) and slaps him hard. "What did you do? What did you do to her?"

"Nothing! Nothing! I can't remember... she was waiting..." He shakes his head. "Only it wasn't me, not really. I haven't been myself the whole day. It's like—"

"Like you're carrying a passenger around inside you," she finishes. That's what she'd sensed when he walked in. She should have done something about it then, should have tried to kill him – only she wasn't quite sure how, not knowing exactly what it was – and she'll admit there was genuine reluctance to take his life, and not just because he'd leave a mess to clean up. She clears her throat. "Do you remember when you felt the change?"

"After I read that book."

"Right, you're going to have to be more specific. There are rather a lot in the palace."

"There was one waiting for me on my bed, nicely wrapped." He shrugged. "Assumed it was a present. How do you know how many books are in the—"

"Nice life you've got, random presents being left around," Millie interrupts, words sounding hollow even to her – that was her life, before it all fell apart. She'd found just such a gift, once.

"That much I do recall. *San't Marten's Book of Mild Melancholy*. The first line is—"

"'Death is the only true love.'" Millie Broad sighs. "It's a trap, that book. A spell, really, the entire thing. There's a demon bound inside, pops up like a jack-in-the-box when read. Makes the reader murder others – loved ones, friends, whoever the spell names."

"Who would write such a thing? Who would leave such a thing?"

"Someone who did not wish you well." Millie frowns. "You wanted me to 'bring them back'. Who's *they*?"

"I don't remember."

"I think you're lying."

For a while she doesn't know if he's going to answer. Then, he almost coughs out, "I think I hurt my family: my uncle, his wife."

And he looks so miserable and so young that her heart gives a squeak of sympathy, something she was sure had been drained altogether these past years.

"I... know I did."

"I'm sorry," she says. "Look, we need to go."

He nods. "There'll be soldiers coming soon enough. Looking for me."

Millie stares at him with bitter amusement, sympathy draining away. "Do you really think so? Because when my family was slaughtered, no one came to our aid, and no one delivered justice. Your uncle simply walked in and took over, didn't even change the livery on the household servants, declared you his heir, took a fresh wife from the pile of noble houses waiting for their chance." She laughs. "We need to go so I can find an answer before someone replaces your uncle the way he replaced my father."

"Your father? You're her? The Lost One." He stares. "You know my uncle had you written out of the records? Because you couldn't be found, he decided the best thing to do was erase you."

Millie hadn't known that. Why would she? Did it matter? When she could barely recall the name she'd been born with? When she was so thoroughly Millicent Broad, owner of The Bureau? Or rather, of a burning business? A pile of ash? To gain herself a moment, she turns her head, lifts her hair and shows him the scar where Faustus put a burning brand to sear away the tattoo. Over the years something had happened, as if he'd burned it into the skin, though these days it was pale, like a raised cicatrice.

They *should* get moving, but she's got questions and they're demanding attention. "So now you know. Now you can get rid of me."

"I wouldn't! I'd never… I only became crown prince because my uncle has no sons. I was quite happy on my parents' farm – oh, they call it an estate, but if the livestock wander into the kitchen on a daily basis, it's a farm." He throws his hands up. "The moment his latest consort delivers a boy, I'll be finished. The best I can hope for is being castrated and sent to service in the archival holds. Or the best I could have hoped for before…" He narrows his eyes. "Wait. How did you know about the book, how it starts? That's a very specific piece of knowledge…"

Millie blinks hard. "Because when I was five, I found such a gift, too."

His eyes widen in understanding of what goes unsaid.

She changes the subject. "When the spell activates, that version of the book's destroyed, the demon takes a host. When the deed is done, the demon disappears. Yours is gone now."

"Are you sure?"

She nods. "Whatever you – it – asked Pandora to do? There were enchantments and wards laid over The Bureau by the original owners that won't allow certain things to happen. And Pandora… poor stupid girl. She was consumed by the reaction – the demon jumping to her, a better and more powerful vessel with all the medium magic in her, precisely the sort of thing that's not allowed. It threw you out of the loop in doing so – and then the wards were lit up."

"But someone still sent me *San't Marten's Book of Mild Melancholy*."

"Not something done lightly or accidentally, unless you're very stupid." She pauses. "But why did you come to The Bureau?"

He shrugs. "It wasn't me. An imperative."

"Huh. Interesting," she says. "An order folded into the demon folded into the book. I think it wanted me, but it went with Pandora when offered. Curious. Not a very targeted thing, then. Not a skilled practitioner, just someone who knew enough to do damage."

"So…?"

"So, we should get out of here before someone sees us anywhere near this awfully large and destructive fire and all the damaged property." She begins to crawl across the soft, unstable surface. "Oh, and let's avoid any patrols – if they find us, they'll just put you on the throne and it'll take ages to sort this out."

She steals a cloak hanging from a washing line somewhere in the mean streets – he's already got one – and makes a mental note to come back and replace it when she can, or leave coins on the doorstep at a later date. They wander the streets, hooded like assassins, ducking in and out of the mouths of alleys, bolting across brightly lit streets, doing their best to stick to the deeper darkness wherever they can. They manage to avoid the patrols and firemen, shouting, hauling buckets of water in the direction of the blaze. Millie hopes hard that the fire's contained, for everyone's sake. Almost at their destination, however, a band of heavily armed guardsmen round the corner, catching the pair passing beneath an unavoidable streetlamp. Millie pushes the prince against a wall without thought, brings her face close to his, hisses, "Hush."

He murmurs "Well, this is familiar" and pulls her into a kiss before she can snarl at him.

The guardsmen are well and truly gone by the time Millie comes up for air. She didn't even hear – or hardly heard – the coarse comments about joy-walkers and their clientele, exhortations to take a room somewhere, and requests to be next in line. The prince doesn't seem to want to let her go and she'd admit, if anyone had the breath to ask, that she feels the same. But there's a problem to solve, so she puts a hand flat on his chest (doesn't quite manage to make herself push him away, just pats the muscles there), and sighs. "Later."

He moans and nods reluctantly.

When Millie at last knocks on the copper-banded door inside the Inn of the Painted Face, Faustus takes even longer to answer than before and she wonders if either he suspects it's her again and is waiting for her to leave, or if he's gone altogether. If he'd heard the explosion, or news of the fire, and in a fit of caring has run through the streets to see if she's safe; or in a fit of terror has left the city at long last. When he does finally appear, his eyes go terribly wide in disbelief. She pushes her way inside, dragging the crown prince behind her. Faustus looks doubly surprised when he sees the young man.

"Did you hear?" asks Millie.

"What?"

"The explosion."

"Uh. No. Nothing."

Millie can tell he's lying. She tilts her head, stares. For a moment it's like he struggles to select a train of thought, then seems to give up, shrugs. "Honestly, I didn't think you'd survive. You're like a rat or a cockroach."

It feels like a slap, even though there's never been any gentleness from him over the years. But he had saved her, and she'd always thought it meant *something*, some rough kind of caring.

"But you rescued me," she says dumbly, as if the betrayal cannot be believed.

"I'll admit it was irritating, to find you alive, but it's worked out. An insurance policy, small and portable. A source of income when needed. And now you've conveniently delivered my next problem here." He shakes his head. "I must get better with those bloody books."

"Why? Why do that now? Why do it then?"

"Don't you ever get tired of living down here?" Faustus shouts. "All the darkness, all the time! It's maddening. I want the sun again, I want to be able to show my face without fear of being found! Of being recognised and punished!"

"By whom?"

He points at Augustus, who looks perplexed. "His uncle! My traitorous co-conspirator. He promised me... promised me every bit of power my heart desired, promised not to ignore me like *your* father. If only I did this one little favour for him, cleared his path, oh, what a glorious empire we would build."

"The book. You left the book for me. You left a book for him."

"And didn't it work beautifully? What a good little girl you were, so suggestible, putting the poison in the soup. All your brothers and sisters, your parents, gone in one fell swoop." Faustus looks at Augustus with less enthusiasm. "You only had to get rid of your uncle and his wife," he says almost to himself, shakes his head, baffled. "But my little Millie, a mass murderer at the age of five!" He shakes his head again. "Then I saw my old friend marching towards me with death in his eyes... when he should have been thanking me."

"And you grabbed me and ran."

"Still haven't worked out how to make the possessed commit suicide afterwards, though."

"You can't – demons are surprisingly lifeward," Millie says absently, then blinks to try and rid herself of the image of her family slumped over the dining table. "But once they're gone, sometimes the killers kill themselves." She looks at Gus, understanding dawning. "I think he meant demon-you to kill me, but you-you simply asked me to bring them back." Millie stares at Faustus again. "So, what now?"

"A new age. The librarian-king. The magician-king." He raises his arms grandly, as if he's not in a dingy little kingdom that smells like booze and sweat and a man who's stewed himself and his brain for fifteen years.

"You're a better bookbinder than you ever were a magician. Or a librarian for that matter." Millie rolls her eyes, and steps in front of the crown prince. In the seconds Faustus takes to drain his drink, his eyes off her, she waves her hands, circling herself and Augustus; the line of salt forms.

"I've learnt some things." He claps his hands together, chants a low-voiced spell. From the table where all the sharp bookbinding tools rest, four knives fly up, hover for a second, then speed towards Millie and the prince – and fall when they hit Millie's protective barrier.

"You were so dismissive of my Witches, Faustus, but they taught me more than you'll ever know." Calmly, Millie takes one of her knives and slices her palm, makes a fist and pumps it so the blood pools hot and warm; blood magic for the worst sort of thing. She fixes Pandora's face in her mind, that peaky, sneaky face with its ambition and its drive and its intelligence blunted by those things, the dusting of freckles, the curling red hair. She thinks of the Witches' lessons, how to call up a revenant from only the memory of them, how to sing a body into being long enough for it to do damage. Soon enough, Pandora is gazing at her erstwhile employer, looking for the last very specific instructions.

"Him. Faustus Belisarius. He's the one who did this to you. Take your vengeance on him, then go to your rest."

And the temporary thing of flesh and blinding rage becomes a whirlwind of blades made of bone, turning upon the thin man.

Pandora, or what was once her, makes short work of Faustus – there's not much of him for a meal – slicing and dicing, then descending on the wet, red remains. Millie's stomach turns at the sound of the feasting, but they cease soon enough and the revenant fades away.

Millie and Augustus stay in place for some time, until the prince puts his hands on her shoulders and turns her to face him. He wipes tears from Millie's cheeks; she hadn't realised she'd begun to cry. "I shouldn't be so stupid. And I don't really know who I'm weeping for."

"You thought you meant something to him. It's entirely understandable."

She sags against him, breathes in his scent, lets his arms hold her up and lets herself think, for the barest sliver of a moment, that this might last. There's a lot to consider, knowing what she does now, guilt and grief she's carried more than half her life for something not her fault. But there are other, more pressing things needing to be done, so all that must wait. She forces herself to straighten, step away. "Well, I suppose that's that. You'll be going to claim your throne, then?"

"Oh. No. No way. Not for anything in the world. It's your throne, really. You take it."

"I don't want the bloody thing!"

"Then… we leave? Go elsewhere? I like the idea of a farm but not the actual farming. So, another city? Travel for a while?"

Others, she supposed, might be driven by a sense of duty – noble obligation – to stay, to rule, but she'd not been brought up that way, and he'd never wanted it. "Are you asking me to run away with you?"

"Suppose I am. I mean, your house is on fire, your business all gone..." Augustus grins, then sobers. "When did you last make a choice for yourself? The little I know of you: possessed by a murder demon, kidnapped by a librarian, sold to Witches and inherited their business. What would *you* like to do?"

She thinks about leaving a life below the sunline and living in the light once more. She thinks about him, that she'd like to know him better. And she thinks about the cities with banks that hold some of her money, any of which would be perfectly good places to start.

GOOD DEEDS AND THEIR MAGICAL PUNISHMENTS

By

HANNAH NICOLE MAEHRER

CHAPTER 1

Elizabeth Fellowes hated noise.

Which made her current living situation in New York City either a cruel act of fate or the result of her own nonsensical choices — knowing herself well enough to weigh the possibilities, both options were on the table. As was the silverware she'd been rolling into the soft cotton napkins for the last hour. A silver fork slipped from her grasp and clattered to the ground, the noise ringing unpleasantly in her ear.

She glared at it like it had done something offensive rather than being a victim of her sweaty palms and butter fingers. Bending low to pick it up, a strand of light brown hair tickled her exposed collarbone. Brushing it back in a huff, she tucked it behind her ears as a pair of nonslip black sneakers appeared before her. Her eyes rolled. First the fork and now this? The universe was punishing her for not holding the elevator for Mr Lennings that morning, but she'd been in a hurry, and Mr Lennings liked small talk.

Elizabeth believed small talk to be a section of hell carved out on earth just for her personal torment. Her habit had always been to get to the point with as few clipped words as possible to end the interaction swiftly so she didn't say something mortifying to screw it up.

"Bette, still here? Were you waiting for me? And on your knees, no less." Randall, a fellow server who had been at Madame Rose's far longer than Bette, gave her a slimy smile. She winced like she'd just experienced something revolting.

Randall seemed to have that effect in general.

Placing the fork gently back on the table, she straightened her aching back, attempting to stand taller than the man leering down at her. "Why would I be waiting for you, Randall?" She said it curiously, as if she didn't know what he'd been suggesting, blinking her wide brown eyes at him.

Bette found it much easier to act as if she didn't understand people's meanings when they were trying to offend her. It was nothing if not entertaining, watching them stumble at her lack of comprehension with slight panic at the prospect of explaining themselves.

Randall wiped underneath his nose with the back of his hand, his eyes roving to the ceiling. "I was just teasing you, Betty girl. Boss told me you're cut and can head home. It's dead tonight."

It wasn't, of course – dead that is. They were in the Lower East Side of New York City, the place was still packed with people, and Bette was almost certain Randall was trying to be rid of her so he could commandeer her section. Well, fine. She was at the end of her rope, she'd surrender it happily.

Pasting a small smile on her face, she brushed her damp palms against her black apron. "That's so considerate Randall," she said pleasantly. It wasn't. "I'm so appreciative." She wasn't.

But she'd already sacrificed enough to the restaurant gods for the evening; the red wine stain on her new white shirt was ample proof. Courtesy of a patron who'd drunk her weight in merlot and was generous enough to 'share' it with Bette.

It had been the woman's birthday and Bette had to assure her for fifteen agonizing minutes that it was fine, and she could get a new shirt and 'no this isn't a big deal, I promise you it happens all the time.' The woman had relented and given her a hug and pathetically Bette almost wept into her shoulder at the contact.

She couldn't remember the last time someone had hugged her, and she hadn't realized how much she missed it until a drunk stranger was holding her tight and patting her back.

It wasn't a cry for help. More like a scream.

Without a backward glance, she kept her middle finger clenched tightly to her palm in the tentative hopes she wouldn't flip anyone off on her way out. The evening summer air was balmy and damp. The sweat she'd just wiped from her palms was now seeping from the top of her forehead and the back of her neck as she re-tied her thick hair away from her face.

Only three more months.

If she continued making the tips she was, she'd only need to do this for three more months before she could finally afford the down payment for the small cabin she'd been eyeing in the Poconos for the last year. The real estate agent had warned her that it was a fixer-upper, that she'd be secluded, away from the major roads and therefore cut off from most of civilization.

Her co-workers had called her out of her gourd, and maybe she was, but the city had held no appeal since her parents passed.

The paramedics had called it an accident. To her, it was the day she was forever altered. Sweet Bette had both her wings clipped when she'd woken up with two parents and had gone to sleep with both dead.

There was no point staying in New York when every time she closed her eyes, she saw their faces. Her sweet father with his horrific jokes, her mother with her zany tarot readings, and the beating heart in Bette's chest that missed them so much it was difficult to breathe.

Her hand absentmindedly rubbed her chest as she walked, block by block, street by street. The lights and the people passing were all blurring together as she made her way to the rent-controlled apartment that had been on loan to her from a family friend. Something most New Yorkers would kill for, and she was desperately trying to leave it behind.

But grief didn't leave much room for logic, only for dull, phantom aches.

She passed a comedy club pizza place she used to go to with Emma, her high school best friend with journalistic aspirations. Bette had received something like twelve unanswered text messages from Emma since the funeral. The last was a gentle, '*I know you're hurting. Call me when you're ready to talk.*' Bette had figured, even then, that she'd never be ready to talk about it. So, she never called.

Her sneakers made scuffing sounds against the pavement as she turned onto her street. Ivory overgrowth sprouting up between the cracks in the brick buildings' architecture made the dimly lit street look romantic in a way that caused her chest to constrict. It was irritating and inconvenient, that every positive emotion seemed to only last a moment before her piercing guilt set in.

Bette halted to pluck one of the ivy leaves and twirled the green stem between her fingers as she picked up her pace. She needed mind-numbing television, greasy takeout, and the quiet company of her goldfish, Max. The crowds on the street had thinned out to only a few stragglers and even more dimly lit sidewalks. This was the part of the walk where her hand drifted to her pockets and put one finger on the plastic tab above her pepper spray, the part of the walk where she became acutely aware she was a young woman traveling alone at night.

That awareness always lived inside her, but there were moments of heart-pumping adrenalin that made the starkness of that fact stand out with a little too much clarity. The hairs on the back of her neck stood on end as she rounded another corner and saw two men booking it down the sidewalk toward her.

She side-stepped them, trying to keep her expression even, and they passed her without a second glance. It made her feel silly, but she'd rather be silly than careless.

"Oh dear." Bette halted and turned her head at the distressed voice echoing behind her. The two men may not have been coming for her, but they'd neglected to see the elderly woman in their path as they knocked into her shoulder, causing her blue glasses to fly off her nose and onto the sidewalk.

Keep walking, Bette.

The old woman was squinting down at the ground, her eyes tinged in panic as she searched for the discarded lenses. Surely, she'd find them. Bette should keep walking. Bette shouldn't be standing there, thirteen paces up the street, frozen and staring, willing the woman to find the lenses so she could continue with a clear conscience.

But Bette stood there, because despite her parents being gone, despite any trace of them being left on this earth, they'd left their goodwill behind to live on in her. It was the strongest piece of them she still held.

Strongest, and most irritating.

After the sixth person – and yes it *was* six, she'd counted them in bubbling anger – had passed the old woman by without a second glance, the last person took a wide step over the woman's glasses without breaking pace. That was what propelled Bette to turn around, back to the old woman, who looked on the verge of tears.

"It's alright," Bette said gently, giving her a small smile and laying a hand on her arm to still her shaking. Bette's parents were the storm; they had always called Bette the calm. *'Better-than-medicine Bette'* had been her father's favorite nickname for her. She tried to summon that side of herself now, though she feared her presence no longer served as a remedy. Bending low, she picked up the glasses and took the woman's hand, gently placing the lenses in her age-spotted palm.

"Here you go," Bette said, her sincerity surprising her after so long in a haze of robotic interactions. "These streets aren't lit enough; I can barely see my shoelaces."

Up close, she noticed the older woman was in clothing that

would be deemed strange if they were anywhere outside New York City, like she'd just hit the Renaissance faire or Comic Con as a DnD character. "I like your outfit." Bette offered the compliment before letting out a nervous chuckle. The woman didn't answer, just quietly placed the glasses back on her nose. "Did you just come from somewhere fun?"

The woman remained silent, twirling the end of a long, gray braid, hazel eyes crinkling as they roved up and down Bette's person. "Hmph. I didn't think it would be someone so young. Odd."

Bette's brow furrowed. "I'm twenty-eight."

"You seem tall." The old woman tapped her chin. "Like a statue. Can you turn?"

Bette's first voluntarily initiated social contact in months, and she was being inspected like grocery produce. "I'm average height— Excuse me!" She yelped as the old woman lifted Bette's arm and inspected her hands. "Ma'am, please let go." The grip wasn't tight, Bette could certainly pull free, but this whole thing was so irrationally peculiar she couldn't help but raise an eyebrow. The street was dim, but still littered with people, so she didn't feel necessarily unsafe. And despite her better judgement, she was entertained.

"You're rather scrawny. Do you eat?" The old woman dropped her arm and *tsked*.

Bette let out a laugh that sounded like it had been dragged out of early retirement – unused, raspy, and a bit unnatural. "I eat plenty, thank you!"

"Never mind. Outsides can always change. It's the insides that are stubborn, and your insides don't need any changing. *Hmph*." The woman adjusted her glasses, snapping a crooked finger in the air. "You'll do."

Bette wasn't entertained after that.

The entire street vibrated and rattled until every person, every blowing branch of the gated trees, even the pigeons midflight... froze. As did the blood running through Bette's veins. It was ice. She was ice. This was it; the repressed grief had finally gotten to her. She had descended into full-blown hallucinations. That, or she'd been drugged.

It was a toss-up which was worse.

"What— I don't— What did you do? What's happening?" Her heart was pounding in her ears, her instincts screaming at her to run, but she couldn't. Her feet were stuck, her hands clasped together over her mouth.

The old woman waved her own hand over the ivy-covered brick wall. Bette watched in horrified wonder as a bright, beaming swirl of lilac light sparkled there, covering the brick with a large misshappen circle. "Worry not, Bette. I'll explain when we return to Magic Grove through the portal." The woman gripped her hand and dragged her forward.

Bette went along in a daze, her whole body screaming at her to stop, but it was like her limbs were not following her commands. "How do you know my name? Have you been stalking me? Is this a kidnapping scheme? What are you—"

"You're wearing a nametag, dear."

Bette glanced down at the pin at the top of her stained shirt. Oh. The realization was embarrassing perhaps, but not her largest obstacle. "What is that? What's a portal? And what's Magic Grove? And why did you—"

The old woman rolled her eyes as she dragged them both forward into the beaming light. On the heels of Bette's drowning screams, she only heard one sentence from the old woman's mouth.

"Mortals ask all the wrong questions."

CHAPTER 2

Lord Fenmore Majos' mother was missing.

This fact might have sent other lords in Magic Grove – a magical realm parallel to the mortal one – into great alarm at the prospect of what could've happened to their elderly mother. Lord Fenmore's case was rather different in that when his mother went missing, he didn't so much worry for what happened to her, but what would happen to everyone else.

The argument they'd had the night before would only be fuel for her destructive magical tirade.

"Jorge!" Fenmore bellowed up the great hall of the estate house, running a hand through his wild red locks that needed to be shorn imminently.

His butler appeared, looking sheepish and startled – his mother's signature if he'd ever seen it. "Yes, My Lord? How may I be of service?" It was odd to take on any sort of authoritative role over the graying butler. Said butler had known Fenmore since he was no more than a babe. If someone had watched you spit up your mushed carrots, it became significantly more difficult to hold any sort of dignity before them.

But Fenmore had to try, because if there was one person Jorge was more loyal to than Fenmore, it was his mother. "Have you seen the Dowager Louise?"

Jorge swallowed so hard Fenmore could see his throat bob. Fenmore placed his hand on the smooth, cool wood of the large front staircase. "Jorge, I might remind you that I am the Lord of this land *and* this house. I bid you to tell me where my mother has gone before I find out for myself."

With his chin held high, Jorge stared straight ahead at the old clock mounted on the wall. Clearing his throat, his butler's back straightened more (if that was even possible). "My Lord, I fear for her ladyship's wellbeing if I were to tell you the truth of—"

But before the sputtering butler could say another word, a large, beaming portal appeared in the far wall, his mother hurtling haphazardly through it, her gray hair askew and a wide, alarming grin on her face. "I've done it, Fenmore! I've done it!"

A more disturbing sentence had never been uttered.

He kept his face blank, his voice calm, his body still, showing no weakness. His mother could sniff out fragility like a hound on a scent. He would be damned before he'd allow her to win this game of wills they'd been playing for the last month. "I bid you be more specific, Mother. What is it exactly that you've done?" He tucked his shirt in as he spoke, as if he was bored, as if it didn't matter what her response was. Nothing would crack his unbreakable mien.

That is, nothing but a young woman falling through the portal straight to her hands and knees, a curtain of mousy brown hair falling over her face, her ragged breaths echoing in the silence.

He sighed, controlling his surprise, controlling everything the way he always had to. His mother wasn't stable enough to take proper care of the lands and the tenants that relied upon them.

After Fenmore's father passed when he was just a boy, he'd become the only member of the household with any sense of responsibility.

"Mother, have we resorted to kidnapping now?" He took a few steps closer, the rug in the entryway softening the sound of his footsteps as he approached. "I'm certain the mortals you so desperately want to rub elbows with would frown upon this."

His mother *tsked*. "Kidnapping is for children. This one's too old for kidnapping."

That comment seemed to shock the woman from her stupor, her head whipping up, long soft tresses of hair cascading down her back as she stood. "First of all, as I said, I am twenty-eight. That is not old by anyone's standard. Secondly, the definition of kidnapping is to take someone against their wishes. Which you have, because I did not *wish* to be thrust into that weird light thing that made my stomach feel like it was doing a backflip – only to land in a house that looks like it was designed in the Middle freaking Ages!"

The woman breathed out a hard exhale before turning her head toward him, giving him a first glimpse at her face. Whatever hardened indifference he felt seeped away as his lips parted in quiet, startled awe. She was… lovely.

Her tan cheeks were tinged red from her anger, her brows drawn together, her lips the color of the pink rosebuds just sprouting in the estate's garden. He took a step toward her, then another, his legs moving of their own accord. His resolve was disappearing. In the whole of his thirty-six years in the world, he couldn't recall a single time he'd had such an instantaneous reaction to another person. As he edged closer, he watched her brown eyes widen – shining against the light from the chandelier above them, making her look doe-eyed and innocent.

And then she pepper-sprayed him.

"Stay back!"

"Fuck!" Fenmore bellowed, rubbing at his eyes, which only seemed to make the stinging agony worse. "What was that?"

"Pepper spray, you creep!"

The burning in his nose and throat was suffocating, and the thick tears his eyes were producing turned the beautiful woman before him into a blurry blob. Good. He could argue with a blob. She'd done him a favor really.

"Oh, my Fenmore!" He couldn't see but he could hear his mother laughing. "I brought her to prove to you that you are wrong about mortals. I fear this is a rather rocky start, however."

"Why do you keep saying mortals as if the both of you *aren't?*"

There was a pitch of frustration in the woman's voice on the last word that made his lip curl up despite the pain. She was handling the magical world better than most mortals did; he'd give her that, if nothing else.

"My dear, my son and I have made a wager. I'm afraid I'm putting all my stakes on you to help me win it!"

A blur appeared at his side that Fenmore could only assume was Jorge. His suspicions were proved correct as a glowing cloth was placed in his hands. "This should be just the thing, sir." He rubbed the magical fabric over his eyes, and the stinging abated immediately as the healing magic did its work.

When Fenmore could finally see properly again, the tableau before him was like a badly written play. His mother was gesticulating wildly, his butler was inching behind a potted plant so he wouldn't be seen, and the girl—

The girl was still lovely, despite trying to blind him.

Damn it.

"We have very little time so I'm going to explain this promptly, dear." She took the girl's hand, and she just stood there, staring at her fingers clasped in his mother's. "My son has convinced himself that mortal kindness does not exist and it's just a ruse you put on to seem decent. I think that's baloney!"

The girl let out a startled laugh and Fenmore's heartrate picked up speed coincidentally at the same time. "Baloney?"

"Yes, baloney! So, I told Fenmore I only needed two days to prove to him that mortal kindness does exist. You showed me kindness by picking up my glasses when sixty other people that day passed me by, failing the very same test."

Her pink lips dropped open. "*Sixty?* Sixty people passed you before me? And none of them helped you?" She kicked the tip of her black shoes against the ground before groaning. "Why are you like this, New York?"

"Because mortals have a tendency to be selfish and judgmental," Fenmore chimed in, his voice sounding somewhat level despite the panic he was feeling, but he was a lord and a gentleman. She raised a brow at him as he bowed stiffly. "Lord Fenmore Majos, Miss…?"

"Bette Fellowes, or Elizabeth if we want to stand on formalities." She seemed to be mocking him as she dipped into a curtsey, but there was a glimmer of life in her eyes that hadn't been there when she'd arrived, and he rather enjoyed it.

That's a problem.

She sniffed, curiosity and conflict passing over her face. "Say I believe you. Say I believe that this is some sort of magical world, and you two aren't mortal, and that towel just healed your eyes in two seconds… What are the terms of the bet?"

He gaped. "After all this? That is your first concern?"

She shrugged.

He rubbed his temples, an aching pressure building there. "It wasn't serious, it was the result of an argument."

But it was no use. His mother was already guiding Elizabeth down the hallway to the main sitting room. "If we win the bet, Fenmore must spend a year in the mortal realm. Most of the magical beings here do at least a year or two so they can understand a world without magic, but my stubborn son refused and now he's emotionally stunted."

"Mother!" Fenmore growled.

The light of the sitting room spilled in as they passed a broom sweeping on its own and a pen corresponding to letters from tenants and fellow lords. "See? He's so angry! My goodness."

Fenmore rolled his eyes, walking past both to open one of the windows. He was beginning to feel cloistered with so many adversaries in one room. It became even more necessary when he brushed past Elizabeth, a prickling sensation going up his arm at the contact. His eyes widened, as did hers, before they both quickly looked away.

Elizabeth took a seat and accepted a glass of water from Jorge with a small smile and a polite, "Thank you so much." Her wide brown eyes turned to Fenmore. "And if we can't prove it? What do you get if you win?"

He grinned at her and watched in satisfaction as she sucked in a sharp breath. "I never have to go to the mortal realm, nor does anyone else on my lands... and, of course, the joy of being right. Mortals are selfish and self-serving to their core."

This seemed to anger her. Color rose to her face as she stalked forward, poking his chest with her smallest finger, a challenge in her eyes. "You're going to eat those words, Fender."

The laugh that surged out of him was so quick and unexpected, it startled him. "It's Fenmore."

"Whatever. By the time I'm through with you, you'll have mortal kindness shooting out your butt."

Another startled laugh shook him, and his mother joined in, looking far too gleeful for comfort. "So, you'll do it?"

Elizabeth nodded, resolved. "Yes."

Fenmore grinned now, knowing how fruitless this task was about to become for both his mother and this strange woman with her daunting eyes. "You are down to a day and a half. I look forward to watching you fail."

Elizabeth grinned herself. "How funny." She planted her hands on her hips, drawing his attention to the gentle curves there.

"I was going to say the same to you."

CHAPTER 3

Bette was still unconvinced that she hadn't been drugged or wasn't suffering some sort of psychotic break that had resulted in a very elaborate illusion of being dragged to a magical place with seemingly human people claiming to be immortal.

But she'd tried to blink it away enough times that the act had begun to give her vertigo and ended up being pointless, because the immortal people still stood there.

One was the old woman with an oddly comforting warmth and the other was a man... who was quite unfortunately very attractive. He looked like an actor; someone you'd see on the screen and think was good-looking in that unreal, unattainable sort of way. It only mildly helped that he didn't seem to carry himself like that. He didn't appear to understand the magnetic power he possessed behind the ice blue of his eyes or the sharp planes of his face.

Bette unfortunately didn't have that level of ignorance. His beauty was grating and lit a fire under her skin that she hadn't thought herself capable of feeling any longer. The emptiness of grief abated for a moment to make room for other feelings, like outrage, anger, frustration, lust...

Scratch that last one.

She sat in the magical parlor, watching the broom sweep its way back and forth, mild alarm melded with amusement. Louise – or at least she assumed that was her name, based on the mutterings of their butler – had exited the lavish sitting room promptly, leaving her alone with the man who was staring a hole in her head like she was a zoo attraction. "Why are you staring?"

He lifted an auburn brow. "Why are *you*?"

She narrowed her eyes and clicked her tongue. "Why don't you believe in mortal kindness, Fender?

He let out a world-weary sigh. It made her a little giddy. "I told you, it's Fenmore."

"You're evading the question." She sniffed; the air smelled like freshly baked pastries and flowers, likely wafting in from the large garden outside. She was beginning to affirm to herself that this world had to be real, because despite her love for stories, Bette's imagination simply didn't stretch this far.

Fenmore took a seat in the ornate chair across from her, folding his arms. His posture was ramrod-straight like he was fresh out of one of her mother's old Regency novels. "I have seen nothing to the contrary."

"You have never been to the mortal world. Of course you haven't." Bette rolled her eyes as the polite butler with the crinkled hands and warm smile set down a plate of blueberry scones. She gave him the same beaming grin she gave anyone offering her pastries. "Thank you, this is very kind."

"Of course he is." Fenmore gave her a cocky smile that she had a feeling he did just to anger her. "He's not mortal."

She laughed, a snort coming out of her nose. If she didn't know better, she would have sworn his eyes lit up, his head perking like he'd heard something worth listening to. "Are you saying because your world is full of magical beings, it somehow makes you morally superior?"

The light she thought she'd seen flickered out. He stood and turned away from her, pretending to inspect a book on the large wooden bookcase in the corner. "The people in our realm, the immortals, the magics if you will – we see each other as a unified community. Everyone takes care of each other, and everyone helps whoever is in need."

She stood now too, walking toward him. Something about his voice struck a chord inside her. Almost as if something within him was calling to something within her. "How can you know mortals don't do the same?"

"Because they didn't when my father did his year-long stint in the human realm."

He turned toward her and she sucked in a breath; his blue eyes were hardened like ice. "A mortal hit him while he was driving one of your vehicles. They had consumed alcohol and, despite your laws decreeing otherwise, they got behind the wheel." It hurt her beyond comprehension, the echo of pain in his eyes that she'd seen in the mirror for the last four months. She waited for him to finish, still as granite. "Because that mortal made such a selfish choice, the car hit the one my father was in." His blue eyes glazed over. "And killed him."

CHAPTER 4

It was too much for Fenmore. The feelings he'd experienced reliving his father's death all those years ago, the look of what he could only assume was pity in Elizabeth's eyes, and in the room where his father had once told him stories of all the adventures they'd have. He couldn't take it.

"Fenmore…" Elizabeth started, taking a step toward him, raising a tentative hand to his shoulder. He wanted to move away, but her intoxicating scent froze him in place. His brow furrowed as he stared down at her. "I'm s—"

He didn't let her finish before he was shaking off her hand and walking in ground-eating strides for the door. *'I'm sorry'* was a phrase he'd grown so accustomed to over the years, he could practically hear it ringing in his ears each night before he went to sleep. Everyone was sorry when his father died. His mother, the foolish driver, Jorge, the people on his land, and no one sorrier than Fenmore, who had lost his father and any chance at a normal childhood in one fell swoop.

"Wait!" she called; it reminded him of honey. Smooth, sweet, until it rotted your teeth and gave you a headache.

Fenmore yanked on the door and— it was locked. *NO.* "She didn't!" he growled, attempting to leave through the open window before he was thrown to the ground by the magical barrier his mother had put up to keep him from sneaking out as a child. "Mother! Surely this is cheating!" he yelled, elbows propping him up.

Elizabeth appeared at his shoulder, crouching down, a soft look on her face as she winced apologetically. "She locked us in, huh?"

"She's a menace." He grunted, stiffening when he felt Elizabeth's hand close around his arm. "I *am* sorry you were dragged into it. Despite your enthusiastic agreement."

She helped him to his feet with a small smile that made his insides turn over. "I wouldn't say anyone is necessarily enthusiastic about kidnapping. But I haven't had this much fun in a while, so I suppose I deserve it."

He turned toward her, their faces much closer than they ought to be; he needed to move away. Why was she so mesmerizing? Why couldn't his mother have brought an old man or someone less…

Just that… someone less.

"Why?" He echoed the word aloud.

She scrunched her nose and tilted her head, a wave of hair falling over her shoulder. His hand itched at his side to brush it back. "I just told you—"

"No. Why haven't you had fun in a while?" Fenmore wasn't sure it mattered, but he watched emotion play in different parts of her face. First the twitch in her brow, then the shuttering of her eyes, and her pressed-together lips.

Which he should *not* be staring at.

She swallowed. "It doesn't matter very much, does it? I'm selfish and lack all sense of kindness. You probably think I deserve to have no fun."

He scoffed in indignation as she moved away from him to take a bite of one of the scones, making a humming sound that raised the hairs on the back of his neck. "I didn't say that."

"But mortal kindness doesn't exist. Does it?" She blinked those innocent doe-eyes again, but this time they looked rather threatening. This woman was lethal. But he'd be damned if he'd fall for it. Even if he wanted to, he couldn't go to the mortal realm for a whole year. The estate would fall to shambles in a day and his mother would have the furniture talking to each other within the week.

His words had to be careful, lest he lose the bet when it still had many hours to go. "A good try, I'll admit. But I won't be defeated so easily. I've been resolved in this opinion for years; you won't undo it in a matter of two days."

The sun was setting rapidly. Excellent.

The light hitting the window, landing squarely on Elizabeth, made her skin flush and her hair glow around her like a crown made of sunlight.

Less excellent.

She smiled again, but this time it looked sad, and it made his heart clench in his chest. He didn't want to upset her; he didn't want to care either. A horrible little circle his mind was forming. "I don't need to change your opinion. I just need to prove that you're wrong."

"And you think that's achievable?"

"I know it is," she said, a certainty in her voice that set him on edge.

"What are you planning?" There was warning in his words as he grabbed a scone himself, taking a large, angry bite.

That little glimmer had returned to her expression, and he felt an alarming sense of relief. Relief that turned to heat shocking his limbs as she reached her hand up and used her thumb to brush bits of crumbs from his mouth.

"I... I'm planning to show you how kind us mortals can be." A ragged breath escaped his lips, and a red flush climbed her neck as her own breath hitched.

He could hardly believe his mind could form full sentences while also imagining how good it would feel to close the distance between them and lay his lips on hers.

"How?" he asked, unable to hide the shakiness.

"You've seen mortals at their worst. I'm going to show you them at their best," she said, looking confident and beautiful.

And all magic help him...

He almost believed her.

CHAPTER 5

"So, you're a servant, essentially?"

Bette laughed into her hand, staring up at the ceiling. Her feet up on the couch, her head propped on the pillow. They'd talked through the night, exchanging stories of their lives. She told him about her job, her life in New York City, where she went to school, how she used to want to be a teacher before she realized that college courses were about as palatable as pulling teeth.

She'd learned that he hadn't attended university due to his responsibilities on the estate; that he loved his mother, despite all the ways he complained about her antics; that he'd never been in love, even with the girl he courted through autumn and winter three years ago. He was playful when he let his guard down and that was beginning to feel dangerous. It was just as well he called her a servant; it would end her ridiculous infatuation.

Except, bizarrely, it made her like him even more.

"I'm a serv-*er*." The lord was sitting on the floor, back to the couch across from the one she was laying on. "It's entirely different."

"Ha!" He pointed, the sudden movement making his auburn locks fall into his eyes. He ran a hand through them as she raised a brow at the outburst. "Point proven again. You are working for an establishment that has tricked you into believing that you're not serving the public."

She chuckled again, something she'd done an increasing number of times since arriving there. "They haven't tricked me. I'm aware I'm serving the public, but servant implies that I'm lesser than the people I'm bringing the food to. In the mortal world, your job doesn't define your standing in life." Bette rubbed a hand over her tired eyes; sleep had evaded her all night. She hadn't wanted to miss any of his stories. She liked talking to him. "Or at least... it shouldn't."

He was staring at her in that contemplative way again, his sleeves had been rolled up to reveal strong forearms smattered with hair. His perfect attire when she'd met him was wrinkled, his pristine white shirt knocked askew to reveal part of his chest. "That's— I agree with you."

Bette gasped, clutching her chest. "And the world didn't end?"

He rolled his eyes, but there was a smile playing on his lips. "Funny."

She'd made a joke. When was the last time she'd joked about anything? Perhaps the magic in this world was doing something to her. Perhaps – like the cloth over his eyes earlier – it was healing her heart at a rapid rate.

"Anyways, it's a good job. Good enough to help me make enough money to eventually move out of the city and somewhere quieter."

He frowned, shadows from the late night appearing under his eyes as light from the rising sun flooded the room. "I thought you enjoyed the city."

Her stories would indicate that, as she'd decided to omit the one that made her hate it. She shrugged, trying to appear unbothered, but she could tell she hadn't convinced him. He straightened, looking at her sharply. "I need a change. The Randalls of the world can be tolerated, if it ensures I get it."

His attention had been rapt on her before, but now it was so intensely burning against her skin she had to sit up to rub her hands down her arms, avoiding his penetrating gaze.

"Who is Randall?" His voice sounded dismissive, but when she peeked over at him he was rigid.

She licked her lips. "A guy I work with. A total pig, to be honest. My shift before your mother hijacked me— It ended with a joke he made about me being on my knees for him." She shivered at the memory, disgust twisting her features, unsure of why she was confiding her frustrations about the sexist remarks she experienced in her workplace.

It's his detachment, she told herself. *His ability to remain calm and unfeeling.*

When Bette looked to where he'd been sitting, however, he was gone. "Where did you— Fender! What are you doing?"

Fenmore was making grunting, growling sounds, almost like an animal as he pulled and tugged at the door with all his strength. "Open it, Mother! Open the door *now*!"

What a humbling response to her vulnerability. She gaped. "My goodness, I wouldn't have told you if I thought you'd be so offended!"

He whipped around and she nearly fell at the fury in his expression. His chiseled jaw was locked, his fists clenched at his sides, nostrils flared as he breathed heavily. "What is the name of the dining establishment?"

She nearly choked on her own spit. "Madame Rose's. Why – why do you want to know?"

"I'm going to eviscerate the little weasel." His arms were flailing in angry gestures, one fist pounding against the door once more. "Open up, Mother! I must commit a murder!"

Bette was almost too shocked to move. Was he outraged... on her behalf? "You can't!"

"I assure you, I can," he said, a sort of mad light in his eyes. He pounded on the door again, so hard she thought the wood might splinter off into his fist. She bolted forward and clutched it between both hands.

"No one should treat you in such a disgusting, appalling, disrespectful manner and have it dismissed so lightly," he said, with such anger in his expression. Anger for her because he... cared.

It was why she stood on the tips of her toes, releasing his fist to clasp her hands over his face.

And kissed him.

CHAPTER 6

Fenmore felt a rage like no other, quickly followed by heart-stopping shock.

Elizabeth's lips were warm, as were her hands as she clutched his cheeks. He was too stunned to move, to do anything but stare as she slowly pulled away, only inches. "No one has cared for me like that in a long time. I haven't known how to let them," she whispered.

She gave a shaky half-smile, and it was like he hadn't known what it was to live before now. Didn't understand the sounds or the smells. The patterns of the world had been so unclear before her lips touched his and he hadn't even known.

And he wanted more.

With a low groan he gripped her hair in a hand, clutching the back of her head as she brought her honey lips back to his. She made a small squeak of surprise but quickly responded in kind as she slid her hands along his shoulders, hands traveling underneath his shirt. They were cold against his skin, making him shiver as she moved them over the muscles in his stomach and chest.

They parted again, Elizabeth eagerly pulling at the fabric of his shirt, her lips swollen from his, her lids heavy and sultry in a way that nearly buckled his knees. He pulled the blasted garment over his head, satisfaction coursing through him at the hunger in her gaze. "I've never felt so—"

"I know," he rasped. "I've never felt it either." He touched a piece of her hair and tucked it behind her ear, her cheek leaning into his hand like his touch was a necessity.

"The bet," she murmured. "We probably shouldn't keep going."

Fuck the bet! he wanted to say, but nodded. Fenmore's being felt as if it only existed to do her bidding, to fulfill her wishes. "I'll stop if you want to."

She shook her head, moisture building in her eyes that mangled his heart. "I don't want you to stop."

That was all he needed.

His lips were on her then, everywhere. Her lips, her cheeks, her neck, her shoulders. The little sounds she was making only spurring him on as he went to grip the hem of her stained white shirt, looking into her eyes before he went further. She gripped the hem herself and pulled it over her own head, before undoing a clasp in the back of her half-corset, dropping it to the ground, revealing her breasts.

Everything around him was merely noise, his only focus on her. He was on fire. He moved forward and so did she, his arms under her legs, lifting her up to wrap them around his waist. Their lips meeting again as they both breathed a sigh of relief. "Please," she whispered, "I need you."

He knew what she was asking, what she wanted as he lowered them both to the sofa. As Fenmore leveled over her he was in awe, pulse pounding. He claimed her mouth before moving his attention to her chest, lips closing over one of her nipples as she gasped and arched beneath him.

The sound snapped something inside him. He moved away to stare into her eyes, a tenderness there he'd never witnessed in the whole of his bitter life. "Elizabeth, I think I— I think I need you, too."

She gave a tiny smile and pulled him back down to her. They were a tangled haze of hips and arms, and legs. All he knew was sensation when he joined with her, as they moved against each other.

He'd be altered by this. It would change the very material of his being. Whether he'd known it or not, the minute her brown eyes locked on his, she'd revived something in him he'd thought was long dead.

Hope.

CHAPTER 7

Bette had just had sex with her elaborate hallucination.

But it hadn't been just sex. She'd had 'just sex' many times before this, mostly unimpressive, if mildly satisfying. This was different, this felt like her heart was involved, her very soul.

His hand was moving over the back of her head as she lay draped on top of him, naked. They'd been arguing the day before and now they were stuck to each other like glue. She pressed a gentle kiss to his chest before laying her hands on him to lever herself up. His pupils were bigger, eating up most of the blue of his irises. "I didn't know that was going to happen," she said with a smile.

He pulled her up, laying his lips gently to her forehead. "I didn't either, but I can't say I'm sorry that it did. I've felt an unreal pull toward you since you pepper-sprayed me."

She nodded earnestly. "That really does it for you, huh?"

He snorted and grinned wide. She took in the sight greedily, hoping privately she could make him do it again. "I am a man of simple tastes."

She giggled, sitting up to retrieve her clothes, squealing when he pulled her back down. "I was going to get dressed." She flicked his shoulder.

"A horrid idea, really." He frowned, but his eyes were full of mirth.

She huffed, amused at his playfulness. "I can't stay naked forever."

He leaned them both up, pulling her in for a kiss. She could tell he'd meant for it to start slow, but it ended with both of them clutching at each other, breathless. "You can. I'll write it into law immediately."

The full light of day was upon them now, her stomach hollowed and making the most atrocious noises. "I think that would cause quite the stir during my shift at the restaurant on Saturday," she jested as she pulled on her clothes. Fenmore had begun to do the same when he froze, pants over his hips, shirt in his hands.

"You're returning, then?" He looked grim and it made her panic.

"Of course I am. I have a job and responsibilities and a goldfish that I hope won't die after one missed feeding."

His expression didn't change as he pulled the shirt over his head, hair more tousled than before. The distance between them was becoming more obvious as the silence trickled in.

"I was thinking," she started, trying to choose her words very carefully. "That when you come for your year's stint in the mortal world, perhaps you can come to New York? I can show you all my favorite places and then maybe you can show me all your favorite places in your realm."

The Fenmore that had just been tenderly running his hands through her hair and kissing her forehead was gone. "Elizabeth, I won't be doing a year in the mortal realm. I won't ever be going there. You didn't win the bet."

She went rigid and pain spiked in her stomach, a thickness in her throat that made it difficult to breathe. "I wasn't talking of the bet. I was speaking of you and me."

He gripped the wall, like he needed its support to grit out the next words. "If you return to the mortal world, there can never *be* a you and me."

She flinched like he'd struck her, hand closing over her mouth. Fenmore's eyes widened like the hurtful words had been said by someone else. "Elizabeth... no, that's not what I meant."

A white-hot heat prickled up her neck. "Oh my God. You— Oh my God!" She fled to the door, pulling frantically at the knob. "Let me out! I want to leave! Now!"

"Elizabeth, please." Fenmore's voice was gentle, his hands on her shoulders as he turned her around, looking like he'd just been dragged over hot coals. "I'm sorry, that was callously put. I only meant to offer you a place here, in our realm. I want us to continue together. I want to hear more of your stories and your jokes and see more of your smiles. I want to spend days laughing with you and nights kissing you. I want you so badly I feel it in my veins. I think I could fall—"

"No!" she yelled, spinning around and shoving him away. His eyebrows shot up his forehead, hands raised in gentle surrender as she carried on, angry tears burning her eyes. "Do you believe that mortals are capable of kindness?"

He ran a hand down his face, blowing out a harsh breath. "Elizabeth, please, you don't understand what I've always known of the mortals in your realm. I promise I don't think that of you."

"You should," she said, numbness washing over her. "I am just like any other mortal in my realm. I make mistakes. I say the wrong thing. I hurt people. I can be hateful and callous and bitter and so angry I feel like I'll *die*."

Fenmore shook his head but she continued, unable to stop her tirade. "All mortals are this way, all people, all *humans*. Kindness and goodness aren't something someone is born with, it's a choice that we make every single day and sometimes we don't get it perfect. Sometimes we stray and mess up and learn how to be better to each other. But the difference between us and you? We may be more flawed, but we still *try*."

His lips parted, but no words came out, as if she couldn't have shocked him more if she'd pulled out a bucket of cold water and dumped it on his head.

"I won't stay and be with someone who doesn't understand the power of a second chance. Not when good people exist. Not when my parents existed once."

His hand reached for her, sensing the distress now coming off her in palpable waves, but he saw her wince and immediately pulled it back. "What happened to them?" he asked softly.

The irony of it all nearly made her laugh. "They were on their way to look at a cabin for sale in the Poconos. They were driving on the backroads, and they found a sixteen-year-old girl alone and hysterical in her car because her phone died and she had a flat tire. My parents didn't see who was in the car, they just pulled over when they saw it, because they thought someone might need help."

Fenmore didn't speak, just watched her with an intense expression she didn't have the will to decipher. "They were rounding the car to get the jack from their truck when another car came and veered off the road." She looked him in the eye as she said, "The EMTs pronounced them both dead on the scene. They were hit..."

Fenmore's eyes glistened.

"By a drunk driver."

The door to the room cracked open. Bette didn't hesitate to slide through it before it was fully open. "Elizabeth. I'm sorry, please, I beg you—"

She stalked down the hall, back to the entry, ignoring Jorge's concerned expression, right to the woman who'd brought her here to peel the scab off, leaving the wound wide open. "I want to leave. Now."

Louise frowned, not arguing. "Very well, child." She opened the portal with a wave of her hand. "I'm sorry for the distress I've caused you. I merely wanted to help him."

The glowing light appeared all over the wall and Bette wiped away the tears still burning her eyes. "You cannot help someone who doesn't want to be helped."

"Elizabeth!" Fenmore yelled behind her, gripping her arm, not enough to be painful but to turn her toward him. "Please try and see my point of view. It took sixty people for my mother to find you. Sixty people that ignored her on the street before she found one who would help her."

"You don't get it." She smiled sadly, bringing a hand up to his face. His eyes closed at her touch. "Being mortal isn't about the sixty people who won't help you."

She stepped back and Fenmore's eyes shot open.

"It's always about one person that does." Bette jumped through the portal and whispered in a broken voice, "Goodbye Fenmore."

CHAPTER 8

Bette wrung her hands together nervously before knocking on the white apartment door. Emma had known it was her and buzzed her in anyway; hopefully that meant her friend would at least hear Bette out.

The door flew open, and her best friend stood there, still stunning with her curls pulled up into a silk bonnet, wearing her mermaid flannel pajamas that she'd had since they were twenty-three. "Bette." She smiled; her face going vibrant the way it always did when she smiled. Light would glow off her brown cheeks, her eyes would crinkle at the corners, and she became the center of the room. Emma was light when she was happy, and she was happy to see Bette.

Bette promised herself she'd keep it together long enough to apologize, but she couldn't, not when the warmest person she knew was beaming at her like she hadn't ignored her texts for four months. She broke right in front of Emma as she said, "I want to talk about it."

"Oh honey." Emma pulled her into the tightest hug she'd ever had, stroking her hair gently. "Come in. We'll have tea and you can talk for however long you want."

"Can we have wine?"

Emma's laugh was like medicine. "Oh, thank God. Yes, let's have wine."

After a long night of reminiscing about her parents, remembering them fully with someone who'd known them and loved them too, Bette fell asleep with a smile on her lips.

The next day, at the end of her shift, she felt lighter, happier. She'd decided to pause her plans to leave the city. She wanted to re-learn it without grief and anger clouding her judgement, wanted a chance to start fresh and live her life again, keeping the memory of her parents alive and well.

Randall was possibly the only thing ruining her calm and tranquil peace of mind. "Betty, what do you say we get a drink after we clock out tonight? I think a night with me would... loosen you up." He slung an arm around her shoulders. His overwhelming aftershave made her nauseous.

She didn't pretend to not know what he meant this time. Bette shoved him away and rounded on him. "Randall, I think you are disgusting."

Randall's jaw dropped. "What?"

"I think you are rude, disrespectful, and just plain repulsive. I do not and never will want to be around you beyond a professional work capacity, and to be honest I don't even want to do that either. My life would be happier if I never laid eyes on you again."

Randall's nostrils flared, his face turning bright red. He raised his clenched fist, as if to strike her. "You rude bitch!" But his hand was caught by someone looming behind him. Someone who was squeezing the life out of Randall's wrist.

Someone tall, with red locks and blue eyes hard as granite.

"Fender?" She gaped, shocked at seeing him there, in her world. That Randall was seeing him too and not enjoying it, by the look of fear on his face.

"What did you call her?" Lord Fenmore released Randall's hands and shoved him against the wall.

The only other server who'd stayed on for closing was a college student named Christy, who looked a little like she was watching a soap opera unfold. "Who's the guy dressed like Mr Darcy?"

Bette choked and surged forward, grabbing Fenmore's arm. "You can't hit him."

Fenmore softened when he turned to her, but hardened as Randall tried to run. Fenmore shoved him against the wall again. "You called my girlfriend a bitch."

"Your girlfriend?" She was hallucinating again. She really needed to get to the doctor.

Fenmore furrowed his brow as he looked her up and down. "That's what mortals call it, yes?"

Bette felt dazed in her response. "Yes but—"

Fenmore gripped Randall's shirt and raised him up the wall. "If you ever make another mortal feel uncomfortable and I find out about it, I will send you to the realm with a thousand poisonous spiders and let them devour you slowly."

Christy clapped. "Oh, that's a very creative threat."

"Christy, stop it!" Bette chastised. "Fenmore, please let him go."

"Not until he promises."

"I promise, man! Just leave me alone!" Randall whined.

Fenmore nodded. "Very well." He dropped Randall like a sack of potatoes before putting himself in front of Bette, dropping to his knees.

Christy gasped. The gossip in the kitchens tomorrow was going to be wild.

"I've come to beg your forgiveness and ask you please, for a second chance," Fenmore said, head bowed in deference.

"You came to the mortal world... for me?" She blinked back tears as Christy dragged Randall away to give them privacy in the empty restaurant.

"As soon as you left, I realized what a fool I've been. I've held my resentment of mortals for so long I panicked at who I'd become without it." He stared into her face, with affection and longing that made her come down to her knees too. He put his hands in hers. "You were right about all of it. It's not about the people who do wrong, we must focus on those who do right. On choosing to be good and kind, not existing that way. Apparently even immortals make mistakes, because I foolishly let you go when you were offering me everything I've ever wanted."

"You did make a huge mistake," she said seriously.

His hope visibly dwindled. "I did."

"You'll probably make more." Her lips curled upwards, and he caught on to the path she was leading them down immediately.

He took one of her hands and placed it over his heart. "I absolutely will." He grinned his widest, most brilliant grin. "I am relying on your mortal goodness to kindly allow me to learn from them."

Bette kissed him, then, with a smile on her own face. He sighed into her mouth, hands cradling her head as he leaned his forehead against hers. "You lost the bet."

He kissed her again, whispering, "Happily."

She pulled back, feeling euphoric and full of hope. "Well, you have at least a year here before we go back to visit the magic realm. What do you want to do first?"

Fenmore looked sheepish and adorable as he asked, "I'd like to try pizza, I think."

She took his hand, both rising from the floor together, looking at each other with a powerful emotion neither of them named.

But they both knew what it was.

She smiled, taking his hand. "I know just the place."

THE LARKSPUR

By

MEGAN BANNEN

'The Larkspur' is set in the same world as my novel The Undertaking of Hart and Mercy *and the subsequent books in that series; however, Sterling's story takes place in a different time and location within the Tanrian Marshals universe. Many readers will notice a hint of Emmuska Orczy's* The Scarlet Pimpernel *in these pages, but more than anything, this tale is a loose reimagining of one of my favorite comfort reads,* The Blue Castle *by L. M. Montgomery, the author of* Anne of Green Gables.

Sterling Valancy sat across from his wife at the kitchen table, both of them staring at the scarred wood between them.

"You didn't die," Bernadette said at last.

"I didn't die," Sterling agreed numbly.

"Again."

It was a reasonable observation. Votary Trent had assured

Sterling that any accident might befall him before the year was out, yet here he was ten months later, alive and, quite frankly, well. For someone on the verge of death, he had demonstrated a remarkable propensity for survival.

This time, he had been buying Bernadette a bag of honey-roasted almonds — her favorite — when a pianoforte nearly crushed him in the street, the beast of an instrument having come loose of its harness during a botched third-floor delivery. He could still hear the cacophony of wood and keys and strings as it slammed onto the cobblestones not three feet from where he stood.

The evidence was difficult to ignore, and the niggling suspicion that he might live out the year — and possibly many, many years to come — loomed over Sterling like a specter. What if the oracle had made a mistake? What if his brilliant, vivacious wife — who had only married him out of pity — was now stuck with him?

Without another word, Bernadette got up and closed herself in her study, never to emerge. Sterling could hear her pacing incessantly through the thin wall while he busied himself with the homey rituals he had come to cherish — the washing of their dishes, the dusting of their shelves, the tidying up of Bernadette's chaos. Eventually, he took himself to bed, feeling completely adrift as he lay alone, longing for his wife. She was only in the next room, and yet she might as well have been on the moon.

If I am not going to die, I shall have to return to Uncle Stickles' house, he thought, a prospect that knotted his guts. He had lived under the thumb of his uncle's charity from infancy, he and his mother having moved in when Sterling's father died two months after his birth. Uncle Stickles, who seemed like a veritable immortal, clung to life — and his money — with a skeletal death grip, so Mama had fussed over Sterling throughout his twenty-six years, worried that he would die before inheriting his uncle's modest fortune.

You must not go out of doors, Lambie! You know how susceptible you are to colds and fevers.

You must not exert yourself, Lambie! You know how weak your constitution is.

But how Sterling had wanted to exert himself, to play like other children and run and climb trees.

Get down at once, Lambie! You know you are liable to break your neck!

And so, earlier that year, when Sterling had found out that his life was about to end before it had ever begun, he left Mama and Uncle Stickles to apprentice himself to Abel Roring, the blacksmith. For the past ten months, he had relished the work of his body – the pumping of the bellows, the pounding of a hammer, the hefting of iron.

And the people who came in and out of the smithy each day! Abel was friends with everyone within a mile's radius, and they loved to drop in, if only to say hello, each one with a life as colorful as Sterling's old existence had been drab. There was Chauvelin, for example, the Golois wool merchant, who had defected to Stenland years ago and always seemed to have a bottle of wine and a loaf of bread on him. And of course, there was Bernadette Snaith, the peddler, who cussed like a sailor and cared not one jot what anyone thought about her.

Sterling had walked out of his old life, and Bernadette had stepped into his new one like a miracle.

But if the oracle was wrong, he would have to return to the dreary townhouse in Benchley Square, where the ancestral altar groaned under the weight of the gods knew how many dusty birth keys; where his mother's scraggly fern soldiered on in the anemic light of the entry hall, shedding yellowed leaves like half-hearted flags of surrender; where the hoar, cast-iron stand beside the front door hosted two outmoded umbrellas; where the grandfather clock at the foot of the stairs ran two minutes late by mid-afternoon, its pendulum swinging ponderously in its mahogany case. How that clock had driven him nearly to madness some days with its insistent ticking away of his time, as if to say, "Here is another second of your life wasted, Sterling, and another, and another."

He would once again have to sit in the drawing room every afternoon, reading a novel hidden behind some dry ecclesiastic text to the grating rhythm of his mother's knitting and the wheezing coughs of Uncle Stickles, who read political newspapers that made Sterling want to pull out his own hair. And all the while, the porcelain lamb figurine, which his mother had purchased out of drippy sentimentality because it reminded her of 'her Lambie,' would sit on the side table and stare at him reproachfully, as if to say, *How pathetic you are.*

As memories of his woebegone existence under his uncle's roof flooded his mind, he drifted into a fitful slumber. When he awoke early the next morning, he instinctively knew that Bernadette was not at home. There was a stillness to their ramshackle cottage when she was not in it. Sterling felt much the same. He had been a hollowed-out shell of a man before Bernadette had come along to fill him to the brim with life and living.

He had only mustered the bravery to ask for her key in marriage because he'd had nothing to lose – or so he had thought – and she had only accepted him out of pity, knowing full well she would not be shackled to her husband for long.

Unless the oracle had made a mistake.

Sterling rather hoped a bolt of lightning might strike him to prove his suspicions incorrect as he hailed a hackney to take him to Three Mothers Temple.

※

"So… I am *not* out of luck?" he asked in miserable disbelief as he slumped in the pew. The oracle's votary, a middle-aged woman with golden demigod eyes, regarded him from across the altar in the Bride of Fortune's oracular as if he were a boy in short pants, covered in mud, clutching a frog in his grubby hands and begging, *Please may I keep him?*

"Why would you think that you were out of luck?"

"Because you *told* me that I was out of luck!"

"I… I am afraid that I have not the pleasure of understanding you."

Obviously, Sterling had met Votary Trent before, but he still found her eyes unsettling as she blinked at him. When he was eight years old, he had asked his uncle how one could tell if a person was a demigod.

Eyes and size, boy, the old man had answered with a dry laugh, and while that assessment rang somewhat offensive to Sterling's adult ears, it was not entirely inaccurate. In addition to having yellow irises, Votary Trent was indeed quite tall.

Sterling slid the letter, dated ten months earlier, across the altar to her. It read:

Mr Valancey,
I apologize for the late arrival of this missive. I was unexpectedly

called away from my work on a personal matter of an upsetting nature. It will be some time before I am able to return to temple, but your situation is such that I feel I must write to you at once.

I have consulted the oracle on your behalf, and, with a heavy pen and a heavier heart, I write to inform you that the Bride of Fortune has intervened in your present circumstances as much as she is able to. The sad truth is that what little luck you may have had in this life is about to run out. I regret to inform you that you have, at most, a year to live.

It is my professional opinion that you should avoid perilous situations at all costs. Leave your house but sparingly and safely secure all sharp objects. Do not walk under open windows. Bodies of water should be avoided at all costs. Etc. And I advise you to put your affairs in order at your earliest convenience.

I am sorry to be the bearer of bad tidings, Mr Valancey, but it is with the utmost sincerity that I wish you all the best for the life you have left to you.

Sincerely,
Sarah Trent, Votary of the Bride's Oracle.

The votary blanched as she held the letter in her slim hands. "Oh dear. I'm afraid there has been a misunderstanding. As I recall, I was called away quite suddenly during your visit. My niece was gravely injured in a sea polo match, you see, and in my disturbed state, I must have mixed up the envelopes. This letter was intended for a Mr *Sherwood* Valancey of Hellebore Corners. He came to the oracle the same day as you and was felled by an infected paper cut not two weeks later. But see here? He spelled Valancey with an *e*. Didn't you notice?"

"I assumed you simply misspelled my name," Sterling said faintly as his marriage and, therefore, his joy, slipped away from him like water trickling between his fingers.

Bernadette, he wailed in the privacy of his mind, his heart already a bruise and careening toward a decimated pulp. He would beg her for forgiveness. He would grovel – gods, would he grovel – but even if she forgave him, she would not want him. She never had.

Perhaps sensing Sterling's inner turmoil, Votary Trent came to sit on the edge of the altar, her goldenrod eyes gentling.

"If you don't mind my saying, Mr Valancy, you appear far more hale and hearty than you were the day you came to consult the oracle. The past several months seem to have agreed with you."

"Yes, I've been doing the things I always wanted to do. I took up blacksmithing. And I got married." Sterling's morose tone did not match the words coming out of his mouth.

The votary placed an encouraging hand on his shoulder. "You're a lucky man, then. Go home to your wife, and tell her the good news."

His wife.

Sterling buried his face in his hands.

༺༻

Bernadette had yet to come home by the time Sterling returned. Salt Sea and all the gods of death, what must she be thinking? That he had swindled her? Trapped her?

He was surprised by how badly he wanted to explain the horrible misunderstanding to her in person. He would have expected himself to be more cowardly than that. But since he had no idea when she would return, and since he could not rightfully call this precious rundown cottage his home any longer, he would have to leave her a letter instead.

A pathetic, inadequate letter.

He took his linen handkerchief from his coat pocket and dabbed his eyes. Tears would not serve him now. What he needed was a pen and paper.

Finding either proved depressingly daunting. Sterling used an old pencil to jot down the market list each week on the small notepad in the cupboard drawer. Both the pencil and the notepad seemed woefully insufficient for the task at hand, but, short of searching Bernadette's study – a room he was forbidden to enter as a part of their marriage agreement – he could not locate a proper pen nor a sheet of paper anywhere in the cottage, much less a pot of ink.

He gazed down at the dull pencil sitting atop the newspaper. Bernadette had used it to draw a preposterous mustache and a pair of horns on an image of the Larkspur, the anonymous hero who risked life and limb to help demigods escape the bloody revolution in the country of Gol. Unsatisfied with rejecting only the Old Gods, the Golois had decided to reject the New Gods and demigods, as well. They were imprisoning and executing the hapless offspring of immortals left and right… unless the Larkspur managed to sneak in and steal the demigods from underneath their noses.

"Spare me," Bernadette would moan whenever Sterling attempted to read aloud excerpts from the newspaper, recounting the Larkspur's outlandish exploits. She would roll her beautiful blue eyes at him before snatching the paper out of his hands, straddling him in his armchair, and kissing him until he could barely remember his own name, much less the derring-do of the Larkspur.

As he thought of Bernadette in his arms, a sharp pang of loss and regret rattled through his ribcage. He looked to the door of her study, which was closed as always. Sterling had long suspected his wife of being a smuggler rather than a peddler, but he had never questioned her stipulation that he stay out of her business affairs and, therefore, out of her study. He'd even joked about it, calling the mysterious room her 'Den of Iniquity'. But now he needed to write her a letter, and with nothing better than a pencil and a small, wrinkled notepad at hand, he would have to enter the forbidden study in search of proper writing supplies.

I have already broken faith with Bernadette by living, even if I had not meant to, he thought. *What is one more transgression?*

Either Bernadette trusted him more than he deserved, or she had been in such a rush to get away from him that morning she'd forgotten to lock the door. In either case, Sterling entered the Den of Iniquity with ease.

The room was small but remarkably tidy. There was a business-like oak desk with a neat stack of papers and a well-made wooden chair atop a worn wool rug. When Sterling drew aside the curtain covering the single window to let in sunlight, the glass was clean, the sashes dusted. It was very unlike Bernadette to be so neat. Throughout the rest of the cramped house, she was an invasive vine, leaving tendrils of herself wherever Sterling looked – teacups on the mantel, earrings on a cupboard shelf, her drawers wherever it was they had last made love.

He did his best to ferret out what he needed without looking too closely at the rest of the room. He found a pen and a sheaf of rather fine paper, and a bottle of ink in one of the desk drawers. The words did not come easily, however. He had three false starts full of apologies and groveling before he gave up and opted for the plain truth.

> *Dear Bernadette,*
>
> *I went to the Bride's Oracle today. Ten months ago, she mistakenly sent to me a letter intended for a Mr Sherwood Valancey... with an 'e'. I do not have bad luck after all!*
>
> *Please believe me when I tell you that it was never my intention to trap you in a marriage you did not want. I will, of course, grant you a divorce without argument. Your fortune is yours. Your life is yours. I would not dream of remaining in your way any longer.*
>
> *Thank you for your generosity, for sharing your home and your kindness with me all these months. I will always look back on this time as the luckiest of my life.*
>
> *Yours,*
> *Sterling*

He would not write to her of his love, much as he wanted to, because that would be unfair of him, manipulative even. She owed him nothing, and he did not want her to feel guilty for letting him go.

The heavy task completed, Sterling leaned against the back of the chair, making it creak ominously. He could almost hear Bernadette's laughter when he had told her that his mother called him 'Lambie.'

Lambie! she had cackled. *You are more like a bear!*

But in his mind's eye, Sterling had never stopped thinking of himself as a lamb. He could probably lift Bernadette over his head — and she was not insubstantial herself — but he knew that between the two of them, his wife was the strong one really.

As he mulled over the empty, Bernadette-less future stretching out before him, his eyes drifted to the large, framed maps upon the wall in front of the desk. One was a detailed, topographical map of Gol, the country across the Middlemark Sea from Stenland, the roiling land where the Golois were hunting down demigods and killing them for the crime of being born half-divine. The other was a naval chart of the Middlemark Sea and all the ports of call along the Golois and Stennish coastlines.

Sterling had always assumed that Bernadette brought her illegal wares back and forth between Stenland and the landlocked countries to her north and east. Few were brave enough to land on Golois shores these days for fear of being accused of having divine origins. Many had lost their lives to such baseless accusations. Bernadette was fearless, to be sure — it was one of the many reasons why Sterling loved her — but she was not so foolhardy as to put herself in mortal danger.

Was she?

Suddenly anxious, Sterling got to his feet and began to pace. What if Bernadette's delay in returning home had nothing to do with his lack of bad luck? What if something — or someone — had waylaid her? What if she was trapped in some fetid Golois prison cell, unable to call for help, at this very moment?

What if it was already too late?

This last thought brought him up short as his blood froze in his veins. But no, he was being ridiculous. She could not have made it to the coast and sailed the Middlemark Sea in a day, so she most certainly was not rotting in a Golois dungeon. And Bernadette had too much sense to get herself caught up in something truly dangerous.

As his panic subsided, he found himself staring at a small altar to the left of the study door. Most homes kept the family altar beside the front door, not hidden away in a back room. Sterling had always assumed that Bernadette's lack of a family altar indicated a lack of family, period. He'd once asked her about her parents, but her eyes had gone uncharacteristically sad and distant.

"It's complicated, Bear," she had told him, stroking his bearded cheek with an equally uncharacteristic tenderness.

He hadn't pressed her on it at the time, not when she'd touched his cheek so affectionately and called him Bear. But now that Sterling stood before Bernadette's family altar, he could not see what was so complicated about it. Only one ancestral birth key winked at him from the shelf. Beside it sat an old-fashioned portrait-in-miniature of a man, presumably Bernadette's father. The resemblance was obvious. He had the same thick, dark hair, the same arched eyebrows, the same long nose. His eyes were different, however — large like hers, but brown, so unlike the startling blue of Bernadette's. He appeared to have her more adventurous taste in fashion, too, as evidenced by the height of his stiff collar, the busy pattern of his waistcoat, the many folds of his cravat, and the vibrancy of his delphinium boutonniere.

The only other objects on the altar were a dish of salt water — a symbol of the death god known as the Salt Sea — and a yellowed, postcard-sized painting of the Bride of Fortune. The god's iconography made her easily identifiable — her hands held out as if they formed the two sides of a scale, good fortune balancing out the bad; the vineyard vines tumbling at her feet, representing prosperity; and the key she wore around her neck as was the custom of all brides and grooms on their wedding day, the symbol of two people uniting their fortunes. Only, in the god's case, she united her fortune with all humanity.

Sterling and Bernadette had exchanged birth keys eight months ago beside the Bride of Fortune's altar at the temple in Ironworks Street. It had been the happiest day of Sterling's life up to that point, and every day thereafter had been better than the last. Today being the notable exception.

Sterling swallowed hard against the urge to cry as he folded the letter in half and wrote *To Bernadette* on the back of it. He had lingered too long in her private room, a place to which he had no right, especially now, so he returned to the main part of the house, closing the door behind him. He set the letter on the kitchen table and packed up his few belongings. Before he left, he opened the small, lacquered box on the fireplace mantel. Inside, their birth keys sat side by side, one gold and one silver, hers slightly larger than his.

They belong together, some inner, stubborn voice insisted, but his conscience knew better. Even so, he was tempted to leave his birth key in her care. When he died, he wanted his key to end up on the sparse altar in Bernadette's study, not relegated to the back corner of an altar belonging to a distant relative who had never respected him in life and would undoubtedly never honor him in death. But it would not be fair of Sterling to expect Bernadette to keep it, so he picked it up in his thick fingers and put it in his waistcoat pocket, thinking that he might as well reach down his gullet and pull out his own heart.

With nothing left to do, he inhaled deeply, memorizing the scent of home – of her – before letting himself out.

A half-hour after leaving behind the only real home he had ever known, Sterling teetered on a barstool with a frothy pint glass in front of him. He rarely drank – certainly not during daylight hours – and he could count on one hand the number of times he'd consumed beer in his life. But given his sudden change in circumstances and his reluctance to return in defeat to his mother and uncle, his feet had taken him to a nearby pub rather than to his uncle's townhouse when the hackney dropped him off.

Unfortunately, the pub was located in a respectable part of town, so it was inadequately seedy for his present disposition. Also, he hated beer, but since he had always thought of beer as the beverage into which one drowned one's sorrows, he had ordered a pint. He forced himself to take several gulps. Honestly, the stuff was vile.

The barkeep appeared before him, a pretty, fresh-faced woman in her late-twenties or early-thirties, probably the wife or the daughter of the pub's owner. She held out her hands like two sides of a scale, weighing the options as she asked, "Which do you think is better? Beer or port?"

"Port."

"Thought so."

She whisked away the barely drunk pint and replaced it with a narrow port glass into which she poured the rich, red wine Sterling preferred.

"Thank you," he murmured, flushing with embarrassment.

How marvelously transparent you are, Bernadette had told him early in their acquaintance, when he had first left his family's home to live what little life he had left on his own terms. His mother and Uncle

Stickles had promptly disowned him. He had felt sadder about this turn of events than he would have thought, the emotional state that had prompted Bernadette's comment. From the mouths of most, the word *transparent* would have been an insult, but Bernadette Snaith appreciated people who didn't hide who and what they were. And for his own part, Sterling had relished being seen at last.

It was the moment he knew himself to be in love.

"What's the matter? You look like someone drowned your kittens," observed the barkeep with a face full of sympathy, as Sterling took a draught of port.

"I'm not going to die," he answered mournfully.

"I hate to be the bearer of bad tidings, but I think it likely you *will* die someday."

"But not soon."

"You cannot know that either."

Sterling regarded her with bleary eyes. She seemed oddly familiar, although he could not recall when and where he had seen her before.

"Aren't you meant to be comforting me?" he asked.

"Death *is* a comfort. Your life is not meant to go on and on without end. Imagine how terrible that would be." She polished the countertop as she spoke, as if this were the sort of conversation she carried on all the time. And who knew? Given her line of work, perhaps it was.

"Who are you? Grandmother Wisdom?" he joked, albeit weakly, referring to the god who gave humanity the gift of understanding mortality so that people would better appreciate life.

"Ha! Can you imagine? Ha ha!" Her eyes sparkled with amusement, reminding Sterling of Bernadette's eyes, although his wife's were much bluer and much lovelier. He ought to laugh along with the kind barkeep, but if anything, his spirits sank lower. He took another gulp of port.

"Hmm," said the woman, her face falling as she studied Sterling's miserable countenance. "Perhaps you would be better off at temple, rather than hunkered down in a pub with a glass of port and a measly barmaid to keep you company. Go make an offering to some god or other. You look like you need to ask for the Bride of Fortune's favor."

Sterling snorted. "I need no more favors from that quarter, I can promise you that."

"Oh? What favors has she given you?"

"Only one, and she has already taken it back."

"Are you certain about that?"

"Do you doubt me?"

"Yes, actually, I do." She leaned her elbows on the counter and lowered her voice, her mien conspiratorial. "Let me ask you this: If the Bride of Fortune stood before you now, what would you ask of her?"

His knee-jerk response was *Bernadette*, but he thought better of it. Even as the port began to muddle his brain, he understood that he could not very well ask for a person. Bernadette had her own thoughts and hopes and dreams. How could he call affection that was not freely given 'love'? He could not. And since he did not want anything or anyone besides Bernadette Snaith, he had no choice but to answer, "I don't know."

The barkeep nodded sagely. "Well, that is a good start. Most people ask for the moon. Cure this disease. Make this person fall in love with me. Stop the People's Republic of Gol from hunting me down and cutting off my head. But the truth is that, in a world full of free will, even a god has limits. And really, it's the little things that end up mattering most – the day-to-day banalities, barely noticeable in the moment, that add up to something extraordinary."

Sterling had the strangest sensation that the pub had faded away and there was nothing in the universe besides himself, the woman across from him, and the long bar that separated them. The lunchtime conversations carrying on behind him became muted, forming a bubble of soft sound that surrounded them like a blanket.

"I will give you an example," she continued. "Imagine a mother and a daughter. The daughter is intelligent and curious, but she struggles to fit in among her peers. They bully her mercilessly at school. The child wants her mother to intervene. But what happens to children whose parents never allow them to stand up for themselves or to use their own voices?"

The conversations around them grew fuzzier as Sterling dredged up memories of his own childhood, of being cosseted by his mother, of his sense of self shrinking as his peers mocked his size and his doughy round cheeks.

"They become weak-willed," he answered, his voice hardly above a whisper. "They come to believe that they have no power over their own lives."

In short, children whose parents never allowed them to stand up for themselves or to use their own voices became Sterling Valancy.

"Exactly. Now imagine that same intelligent, curious girl growing into a woman who demands respect from everyone and who does not suffer fools. What might that woman accomplish? Whom might she help in a world made so trying and difficult and sad by the Old Gods?"

The barkeep leaned closer, and as she did so, the pendant of her necklace swung between them – a small golden key.

"It's the little things that bring good fortune, Sterling. Sometimes luck comes in the form you least expect."

"How did you know—?"

"Go home, son."

She squeezed his arm, and he awoke with a start as the sounds of the pub came flooding back into his ears. He lifted his head from the bar to find a mostly full beer glass sweating at his elbow rather than a glass of port. He must have fallen asleep, precariously balanced on his barstool.

Already the dream was fading, but he could remember the last thing the dream-barmaid had told him: *Go home, son.* And so he paid his tab and made his way to the only home he had left.

Sterling stood on the stoop, staring at the plain wooden door painted the same dismal gray it had always worn, set into the stolid stonework that made up his uncle's dreary townhouse. He had spent the first twenty-six years of his life in this place, but he had never known what it meant to come home until he had married Bernadette. Now, he saw that his childhood home was little better than a debtor's prison. And yet, here he was, his life having come depressingly full circle.

Should he knock? It seemed a bizarre thing to do when his mother lived on the other side of the door, yet she and Uncle Stickles had made it clear that he was no longer welcome.

What would Bernadette do? he wondered.

To Old Hell with them. Go in, she spoke in his mind as clear as a bell. He went inside.

At first glance, nothing had changed. There was the altar with its rusting keys. There was the flagging fern. There was the ancient umbrella stand. There was the grandfather clock with its monotonous tick-tocking. Gods, it was almost physically painful to be standing in this entry hall once more, but Sterling's chagrin at returning to his uncle's house was nothing compared to the shame he felt in trapping poor Bernadette. It would cost a fortune to divorce, and the Unknown God knew where either of them would find the money. He would rather face his relatives' condemnation than his own betrayal of Bernadette's trust, so with that lowering thought in mind, he stepped into the drawing room in search of his mother and uncle. There they perched on the same uncomfortable chairs upon which they sat every afternoon. Uncle Stickles clutched a copy of this week's edition of *The Sanctimony* (his newspaper of choice) in his arthritic hands, while Mama's needlework basket sat at her feet, ready for another endless afternoon of knitting hats and mufflers and mittens for the 'poor wretches' who had brought their ill fortunes upon themselves, in her humble opinion. The ridiculous porcelain lamb stared at Sterling from the side table, its doe-eyes as empty as he felt. Whiling away another afternoon of his one precious life in this stifling parlor might have crushed his soul had it not been for one notable exception to the sameness of the drawing room.

Bernadette was here.

More specifically, Bernadette stood beside the fireplace in the clutches of the narrow-faced wool merchant, Chauvelin, who held a knife to her throat while Mama and Uncle Stickles watched on in scandalized horror.

Sterling stopped breathing. His heart could not seem to decide if it should gallop out of his chest or stop beating altogether as he stared uncomprehendingly at the scene before him: Bernadette was in his uncle's drawing room with Chauvelin, who held her at knifepoint – Chauvelin, that good-natured fellow they had enjoyed chatting with on market day; Chauvelin, whom they had once invited into their home when his old wagon had a broken axle. Bernadette was taller than the wool merchant, but to Sterling, the man seemed like a giant as he pressed the blade against the smooth column of his wife's neck, her untidy hair dangling tendrils around the sharp steel. There was an intensity in her blue gaze, as if she were trying to convey an important message to Sterling, but his mind could make no sense of it. All he could do was stand and stare and then stare some more.

It was Chauvelin who broke the silence with words uttered in his sibilant, Golois accent. "Good day to you, Mr Valancy. Or would you prefer that I address you by your sobriquet?"

Flabbergasted, and more than a little panicked, Sterling could only repeat the same words Votary Trent had spoken to him this morning. "I... I am afraid that I have not the pleasure of understanding you."

"The Larkspur, my dear sir."

The answer did nothing to improve Sterling's understanding. "The Larkspur?"

Chauvelin inclined his head.

"What about the Larkspur?"

"Do not feign innocence with me. I already know all."

The clock in the entry hall ticked away the seconds as the cogs and wheels of Sterling's brain got to work. The maps in Bernadette's study. Her smuggling operation. All the times she had been gone for days on end without explanation. The painting of her father on her altar with a boutonniere of delphinium blooms. And what was the common name for delphiniums?

Larkspur.

And there was the other object on the altar, too, a painting of the Bride of Fortune. And now Bernadette's extraordinary blue eyes were boring into his.

Demigod eyes.

And what was the Larkspur smuggling out of Gol?

Demigods.

Salt Sea and all the gods of death, how on earth had Sterling failed to piece it together? Bernadette was his wife, the treasure of his heart! And yet, he could not have concocted this turn of events in his wildest imagination. He had merely thought her eyes lovely; he had never considered that her periwinkle irises might come from a divine parent – the Bride of Fortune, no less! Why would he? And why would he suspect Bernadette of being the Larkspur when she hated the newspaper accounts and drew goatees on the heroic images dreamed up by the newspaper artist?

And why would this Golois blackguard in his uncle's drawing room think that Sterling, of all people, was the Larkspur, when obviously his wife was a thousand times braver than he would ever be? He decided the question was worth asking aloud.

"You believe *me* to be the Larkspur?"

"It is not a matter of belief, sir. I know it to be true. We have tracked your movements. You have been followed all the way to your domicile on numerous occasions."

But of course, it was not Sterling's movements they had tracked;

the Golois spies had been following Bernadette.

In a display of inappropriateness that was both stunning and typical, Uncle Stickles burst out laughing. "Sterling? The Larkspur? I say, what a good joke!"

"Do hold your tongue, Uncle!" whispered Sterling's anxious, birdlike mother, wringing her bony hands. It was difficult to say what she found more alarming – the man from Gol wielding a knife in the drawing room or the possibility that one of her respectable acquaintances might discover that she had breathed the same air as Sterling's scandalous wife.

"Come now, Amelia, the man cannot be serious. Sterling has the backbone of a slug. The boy is afraid of his own shadow. Why, you call him Lambie, for gods' sake. Never saw a more chicken-hearted child in my life. And this bird-witted, mutton-headed widgeon thinks *he's* the Larkspur? That man belongs in the asylum, not my drawing room."

"Exactly, sir," said the wool merchant-*cum*-secret agent. "That is his particular gift. He is so meek, so unassuming that no one would ever suspect him of flying in the face of Golois law and illegally transporting convicted felons across the border."

Sterling had no idea how to proceed. He knew only that he needed to get the knife away from Bernadette's throat. Before he could overthink matters, he replied, "Nothing about holding innocent demigods against their will is lawful, Chauvelin."

"So you admit that you are the Larkspur?"

"Yes."

"What are you doing?" Bernadette hissed at him.

"It's too late, my dearest. Our clever friend has found me out."

"He's lying, Chauvelin!" she tried to tell her captor, but why would a man believe a woman when another man was telling him what he wanted to hear? It was one of her greatest pet peeves about men.

A sense of peace settled over Sterling. His self-pity evaporated, replaced by a single-minded focus on keeping Bernadette safe. "What do you want of me?" he asked Chauvelin.

"I want you to rot in Old Hell. Short of that, here are your instructions: Make your way to the pier within the hour. Tell no one where you are going. You will be watched. At the docks, you will find a packet called *La Prospérité*. Present yourself to the crew."

"What is my final destination?"

"Use your imagination."

Unfortunately, Sterling had an excellent imagination, but even his mental conjurations of a Golois dungeon could not make him veer from his chosen path, not when Bernadette's life hung in the balance. "And my wife? My family?"

"Will live as long as you do as you are told."

So this was the end. Sterling would be held prisoner on a packet until he made it to the shores of Gol, and gods knew what would happen to him there. He could only assume that Grandfather Bones would be separating his soul from his body and the Warden would be opening the door to the House of the Unknown God for him sooner rather than later. And all because a Golois spy could not fathom that a woman could be a hero.

Well, Sterling was more than happy to pay for the man's ignorance if it meant saving Bernadette. He gave her a wistful smile and said, "How could I ever have thought myself unlucky when I have had you in my life?"

"No! Don't you dare do this!" Bernadette struggled to get free.

"Chauvelin, you bloody shit-sack, you have it all wrong! I am the L—"

Sterling's mother gasped as the bloody shit-sack in question slapped his hand over Bernadette's mouth and dug the tip of his blade into her skin, causing a slim rivulet of blood to drip down her neck.

For the second time that day, Sterling's surroundings seemed to fade away. There was only Bernadette and Bernadette's blood and the fool holding the knife.

It's the little things that bring good fortune, Sterling, a voice spoke in his ear.

This was no memory. He heard the words as if the speaker were right beside him. A force outside of himself directed his gaze to the cloying lamb statuette on the table to his right.

Sometimes, luck comes in the form you least expect.

It all happened so quickly.

He picked up the horrid lamb and flung it with all his might. The porcelain hit the wall beside Chauvelin's head and burst into a cloud of white shards and powder. The Golois bastard cried out and let go of Bernadette to cover his injured eye as he howled in pain. Sterling crossed the drawing room in three long strides, took the man by his neck, and slammed him against the wall with a hand made thick and callused and strong in the smithy.

"This isn't over," Chauvelin wheezed, his left eye streaming blood.

"You're right," said Bernadette, but she kept her warm gaze on Sterling as she spoke. "This is only the beginning."

Ten minutes later, Chauvelin was tied up; Uncle Stickles was hailing an errand boy to alert the constabulary to the presence of a lunatic raving in his water closet; Mama was drooping in her chair with her smelling salts clutched tight; and Sterling and Bernadette were in the kitchen, where the former was dabbing at the cut on the latter's neck with a clean, damp tea-towel.

"What must you think of me?" Bernadette asked him.

"My thinking about you has not changed in the slightest. Only now I know that you are a demigod who has risked her life to save others like yourself from the clutches of the Golois government."

The cut was not deep and had stopped bleeding. With no further excuse to touch her, Sterling took a step back. "I don't suppose you saw my letter?"

"Oh yes, I returned home to find that insulting piece of paper in place of my husband. I came racing here to haul you back to our cottage where you belong, but that fool Chauvelin followed me, and the instant I stormed the drawing room, he had a knife at my throat."

"So you know that the oracle made a mistake, that my luck is perfectly fine?"

Bernadette took him by the shoulders and shook him. "That's a *good* thing, you ridiculous sap-skull!"

She grabbed his face in both hands and kissed him with a ferocity that sent them both staggering against the dry sink.

"'Divorce'?" she cried when she came up for air. "Just you try to get rid of me!"

"I don't want to divorce you," he admitted sheepishly

"Then don't. Although, if you had an ounce of sense, you would. I am a very dangerous outlaw."

"Then it is just as well that I'm a ridiculous sap-skull." She pressed her forehead to his, and he put his arms around her waist, hardly daring to hope for a happy ending.

"I watched that pianoforte nearly flatten you, and I understood all at once that I had gone and fallen in love with my own husband. Can you imagine?"

"Yes, actually." Sterling's heart expanded so quickly in his ribcage that he was finding it difficult to breathe.

"When I realized that I might be able to keep you for a while longer, I didn't know what to do or think. It was one thing to marry you when I thought you were going to die. It's quite another to let myself love you when I know that my work could endanger you. I almost got us both killed this afternoon, and your family to boot!"

Perhaps these were valid concerns, but all Sterling heard was 'love,' so he kissed his wife until he was tempted to sling her over his shoulder and carry her to his ugly old bedroom upstairs. It was high time someone made good memories in that room.

"Your family is terrible, by the way," she informed him as he pressed his lips to the sensitive spot behind her ear.

"Yes, they are. Speaking of family..." He lifted his head to grin at her. "I believe I met your mother."

"Did you? *I* haven't seen the Bride of Fortune in ages." Bernadette sighed in fond exasperation before she kissed the tip of Sterling's nose. "Lucky you."

ROSEBUD

By

KATHERINE ARDEN

It was January when we came to Brussels, my sister and my aunt and I, although the War had ended in November. My father had gone ahead of us, saying he would have a place ready, and indeed he had taken a house. But he had no notion of housekeeping or organization, and so we were none of us surprised to find the house – while surprisingly large and surprisingly grand – to be nearly bare of furniture, except for a few pieces half-buried in grime, their dust sheets long since hauled away for bandages. Susan, of course, was enchanted by the vast, echoing spaces, and the dust did not make her sneeze. She danced round the ballroom, startling three bats out of their roost, leaving footprints in the slippery dust, curls round as candlesticks coming loose and looping down her back. "Isn't it beautiful?" she said.

Honestly, I couldn't see it; I had been sneezing from the moment I set foot in the house, my eyes were streaming, and it was dark to begin with. The January dusk came quickly, and in those lean days of rationed oil, the streetlights did not come on. When I put a hand to the light switch it rattled and clicked and spat and flickered, showing the ballroom in uncertain pieces: molding and cornices, peeling gilt and the shredded remains of rose-trellis wallpaper, a floor of glorious parquet, splintered and softened and scraped by careless, booted feet, with electric lines and phone lines stapled higgledy-piggledy to the moldy wall. In my wavering vision, it looked cold, and sinister.

"Wretched man, that father of yours," said Aunt Irene, who had sneezed twice, tidily, and then put her handkerchief away. I was still leaning on the doorframe, not so much sneezing as attempting to expel the contents of my skull through my nose. "Tells us he's let an historic house. Well, historic it is. Historic enough to choke on." She patted me on the back while I wheezed. "There, there dear, it will pass soon enough. Sue, come back this instant!"

Susan was already darting back across the floor, dancing a wild waltz with her shadow, and the unshaded light, still crackling and flickering, turned her high-colored face garish, made cobwebs of her swinging hair. She was smiling. "I think it's lovely," she said. "Did Father say why it was historic?"

"No," said Irene. She sniffed. "You know how he is. Too busy planning the fate of the world."

Our father was a diplomat, and young to have a pair of grown girls – I was twenty and Susan was hardly younger. He'd married young and lost our mother young and with the excuse of his grieving widowhood, buried himself, with some relief, in work. He had always been easier with his colleagues than with our mother, and I never saw him happier than when he had them over for dinner in Washington, in our big house on Church Street, bought with Mother's money.

We had a series of stand-in parents, mostly from our father's side, in the years after Mother passed, with varying degrees of discipline; from Aunt Agatha, who wore pearls and strong scent and had been on the stage long ago, and who let us streak our faces with rouge and play mad games about the house, to Cousin Lettie, who did not like children at all and considered it her duty to change us into properly dressed waxworks, demure and preferably speechless.

The result of all this was that we went from a little haphazard to absolutely ungovernable, until finally we humiliated our father before his particular friend, Colonel Cooper, and Aunt Irene came to take charge, and told us she would not leave again until we were grown.

We hated her, of course, and spilled out all our spleen at feeling unwanted upon her, but she was perfectly unmoved and after we stopped complaining, we benefited greatly from the settling-down of the house. Susan was the great beauty of the world; as like a kitten as any girl could possibly be, the kind of girl who looks a coquette well before she is one, and must be ferociously defended by all her relatives against the sort of wretches who read coquetry in the easy manners and rosy cheeks of a girl not yet fourteen. So Irene watched over her fiercely, and I did too. No one has ever yet read coquetry into *my* long-nosed face, framed with spectacles, a book always clasped before me like plate-armor, and besides, since my sister was beautiful, and easy in company, it comforted me to think that I was the clever, worldly one, who must keep her from the evils of society that I had read all about.

Perhaps predictably, Susan turned eighteen and made a mockery of all our hovering by falling in love.

He was a secretary in our father's office, older than us, but not old enough to be a proper catch with money and position. Susan spent three weeks avoiding me and Aunt Irene, creeping in at odd hours and getting away with it, adroit as she was and quick-tongued and of course ravishing. To be ravishing makes everything easier, and whoever says not is lying. But the more she crept around, the more I wanted to know what she was doing, and it was I who caught her, in the end. She'd invited Mr Lewis into her own bedroom, sneaking him up by the stairs, and when I went up to borrow some thread, I found the door locked. But there was no key in the keyhole and so when I looked in, I saw them there, clasped together on the bed, his hands in her hair, hers tangled in his clothes.

I did not cry out at once, only stared in shock – I felt a jolt all through me and perhaps a little envy, for they looked as passionate as anyone in my beloved fictions. And then I was just angry at the wretch for imposing on my sister's innocence, no matter how happy she looked. I meant to creep away and tell Aunt Irene at once, but must have made some sound at the keyhole, for my sister gave a soft cry, and Mr Lewis strode across the room and flung open the door.

"Alice," said Susan, straightening up on the bed, drawing the front of her dress together. "What are you doing?"

I could not find my voice. She'd undone the buttons of his shirt, and his tie was loose; his jacket was thrown crumpled over a chair. The notch of his clavicles, the smooth skin above her breasts, were glossy with sweat. Susan got to her feet, straightening her skirt, her white face going red. "Alice, go away." A mark like a strawberry showed below her collarbone, where his mouth had drawn the blood up near the surface of her thin, fair skin.

Mr Lewis took Susan's hand, and said placatingly, "Alice, I see you are angry. But there's no offense meant. I love your sister."

Finally I found my tongue, although perhaps it would have been better if I stayed mute. "Love?" I said, drawing myself up. "This is not love but – but animal fornication—" which was a phrase I'd read in a book and chased eagerly through several more, "And you, sir, are taking advantage of my sister's innocence!"

I spat this out, full of righteousness, arms crossed, my feet planted in the doorway. But Mr Lewis made no answer. His lids only dropped a fraction, as though my opinions were not worth his reply. Susan didn't say anything either; they looked at each other like I wasn't even there. Mr Lewis put a hand up, very carefully, and laid his palm across the scarlet mark on my sister's breastbone, and she raised both her hands to hold him.

"I'll talk to my father," she said, smiling.

"I'll come back when you do. Or when you call. Or even if you don't," he said. They didn't even look ashamed, they looked *mischievous*, and I felt my outrage climbing again.

"Sir, I will scream," I said, rather desperately, thinking of books again; a little old-fashioned maybe but to scream was a proper response to an interloper, according to my reading. But I was still thrown off by their faces. They ought to have looked guilty instead of giddy, and I hesitated in a sort of childish incomprehension. Mr Lewis just touched Susan's flushed lower lip and smiled at her, and I felt like a joke standing in the doorway, gawky, unlovable, and torn between simple outrage and the desperation to be desired myself.

He said to Susan, "I could go to your father tonight."

"He's at Colonel Cooper's; he often stays the night when they get to jawing," said Susan, which was true. "Alice, would you leave now, please?" She was using the coaxing tone that I'd yielded to all her life, but that night my indignation was stronger than my affection, so I opened my mouth and screamed like a teakettle.

Mr Lewis swore and laughed and kissed Susan, whispering something in her ear, before snatching up his coat and tie and shoes and jumping, still laughing, for the window. In that moment, he was as far from the rather colorless young man of my father's office as could possibly be imagined, and I was jealous all over again.

Susan watched him go, just as Aunt Irene came running up and her reaction was exactly as I could have wished; she took one look at my flushed, radiant sister, with her blouse askew and her hair lifting in loose curls in the wind from the window, and she cried out, in throbbing tones just suited for one of my romances, "What have you been *doing*?"

"Oh, I'm tired of both of you," said Susan. "I am going to talk to Father in the morning." And she walked across to the bedroom door, pushed us out, and turned the key. This time she left it in the lock, but although Irene and I waited for what felt like hours, Mr Lewis did not come back.

Susan never had a chance to speak to Father. For war was declared three days later and the first I heard of it was from Susan sobbing in her room the day after that. "Dearest," I said, running in, "are you all right?"

"The States are joining the war. He is enlisting," she said, curled in on herself on the quilted counterpane, her body as racked with grief as it had been taut with joy on that same bed a week ago. She sniffed and lifted her wet face to look at me. "And you needn't say you're pleased. I think I'd slap your face for you if you did."

"I'm not," I said, holding both her hands. "Believe me I'm not. I wanted to protect you and now you are crying."

She collapsed onto my shoulder at that, and I held her very tightly.

They did not see each other for two years, although letters went to and fro by the boatload. I had begun to think he did actually love her, just from the sheer volume of correspondence, but then in the last six months he did not write at all. His mother wrote once, to say he was wounded, and then silence.

My sister went about for weeks like an alabaster figurine of Desolation. I hated him all over again, worse than ever, seeing the color in her fade, her disinterest in anything except the daily mail. The war had ended, and still there was this silence. I was sure he'd run off with someone.

Susan revived suddenly, however, when Father was posted to the Embassy in Brussels. She begged for us to go too, said that it would be a wonderful opportunity to practice our French and learn Flemish. Glad to see her taking an interest, I joined my voice with hers, to persuade Father to take us both, and Aunt Irene.

And now here we were. Father had rented this grand old house for us, achingly beautiful, bats in the ballroom, quite unlivable. On that first night, tossing on my dusty mattress, I wondered very much if I'd done right by my sister, trying to get us all out of Washington.

But Aunt Irene was a woman to make the best of things, and she had no intention of letting a mere house get the better of her. She set to work on scrubbing at once, and scolded me and Sue into helping her. But Susan was sly; she poked at the baseboards with a rag, but the instant she could get away she trekked off with nothing but a few francs in her pocket and all our years of haphazard education in French crammed, strongly accented, into her skull. When she came back, she cut through all our furious lectures to say that she'd volunteered at one of the soldiers' hospitals in Brussels.

I tried going with her for a day or two, because I was worried about her, and nursing sounded more glamorous than scrubbing – and anyway, she and I had always done everything together: learning and loving and playing and fighting. But I couldn't bear the hospital. The patients were all old soldiers, wounded in the last months of the War, their faces clammy-pale, or greenish, or yellow-tinged. Sometimes they screamed for no reason, and sometimes they clutched at you, smelling of carbolic and blood, and sometimes they were angry at you, for no other reason than you were walking and they weren't. I read to them instead of properly nursing, because I found that I could not bear the sight and smell of their wounds. There was one boy, I remember, called Lenny, who listened with vast owl-eyes in a wizened face when I read him limericks to make him smile. He used to joke fluently in return, leave me panting with laughter, every face in every bed agrin, and he told me about his mother and his sister and how he'd sold insurance subscriptions before he was called up.

I think I stayed in the hospital for him; certainly, I came back every day for a week, reading material in hand, hating the war worse with every hour, wishing I were a girl in a story where time could be wound back to some vague, beautiful Before, when these men were whole and my sister was happy.

But I was not, of course, and one day Lenny simply wasn't there anymore and they were too busy to do more than point at where they'd put him in the cemetery. I didn't have the strength to volunteer again after that. Susan had taken to staying out late, coming home smelling dreadful, and when Aunt Irene asked what she'd been up to, Susan said, "Nursing," which in those days was an unanswerable excuse.

I was happy enough to go back to scrubbing, myself.

You'd think I would have started cleaning in some useful room; my bedroom, say, or Sue's, or the little sitting room with chipped walls the color of Himalayan poppies. Irene was responsibly ploughing through the kitchen and parlor. But I decided that first I wanted to clean the ballroom.

Most of that great house had been rendered quite practical in the years of the war. The froth of its colors, the frivolity of its cornicing, had been sacrificed to telephone wires and lumber rooms; the bedstead in my room was the same curving iron that, I imagined, went to fashion trench-knives.

But somehow, the ballroom had resisted the swift spring tide of the changing world; not even dust or mice or softening wood could touch its essential atmosphere of lugubrious grace. One could imagine anything in that ballroom: knights or lovers or even a world where Lenny was still selling insurance and war was only an excuse for gallantry amongst the brave.

No one ever thought of me as romantic, not with Susan around wearing her heart on her sleeve and looking like a fairytale princess. I was the sensible one. And yet, my imagination ran riot far more often than hers. So I imagined and scrubbed and scrubbed more, wondering where Susan was and telling myself I didn't care, that I should see her presently, and anyway, here was the parquet coming clean at last. Finally it was free of dust, although it would have been waxed, I thought, for a grand ball. I rose from my grubby knees before one of the great, tarnished mirrors, and saw with fascination that the vast spaces of the ballroom had lent grace even to me. My pinched, bookish face looked austere and wide-eyed and young. And since there was no one to see, I curtseyed, awkwardly, to my own reflection and said, "Yes, I will have this dance," and took an invisible hand and swept myself off into an invisible waltz, spinning round the clean floor and laughing, and then I heard it: music – violins and viols keeping time with my steps – and I spun to it, my heart beating faster and faster, until Susan's voice broke my reverie.

"Alice – Alice," she called, and I lurched to a halt, nearly falling, and terribly embarrassed.

"What do you mean, being gone for hours on end and then creeping up—" I began, and ordinarily, she'd have teased me for my silliness.

But now she just said, urgently, with a smudge of dirt on her nose, "I've found him. I'm bringing him here."

I did not understand at all, but she added impatiently to my puzzled face, "Art, of course. Arthur. Mr Lewis. I found him. He was in hospital and I'm bringing him here."

I stared. "Mr Lewis? But he – he abandoned you, he – I was sure he'd run off with someone!"

Susan drew herself up fiercely, and I saw with a fearful little pang that the strain had begun to print marks like craquelure on the skin round her eyes. He was making her old before her time, the wretched man. "He didn't. He thought I shouldn't be burdened with him, that's why he wouldn't write back. But I hounded everyone I knew until someone told me where he was."

"Burdened with him?" I said, still blank.

The lines around Sue's eyes deepened fractionally. "He was hurt. His face is different."

I didn't see Mr Lewis' face that night, or for many nights thereafter. He was brought in late, after Susan and Aunt Irene and I had a frantic four hours' work airing another of the boarded-up bedrooms; his face was swathed in bandages from cheekbones to chin, and his eyes were horrible. They were haunted, but not in the way that eyes were in books: patiently borne suffering that lent a face noble character. They were lifeless as two holes, and even when Susan smiled with all her bright beauty and smoothed the blanket round his shoulders, well, he looked straight through and past her and I saw her lips quiver.

I tried to help her that night, when she got him settled, but I don't think I did much good. I kept imagining terrible voids under the concealing bandages and I could not bring myself to look into the flat, dead coins of his eyes. Finally she told me I was clumsy and sent me away. I went, but I held her when she came to my room and wept afterward, and eventually we fell asleep like children together on my creaking bed, with the door open, at Sue's insistence, in case Mr Lewis cried out in the night.

The open door is perhaps why we heard the music.

I heard it first; I distinctly remember sitting up, thinking I'd dreamt the same disembodied melody that I'd whirled to in the forenoon. But I wasn't dreaming now. The music pressed on my ears, unbearably beautiful in a place and a year starved for beauty. I shook Susan awake. Dried tears had glued her hair to her face. "Alice?" Her face changed as she heard it too. "A gramophone?"

I shook my head, listening for all I was worth. No gramophone could *surround* you with music, so. I yearned with every fiber to know where it was coming from.

"Come on," I murmured. "It's in the ballroom, surely."

Sue hesitated. "Art might need me."

"He'll be all right," I insisted. "Just a look."

So we pulled our wrappers around us against the dank chill of the corridor and crept towards the ballroom, drawn by the sound. With my sister beside me, it was just like before. Before the war, before Susan had to go and fall in love with someone who had made her happy for moments and made her cry for months. I had longed for that Before with all my heart; this perhaps was as close as I would ever get.

We tiptoed up to the ballroom archway like children, then stopped, awed.

"Is it real?" whispered Susan.

The ballroom wasn't empty anymore. It was bursting with color, like a world tinted sepia had come suddenly to life. It was also packed with people. The music that had drawn us from our beds mingled now with their raised voices, speaking English, their laughter. They were all in ball-dress straight out of one of my romances, high-waisted dresses, scarlet uniforms. The gowns were like drooping flowers, colored saffron and ivory and raspberry and lime. Everywhere I looked I saw gallant faces and fans and curls and jewels like hoarfrost at dawn, and garnet-colored wine casting rosy shadows. It was utterly impossible. It was the loveliest thing I had ever seen.

I stared.

Sue stared.

"Are we dreaming?" said Sue. She looked a little fearful. She'd begun to step back towards the safety of that shadowed corridor, the quotidian smell of dust.

But I reached out and caught her hand, held her where she was.

"Maybe," I whispered back. "But with such dreams, who wants to wake up? Do you think they'd let us dance?" I couldn't take my eyes off that glorious ballroom.

"Can they even see us?" demanded Sue. "Are they ghosts? Are they real? Maybe something horrible will happen if we go in."

I was silent. It was true, no one had looked our way. I was the furthest thing from a lady just then. I was wearing a nightgown. My toes wiggled in their sagging wool socks. If it was a dream, all that wouldn't matter. But was it a dream? It was probably a dream.

"I should be getting back," said Sue.

"He made you wait," I said, eyes still on the dancers. "He made you cry. He made you crawl through all of Brussels, looking, and now he won't look you in the face. Maybe they'll let us dance. If it's a dream, they won't notice our nightdresses."

Susan said nothing. But she stopped moving back. The ballroom before us was as bright and pure as a meadow at sunrise, its people nodding like flowers.

We stepped tentatively into the room.

Nothing happened. No one looked. We took three steps, four, and then, one person smiled, a gentleman bowed, a woman gave us a curtsey and a friendly greeting, and without quite knowing how it happened, the party swept us up. Soon Susan was dancing, even laughing. She'd always been a fine dancer. I considered myself too clumsy to dance, too awkward to ask, despite all my dreams of romance, and so at first I tried to watch over her, as I had always done at parties, happy just to be in this glorious reverie that I knew I'd remember all my life.

I stood quiet, drinking some of the rose-red wine and watching my sister, when I saw a gentleman watching me.

He had quite an ordinary face, teeth a little crooked, big chin and bony jaw, with fair hair tied back like men used to do. When I caught his glance he lifted his own glass in salute and began to walk towards me.

I'd have flushed and turned away, if I were awake, but everything was weightless there as in the way of dreams, where actions have no consequence. Suddenly bold, I lifted my glass to him in return and he smiled. "Major Edward Griffiths, fifteenth Hussars," he said to me, with a bow. "I do not believe I've had the pleasure, miss—"

"I'm Alice," I blurted, and felt my face flame, shyness knotting my tongue.

He looked taken aback, and of course a well-bred man in an officer's red coat *would* be taken aback to be so baldly introduced, but his eyes were warm on my face, and he said, "Well then, Miss Alice, I am glad to meet you. May I have this dance?"

Dancing, in company, was one of those other things that had frightened me at home, and that I almost never did. My natural awkwardness aside, I'd always felt that there is danger in dancing, that to dance with one man or another is an irrevocable decision – do you favor him or not? – and that decision can lead to another and another – three dances then four, then calls and drives then a wedding and a house and a child. And every single one of those steps was just one more trudging pace away from that supreme, longed-for moment, in a ballroom in candlelight, when anything in the whole world was possible.

But there was no weight of decision on me that night. Dreams have no tomorrow. I looked for Sue, saw her smiling up into her current partner's face, but even that did not worry me, for once.

I took the offered hand of Edward Griffiths, and he whirled me out onto the dance floor.

Perhaps it was the silkiness of the floor, so unlike the scraped thing I had scrubbed that day, or perhaps it was the momentary lifting of my shyness. But I've never danced so well, nor agreed with a partner so well. I do not even know how long we danced, and we talked, breathlessly, the entire time.

"Where are you from, my mysterious Alice?" he asked me.

"America," I said. "From California." Which I was not, but it made his eyes go large, and from there we were off, exchanging stories. I could be anyone at all to him. Anyone I wished to be, and it was the headiest feeling.

Very sincerely, he told me of his mother and a brother not yet in long trousers, a sister of a hoydenish disposition who had painted a whole sketchbook of scurrilous watercolors, to her mother's despair. He had me laughing louder than my dying soldier ever had.

I don't know how many hours passed before I realized how warm I was, how I'd begun to flush every time our eyes met. He smelt of wool and gold bullion and the faint cedar scent of the clothes-press, to keep away the moths. And of himself, the smell of his body. He was taller than me, broad and strong under his scarlet coat, and his blue eyes were brilliant when he looked at my face. When he drew me nearer still, I went pliant as an apple-branch, and the warmth of his hand sank through his dancing glove and through all my layers of clothing into the skin of my back.

But even as we stared at each other, with me thinking, heartbroken, *I've fallen in love at last, and it's only a dream*, the rhythm of the dance was faltering. I saw servants in wigs running. A very grand gentleman, with epaulettes, got up abruptly and left the room. Four others followed.

And Edward, dear Edward, as I called him in my thoughts, lifted his head, although his arm was still round my quivering body, and said, "Something is wrong." Couples all over the dance floor were coming to a halt; one girl in china blue burst into tears. Edward's arm tightened around my waist and then the grand gentleman with the epaulettes came back into the main ballroom, wearing a great caped traveling cloak over his beautiful ball-clothes.

"He's on the march," this gentleman said simply. "We shall meet him at Waterloo. Come now, all of you."

Edward's face was full of high color. "We shall beat him there; I make no doubt. And then I shall see you again, my angel." And, before I could protest, or even really understand, he crushed his face to mine, a shocking kiss that seemed to rend my veins with flame and remake me into liquid. He seized a white rosebud from the nearest vase, pressed it to his lips and tucked it into the mess of my dance-snarled hair. Then he was gone, hurrying across the floor with an eager step; nearly all the men were going, and the music was dying with them. Susan was coming across to me, limping on her slippered feet. "I don't understand," she said, but I hardly heard her, my eye following broad young shoulders, and a head of fair, tied-back hair.

And I blinked and I think Susan blinked and we were standing, sweat-drenched and shivering in an empty ballroom with only ourselves, reflected endlessly stunned in the tarnished mirrors. As we stood staring at each other like ninnies, Susan gasped and pointed to me. "Alice…"

And I, reaching up, following her pointing finger, touched silken softness in my wild hair, and nearly fainted. For there, caught up in the mess, was one perfect white rosebud.

I wanted for Sue and I to talk about it right away, of course. It was the finest and strangest thing that ever happened to us in the whole course of our lives, and *not* a dream. Was not my rosebud proof? But she had to go back to Mr Lewis. I went to my bedroom, but I didn't want to get dressed and have an ordinary day – my whole soul rebelled at the thought of an ordinary day – where washing and visiting and reading might dim the bright images in my mind. So I went to bed and wrapped myself in all my quilts at once, like a caterpillar, and there I slept, full of hazy dreams. Aunt Irene woke me just before luncheon, saying that Father was home to eat with us, for once, and that even Mr Lewis had agreed to come and sit at table, although he did not choose to actually eat in company, and was I sick, to still be in bed?

I would have said I am sick, and sunk straight back down, for the world felt particularly cold and dusty outside my quilts and my imaginings. But a question had occurred to me sometime in my dazed slumber, and it was wanting an answer that got me up and made me pin up my hair and reluctantly take off my nightgown, which smelled, oh so very faintly, of beeswax and wool and roses. Getting out of bed instantly reduced my memories of the night to a misty blur. I wanted to cry and leap back in, but Aunt Irene was tapping her foot outside, so I went.

Mr Lewis sat gaunt and strange and silent at table, his face tied up tight in its bandages, and my father was making conversation with that unthinking flow he'd learnt in Washington. Susan sat on Mr Lewis' other side, and I could almost see the air quiver in the space between their bodies, alive with all that they were not saying.

It was not so with my Edward, I thought, complacently – we talked like old friends. The question that had occurred to me in my dreams was still with me and that was, *if the grand ball was not a dream, is it a memory? A haunting? A symptom of brain-fever?* So I said ingenuously, "Father – was there ever a grand ball in this house? There must have been. The ballroom is so lovely."

Sue gave me a hard look, but Father and Aunt Irene smiled – probably they thought I was being gracious, filling the razor-edged silence with innocuous conversation. My father said instantly, "Why yes – didn't I say? I was sure I said – it's why I took this house, I thought you girls would like it. This is the house where the Duchess of Richmond had her ball." Aunt Irene nodded, but seeing me and Sue tolerably blank, with the bandaged Mr Lewis as ever unreadable, he went on: "Well, of course it was during the Napoleonic wars, when the Duke of Richmond was in charge of the troop defending Brussels. The duchess came to join her husband for the summer season and gave her ball for Wellington's officers." My father was a fine speaker; he had no ambition to be an ambassador or run for Congress, but he could still turn a story better than anyone I'd heard. "It was the grandest ball in history, they said later. Wellington came, and all the senior staff of the allied forces, and they danced until midnight with waltzes and gallopades and reels, before they went in to supper. But Wellington received a note at supper to say that Napoleon had stolen a march on him, had advanced to Quatre-Bras and the army must march instantly to meet him at Waterloo. And so they did. The officers left straight from here, straight from the ball. Many officers fought in evening clothes, and so died."

I felt the blood creeping in fear towards my heart, leaving my toes and fingers cold. "Died? The next day?"

"Many of them, yes," said Father.

I wanted to ask more, but Susan had turned aside to talk to Mr Lewis, who did not answer but got up stiffly and walked away. Sue bit both her lips nearly bloody and I held her hand under the table, with rage at war and the world in my heart. I asked no more questions. Perhaps I didn't want to know. I could not imagine Edward as I'd seen the men in the hospital, gray and stinking and empty. With eyes like holes, like Mr Lewis' eyes. Or splintered bone and blood on trampled earth. My whole being shrank in horror at the thought.

Later that night Susan and Mr Lewis quarreled. I did not mean to listen, of course; I am not actually a girl who listens at keyholes, except when it's particularly warranted. But I could not help hearing; her voice was raised, and so was his, quite unmuffled, so that I thought his bandages must be off. His fine, deep voice was hard-wrought with tension. "Will you give over? Must you take me in like a dog? I did not write you because I wanted you to forget me."

And Susan, almost spitting like a cat in her fury, answered straight back, "Well, I did not, did I? How could I? Didn't we make promises?" She might have stamped her foot, which would be very like Sue, the sound muffled by a sock on a floorboard.

"You made promises to a different man, my girl," he said. "In a different world. Do you think I love you so little that I'd tie you to a monster? What do you think we can have together, if your husband cannot go outside without the little children screaming?"

"Well then, if they scream I'll smack them and make them stop," said Susan furiously. "And you'll have your own children." Her voice broke on a sob, and I tried to imagine what Mr Lewis was doing, probably shaking his head, for his next words were, "It's no good, Sue. I'm for a boat as soon as I can walk about reliably, straight off to where no one knows who I was. It's better that way."

"And what about me?" she demanded. "Where do I fit, in all your grand plans?"

"You marry a fine gentleman, who's whole from hair to heel, and you have little girls as pretty as any that ever were and you *forget*. You're not being sensible now, you're like a kid with a lost puppy, so I'm being sensible for both of us. Go away, Sue."

He must have turned his back, or some such thing, for I heard a moment of silence, and then Susan's footsteps as she left his room and closed the door. She ought to have slammed it, but there was only the click, and her footsteps as she passed her own room and came to mine. She saw my face, naturally, although I was trying for an attitude of unconcern, and she said, "I suppose you heard, you little spy," but the rancor in her voice was not directed at me.

"Yes," I said.

Susan was silent. Her face was hard and pale and dry, lifeless as a world in drought when all the moisture has gone deep underground. She didn't cry.

"I'm sorry," I ventured. "But if his face is very bad, then – perhaps it's for the best?" I said this quite tentatively, half-expecting an explosion, but she was quiet. "He wants you to have a fine life," I added with more confidence.

"And yet," said Susan, getting up with a kind of macabre gaiety, "no one can explain to me why you and he and Aunt Irene and Father are all better qualified than me to decide upon the kind of fine life I am to have. Do you think we will hear the music again later?"

I'd more than half convinced myself it had been a singular event, a memory preserved in the ballroom's walls, a one-time haunting. But I said, on the wings of my desire, "We might. I hope we do…"

We waited up that night, and in a fit of fierce optimism I put on a party dress, although Susan merely watched me in tolerant silence. But she did up the back of my dress when I asked her to, and wove the white rosebud into my hair. We heard the clocks sound at midnight, and I was at the highest pitch of tension, and I think Sue was too, although we never said a word to each other, and then, after the sound of the clock in the foyer died away, we heard the music in the ballroom.

We went together, clasping hands, and it was just the same as the night before: flowers and perfume and the smell of a fine supper, lamplight and candlelight combining to make of it a dreamland. As before, Susan was instantly borne off, laughing wildly, into the dance; I glimpsed her waltzing with a tall highlander, her wrapper flying alongside his kilt, and then, as before, a deep, tender pair of blue eyes caught my own.

"I have not had the pleasure," he said to me, very softly, and for an instant I was sad, thinking, *he doesn't remember.* And then I realized I could meet him properly this time, with none of the girlish gaucherie that had tongue-tied me the night before, so I curtseyed and said, smiling, "Nor have I. But may I hope to remedy that?" And I saw his eyes kindle with a kind of wondering fire.

That night I told him I was an heiress from New York, and for the space of the dance, I even believed it. We danced until dawn, again. Susan with her partners, and me with my Edward, my body drawn heedlessly to his. By the end of the dancing we were clinging together, both of us half-dazed with love and wanting. And when, just as before, the word came that they must march, he kissed me on my wet eyes and then, after a pause, full on my quivering lips.

I wept to watch him go, and I also thought my heart would stop with joy, even as the men disappeared one by one and the room went silent once more. For if we'd had two nights then why not three?

Next moment, I found myself standing with Susan in the empty ballroom. I looked down and saw without much interest that my feet were bleeding, and so were my sister's. A small price, for such delights. We went to bed, both of us this time, and slept until Aunt Irene woke us with consternation and asked what ailed us.

After that we went to the ball each night. I think Mr Lewis was getting stronger, for certainly I heard his voice more often, less and less muffled by bandages, and Susan still went to him dutifully and tended him. But there was no fire in her voice, hardly any interest, even, and finally one day, I heard him say, "Are you all right, Sue? You're limping."

"As though you care," said Susan, in a flat voice, and left him soon after, to come to me. Our feet indeed were rather rough, for every night we went to the ballroom to dance. I think Susan did it to forget Mr Lewis, to lose herself in the whirl of all those beautiful men's admiration, but I of course did it to be with my Edward.

"I am a general's daughter," I would tell him. Or sometimes, "I'm a bluestocking naturalist."

And no matter what I said, or how we met, or who I seemed to be, every night we fell in love again.

I was the luckiest girl alive.

It's true that once or twice I was put out with him – when there was some fact of my life, some preference that he'd learnt a dozen times and still did not remember. I knew what he liked at supper, knew his sister's name. Treasured the truths of him like hoarded pearls. Wept sometimes, that he could never know me so. But then I would have a nightmare, in my long sleep after the ball was done, that I was back in that Brussels hospital, with wounded and broken men on either side, and they all had Edward's face. And I would be reminded anew that perhaps Edward did not know me, but that there was also no chance for us of heartbreak or despair or betrayal. That horrible battle was always tomorrow, but at least it was never today.

Aunt Irene demanded, "What has happened to you?" and I heard Mr Lewis say, with horror, "Christ almighty, Sue, your feet."

"It's nothing."

"It's not nothing. You're skin and bone, and your face—"

"It's nothing!" cried Sue. "You told me to be nothing to you and so I am! Nothing!"

I agreed with her, silently. Nothing mattered, nothing could possibly matter in this wrecked and dusty world. We only lived for the night, for those hours before the end, when all was yet perfect.

Another night came. By now Sue and I were putting on our party dresses together, laughing as we did our hair. Susan dabbed rouge over our cheekbones, and if I was momentarily disturbed at how starkly the rouge stood out on my pallor, like a corpse's makeup, I forgot it soon enough, in favor of putting perfume on my neck.

"God," said Sue. "How the time does crawl. I want to dance with my highlanders again." She was twitchy, eager, and so was I, imagining how I would be to dear Edward tonight, if I would meet him as a tempestuous storm of a woman, or a sweet, shy girl, knowing he would love me instantly regardless.

And sure enough, at midnight, the music started and we ran through the hallways, laughing. During the day our feet did hurt abominably; I was worried I'd glimpsed a little speck of bone in the ruin of my blisters, but I hid them carefully from Father and Aunt

Irene, and anyway it didn't matter at night. Our feet never hurt at night.

The ballroom had become more familiar to me than any bedroom I'd ever had; the rose-trellis pattern on the wall, the parquet of the floor, the faces of the dear musicians. Sue and I separated, as was our custom. She was instantly engulfed in admirers, and I went straight to Edward. I had decided I wanted to be myself that night, more or less: bookish and sharp and serious. But he still greeted me with courtesy and listened to my opinions and laughed at my jokes.

Every night he fell in love with me. Every night I loved him more.

He does not know you, a voice in my heart whispered, but I shoved it away. He did not need to.

Standing on the edge of the dance floor, on the precipice of that joyful whirl, I said, my voice shaking with feeling, "I wish the night would not stop."

"Then let it not stop," he said, smiling down at my face, and we pelted out into the dance.

But something was wrong.

Cries suddenly arose from every part of the ballroom; the music lurched to an ungainly halt, and the dancers stumbled into each other as the rhythm faltered and died. Dear Edward kept me from grief with a hand on the small of my back. Then he put his hand on his ceremony-sword, saying, "What the devil is this?"

For a monster had come to the ballroom.

The monster stood in the middle of the dance floor, head a little bowed. His hair was thick and dark except where it had been seared away. His face was young and kind and ordinary except where it was seamed with wormlike scars that twisted up his mouth; one ear was a lump, one eye was glass.

Women screamed; the atmosphere of wondrous unreality was shattered. I felt my stomach close and cramp. As though time in its damnable marching had been given a face and come with funereal tread into my sanctuary.

And the monster said, "Sue? What is this? What are you doing? What is this place?"

To my horror, my sister stepped out of the throngs of frightened people. "Does it matter? What are you doing here?"

"I came looking for you. I was afraid for you."

"You don't have the right to be afraid for me!" she cried. "You gave me up! Go away and let me dance!"

She tried to dart back among the highlanders, and I breathed a sigh of relief, but the monster caught her round the waist and held her to him. "No," he said. "Can't you see it? No. Whatever this place is, it's not real. It's killing you."

She laughed wildly. "Not real? It's more real than you and I. You told me we were nothing, but this – this is something, at least."

He shook her a little. "No it isn't. I may be half-blind now, but I can see that clear enough." The unmarred side of his face mingled wonder and nostalgia and a well-marked contempt when he looked us all over, all the beauties of that perfect night, and I had never hated him more. "It's just pretty shadows. And you're everything, Sue. Everything in the whole world."

"No I'm not. You shoved me away. I love you and you said it was nothing!"

"Because I knew that if I admitted that I love you still, I would catch you and hold you and keep you, even if it was your ruin. I didn't want to do that. Not to you, never to you, my love."

She was starting to cry. "I wanted you to." I saw their tears mingling and I thought with horror that he would make her do it, would drag her with him back out into the terrible daylight, to love a man who has lost his ear and his eye and all his joy, where days would turn to weeks turn to months turn to tears… "Sue!" I screamed, trying to reach her, clutching on to Edward's hand, as I pulled him along the floor. "Sue, come here, come back, tell him to go away." I was crying too.

Susan reached out to me, but Edward was an anchor, dragging on my arm. I could not reach my sister's hand without dropping his. Susan's fingers brushed mine, but that was all, and then Mr Lewis caught her round the waist and pulled her to him, and next moment she was gone from the ballroom, gone as though she'd never been.

I suppose these last words must be mine. Arthur and I found ourselves quite alone, standing in our nightclothes in that infernal ballroom, but there was no music and no lights and no flowers and no candles. Just the electric bulb, swinging, and the sound of a mouse as it ran along the wall. My feet were all over blood.

There was no sign of Alice.

I hurt my fists on the mirrors and sobbed out her name while Art held me. But there was no answer. No sound of voices, nor of music. Only a horrible, scratchy silence. The daylight was trickling in through the shuttered windows when at last Arthur picked me up, strong despite his poor face, and carried me away.

There was an investigation, of course. The poor old frozen garden was quite dug up. They didn't find her, though. No one ever found her.

Art and I got married. We stayed in the house for weeks, in Brussels for months. At first I'd go back every night, to listen for the music and call out to my sister.

But she never answered.

Do you hear me Alice, my dear wretch? I hope at least you are happy in your ballroom of dreams and of dust, and that you still hear music where I only hear a mouse's scurrying.

Alice, tell me you are there.

Alice.

I stayed in the ballroom all night, that last night in Brussels, and Arthur stayed with me, so fiercely alive, after the cobweb dreams of the Duchess of Richmond's ball. I must have dozed off near dawn, for I had nightmares of my sister weaving through dancers, just out of reach, her hair unmistakable, her smiling face gray. I woke up calling her name, and Art woke with me and whispered, "Sue – look."

I looked, and looked and was utterly silent, except for my tears. Alice was gone. But I'd woken up with a single white rosebud, tight-furled, never to bloom, caught between my fingers.

ABOUT THE AUTHORS

OLIVIE BLAKE is the *New York Times* bestselling author of *The Atlas Six, Alone with You in the Ether, Masters of Death*, and other works of adult contemporary sci-fi and fantasy. As Alexene Farol Follmuth, she is also the author of the young adult rom-coms *My Mechanical Romance* and *Twelfth Knight*. She lives in Los Angeles with her husband and goblin prince/toddler.

MELISSA MARR writes fiction for adults, teens, and children. Her books have been translated into twenty-eight languages and been bestsellers in the US and overseas. If she's not in the desert she currently calls home, she's either at the nearest body of water or on her annual visit to Scotland.

KELLY ANDREW lives outside of Boston with her husband, two daughters, and a persnickety Boston Terrier. She has a Bachelor's in Social Work, but received her Master's in English & Creative Writing. When she's not writing she enjoys obsessing over a good book, soaking up family time, warming herself in various toasty lodges while her husband skis, and getting intentionally lost in the woods.

TASHA SURI is the World Fantasy Award-winning author of the Burning Kingdoms Trilogy, the Books of Ambha Duology, *What Souls Are Made Of* and *Doctor Who: The Cradle*. Once a librarian, she is now a part-time writing tutor and a full-time cat and rabbit wrangler. She lives with her family in a mildly haunted house in London.

KELLEY ARMSTRONG is the author of the Rip Through Time and Rockton mystery series. Past works include the Otherworld urban fantasy series, the Cainsville gothic mystery series, the Nadia Stafford thriller trilogy and the Darkest Powers & Darkness Rising teen paranormal series.

KAMILAH COLE is a national bestselling, Dragon Award-nominated Jamaican American author. She worked as a writer and entertainment editor at *Bustle* for four years, and her nonfiction has appeared in *Marie Claire* and *Seventeen*. A graduate of New York University, Kamilah lives in the Pacific Northwest, where she's usually playing *Kingdom Hearts* for the hundredth time, quoting early *SpongeBob SquarePants* episodes, or crying her way through Zuko's redemption arc in *Avatar: The Last Airbender*. You can connect with her on social media at @wordsiren or on her website *kamilah-cole.com*.

ELIZA CHAN is a Scottish-born speculative fiction author who writes about East Asian mythology, British folklore and reclaiming the dragon lady. Her *Sunday Times*-bestselling debut novel

Fathomfolk – inspired by mythology, East and Southeast Asian cities and diaspora feels – was published by Orbit in 2024. The sequel *Tideborn* will be published in 2025. *Harbour of Hungry Ghosts*, *Babel* meets *The Witcher* in a historical fantasy set in mid-Opium War era Hong Kong, has been announced for 2026.

She has been a medical school dropout, a kilt shop assistant, an English teacher and a speech and language therapist, but currently spends her time tabletop gaming, cosplaying, crafting and toddler wrangling.

Find out more on her website *www.elizachan.co.uk*.

A. C. WISE is the author of the novels *Wendy, Darling* and *Hooked*, the novellas *Grackle* and *Out of the Drowning Deep*, and the short story collection *The Ghost Sequences*, among other titles. Her work has won the Sunburst Award, and been a finalist for the Nebula, World Fantasy, Stoker, British Fantasy, Locus, Aurora, Shirley Jackson, Lambda Literary, and Ignyte Awards. In addition to her fiction, she contributes regular review columns to *Apex* and *Locus Magazine*.

ANGELA 'A. G.' SLATTER is the author of six novels, including *All the Murmuring Bones*, *The Path of Thorns* and *The Briar Book of the Dead*, as well as twelve short story collections, and three novellas. She's won a World Fantasy Award, a British Fantasy Award, a Shirley Jackson Award, three Australian Shadows Awards, and eight Aurealis Awards. She has an MA and a PhD in creative writing. In 2023 she collaborated with Mike Mignola on a new series from Dark Horse Comics, *Castle Full of Blackbirds*, set in the Hellboy Universe. Her seventh novel, *The Crimson Road*, will be published in 2025 by Titan Books. *www.angelaslatter.com*

ABOUT THE AUTHORS

HANNAH NICOLE MAEHRER – or as TikTok knows her, @hannahnicolemae – is a fantasy romance author and BookToker with a propensity for villains. When she's not creating bookish comedy skits about Villains and Assistants, she's writing to Taylor Swift songs. Her biggest passions in life include romance, magic, laughter, and finding ways to include them all in everything she creates. Most days you can find her with her head in the clouds and a pen in her hand.

MEGAN BANNEN is a *USA Today* bestselling author of award-winning speculative fiction. Her work has been selected for the RUSA Reading List, the Indies Introduce list, and the Kids' Indie Next List, along with numerous best-of-the-year compilations. As a former public librarian, she has spent most of her professional career behind a reference desk, but she has also sold luggage, written grants, collected a few graduate degrees from various Kansas universities, and taught English at home and abroad. She lives in the Kansas City area with her family and more pets than is reasonable.

KATHERINE ARDEN is the *New York Times*, *USA Today* and *Sunday Times* bestselling author of the Winternight Trilogy and *The Warm Hands of Ghosts*. She is also the author of the Small Spaces Quartet, an award-winning series for children. The first book of the Winternight Trilogy, *The Bear and the Nightingale*, was named by Amazon as the best science fiction and fantasy novel of 2017. The trilogy has been nominated for the Locus and Nebula awards, the Vermont Book Award, and four Goodreads Choice Awards. The Winternight Trilogy has been translated into over twenty-five languages. RL Stine called *Small Spaces*, the first book in the Small Spaces Quartet, 'terrifying and fun.' It was named a best book of 2018 by *Kirkus*, *Publisher's Weekly*, the Chicago Public Library system, and the American Library Association, as well as being nominated for student book awards in over twenty-five states. It is the winner of the Golden Dome award in Vermont, the William Allen White award in Kansas, the Nene award in Hawaii, as well as student voted awards in Idaho and Nebraska. Born in Austin, Texas, Arden studied Russian in Moscow, taught at a school in the French Alps and worked on a farm in Hawaii. She currently lives in Vermont, where she writes, hikes with her dog, skis, and continues to expand her vegetable garden and extensive beds of perennial flowers.

ABOUT THE EDITORS

MARIE O'REGAN is a British Fantasy Award and Shirley Jackson Award-nominated author and editor, based in Derbyshire. She was awarded the British Fantasy Society 'Legends of FantasyCon' award in 2022. Her first collection, *Mirror Mere*, was published in 2006 by Rainfall Books; her second, *In Times of Want*, came out in September 2016 from Hersham Horror Books. Her third, *The Last Ghost and Other Stories*, was published by Luna Press early in 2019. Her short fiction has appeared in a number of genre magazines and anthologies in the UK, US, Canada, Italy and Germany, including *Best British Horror 2014*, *Great British Horror: Dark Satanic Mills* (2017), and *The Mammoth Book of Halloween Stories*. Her novella, *Bury Them Deep*, was published by Hersham Horror Books in September 2017. She was shortlisted for the British Fantasy Society Award for Best Short Story in 2006, Best Anthology in 2010 (*Hellbound Hearts*), 2012 (*The Mammoth Book of Ghost Stories by Women*), and 2023 (*The Other Side of Never*). She was also shortlisted for the Shirley Jackson Award for Best Anthology in 2020 (*Wonderland*). Her genre journalism has appeared in magazines like *The Dark Side*, *Rue Morgue* and *Fortean Times*, and her interview book with prominent figures from the horror genre, *Voices in the Dark*, was released in 2011. An essay on *The Changeling* was published in PS Publishing's *Cinema Macabre*, edited by Mark Morris. She is co-editor of the bestselling *Hellbound Hearts*, *The Mammoth Book of Body Horror*, *A Carnivàle of Horror – Dark Tales from the Fairground*, *Exit Wounds*, *Wonderland*, *Cursed*, *Twice Cursed*, *The Other Side of Never*, *In These Hallowed Halls*, *Beyond & Within: Folk Horror Short Stories*, and *Death Comes at Christmas*, as well as the charity anthology *Trickster's Treats #3*, plus editor of the bestselling anthologies *The Mammoth Book of Ghost Stories by Women* and *Phantoms*. Her first novel, the internationally bestselling *Celeste*, was published in February 2022. Marie was Chair of the British Fantasy Society from 2004 to 2008, and Co-Chair of the UK Chapter of the Horror Writers' Association from 2015 to 2022. She was also co-chair of ChillerCon UK in 2022. Visit her website at *marieoregan.net*. She can be found on X @Marie_O_Regan and Instagram @marieoregan8101.

PAUL KANE is the award-winning (including the British Fantasy Society's Legends of FantasyCon Award 2022), bestselling author and editor of over a hundred and fifty books – such as the Arrowhead trilogy (gathered together in the sellout *Hooded Man* omnibus, revolving around a post-apocalyptic version of Robin Hood), *The Butterfly Man and Other Stories*, *Hellbound Hearts*, *Wonderland* (a Shirley Jackson Award finalist) and *Pain Cages* (an Amazon #1 bestseller). His non-fiction books include *The Hellraiser Films and Their Legacy* and *Voices in the Dark*, and his genre journalism has appeared in the likes of *SFX*, *Rue Morgue* and *DeathRay*. He has been a Guest at Alt.Fiction five times, was a Guest at the first SFX Weekender, at Thought Bubble in 2011, Derbyshire Literary Festival and Off the Shelf in 2012, Monster Mash and Event Horizon in 2013, Edge-Lit in 2014 and 2018, HorrorCon, HorrorFest and Grimm Up North in 2015, The Dublin Ghost Story Festival and Sledge-Lit in 2016, IMATS Olympia and Celluloid Screams in 2017, Black Library Live and the UK Ghost Story Festival in 2019 and 2023, plus the WordCrafter virtual event 2021 – where he delivered the keynote speech – as well as being a panellist at FantasyCon and the World Fantasy Convention, and a fiction judge at the Sci-Fi London festival. A former British Fantasy Society Special Publications Editor, he has also served as co-chair for the UK chapter of the Horror Writers Association and co-chaired ChillerCon UK in May 2022.

His work has been optioned and adapted for the big and small screen, including for US network primetime television, and his novelette 'Men of the Cloth' was turned into a feature by Loose Canon/Hydra Films, starring Barbara Crampton (*Re-Animator, You're Next*): *Sacrifice*, released by Epic Pictures/101 Films. His audio work includes the full cast drama adaptation of *The Hellbound Heart* for Bafflegab, starring Tom Meeten (*The Ghoul*), Neve McIntosh (*Doctor Who*) and Alice Lowe (*Prevenge*), and the *Robin of Sherwood* adventure *The Red Lord* for Spiteful Puppet/ITV narrated by Ian Ogilvy (*Return of the Saint*). He has also contributed to the Warhammer 40k universe for Games Workshop. Paul's latest novels are *Lunar* (set to be turned into a feature film), the YA story *The Rainbow Man* (as PB Kane), the sequels to *RED* – *Blood RED* & *Deep RED*, all collected in an omnibus edition – the award-winning hit *Sherlock Holmes & the Servants of Hell*, *Before* (an Amazon Top 5 dark fantasy bestseller), *Arcana* and *The Storm*. In addition, he writes thrillers for HQ/HarperCollins as PL Kane, the first of which, *Her Last Secret* and *Her Husband's Grave* (a sellout on Waterstones.com and at The Works) came out in 2020, with *The Family Lie* released the following year (all three novels were Amazon sellouts). His books have been translated into many languages, including French, German, Spanish, Ukrainian, Turkish, Czech, Bulgarian and Polish. Paul lives in Derbyshire, UK, with his wife Marie O'Regan. Find out more at his site *www.shadow-writer.co.uk*, which has featured Guest Writers such as Stephen King, Charlaine Harris, Robert Kirkman, Catriona Ward, Dean Koontz, Sarah Pinborough and Guillermo del Toro. He can also be found @PaulKaneShadow on X, and @paul.kane.376 on Instagram.

ACKNOWLEDGEMENTS

And now for the important bit – our opportunity to say thank you. Firstly, to all the authors for their contributions, to Katie Dent for getting the ball rolling, and all the team at Titan. Finally, thanks to our respective families, without whom etc.

For more fantastic fiction, author events,
exclusive excerpts, competitions, limited editions and more

VISIT OUR WEBSITE
titanbooks.com

LIKE US ON FACEBOOK
facebook.com/titanbooks

FOLLOW US ON TWITTER AND INSTAGRAM
@TitanBooks

EMAIL US
readerfeedback@titanemail.com